FOR A

FEW

DEMONS

MORE

BOOKS OF THE HOLLOWS

FOR A FEW DEMONS MORE

Kim Harrison

An Imprint of HarperCollinsPublishers

FOR A FEW DEMONS MORE. Copyright © 2007 by Kim Harrison. All rights reserved. Printed in the United States of America. No part of this book may be used or reproduced in any manner whatsoever without written permission except in the case of brief quotations embodied in critical articles and reviews. For information address HarperCollins Publishers, 10 East 53rd Street, New York, NY 10022.

HarperCollins books may be purchased for educational, business, or sales promotional use. For information please write: Special Markets Department, HarperCollins Publishers, 10 East 53rd Street, New York, NY 10022.

FIRST EDITION

Eos is a federally registered trademark of HarperCollins Publishers.

Designed by Sunil Manchikanti

Library of Congress Cataloging-in-Publication Data has been applied for.

ISBN: 978-0-06-078838-4
ISBN-10: 0-06-078838-0

07 08 09 10 11 WBC/RRD 10 9 8 7 6 5 4 3 2 1

To the guy who knows that the rose is more
beautiful with the thorns still on it

I'd like to thank two people who have been with me from almost day one, whose combined efforts and business savvy have been so instrumental in putting me somewhere I never dreamed possible my editor, Diana Gill, and my agent, Richard Curtis.

☉ ΠΕ

Hammering my fist against the back of my closet wasn't one of my more pleasant dreams. Actually, it hurt. The pain broke through my comfortable sleepy haze, and I felt the primitive part of me that never slept coolly measuring my slow gathering of will as I tried to wake up. With an eerie feeling of disconnection, I watched it happen, even as in my dream I tore the clothes off the rod and threw them to my rumpled bed.

Something, though, wasn't right. I wasn't waking up. The dream wasn't passively shredding into hard-to-remember bits. And with a jolt I realized I was conscious but not awake.

What in hell? Something was really, really wrong, and instinct sent a pulse of adrenaline thorough me, demanding I wake. But I didn't.

My breath was quick and ragged, and after I emptied the closet, I dropped to the floor and tapped my knuckles on the boards for a secret compartment I knew wasn't there. Frightened, I grasped my will and forced myself awake.

Pain reverberated through my forehead. I sprawled, all my muscles going flaccid. I managed to turn my head, and my ear stung instead of my nose breaking. Hard wood pressed against me, cold through my pajama shorts and top. My cry came out as a gurgle. I couldn't breathe! Something . . . something was in here with me. In my head. Trying to possess me!

Terror smothered me like a blanket. I couldn't see it, couldn't hear it, could hardly *sense* it. But my body had become a battlefield—one where I didn't know how to win. Possession was a black art, and I hadn't taken the right classes. *Damn it, my life isn't supposed to be like this!*

Utter panic gave me strength. I tried to mobilize my legs and arms under me and push. I managed to rise to my hands and knees, then fell into my bedside table. It crashed to the floor and rolled to the empty closet.

My pulse hammering, the fear of suffocating overtook me. I managed to stagger into the hallway, looking for help. My unknown assailant and I found common ground and, working together, we took a breath that escaped in a choked cry. *Where the devil was Ivy? Was she deaf?* Maybe she hadn't yet come in from her run with Jenks. She'd said they'd be late.

As if bothered by the cooperation, my attacker gripped harder, and I collapsed to the floor. My eyes were open, and the red sheet of my hair stood between me and the end of the dusky hallway. It had won. Whatever it was, it had won, and I panicked as I found myself sitting up with an eerie slowness. The thick scent of burnt amber hung in my nose, rising from my skin.

No! I cried in my thoughts—but I couldn't even speak. I wanted to scream, but my possessor made me take a slow, sedate breath instead. *"Malum,"* I heard myself curse, my voice carrying an odd accent and a sophisticated lilt that had never been mine.

That was the last penny in the jar. Fear shifted to anger. I didn't know who was in here with me, but whoever it was, was going to get out. Right now. Making me speak in tongues was just rude.

Falling into my thoughts, I felt the barest brush of someone else's confusion. Fine. I could build on that. Before the intruder could figure out what I was doing, I tapped the ley line out back in the graveyard. Stark, foreign surprise filled me, and while my assailant struggled to break me from the line, I formed a protection circle in my thoughts.

Practice makes perfect, I thought smugly, then braced myself. This was going to hurt like hell.

I opened my thoughts to the ley line with an abandon I'd never dared before. And it came. Magic roared in. It overflowed my chi and poured into my body, burning my synapses and neurons. *Tulpa,* I thought in agony, the word opening the mental channels to spindle the energy.

The rush would have killed me if I hadn't already burned a trail of nerves from my chi to my mind. Groaning, I felt the power sear anew as it raced to the protection circle in my thoughts, expanding it like a balloon. It was how I spindled ley line energy to use later, but at this rate it was like diving into a vat of molten metal.

An internal yelp of pain resounded in me, and with a mental push that I mirrored with my hands, I shoved away from myself.

A snap reverberated through me, and I was free of the unknown presence. From the church's belfry above came the sound of the bell tolling—an echo of my actions.

Something rolled and bumped down the corridor to crash into the wall at the end of the hall. I gasped and pulled my head up, then groaned in pain. Moving hurt. I held too much ley line power. It felt as if it had settled in my muscles, and using them squeezed the energy out.

"Ow," I panted, very aware that something at the end of the hall was standing up. But at least now it wasn't in my head. My heart beat, and that hurt, too. Oh God, I'd never held this much power before. And I stank. I reeked of burnt amber. What the Turn was going on?

With a pained determination, I squeezed the protection circle in my mind until the energy slipped back through my chi and into the ley line. It hurt almost as much as taking it in. But when I unspindled the ever-after from my thoughts to leave only that which my chi could hold, I looked up past the snarls of my hair, panting.

Oh, God. It was Newt.

"What are you doing here?" I said, feeling coated in ever-after slime.

The powerful demon looked confused, but I was still too out of things to appreciate its shocked expression: either a smooth-faced adolescent boy or a strong-featured female. Slender of build, it stood barefoot in my hallway between the kitchen and the living room. Squinting, I looked again—yeah, the demon was standing this time, not floating, its long, bony feet definitely pressing the floorboards—and I wondered how Newt had managed to attack me when I was on hallowed ground. The addition to the church, where it stood now, wasn't sanctified, though, and it looked bewildered, wearing a dark red robe that looked somewhere between a kimono and what Lawrence of Arabia might wear on his day off.

There was a soft blurring of black ley line energy, and a slender obsidian staff as tall as I was melted into existence in Newt's grasp, completing the vision I remembered from the time I had been trapped in the ever-after and had had to buy a trip home from Newt. The demon's eyes were entirely black—even what should be the whites—but they were more alive than any I'd ever seen as they stared at me unblinking down the twenty feet that separated us—twenty tiny feet and a swath of hallowed ground. At least I hoped it was still hallowed ground.

"How did you learn how to do that?" it said, and I stiffened at the odd accent, the vowels that seemed to insert themselves into the folds of my brain.

"Al," I whispered, and the demon's almost-nonexistent eyebrows rose. Shoulder against the wall, I never took my eyes from it as I slid upward to stand. This was not the way I wanted to start my day. God help me, I'd only been asleep for an hour by the looks of the light.

"What's the matter with you? You can't just show up!" I exclaimed, trying to burn off some adrenaline as I stood in the hallway still in the skimpy shirt and shorts I wore to bed. "No one summoned you! And how could you stand on hallowed ground? Demons can't stand on sacred ground. It's in every book."

"I do what I want." Newt peered into the living room, poking the staff over the threshold as if looking for traps. "And assumptions like that will kill you," the demon added, adjusting the strand of black gold that glinted dully against the midnight red of its robe. "I wasn't standing on hallowed ground—you were. And Minias . . . Minias said I wrote most of those books, so who knows how right they are?"

Its smooth features melted into annoyance, at itself, not me. "Sometimes I don't remember the past right," Newt said, its voice distant. "Or maybe they simply change it and don't tell me."

My face went cold in the predawn chill. Newt was insane. I had an insane demon standing in my hallway and roommates coming home in about twenty minutes. *How could something this powerful survive being this unbalanced?* But unbalanced seldom equated with stupid, though powerful and unbalanced did. And clever. And ruthless. Demonic.

"What do you want?" I asked, wondering how long until the sun would rise.

With a troubled look, Newt exhaled. "I don't remember," it finally said. "But you have something of mine. I want it back."

While unknown emotions flitted through and Newt's thoughts cataloged themselves, I squinted down the shadowy hallway, trying to decide if it was male or female. Demons could look like anything they wanted to. Right now Newt had pale eyebrows and a light, absolutely even skin tone. I'd say it was feminine, but the jaw was strong and those bare feet were too bony to be pretty. Nail polish would look wrong on them.

It was wearing the same hat as before—round, with straight sides and a flat top made from a scrumptiously rich red fabric and gold braiding. The short, nondescript hair falling to just below the ear gave no clue to gender. The time I'd questioned what sex he or she was, Newt had asked me if it made a difference. And watching Newt struggle to place a thought, I had a feeling it wasn't that the demon didn't think it was important but that Newt didn't remember what parts he or she had been born with. Maybe Minias did. Whoever Minias was.

"Newt," I said, hoping my shaking voice wasn't too obvious, "I demand you leave. Go directly to the ever-after from this place, and don't return to bother me again."

It was a good banishment—apart from my not having put it in a circle first—and Newt raised one eyebrow at me, its puzzlement set aside with an ease that spoke of much practice. "That's not my summoning name."

The demon jerked into motion. I shrank back to invoke a circle—paltry though it would be, undrawn and unscribed—but Newt stepped into the living room, the hem of its robe the last thing I saw slipping around the doorframe. From out of sight came the sound of nails being pulled from wood. There was a sharp crack of splintering paneling, and Newt swore colorfully in Latin.

Jenks's cat Rex padded past me, curiosity doing its best to fulfill its promise. I lunged after the stupid animal, but she didn't like me and so skittered away. The caramel-colored kitten paused at the threshold with her ears pricked. Tail twitching, she sat and watched.

Newt wasn't trying to pull me into the ever-after, and it wasn't trying to kill me. It was looking for something, and I think the only reason it had possessed me was so it could search the sanctified church. Which boded well as a sign that the grounds were still holy. But the damned thing was crazy. Who knew how long it would ignore me? Until it decided I might be able to tell it where *it* was? *Whatever* it was?

A thump from the living room made me jump. Tail crooked, Rex padded in.

The sudden knocking on the front door of the church spun me the other way to the empty sanctuary, but before I could call out a warning, the heavy oak door swung open, unlocked in expectation of Ivy's return. *Great. Now what?*

"Rachel?" a worried voice called, and Ceri strode in, fully dressed in faded jeans with dirt-wet knees, clearly having been in the garden despite it being before sunrise. Her eyes were wide with worry, and her long, fair hair billowed about her as she paced quickly across the barren sanctuary, tracking in mud from her garden-inappropriate, elaborately embroidered slippers. She was an elf in hiding, and I knew that her schedule was like a pixy's: awake all day and night but for four hours around each midnight and noon.

Frantic, I waved my hands, alternating my attention between the empty hallway and her. "Out!" I all but yelped. "Ceri, get out!"

"Your church bell rang," she said, cheeks pale with concern as she came to take my hands. She smelled wonderful—the elven scent of wine and cinnamon mixing with the honest smell of dirt—and the crucifix Ivy had given her glinted in the dim light. "Are you all right?"

Oh, yeah, I thought, remembering hearing the bell in the belfry toll when I had pushed Newt from my thoughts. The expression "ringing the bells" wasn't just a figure of speech, and I wondered how much energy I had channeled to make the bell in the tower resonate.

From the living room came the ugly noise of paneling being ripped from the wall. Ceri's blond eyebrows rose. Crap, she was calm and sedate, and I was shaking in my underwear.

"It's a demon," I whispered, wondering if we should leave or try for the circle I had etched in the kitchen floor. The sanctuary was still hallowed ground, but I didn't trust anything except a well-drawn circle to protect me from a demon. Especially this one.

The questioning look on Ceri's delicate, heart-shaped face went hard with anger. She had spent a thousand years trapped as a demon's familiar, and she treated them like snakes. Cautious, yes, but she had long since lost her fear. "Why are you summoning demons?" she accused. "And in your sleepwear?" Her narrow shoulders stiffened.

6   KIM HARRISON

"I said I'd help you with your magic. Thank you very much, Ms. Rachel Mariana Morgan, for making me feel worthless."

I took her elbow and started dragging her backward. "Ceri," I pleaded, not believing that her delicate temper had taken this the wrong way. "I didn't call it. It showed up on its own." *Like I would even touch demon magic now?* My soul was already tainted with enough demon smut to paint a gymnasium.

At that, Ceri pulled me to a stop, steps from the open sanctuary. "Demons can't show up on their own," she said, the flicker of concern returning as her white fingers touched her crucifix. "Someone must have summoned it, then let it go improperly."

The soft scuff of bare feet at the end of the hallway cut through me like a gunshot. My pulse catching, I turned, Ceri's attention following mine an instant later.

"Can't—or don't?" Newt said. The kitten was in its arms, paws kneading.

Ceri's knees buckled, and I reached for her. "Don't touch me!" she shrieked, and I was suddenly battling her as she swung blindly, pulling from me and lunging into the sanctuary.

Shit. I think we're in trouble.

I lurched after her, but she jerked me back when we found the middle of the empty space. "Sit," she said, her hands shaking as she tried to yank me down.

Okay, we weren't leaving. "Ceri—" I began and then my jaw dropped when she flicked a dirt-caked jackknife from her back pocket. "Ceri!" I exclaimed as she sliced her thumb open. Blood gushed, and while I stared, she drew a large circle, mumbling Latin. Her waist-length, almost-translucent hair hid her features, but she was trembling. My God, she was terrified.

"Ceri, the sanctuary is holy!" I protested, but she tapped a line and invoked her circle. A black-stained field of ever-after rose to encompass us, and I shuddered, feeling the smut of her past demon magic slither over me. The circle was a good five feet in diameter, rather large for one person to hold, but Ceri was probably the best ley line practitioner in Cincinnati. She cut her middle finger, and I grabbed her arm. "Ceri, stop! We're safe!"

Wide-eyed in panic, she shoved me off her, and I fell into the inside of her field, hitting it like a wall. "Get out of the way," she ordered, starting to draw a second circle inside the first.

Shocked, I pulled myself to the center, and she smeared her blood behind me.

"Ceri—" I tried again, stopping when I saw her intertwining the line with the first, enforcing it. I'd never seen that before. Latin words fell from her lips, dark and threatening. Pinpricks of power crawled over my skin, and I stared when she cut her pinkie and started a third circuit.

Silent, desperate tears marked her face as she finished and invoked it. A third sheet of black rose over us, heavy and oppressive. She switched the filthy gardening blade to her bloodied hand and, shaking, prepared to cut her left thumb.

"Stop!" I protested. Frightened, I grabbed her wrist, sticky with her own blood.

Her head swung up. Blue eyes lost in terror met mine. Her skin was chalk white.

"It's okay," I said, wondering what Newt had done to cause this self-assured, unflappable woman to lose it. "We're in the church. It's sanctified. You built a damn fine circle." I looked at it humming over my head, worried. The triple circle was black with a thousand years of curses that Algaliarept, the demon I'd saved her from, made her pay for. I'd never felt such a strong barrier.

Ceri's pretty head shook back and forth, lips parted to show tiny teeth. "You have to call Minias. God help us. You have to call him!"

"Minias?" I questioned. "Who in hell is Minias?"

"Newt's familiar," Ceri stammered, her blue eyes showing her fear.

Was she nuts? Newt's familiar was another demon. "Give me that knife," I said, wrestling it from her. Her thumb was bleeding, and I looked for something to wrap it in. We were safe. Newt could have the run of the back for all I cared. Sunup was near, and I'd sat in a circle and waited for it before. Memories of my ex-boyfriend Nick rose through me and vanished.

"You have to call him," Ceri gushed, and I stared when she fell to her knees and started scribing a plate-size circle with her blood, tears spotting the old oak timbers as she worked.

"Ceri, it's okay," I said, standing over her in confusion.

But when she looked up, my confidence faltered. "No, it isn't," she said, her voice low, the elegant accent that gave away her royal beginnings now carrying the sound of defeat.

A wave of something pulsed, bending the bubble of force that sheltered us. My gaze went to the half sphere of ever-after around us, and from above came a clear bong of the church bell resonating. The black sheet protecting us quivered, flashing the pure color of Ceri's blue aura for an instant before returning to its demon-fouled black state.

From the archway at the back of the church came Newt's soft voice. "Don't cry, Ceri. It won't hurt as bad the second time."

Ceri jerked, and I snatched her arm to keep her from running for the open door and breaking her own circle. Her flailing hand struck my face, and at my yelp she collapsed to slump at my feet. "Newt broke the sanctity," Ceri said around her sobs. "She broke it. I can't go back there. Al lost a bet, and I twisted her curses for ten years. I can't go back there, Rachel!"

Frightened, I put my hand on her shoulder, but then hesitated. *Newt was female.* Then my face blanked. *Newt was in the hallway—the* sanctified *part.*

My thoughts returned to that pulse of energy. Ceri had once said it was possible for a demon to desanctify the church, but that it was unlikely as it cost far too much. And Newt had done so without a thought. *Shit.*

Swallowing, I looked to find Newt framed by the hallway, well within what had been holy ground. Rex was still in the demon's arms, smiling a stupid cat smile. The orange feline wouldn't let me touch her, but she'd purr while an insane demon petted her. Figures.

With her black staff tucked in the crook of her elbow and draped in her elegantly cut robes, Newt looked almost biblical. Her femininity was obvious once her gender was settled, her black, unblinking eyes placidly taking in Ceri's circle in the middle of the all-but-barren sanctuary.

I crossed my arms over myself to hide my near nakedness. Not that there was that much to hide. My heart pounded and my breath came fast. The demon mark on the underside of my foot—proof that I owed Newt a favor for returning me back from the ever-after into reality last solstice—throbbed as if aware that its maker was in the room.

From beyond the tall stained-glass windows and the open front door came the soft whoosh of a passing car and the twitters of early birds. I prayed the pixies would stay in the garden. The knife was red and sticky in my hand from Ceri's blood, and I felt ill.

"It's too late to flee," she said, taking the knife back. "Call Minias."

Newt stiffened. Rex jumped from her arms to land upon my desk. Panicked, the cat leapt to the floor, scattering papers as she streaked into the hall. Red robe furling, Newt strode to Ceri's circle, slamming her spinning staff into it. "Minias doesn't *belong* here!" she shouted. "Give it to me! It's mine. I want it back!"

Adrenaline made my head hurt. I watched the circle quiver, then hold.

"We have only moments after she becomes serious," Ceri whispered, white-faced but looking more collected. "Can you distract her?"

I nodded, and Ceri began to prepare her spell. Tension pulled my shoulders tight, and I prayed my conversation skills were better than my magic. "What do you want? Tell me, and I'll give it to you," I said, voice quaking.

Newt began to pace the circle, looking like a caged tiger as her deep red robe hissed against the floor. "I don't remember." Confusion made her face hard. "Don't call him," the demon warned, black eyes shining. "Every time I do, he makes me forget. I want it back, and you have it."

Oh, this just gets better and better. Newt's gaze went to Ceri, and I blocked her view.

I had a half-second warning before the demon again jabbed her staff at the circle. *"Corrumpro!"* she shouted as it connected. At my feet, Ceri trembled when the outermost circle flashed into utter blackness as Newt owned it. With a little smile, Newt touched the circle, and it vanished to leave two thin, shining bands of unreality between us and death, dressed in a dark red robe and wielding a black staff.

"Your skills are much improved, Cerdiwen Merriam Dulciate," Newt said. "Al is an exceptional teacher. Perhaps enough that you might be worth my kitchen."

Ceri didn't look up. The curtain of her pale hair hid what she was doing, and its tips were stained red from her blood. My breath was fast, and I continued to turn to keep Newt in sight until my back was again facing the open door to the church.

"I remember you," Newt said, tapping the butt of her staff along the circle where it met the floor. Each jab sent a deeper wash of black crawling over the barrier. "I put your soul back together when you traveled the lines. You owe me a favor." I stifled a shiver when the demon's gaze went past my bare, pasty legs to Ceri. "Give me Ceri, and I'll call it null."

I stiffened. Kneeling behind me, Ceri found her strength. "I have my soul," she stated, voice quivering. "I don't belong to anyone."

Newt seemed to shrug, fingers playing with her necklace. "Ceri's signature is all over the imbalance on your soul," the demon said to me as she moved to Ivy's piano and turned her back on me. "She is twisting curses for you, and you're taking them. If that doesn't make her your familiar, then what does?"

"She twisted a curse for me," I admitted, watching the demon's long fingers caress the black wood. "But I took the imbalance, not her. That makes her my friend, not my familiar."

But Newt had apparently forgotten us. Standing beside Ivy's piano, the robed figure seemed to gather the power of the room into her, turning all that had once been holy and pure to her own purpose. "Here," she murmured. "I came to get something of mine you stole . . . but this . . ." Tucking her staff into the crook of her arm, Newt bowed her head and held it. "This bothers me. I don't like it here. It hurts. Why does it hurt here?"

Keeping Newt distracted while Ceri worked was well and good, but the demon was nuts. The last time I had run into Newt, she had been at least rational, but this was unimaginable power fueled by insanity.

"It was here!" the demon shouted, and I jumped, stifling a gasp. Ceri's breath caught audibly as Newt turned, her black eyes full of malevolence. "I don't like this," Newt accused. "It hurts. It shouldn't hurt."

"You shouldn't be here," I said, feeling airy and unreal, as if I were balancing on a knife's edge. "You should go home."

"I don't remember where home is," Newt said. Vehement anger colored her soft voice.

Ceri tugged at me. "It's ready," she whispered. "Call him."

I pulled my eyes from Newt as the demon began to circle again, dropping my attention to the ugly, elaborate, twin-ringed pentagram drawn with Ceri's blood. "You think calling one demon to take care of another is a good idea?" I whispered, and Newt's pace quickened.

"He's the only one who can reason with her," she said, panicked and desperate. "Please, Rachel. I'd do it, but I can't. It's demon magic."

I shook my head. "Her familiar? Would you have helped Al?"

While Newt chuckled over my nickname for Algaliarept, her demon captor, Ceri's chin trembled. "Newt is insane," she whispered.

"You think?" I snapped, jumping when Newt slammed a side kick into the barrier, her robes swirling dramatically. Great, she knew martial arts on top of everything else. Why not? She'd obviously been around a while.

"That's why she has a demon for a familiar," Ceri said, eyes flicking nervously. "They had a contest. The loser became her familiar. He's more of a caretaker, and he's probably looking for her. They don't like it when she slips his watch."

The lights in my head started to go on, and my mouth dropped open. Seeing my understanding, Ceri tugged me down to her pentagram drawn in blood. Grabbing my wrist, she tuned it palm side up and aimed for my finger with her knife. "Hey!" I shouted, snatching my hand back.

Ceri looked at me, her lips pressed together. She was getting bitchy. That was good. It meant she thought she—we—might live through this. "Do you have a finger stick?" she snapped.

"No."

"Then let me cut your finger."

"You're already bleeding," I said. "Use your blood."

"Mine won't work," she said from between gritted teeth. "It's demon magic, and—"

"Yeah, I got it," I interrupted. Her blood didn't have the right enzymes, and thanks to some illegal genetic tinkering to save my life, I had survived being born possessing them.

The humming presence of the circle above us seemed to hesitate, and Newt made a sound of success. Ceri shuddered as she lost control of the middle circle, and Newt took it down. One thin, fragile circle left. I held out my hand—consumed with fear. Ceri's eyes met mine, stress making her angular features beautiful. I only looked ugly when I got scared. Newt's hand hovered over the last circle, smiling evilly as she muttered Latin. It had become a race.

Ceri made a quick swipe at my finger, and I jerked against the sting, watching a bead of red swell. "What do I do?" I asked, not liking this at all.

Blue eyes dropping, she turned my hand palm down and set it in the circle. The old oak seemed to vibrate, as if its stored life force were running through me, connecting me to the spinning of the earth and the burning of the sun. "It's a public curse," she said, her words falling over themselves. "The invocation phrase is *mater tintinnabulum.* Say it and Minias's name in your thoughts, and the curse will put you through."

"Don't summon Minias," Newt threatened, and I felt Ceri's control over the last circle swell while the demon was distracted. "He'll kill you faster than I will."

"You aren't summoning him, you're asking for his attention," Ceri said desperately. "The imbalance would normally go to you, but you can bargain with Newt's location and he'll take it. If he doesn't, I will."

It was a huge concession from the smut-covered elf. This was looking better and better, but the sun wasn't up yet, and Newt looked ready to tear us apart. I didn't think Ceri could hold her concentration much longer against a master demon. And I had to believe that the demons possessed a way to control this member of their species, otherwise they'd be dead already. If his name was Minias and he masqueraded as her familiar, then that's the way it was.

"Hurry," Ceri whispered, sweat tracking her face. "You'll probably show up as an unregistered user, but unless she's cursed him again, he's likely looking for her and will answer."

Unregistered? I wondered. Licking my lips, I closed my eyes. I was already connected to the line, so all that was left was invoking the curse and thinking his name. *Mater tintinnabulum, Minias,* I thought, not expecting anything to happen.

My breath came in a quick heave, and I felt Ceri's hand clamp on my wrist, forcing my own to stay in the circle. A jolt of ever-after spun from me, colored with my aura. I felt it leave me like a winging bird, and I struggled to hold myself together as I saw it flee in my imagination, taking a portion of me with it.

"I won't let him steal it from me!" Newt shouted. "It's mine! I want it back!"

"Concentrate," Ceri whispered, and I fell into myself, feeling that freed slice of me ring like a bell through the entirety of the ever-after. And like a ringing bell, it was answered.

I'm a little busy, came an irritated thought. *Leave a message on the damned landline and I'll get back to you.*

I shuddered at the sensation of thoughts not my own curling through my mind, but Ceri kept my hand unmoving. Within Minias was a background clutter of worry, guilt, aggravation. But he had dismissed me like a telemarketer and was ready to snap the connection.

Newt, I thought. *Take the imbalance for my calling you, and I'll tell you where she is. And promise you won't hurt us,* I added. *Or let her hurt us. And get her the hell out of my church!*

"Hurry!" Ceri cried, and my concentration bobbled.

Done, the voice thought decisively. Minias's worry sharpened to a point and joined mine. *Where are you?*

My brief elation vanished. *Uh,* I thought, wondering how you give directions to a demon, but Minias's own thoughts faltered in confusion.

What the devil is she doing past the lines? It's almost sunup.

She's trying to kill me! I thought. *Get your ass over here and collect her!*

You aren't registered. How am I supposed to know where you are? I'll have to . . .

I stiffened, jerking my hand out of the circle and Ceri's grip when the voice's presence squeezed my thoughts harder. Gasping, I fell backward onto my butt, my body mirroring my attempt to jerk away from Minias's presence.

". . . come though on your thoughts," a darkly mellow voice said.

"Heavenly Father, save us," Ceri gasped.

My head spun, and I caught a glimpse of Ceri falling backward. She hit her circle, and panic iced through me when it broke in a flash of black.

Oh, God. We're dead.

She met my gaze as she sprawled half upright up on the floor, her eyes saying she thought she had killed us. Newt cried out, and I spun where I was sitting, only to freeze in shock.

Nothing stood between Newt and us now but a man, his purple robes reflecting hers in all but color. He was barefoot, and only now did I remember the flash of those robes coming between me and Ceri as he shoved the elf into the bubble to break it so he could get to Newt.

"Let me go, Minias," Newt snarled, and my eyes widened at his thick-knuckled hand gripping her upper arm. "She has something of mine. I want it back."

"What has she got of yours?" he asked calmly, his back to me. Newt was a head shorter than Minias, and it made her look vulnerable despite the scathing vehemence in her voice. His voice carried the intent sound of a more-than-casual question, and my eyes dropped to the grip he had on her staff, right above her hand. It never eased up, not even as his honey-amber voice spilled into the violated sanctuary like a balm. Soothing, yes, but holding tension, too.

Newt said nothing. I could see the hem of her robe past Minias tremble.

I scrambled up, Ceri finding her feet beside me. She didn't bother to reinstate the circle. What was the point? Minias shifted to block Newt's view. He was focused on her, but I was sure he was aware of us, and he looked like he knew what he was doing. I had yet to see his face, but his brown hair was short, the curls crushed by the same hat Newt wore.

"Breathe," Minias said, as if trying to trigger something. "Tell me what you want."

"I want to remember," she whispered. It was as if we weren't even in the room anymore, so focused were they on each other, and only now did Minias's grip become gentle.

"Then why do you—"

"Because it hurts," she said, her bare feet shifting.

Leaning in as if concerned, he asked gently, "Why did you come here?"

She was silent, and then finally said, "I don't remember." It was agitated—soft and threatening—and the only reason I believed her was that she had clearly forgotten before Minias had shown up.

Minias lost the last of his anger. I felt as if we were witnessing a common but seldom-seen event, and I hoped he would hold to his promise that they wouldn't take us when they were ready to leave. "Then let's go," he soothed, and I wondered how much of this was caretaker and how much was simply caring. Could demons care about each other?

"Maybe you'll remember when we get back," he said, turning Newt as if he were going to lead her away. "If you forget something, you should go to where you first thought it, and it will be waiting for you."

Newt refused to step with him, and our eyes met when Minias moved out of the way. "It's not at home," she said, her brow furrowed to show a deep inner pain and, under that, a seething power held in check by the demon whose grip had slid from her staff to her hand. "It's here, not there. Whatever it is, it's here. Or it was here. I . . . I know it." Anger slipped over her brow, born from frustration. "You don't want me to remember," she accused.

"*I* don't want you to remember?" he asked harshly, his hand falling from her and extending in demand. "Give them to me. Now."

My gaze flicked between them. He had gone from lover to jailer in a pulse.

"I'm missing my cache of yew," he said. "I didn't make you forget. Give them to me."

Newt's lips pressed together, and spots of color appeared on her cheeks. It was starting to make sense. Yew was highly toxic and used almost exclusively in communing with the dead and for making forget charms. Illegal forget charms. I had found a yew in the back of the graveyard by an abandoned mausoleum, and though I didn't commune with the dead, I had left it, hoping that plausible deniability would keep my butt out of court if anyone found it there. Growing yew wasn't illegal, but growing it in a graveyard, where the potency was enhanced, was.

"I made them," Newt snapped. "They're mine! I made them myself!"

She turned to leave, and he reached out and spun her back. I could see Minias's face now. He had a strong jaw, clenched with emotion. His red demon eyes were so dark they almost hid the characteristic goat-slitted appearance, and his nose was strongly Roman. Anger was heavy on him, balancing Newt's own temper perfectly.

Emotions cascaded over them both in a rapid, fluid torrent. It was as if a five-minute argument were passing in three seconds, her face changing, his responding, causing a shift of her mood that was reflected in his body language. He carefully manipulated her, this demon who had removed the sanctity of the church without a second thought, who had turned a triple blood-circle to her will—something that I had been told was impossible but of which Ceri had known Newt was fully capable. I didn't know whom to be more frightened of—Newt, who could plague the world, or Minias, who controlled her.

"Please," he asked when her face shifted to chagrin and her black eyes dropped.

Hesitating briefly, she reached into the pocket of her expansive sleeve and handed him a fistful of vials.

"How many did you invoke when you remembered?" he asked, the vials clattering.

Newt's eyes went to the floor, beaten, but the sly look to her demeanor told me she wasn't sorry about it. "I don't recall."

He jiggled them in his hand before pocketing them, clearly seeing her unrepentant mood. "There are four missing."

She looked at him, real tears showing. "It hurts," she said, scaring the crap out of me. *Newt had inflicted her own memory loss? What had she remembered that she didn't want to?*

Ceri was standing beside me, almost forgotten, and she slumped, telling me that it was almost done. I wondered how often she had seen this played out.

His mood easing, Minias pulled Newt close, the purple of his robe curving around her. Newt folded her arms against herself and let him hold her, her eyes shut and her head tucked under his chin. They looked elegant and self-possessed standing in their strongly colored robes and proud stances. I wondered how I could ever have doubted Newt's gender. It was so clear now, and I spared a thought that perhaps she had subtly shifted her appearance. Seeing them together made a shudder ripple over me. Minias was the only thing holding Newt to her sanity. I didn't think he was just her familiar. I don't think he had ever been *just* anything.

"You shouldn't take them," he whispered, his breath brushing her forehead. His voice was captivating, moving up and down like music.

"It hurts," she said, her own voice muffled.

"I know." His demonic eyes locked with mine, and I shivered. "That's why I don't like it when you go out without me," he said, looking at me but talking to her. "You don't need them." Breaking our eye contact, Minias turned her face to his, his hand cupping her strong jawline.

My arms wrapped around my middle, I wondered how long they had been together. Long enough that a forced burden became one willingly shouldered?

"I don't want to remember," Newt said. "The things I've done—"

A demon with a conscience? Why not? They did have souls.

"Don't," Minias said, interrupting her. He held her more gently. "Promise you'll tell me the next time you remember something instead of going looking for answers?"

Newt nodded, then stiffened in his arms. "That's where I was," she whispered, and my gut clenched at the sound of realization in her voice. Minias froze, and beside me Ceri paled.

"It was in your journals!" Newt exclaimed, pushing him away. Minias fell back, wary, but the demon was beyond noticing. "You've been writing it down. You've written down everything I remember! How much do you have in your books, Minias? How much do you know that I wanted to forget!"

"Newt . . ." he warned, his fingers fumbling in his pocket.

"I found them!" Newt shouted. "You know why I'm here! Tell me why am I over here!"

I jumped when Ceri gripped my arm. Shouting in rage, Newt swung her staff at him. Minias's fingers danced in the air as if babbling in sign language, forming a ley line spell. I felt a huge drop as someone pulled on the line out back, and with a surprising shout, Minias ended his spell by popping the lid to a vial he'd taken from Newt and flinging it at her.

Newt cried out in dismay as the sparkles hung in the air, her anger, frustration, and pain shocking in their depth. And then the potion hit her, and her face went blank.

Sliding to a stop, she blinked, glancing over the empty sanctuary with no recognition in her gaze as it landed on Ceri and me. She saw Minias, then threw her staff to the floor as if it were a snake. It hit with a clatter and bounced. Outside, past the stained-glass windows, the robins were singing in the predawn haze, but in here it was as if the air were dead.

"Minias?" she said, her tone confused and dismayed.

"It's done," he said gently. He came forward, scooping up her staff and handing it to her.

"Did I hurt you?" Her voice was worried, and when Minias shook his head, relief spilled over her, quickly turning to depression.

I felt sick.

"Take me home," the demon said, glancing at me. "My head hurts."

"Wait for me." Minias's gaze flicked to mine, then returned to her. "We'll go together."

Ceri held her breath as the demon approached us, his face down and wide shoulders hunched. I thought briefly about reinstating the circle but didn't. Minias stopped before me, too close for comfort. His tired eyes took in my nightclothes, Ceri's blood staining my hands, and the three circles that had nearly failed to stop Newt. His gaze rose to encompass the interior of the sanctuary, with my desk, Ivy's piano, and the stark emptiness between them. "You were the one who stole Ceri from her demon?" he asked, surprising me.

I wanted to explain that it had been a rescue, not stealing her, but I just nodded.

His head moved up and down once, mocking me, and I fixed on his eyes. The red was so dark that they looked brown, and the characteristic demonic sideways pupil gave me pause.

"Your blood kindled the curse," he said, his red, goat-slitted eyes darting to the blood circle beside me. "She told me about shoving you through the lines last winter." His eyes traveled over me, evaluating. "No wonder Al is interested in you. Do you have anything that might have attracted her?"

"Other than the favor I owe her?" I said, my voice shaking. "I don't think so."

His eyes dropped to the elaborate circle Ceri had drawn for me to contact him with. "If you think of anything, call me. I'll pick up the imbalance. I don't want her coming over here again."

Ceri's fingers on my arm tightened. *Yeah, me neither,* I thought.

"Stay here," he said as he turned away. "I'll be back to settle up."

Alarmed, I pulled from Ceri. "Whoa, hold up, demon boy. I don't owe you anything."

His eyebrows were high and mocking when he turned around. "I owe you, idiot. The sun is almost up. I have to get out of here. I'll be back when I can."

Ceri's eyes were wide. Somehow I didn't think that having a demon owe me a favor was a good thing. "Hey," I said, taking a step forward. "I don't want you just showing up. That's rude." *And really scary.*

He looked impatient to be away as he adjusted his clothing. "Yes, I know. Why do you think demons try to kill their summoners? You're crude, unintelligent, grasping hacks with no sense of social grace, demanding we cross the lines *and* pick up the cost?"

I warmed, but before I could tell him to shove it, he said, "I'll call first. *You* take the imbalance for that, since you asked for it."

I glanced at Ceri for guidance, and she nodded. The guarantee that he wouldn't show up while I was showering was worth it. "Deal," I said, hiding my hand so he wouldn't take it.

From behind him, Newt eyed me with her brow creased. Minias's steps were silent as he moved to take her elbow possessively, his worried eyes darting to mine. His head rose to look past Ceri and me to the open door, and I heard the *lub-lub-lub* of a cycle pulling into the carport. In the time between one heartbeat and the next, they vanished.

I slumped in relief. Ceri leaned against the piano, the flat of her arms getting blood on it. Her shoulders started to shake, and I put a hand on one, wanting nothing more than to do the same. From outside came the sudden silence of Ivy's bike turning off, and then her distinctive steps on the cement walk.

"So then the pixy says to the druggist," Jenks said, the clatter of his wings obvious, "'Tax? I thought they stayed on by themselves!'" The pixy laughed, the tinkling sound of it like wind chimes. "Get it, Ivy? Tax? Tacks?"

"Yes, I got it," she muttered, her pace shifting as she took the cement steps. "Good one, Jenks. Hey, the door is open."

The light coming into the church was eclipsed, and Ceri pulled herself up, wiping her face and smearing it with blood, tears, and dirt from her garden. I could smell the stink of burnt amber on me and throughout the church, and I wondered if I would ever feel clean again. Together we stood, numb, as Ivy halted just past the foyer. Jenks hovered for three seconds, and then, dropping swear words like the golden sparkles he was shedding, he tore off in search of his wife and kids.

Ivy put a hand on her cocked hip and took in the three—no, four—circles made of blood, me in my pj's and Ceri crying silently, her hand, sticky with drying blood, clutching her crucifix.

"What on God's green earth did you do now?"

Wondering if I'd ever sleep again, I glanced at Ceri. "I have no idea."

TWO

I didn't feel good, my stomach queasy as I sat on my hard-backed chair in the kitchen at Ivy's heavy and very large antique table, shoved up against an interior wall. The sun was a thin slice of gold shining on the stainless-steel fridge. I didn't see that often. I wasn't used to being up this early, and my body was starting to let me know about it. I didn't think it was from the morning's trouble. *Yeah. Right.*

Tugging my terry-cloth robe shut, I flipped through the Yellow Pages while Jenks and Ivy argued by the sink. The phone was on my lap so Ivy wouldn't take over as I searched for someone to resanctify the church. I'd already called the guys who had reshingled the roof to give us an estimate on the living room. They were human, and Ivy and I liked using them, since they generally got here bright and early at noon. Newt had torn up the carpet and pulled several pieces of paneling off the walls. *What in hell had she been looking for?*

Jenks's kids were in there right now, though they weren't even supposed to be in the church, and by the shrieks and chiming laughs, they were making a mess of the exposed insulation. Turning another thin page, I wondered if Ivy and I might take the opportunity to do some remodeling. There was a nice hardwood floor under the carpet, and Ivy had a great eye for decorating. She had redone the kitchen before I'd moved in, and I loved it.

The large industrial-sized kitchen had never been sanctified, having been added on to the church for Sunday suppers and wedding receptions. It had two stoves—one electric, one gas—so I didn't have to cook dinner and stir my spells on the same surface. Not that I made dinner on the stovetop too often. It was usually microwave something or cook on Ivy's hellacious grill out back, in the tidy witch's garden between the church and the graveyard proper.

Actually, I did most of my spelling at the island counter between the sink and Ivy's farmhouse kitchen table. There was an overhead rack where I hung the herbs I was currently messing with and my spelling equipment that didn't fit under the counter, and with the large circle etched out in the linoleum, it made a secure place to invoke a magical circle; there were no pipes or wires crossing either overhead in the attic or under in the crawl space to break it. I knew. I had checked.

The one window overlooked the garden and graveyard, making a comfortable mix of my earthy spelling supplies and Ivy's computer and tight organization. It was my favorite room in the church, even if most of the arguments took place here.

The biting scent of rose hips came from the tea Ceri had made me before she left. I frowned at the pale pink liquid. I'd rather have coffee, but Ivy wasn't making any, and I was going to bed as soon as I got the reek of burnt amber off me.

Jenks was standing on the windowsill in his Peter Pan pose, his hands on his hips and cocky as hell. The sun hit his blond hair and dragonfly-like wings, sending flashes of light everywhere as they moved. "Damn the cost," he said, standing between my betta, Mr. Fish, who swam around in an oversize brandy snifter, and Jenks's tank of brine shrimp. "Money doesn't do you any good if you're dead." His tiny, angular features sharpened. "At least not for us, Ivy."

Ivy stiffened, her perfect oval face emptying of emotion. On an exhale she drew her athletic six-foot height up from where she'd been leaning against the counter, straightening the leather pants she usually wore while on an investigation run and tossing her enviably straight black hair from habit. She'd had cut it a couple of months ago, and I knew she kept forgetting how short it was, just above her ears. I'd commented last week that I liked it, and she had gotten it styled into downward spikes with gold tips. It looked great on her, and I wondered where her recent attention to her appearance was coming from. *Skimmer, maybe?*

She glanced at me, her lips pressed together and spots of color showing on her usually pale complexion. The hint of almond-shaped eyes gave away her Asian heritage, and that, combined with her small, strongly defined features, made her striking. Her eyes were brown most of the time, going pupil black when her living-vampire status got the better of her.

I had let her sink her teeth into me once, and though as exhilarating and pleasurable as all hell, it had scared the crap out of both of us when she lost control and nearly killed me. Even so, I was willing to cautiously risk trying to find a blood balance. Ivy flatly refused, though it was becoming painfully obvious the pressures were building in both of us. She was terrified of hurting me in a haze of bloodlust. Ivy dealt with fear by ignoring its existence and avoiding its origin, but her self-imposed denial was just about killing her even as it gave her strength.

If my roommates/business partners could be believed, finding thrills was what I organized both my daily life and my sex life around. Jenks called me an adrenaline junkie, but if I was making money at it and remembered my limits, where was the harm? And I knew to the depths of my soul that Ivy didn't fall under that "looking for a thrill" umbrella. Yes, the rush had been incredible, but it was the self-worth I had given her that told me it hadn't been a mistake, not the blood ecstasy she had instilled.

For an instant, Ivy had seen herself as I did: strong, capable, able to love someone fully and be loved in return. By giving her my blood, I had told her that yes, she was worth sacrificing for, that I liked her for who she was, and that her needs weren't wrong. Needs were needs. It was us who labeled them right or wrong. I wanted her to feel that way all the time.

But God help me, it had been a rush.

As if she had heard my thought, Ivy turned from Jenks. "Stop it," she said, and I flushed. She couldn't read my mind, but she might as well have. A vamp's sense of smell was tuned to pheromones. She could read my mood as easily as I could smell the sharp scent of rose hips coming from my untouched tea. *Crap, Ceri really expected me to drink this?*

Jenks's wings reddened, clearly not liking the shift in topic from how to spend our pooled business money to how to keep our teeth to ourselves, and Ivy gestured with a long, slim hand to include me in their argument.

"It's not that I don't want to spend the money," she said, both soothing and assertive. "But why do it if a demon will take it down again?"

I snorted, turning to the phone book and shifting a page. "Newt isn't *just* a demon. Ceri says she's one of the oldest, most powerful demons in the ever-after. And she's stark raving nuts," I muttered, turning a page to another listing. "Ceri doesn't think she'll be back."

Ivy crossed her arms to look slinky and svelte. "So why bother re-sanctifying at all?"

Jenks snickered. "Yeah, Rache. Why bother? I mean, this could be good. Ivy could invite her mom over for a housewarming. We've been here a year, and the woman is dying to come over. Well, at least she would be if she were still alive."

Worried, I looked up from the phone book. Alarm sifted over Ivy. For a moment it was so quiet I could hear the clock above the sink, and then Ivy jerked, her speed edging into that eerie vamp quickness she took pains to hide. "Give me the phone," she said, snatching it.

The black plastic slipped from my lap, and Ivy drew the heavy book off the table. Retreating to her end of the table with quick steps, she set the directory on her knees and pulled a legal pad from a stack. While Jenks laughed, she sketched a graph with columns headed by phone number, availability, cost, and religious affiliation. Confident we'd be on holy ground before the week was out, I stifled my ire that she had taken over.

Jenks was smiling when he flitted from the windowsill, gold sparkles landing in my teacup before he settled beside it. "Thanks," I said, knowing Ivy would hear me even if I whispered. "I don't think I'm going to sleep again until we're resanctified—and I like sleeping."

Head bobbing in an exaggerated motion, he nodded. "Why don't you just put the church in a circle?" he questioned. "Nothing can get through that."

"It wouldn't be secure unless we removed all the electricity and gas lines coming in," I explained, not wanting to tell him that Newt could apparently get through any circle with enough reason. "You want to live without your MTV?"

"Oh, hell, no," he said, glancing at Ivy when she offered the person on the phone double to get the job done before sunset tonight. Ivy didn't get along with her mother very well.

Tired, I slumped back into my chair, feeling the weight of the insane morning hour fall on me. Jenks's wife, Matalina, had gotten the pixy kids out of the living room, and the sound of them in the garden slipped in with the morning breeze. "Ceri said if Newt doesn't show up in the next three weeks, she'll probably forget about us," I said around a yawn, "but I still want to get the church resanctified." I looked at my chipped nail polish in dismay. "Minias hit her with a forget charm, but the demon is freaking crazy. And she shows up without being summoned."

Ivy stopped talking on the phone, and after she and Jenks exchanged a look, she clicked it off without saying good-bye. "Who is Minias?"

"Newt's familiar." I gave her a tight-lipped smile to soften the shortness of my answer. Sometimes Ivy was like an ex-boyfriend. Hell, she was like that most times, as her vampire instincts fought with her reasoning. I was not her shadow, aka source of blood, but living with her blurred the lines between what she knew and how her instincts said she should feel.

She remained silent, clearly having heard the lack of completeness. I didn't want to talk about it, the fear being too damn close to my skin. Literally. I stank like the ever-after, and all I wanted was to clean up and hide under my covers for the next three days. Having had Newt in my head gave me the willies, even if I'd regained control almost immediately.

Ivy took a breath to press for more, dissuaded when Jenks clattered a warning with his wings. I'd tell the whole story. Just not now. My blood pressure dropped at Jenks's show of support, and, lurching to my feet, I went to the pantry for the mop and bucket. If we were going to have a holy person in our church, I wanted the blood circles gone. I mean, really . . .

"You've been up since noon yesterday. I can do that," Ivy protested, but lack of sleep had made me bitchy, and I dropped the bucket in the sink, slamming the cupboard door under it when I brought out the disinfectant and tossed the scrub brush in.

"You've been up as long as I have," I said over the rush of water. "And you're arranging who's going to bless the grounds. The sooner we get that done, the better I'll sleep." *Something I was taking care of until you butted in,* I thought snarkily as I took off the metallic bracelet Kisten had given me and draped it around the base of Mr. Fish's bowl. The black gold of the chain and mundane charms glittered, and I wondered if I should take the time to try to put a ley line spell into them, or just leave them as something pretty to wear.

The sharp orange scent tickled my nose, and I shut off the tap. My back protesting, I lugged the bucket over the edge of the counter, spilling some. I awkwardly rubbed the mop over the drops and headed out, bare feet squeaking. "It's not a biggie, Ivy," I said. "Five minutes."

The clatter of pixy wings followed me. "Isn't Newt's familiar a demon?" Jenks asked when he landed on my shoulder.

Okay, so maybe it hadn't been a show of support but merely him wanting to feel me out as to what info to give Ivy. She was a worrywart, and the last thing I wanted was her thinking I couldn't go out for a can of Spam without her "protection." He was a better judge of her mood than I was, so I set the bucket by the circles and whispered, "Yeah, but he's more of a caretaker."

"Tink's a Disney whore," he swore, taking a potshot at his infamous kin as I plunged the mop up and down a few times before squeezing out the excess water. "Don't tell me you got another demon mark?"

He left my shoulder when I sent the mop across the floor, apparently finding the back-and-forth motion too much to take. "No, he owes me," I said nervously, and Jenks's jaw dropped. "I'm going to see if he'll take Al's mark off me in exchange. Or maybe Newt's."

Jenks hovered before me, and I straightened, tired as I leaned on the mop. His eyes were wide and incredulous. The pixy had a wife and way too many kids living in a stump in the garden. He was a family man, but he had the face and body of an eighteen-year-old. A very sexy, tiny eighteen-year-old with wings, and sparkles, and a mop of blond hair that needed arranging. His wife, Matalina, was a very happy pixy, and she dressed him in skintight outfits that were distracting despite his minute size. That he was nearing the end of his life span was killing me and Ivy both. He was more than a steadfast partner skilled in detection, infiltration, and security—he was our friend.

"You think the demon will do that?" Jenks said. "Damn, Rache. That'd be great!"

I shrugged. "It's worth a shot, but all I did was tell him where Newt was."

From the kitchen came Ivy's voice raised in irritation. "It's 1597

Oakstaff. Yes." There was a hesitation, then, "Really? I didn't know you kept those kinds of records. It would have been nice if someone had told us we were a paranormal city shelter. Shouldn't we be getting a tax break or something?" Her voice had gone wary, and I wondered what was up.

Jenks lit on the edge of the bucket, wiping a spot to sit before settling himself, his dragonfly wings stilling to look like gossamer. The mop wasn't doing it; I would have to scrub. Sighing, I dropped to my knees and felt around the bottom of the bucket for the brush.

"No, it *was* sanctified," Ivy continued, her voice growing louder, clear over the hiss of the bristles. "It isn't anymore." A slight pause and she added. "We had an incident." Another hesitation and she said, "We *had* an *incident*. How much to do the entire church?"

My stomach clenched when she added softly, "How much to do just the bedrooms?"

I looked at Jenks, guilt rising thick in me. Maybe we could get the city to defray the cost if we refiled as a city shelter. It wasn't as if we could ask the landlord to fix it. Piscary owned the church, and though Ivy had dropped the facade of paying rent to the master vampire she looked to, we were responsible for the upkeep. It was like living rent free in your parents' house when they were on an extended vacation— vacation being jail in this case, thanks to me. It was an ugly story, but at least I hadn't killed him . . . uh, for good.

Ivy's sigh was audible over the sound of my work. "Can you get out here before tonight?" she asked, making me feel marginally better.

I didn't hear the answer to that, but there was no more conversation forthcoming, and I focused on rubbing out the smears, moving clockwise as I went. Jenks watched for a moment from the rim of the bucket, then said, "You look like a porno star on your hands and knees, mopping in your underwear. Push it, baby," he moaned. "Push it!"

I glanced up to find him making rude motions. *Doesn't he have anything better to do?* But I knew he was trying to cheer me up—least that's what I was telling myself.

As his wings turned red from laughter, I jerked my robe closed and sat back on my knees before I blew a shoulder-length red curl from my face. Taking a swing at his smirk would be useless—he had gotten really fast since his stint under a demon curse that made him people-size. And turning my back to him would be worse.

"Could you straighten my desk for me?" I asked, allowing a touch of annoyance into my voice. "Your cat dumped my papers."

"You bet," he said, zipping off. Immediately I felt my blood pressure drop.

Ivy's soft steps intruded, and Jenks cussed fluently at her when she pulled the papers off the floor and set them on the desktop for him. Politely telling him to shove a slug up his ass, she strode past me to her piano, a spray bottle in one hand and a chamois cloth in the other.

"Someone's coming out this morning," she said, starting to clean Ceri's blood from the varnished wood. Old blood didn't flip any switches in living vamps—not like the chance to take it did. "They're going to give us an estimate, and if our credit checks out, they'll do the entire church. You want to pay the extra five thousand to insure it?"

Five thousand to insure it? Holy crap. How much was this going to cost? Uneasy, I sat back up on my heels and dunked the brush. My rolled-up sleeve slipped, soaking in an instant. From my desk Jenks called out, "Go for it, Rache. It says here you won a million dollars."

I glanced behind me to find him manhandling my mail. Irritated, I dropped the brush and squeezed the water from my robe. "Can we find out how much it's going to cost first?" I asked, and she nodded, giving her piano a heavy coat of whatever was in that unlabeled spray bottle. It evaporated quickly, and she wiped it to a shine.

"Here," she said, setting the bottle down beside the bucket. "It will get rid of the—" Her words stopped. "Just wipe the floor with it," she added, and my eyebrows rose.

"Oka-a-ay." I bent back over the floor, hesitating at the circle Ceri had scribed to call Minias, then smeared it to nothing. Ceri could help me make a new one, and I wasn't going to have demonic blood circles on the floor of my church.

"Hey, Ivy," Jenks called. "You want to keep this?"

She rocked into motion, and I shifted to keep her in my view. Jenks had a coupon for pizza, and I smirked. *Right. Like she would even consider ordering anything but Piscary's Pizza.*

"What else does she have in here?" Ivy said, throwing it away. I turned my back on them, knowing that the chaos I kept my desk in drove Ivy insane. She'd probably take the opportunity to tidy it. God, I'd never be able to find a thing.

"Spell-of-the-Month Club . . . toss," Jenks said, and I heard it thunk into the trash can. "Free issue of *Witch Weekly* . . . toss. Credit check . . . toss. Crap, Rachel. Don't you throw anything away?"

I ignored him, having only a small arc to finish. *Wax on, wax off.* My arm was hurting.

"The zoo wants to know if you want to renew your off-hours runner's pass."

"Save that!" I said.

Jenks whistled long and low, and I wondered what they had found now.

"An invitation to Ellasbeth Withon's wedding?" Ivy drawled in question.

Oh, yeah. I forgot about that.

"Tink knocks your kickers," Jenks exclaimed, and I sat back on my heels. "Rachel!" he called, hovering over the invitation that had probably cost more than my last dinner out. "When did you get an invitation from Trent? For his wedding?"

"I don't remember." I dunked the brush and started in again, but the hush of linen against paper brought me upright. "Hey!" I protested, wiping my hands dry on my robe to make the tie come undone. "You can't do that. It's illegal to open mail not addressed to you."

Jenks had landed on Ivy's shoulder, and they each gave me a long look over the invitation in her grip. "The seal was broken," Ivy said, shaking to the floor the stupid little white tissue paper I had carefully replaced.

Trent Kalamack was the bane of my existence, one of Cincinnati's most beloved councilmen, and the Northern Hemisphere's most eligible bachelor. No one seemed to care he ran half of the city's underworld and worked a good slice of the world's illegal Brimstone trade. That wasn't even considering his punishable-by-death dealings in genetic manipulation and outlawed medicines. *My* being alive because of them was a big part of *my* keeping quiet about it. I didn't like the Antarctic any more than the next person, and that's where I'd end up if it got out. That is, if they didn't just kill me, burn me, and send my ashes to the sun.

Suddenly having a demon trash my living room didn't seem so bad.

"Holy crap!" Jenks swore again. "Ellasbeth wants you to be a *brides-maid*?"

Jerking my robe closed, I stalked across the sanctuary and snatched the invitation out of Ivy's hand. "It's not an invitation, it's a badly worded request for me to work security. The woman hates me. Look, she didn't even sign it. I bet she doesn't even know it exists."

I waved it in the air and shoved it into a drawer, slamming it shut. Trent's fiancée was a bitch in all ways but the literal. Thin, elegant, rich, and bitingly polite. We had gotten along really well the night we had breakfast together, just her, me, and Trent caught between us. Course, part of that might have been from my letting her believe that Trent and I had been childhood sweethearts. But she was the one who decided I was a courtesan. Stupid Yellow Pages ad.

Ivy's expression was wary. She knew better than to push me when it came to Trent, but Jenks wouldn't let it go. "Yeah, but think of it, Rache. It's going to be a hell of a party. The best of Cincinnati is going to be there. You never know who will show up."

I lifted a plant and ran my hand under it—my version of dusting. "People who want to kill Trent," I said lightly. "I like excitement, but I'm not insane."

Ivy moved my bucket and mop to a dry part of the floor and sprayed a heavy layer of that unlabeled bottle. "You going to do it?" she asked, as if I hadn't already said no.

"No."

In one motion I swept all the papers off the desktop and into the uppermost drawer. Jenks landed on the clean surface, his wings stilling as he leaned against the pencil cup and crossed his ankles and arms to look surprisingly alluring for a four-inch-tall man. "Why not?" he accused. "You think he's going to stiff you?"

Again, I added in my thoughts. "Because I already saved his freaking elf ass once," I said. "You do it once, it's a mistake. You do it twice and it's not a mistake anymore."

Mop and bucket in hand, Ivy walked out, snickering.

"It's RSVP by tomorrow," Jenks needled. "Rehearsal is Friday. You're invited."

"I know that." It was my birthday, too, and I wasn't going to spend it with Trent. Ticked, I headed into the kitchen after Ivy.

Flying backward, Jenks got in my face and preceded me down the hallway, slices of sunlight coming in from the living room. "I've got two reasons you should do it," he said. "One, it will piss Ellasbeth off, and two, you could charge him enough to afford to resanctify the church."

My steps slowed, and I tried to keep the ugly look off my face. That was unfair. By the sink, Ivy frowned, clearly thinking the same. "Jenks . . ."

"I'm just saying—"

"She's not working for Kalamack," Ivy threatened, and this time he shut his mouth.

I stood in the kitchen, not knowing why I was here. "I gotta shower," I said.

"Go," Ivy said, meticulously—and needlessly—washing the bucket with soapy water before putting it away. "I'll wait up for the man coming over with an estimate."

I didn't like that. She'd probably fudge on the quote, knowing that her pockets were deeper than mine. She had told me she was nearly broke, but nearly broke for the last living member of the Tamwood vampires was not my broke, rather more of a down-to-six-figures-in-her bank-account broke. If she wanted something, she got it. But I was too tired to fight her.

"I owe you," I said as I grabbed the cooled tea Ceri had made for me and shuffled out.

"God, Jenks," Ivy was saying as I avoided my room with my scattered clothes and just headed for my bathroom. "The last thing she needs is to be working for Kalamack."

"I just thought—" the pixy said.

"No, you didn't think," Ivy accused. "Trent isn't some pantywaist rich pushover, he's a power-hungry, murdering drug lord who looks good in a suit. You don't think he's got some reason for inviting her to work security other than his welfare?"

"I wasn't going to let her go alone," he protested, and I shut the door. Sipping the tart tea, I dropped my pj's into the washer and got the shower going so I wouldn't have to listen to them. Sometimes I felt as if they thought I couldn't hear at all just because I couldn't hear a pixy belch across the graveyard. Yeah, they'd had a contest one night. Jenks won.

The water's warmth was wonderful, and after the sharp scent of pine soap washed away the choking smell of burnt amber, I stepped from the shower feeling refreshed and almost awake. Purple towel wrapped around me, I rubbed the mist from the long mirror, leaning close to see if I had any new freckles. Nope. Not yet. Opening my mouth, I checked out my beautiful, pristine teeth. It was nice not having any fillings.

I may have coated my soul in blackness when I had twisted a demon curse to turn into a wolf this spring, but I wasn't going to feel guilty over the beautiful unmarked skin I had when I turned back. The accumulated damage of twenty-five years of existence had been removed, and if I didn't find a way to get rid of the demon smut from twisting the curse before I died, I was going to pay for it by burning in hell.

At least I'm not going to feel too guilty about it, I thought as I reached for my lotion, heavy on the SPF protection. And I certainly wasn't going to waste it. My mother's family had come from Ireland long before the Turn, and from my mom I got my red hair, my green eyes, and my pale skin, now as satisfyingly soft and supple as a newborn's. From my dad I got my height, my lean, athletic build, and my attitude. From both of them I got a rare genetic condition that would have killed me before my first birthday if Trent's father hadn't set himself above the law and fixed it in his illegal genetic lab.

Our fathers had been friends before they'd died a week apart under suspicious circumstances. At least they were suspicious to me. And that was the reason I distrusted Trent, if his being a drug lord, a murderer, and nastily adept at manipulating me weren't enough.

Suddenly overcome with missing my dad, I shuffled through the cabinet behind the mirror until I found the wooden ring he'd given me on my thirteenth birthday. It had been the last one we'd shared before he died. I looked at it, small and perfect in my palm, and on impulse I put it on. I hadn't worn it since the charm it once held to hide my freckles had been broken, and I hadn't needed it since twisting that demon curse. But I missed him, and after being attacked by a demon this morning, I could use some serious emotional security.

I smiled at it circling my pinkie, feeling better already. The ring had come with a lifetime charm reinstatement, and I had an appointment every fourth Friday in July. Maybe I'd take the madam out for coffee instead. Ask her about maybe changing it to a sunscreen charm—if there was such a thing.

The give-and-take of masculine and feminine voices from the

kitchen became obvious as I toweled my hair. "He's here already?" I grumbled, finding a pair of underwear, jeans, and a red camisole in the dryer. Slipping them on, I dabbed some perfume behind each ear to help block my scent and Ivy's from mixing, combed my damp hair back with my fingers, and headed out.

But it wasn't a holy man I found in the kitchen covered in pixy children, it was Glenn.

THREE

"Hi, Glenn," I said as I slumped barefoot into my chair. "Who's pinching your ass today?"

The clearly uncomfortable, rather tall FIB detective was in a suit, which didn't bode well. He had Jenks's kids all over him, which was really weird. And Ivy was glaring at him from her computer, which was mildly troubling. But considering that the first time she met him, she almost bit him in anger and he almost shot her, I guessed we were doing okay.

Jenks scraped his wings, and his kids scattered, rising up through my rack of spelling supplies and herbs in a swirl of silk and shouts that hurt my eyeballs before flowing into the hall and probably out the chimney in the living room. I hadn't seen him on the sill until now, standing by his pet sea monkeys. *How come a pixy has more pets than I do?*

I smiled tiredly at Glenn across the table, trying to make up for my roommate's stellar attitude. There was a paperboard tray with two cups steaming between us, and the warm breeze coming in from the garden was pushing the heavenly aroma of freshly brewed coffee right to me. I wanted one in the worst way.

Ivy's fingers hit her keyboard aggressively as she weeded out her spam. "Detective Glenn was just leaving. Weren't you?"

The tall black man silently clenched his jaw. Since I'd seen him last, he had gotten rid of his goatee and mustache and replaced them with stud earrings. I wondered what his dad thought about that, but personally, I thought it added to his carefully maintained, polished image of young and capable law enforcer.

His suit was still off-the-rack, but it fit his very nice physique as if made for him. The tips of his dress shoes poking out from under the hems looked comfortable enough to run in if he had to. His trim body certainly seemed up to it, with that wide chest and narrow waist. The butt of a weapon glinted from a holster on his belt to give him a nice hint of danger.

Not that I'm in the market for a new boyfriend, I thought. I had a damn fine boyfriend, Kisten, and Glenn wasn't interested, though I'm sure if he "tried a witch, he'd never switch." And since I knew that his lack of interest wasn't born of prejudice, that was cool.

I exhaled, my fingers shaking from fatigue. My eyes went from his expressive brown ones pinched in worry and annoyance to the coffee. "Is one of these mine, by chance?" I asked, and when he nodded, I reached forward, saying, "Bless you back to the Turn." Pulling off the plastic lid, I took a gulp. My eyes closed, and I held the second swallow in my mouth for a moment. It was a double shot: hot, black, and oh so what I needed right now.

Ivy kept typing, and while Jenks excused himself to help the forgotten toddler crying in the ladle back to the stump in the garden, I took the time to wonder what Glenn was doing here. And so obscenely early. It was seven in the freakin' morning. I hadn't done anything to tick off the FIB—had I?

Glenn worked for the Federal Inderland Bureau, the human-run institution that functioned on a local and national level. The FIB was way outclassed by the I.S., the Inderlander-run side of the coin, when it came to enforcing the law, but during a previous investigation on which I'd helped Glenn, I'd found that the FIB had a scary amount of information on us Inderlanders, making me wish I hadn't written up those species summaries for his dad last fall. Glenn was Cincy's FIB Inderland specialist, which meant that he had enough guts to try working both sides of the street. It had been his dad's idea, and since I owed his dad bigtime, I helped when he asked.

No one was talking, though, and I figured I'd better say something before I fell asleep at the table. "What's the run, Glenn?" I asked, taking a sip and wishing the caffeine would kick in.

Glenn stood, his thick hands adjusting his ID badge on his belt. Square jaw tightening, he gave Ivy a wary glance. "I left a message last night. Didn't you get it?"

The depth of his voice was as soothing as the coffee he'd brought, but coming back in through the pixy hole in the screen, Jenks did an about face. "I think I hear Matalina," he said, vanishing to leave behind a sifting ribbon of gold sparkles. My eyes went from the haze of pixy dust to Ivy, and she shrugged. "No," I prompted.

Ivy's eyes switched to black. "Jenks!" she called, but the pixy didn't show. I shrugged and gave Glenn an apologetic look.

"Jenks!" Ivy yelled. "If you're going to hit the message button, you'd damn well better write it down!"

I took a slow breath, but Ivy interrupted me. "Glenn, Rachel hasn't been to bed yet. Can you come back about four?"

"The morgue will have changed shifts by then," he protested. "I'm sorry you didn't get my message, but will you look anyway? I thought that's why you were up."

Annoyance tightened my shoulders. I was tired and cranky, and I didn't like Ivy trying to field my business. In a sudden wash of bitchiness, I stood.

Framed by her new haircut, Ivy's oval face looked questioning. "Where are you going?"

I grabbed my bag, already packed with a variety of spells and charms, then snapped the top back onto my coffee. "To the morgue, apparently. I've been up this late before."

"But not after a night like you just had."

Silent, I pulled my bracelet from around Mr. Fish and wrangled the clasp. Glenn slowly stood, his posture holding a wary slant. He had once asked me why I lived with Ivy and the threat she posed to my life and free will, and though I knew why now, telling him would make him worry more, not less. "Jeez, Ivy," I said, aware he was analyzing us professionally. "I'd rather do it now. Consider it my bedtime story."

I headed into the hall, trying to remember where I'd left my sandals. *The foyer.* From the kitchen Ivy said, "You don't have to go running whenever the FIB crooks their finger."

"No!" I shouted back, fatigue making me stupid. "But I do have to come up with some money to resanctify the church."

Glenn's steps behind me faltered on the hardwood floor. "It isn't holy anymore?" he asked as we emerged into the brighter sanctuary. "What happened?"

"We had an incident." The darkness of the foyer was soothing when I found it, and I sighed when I scuffed into my sandals and pushed open the heavy door to the sanctuary. *Good Lord,* I thought, squinting at the bright glare of a late-July morning. No wonder I slept through this. It was noisy with shrieking birds, and already hot. If I had known I was going out, I would have put on shorts.

Glenn took my elbow when I stumbled on the step, and I would have spilled my coffee if I hadn't replaced the top. "Not a morning person, eh?" he teased, and I jerked away.

"Jenks!" I shouted when my sandals reached the cracked sidewalk. The least he could do was come with me. Seeing Glenn's cruiser parked at the curb, I hesitated. "Let's take two cars," I offered, not wanting to be seen riding in a FIB cruiser when I could be driving my red convertible. It was hot; I could put the top down.

Glenn chuckled. "With your suspended license? Not a chance."

The scuffing of my sandals slowed, and I looked askance at him, bothered at the amusement in his dark eyes. "Crap, how did you find out about that?"

He opened the passenger-side door for me. "Duh, I work for the FIB? Our street force has been running interference for you every time you go out for groceries. If you get caught driving with a suspended license, the I.S. is going to jail your ass, and we like your ass on the street where it can do some good, Ms. Morgan."

I got into the front seat and set my bag on my lap. I hadn't known the FIB had even *heard* about that, much less had been distracting the I.S. "Thanks," I said softly, and he shut the door with a grunt of acknowledgment.

Glenn crossed in front while I buckled myself in. It was stuffy, and I fiddled with the window control to put it down. The car wasn't on yet, but I was irritated. I jammed my coffee in the cup holder and kept messing with the window until Glenn folded his height into the front seat and gave me a look. My brow furrowed in frustration. "It's not fair,

Glenn," I complained. "They had no right to take my license. They're *picking* on me."

"Just take the driver's-ed class and get it over with."

"But it's not fair! They're intentionally making my life difficult."

"Golly, imagine that?" The key slid into the ignition, and Glenn paused to tug a pair of sunglasses out of his pocket and put them on to up his cool factor by about ten. Face easing in relief, he looked down the quiet street shaded with trees almost eighty years old. "What do you expect?" he said. "You gave them an excuse. They took it."

I drew a frustrated breath, holding it. So I ran a red light. It was yellow most of the way. And I went a little fast on the interstate once. But I suppose letting my ex-boyfriend run into me with a Mack truck to help a vampire start his undead existence might be cause for a few points. No one had died but the vampire, though—and he wanted to.

I fiddled with the button again, and Glenn took the hint. Warm air sifted in as the window whined down, replacing the scent of my perfume with the aroma of cut grass. "Jenks!" I called as he started the car. "Let's *go*!"

The rumble of the big car hid the clatter of Jenks's wings as he zipped in. "Sorry about the message, Rache," he muttered as he landed on the rearview mirror.

"Don't sweat it." I stretched my arm along the length of the open window, not wanting to ream him out over it. I'd taken enough flak from my brother for doing the same thing, and I knew it hadn't been intentional.

I settled into the leather seats as Glenn pulled onto the empty street. It would stay empty until about noon, when most of the Hollows started to wake up. My pulse was slow from the early hour, and the heat of the day made me sleepy. Glenn kept his car as tidy as himself; not an old coffee-stained cup or clutter of paperwork marred the floor or backseat. "So-o-o-o," I drawled around a yawn, "what's at the morgue besides the obvious?"

Glenn glanced at me as he yielded to a stop sign. "Suicide, but it's murder."

Of course it is. Nodding, I waved at the I.S. cruiser behind an overgrown bush, then made a bunny-eared "kiss-kiss" to the small Were in fatigues dozing on a bench in the sun watching them. It was Brett. The militant Were had been kicked out of his pack for having failed at kidnapping me a few months ago, so of course I was the one he wanted to pack up with next. It made sense in a warped sort of way. I had bested his alpha; therefore I was stronger.

David, my alpha, wasn't having anything to do with it, seeing as he hadn't wanted a pack in the first place. It was why he'd bucked the system and started one with a witch in order to keep his job. And so Brett was reduced to lurking on the outskirts of my life, looking for a way in. It was flattering as all hell, but depressing. I was going to have to talk to David. Having a militant Were attached to my chaotic life wasn't a bad idea, and Brett truly wanted someone to look to. It was how most Weres were put together. David's protest that Brett was trying to get in good with his original alpha by spying on me to see if I had the Were artifact that had instigated the kidnapping attempt was crap. Everyone believed that it had gone over the Mackinac Bridge, though in truth it was hidden in David's cat box.

Jenks cleared his throat, and when I glanced at him, he rubbed his thumb and fingers together in the universal indication of money. My eyes followed his to Glenn.

"Hey," I said, shifting in my seat, "this pays, right?" Glenn smiled, and, irritated, I sharpened my voice. "It does pay, *right*?"

Chuckling, the FIB detective glanced in the rearview mirror at Brett and nodded. "Why—" he started, and I interrupted.

"He wants into my pack, and David is balking," I said. "What's so important about this body that you need me to look at it? I'm a lousy detective. It's not what I do."

Glenn's square face was heavy with concern as he looked back at me from the Were behind us. "She's a Were. The I.S. says suicide, but I think it's murder and they're covering it up."

I let the air pressure push my hand up and then down, enjoying the breeze in my shower-damp hair and the feel of my bracelet sliding against my skin. *The I.S. is covering up a murder? Big surprise there.* Jenks looked happy, silent now that we were working and the question of money had been raised, though not settled. "Standard consultant fee," I said.

"Five hundred a day plus expenses," Glenn said, and I laughed.

"Try double that, ketchup boy. I have insurance to pay." *And a church to sanctify, and a living room to repair.*

Glenn's attention on the road went distant. "For two hours of your time, that would be what? Two-fifty?"

Crap. He wanted to go hourly. I frowned, and Jenks's wings slowed to nothing. That might pay for the paneling and the guys to put it in. Maybe.

"Okay," I said, digging through my bag to find the calendar datebook that Ivy had given me last year. It wasn't accurate anymore, but the pages were blank and I needed somewhere to keep track of my time. "But you can expect an itemized bill."

Glenn grinned. "What?" I said, squinting from the come-and-go sun.

He lifted one shoulder and let it fall. "You look so . . . organized," he said, and when Jenks snickered, I flung my hand out and bopped Glenn on the shoulder with the back of my fist.

"Just for that, no more ketchup for you," I muttered, slouching. His grip on the wheel tightened, and I knew I'd hit a sore spot.

"Aw, don't worry, Glenn," Jenks teased. "Christmas is coming. I'll get you a jar of belly-buster jalapeño that will knock your socks off if Rachel won't pimp tomatoes to you anymore."

Glenn shot me a sideways look. "Um, actually, I've got a list," he said, fumbling in an inner coat pocket to bring out a narrow strip of paper with his distinctive, precise handwriting on it. My eyebrows rose as I took it: hot ketchup, spicy BBQ sauce, tomato paste, salsa. His usual.

"You need a new pair of cuffs, right?" he said nervously.

"Yeah," I said, suddenly a lot more awake. "But if you can get ahold of some of those zip-strips the I.S. uses to keep ley line witches from invoking their magic, that'd be great."

"I'll see what I can do," he said, and I bobbed my head, satisfied.

Though Glenn's stiff neck said he was uncomfortable bartering law-enforcement tools for ketchup, I thought it funny that the stoic, straitlaced human was too embarrassed to walk into a store that sold tomatoes. Humanity avoided them like the plague, which was understandable, seeing as a tomato had carried the virus that killed a sizable portion of their population four decades ago and revealed the supernatural species previously hidden by the sheer numbers of humans. But he had been forced into eating pizza, real pizza, not the Alfredo crap that humans serve, and it had been all downhill from there.

I wasn't going to give him a hard time about it. We all had our fears. The fact that Glenn's was that he craved something every other human on the planet shunned was the least of my worries. *And if it got me some zip-strips that might someday save my life,* I thought as I settled back into the leather seats, *then it's a secret well kept.*

FOUR

The morgue was quiet and cool, a quick shift from July to September, and I was glad I had jeans on. My sandals popped against the dirty cement steps as I descended sideways, and the fluorescent light in the stairway only added to the bleak feeling. Jenks was on my shoulder for the warmth, and Glenn made a quick turn to the right when he reached the landing, following the big blue arrows painted on the walls past wide elevators and to the double doors cheerfully proclaiming CINCINNATI MORGUE, AN EQUAL-OPPORTUNITY SERVICE SINCE 1966.

Between the underground dimness and Glenn's coffee still in my grip, I was feeling better, but most of my good mood was from the honest-to-God temp name tag Glenn had handed me when we started down the steps. It wasn't the bent, nasty, yellow laminated four-by-six card everyone else got but a real heavyweight plastic tag embossed with my name. Jenks had one, too, and he was obnoxiously proud of it even though I was the one wearing it, right under mine. It would get me into the morgue when nothing else would. Well, besides being dead.

I didn't do much for the FIB, but somehow I had become their darling, the poor little witch girl who fled the I.S. tyranny to make her own way. They were the ones who had given me my car in lieu of monetary compensation when the I.S. called foul after I helped the FIB solve a crime that I.S. hadn't been able to. It had since been ruled that because

I wasn't on the FIB's payroll, the FIB could hire me much as any corporation or individual could. *Na-na, na, na-a-a, na.*

It was the small things that really made your day.

Glenn pushed open one of the double doors, standing aside so I could go in first. Flip-flops plopping, I scanned the large reception room, more rectangle than square, half of it empty floor, half upright file cabinets and an ugly steel desk that should have been thrown away in the seventies. A college-age kid wearing a lab coat was behind it, his feet on the paper-cluttered desk and a handheld game in his hands. A sheet-draped gurney holding a body waited for attention, but apparently some space aliens needed taking care of first.

The blond kid looked up at our entrance and, after giving me the once-over, set his game down and stood. It smelled in here: pine and dead tissue. Yuck.

"Yo, Iceman," Glenn said, and Jenks grunted in surprise when the straitlaced FIB detective exchanged a complicated arm-, fist-, elbow-slapping . . . thing with the guy at the desk.

"Glenn," the blond kid said, still giving me glances. "You've got about ten minutes."

Glenn slipped him a fifty, and Jenks choked. "Thanks. I owe you."

"You cool. Just make it fast." He handed Glenn a key chained to a naked Bite-Me-Betty doll. No way would anyone be walking out with the morgue key.

I gave him an ambiguous smile and headed for another set of double doors.

"Miss!" the kid called, his adopted colorful accent dissolving into farm-boy Americana.

Jenks snickered. "Someone wants a date."

Sandals scuffing, I turned to find Iceman following us. "Ms. Morgan," the guy said, his eyes dropping to my twin name tags. "If you don't mind. Could you leave your coffee out here?" At my blank look, he added, "It might wake someone up early, and with the vamp orderly out getting lunch, it would . . ." He winced. "It might be bad."

My lips parted in understanding. "Sure," I said, handing it to him. "No problem."

Immediately he relaxed. "Thanks." He turned back to his desk, then hesitated. "Ah, you aren't Rachel Morgan, the runner, are you?"

From my shoulder Jenks sniggered. "My, aren't we the famous one."

But I beamed, facing the kid fully as Glenn fidgeted. He could wait. I wasn't often recognized—and it was even more rare that I didn't have to run away when I was. "Yes, I am," I said, enthusiastically shaking his hand. "Pleased to meet you."

Iceman's hands were warm, and his eyes gave away his delight. "Acc," he said, jiggling on his feet. "Wait here. I've got something for you."

Glenn's grip on the Bite-Me-Betty doll tightened until he realized where his fingers were, and he shifted his grip to the tiny key. Iceman had gone back to his desk and was rummaging in a drawer. "It's here," he said. "Give me a sec." Jenks started humming the tune to *Jeopardy!*, finishing when the kid slammed the drawer triumphantly. "Got it." He jogged back to us, and I felt my face lose its expression when I saw what he was extending proudly to me. *A toe tag?*

Jenks left my shoulder, shocking Iceman out of a year's growth when he landed on my wrist so he could see it. I don't think he'd even known that Jenks was here. "Holy crap, Rachel!" Jenks exclaimed. "It's got your name on it! In ink, even." He lifted into the air, laughing. "Isn't that sweet?" he mocked, but the guy was too flustered to notice.

A toe tag? I held it loosely in my hand, bemused. "Uh, thanks," I managed.

Glenn made a derisive noise from deep in his chest. I was starting to feel like the butt of a joke when Iceman grinned and said, "I was working the night that boat exploded last Christmas? I made it up for you, but you never came in. I kept it as a souvenir." His clean-cut face suddenly went nervous. "I . . . uh, thought you might want it."

Relaxing in understanding, I tucked it in my bag. "Yes, thank you," I said, then touched his shoulder so he'd know it was okay. "Thank you very much."

"Can we go in now?" Glenn grumbled, and Iceman gave me an embarrassed smile before returning to his desk, steps fast to make his open lab coat furl. Sighing, the FIB detective pushed open one of the double doors for me.

Actually, I was really glad to have the toe tag. It had been made with the intent for use and therefore was imbued with a strong connection that a ley line charm could use to target me. Better I have it than someone else. I'd get rid of it safely when I had the time.

Past the door was another, to make an airlock of sorts. The smell of dead things grew, and Jenks landed on my shoulder, standing right by my ear and the dab of perfume I'd put on earlier. "Spend a lot of time down here?" I asked Glenn as we entered the morgue proper.

"Fair amount." He wasn't looking at me, more interested in the numbers and index cards slid into the holders fastened to the people-size drawer doors. I was getting the creeps. I'd never been to the city morgue before, and I dubiously eyed the arrangement of comfortable chairs around a coffee table at the far end that looked like a reception area at a doctor's office.

The room was long, having four rows of drawers on either side of the wide middle space. It was storage and self-repair only, no autopsies, necropsies, or assisted tissue repair. Humans on one side, Inderlanders on the other, though Ivy had told me they all had pull tabs inside in case of accidental misfiling.

I followed Glenn to midway down the Inderland side, watching him double-check the card against a slip of paper before unlocking the door and yanking it open. "Came in Monday," he said over the sound of sliding metal as the tray slid out. "Iceman didn't like the attention given to her, so he gave me a call."

Monday. As in yesterday? "The full moon isn't until next week," I said, avoiding the sheet-draped body. "Isn't that early for a Were suicide?"

I met his deep brown eyes, reading a sad understanding. "That's what I thought, too."

Not knowing what I would see, I looked down as Glenn folded the sheet back.

"Holy crap!" Jenks exclaimed. "Mr. Ray's secretary?"

A sour expression fixed on me. When had being a secretary become a high-risk position? No way had Vanessa committed suicide. She wasn't an alpha, but she was pretty damn close.

Glenn's surprise turned to understanding. "That's right," his low voice rumbled. "You stole that fish from Mr. Ray's office."

Irritation flickered through me. "I *thought* I was *rescuing* it. And it wasn't *his* fish. David said Mr. Ray stole it first."

Eyebrows bunched, Glenn seemed to think it made no difference. "She came in as a wolf," he was saying, his manner professional as his eyes lit on only the bruised and torn parts of her naked body. A small but gorgeous koi tattoo swam in orange and black across a high patch of her upper chest, a permanent sign of her inclusion into the Ray pack. "Standard procedure is to turn them back after the first look. It's easier to find the cause of death on a person than on a wolf."

The smell of dead things in a pine forest was getting to me. It didn't help that I was running on empty. The coffee wasn't setting well anymore. And I'd known the SOP, having briefly dated a guy who made the charms to force a shift back to human. He was a geek, but he had lots of money—it wasn't an easy job, and no one wanted it.

Jenks was making a cold spot on my neck, and not seeing anything out of the ordinary—other than her being dead and her arm torn to the bone—I murmured, "What am I looking at?"

Nodding, Glenn went to a low drawer at the end of the room and, after checking the tag, pulled it open. "This is a Were suicide that came in last month," he said. "You can see the differences. She would have been cremated by now, but we don't know who she is. Two additional Jane Wolfs came in on the same night, and they're giving them a little extra time."

"They all came in together?" I asked, going over to look.

"No," he said softly, gazing down at her in pity. "There's no connection other than the timing and that none of them can be found in the computer. No one's claimed them, and they don't match any missing-persons report—U.S.-wide."

From my shoulder came Jenks's muffled voice saying, "She don't smell like a Were. She smells like perfume."

I winced when Glenn unzipped the bag to show that the woman's entire side had been ravaged. "Self-inflicted," he said. "They found tissue between her teeth. It's not uncommon, though they're usually a lot less brutal than this and simply open a vein and bleed out. A jogger found her in an alley in Cincinnati. He called the pound." The faint wrinkles around Glenn's eyes deepened with anger. He didn't have to say that the jogger had been human.

Jenks was quiet, and I searched for cool detachment as I examined her. She was tall for a Were, but not overly so. Big up top, with shoulder-length hair that curled gently where it wasn't matted. Pretty. No tattoos that I could see. Mid-thirties? She took care of herself, given the definition. I wondered what had been so bad that she thought the answer was to end it.

Seeing me satisfied, Glenn opened a third drawer. "This one was hit by a car," he said as he unzipped the sturdy bag. "The officer recognized her as being a Were, and she made it to the hospital. They actually had her turned back to treat her, but she died." Creases appeared in his brow as he looked at her damaged body. "Her heart gave out. Right on the table."

I forced my gaze down, flinching at the bruises and skin split by the accident. IV tips were still in her, evidence of the efforts to save her life. Jane Wolf number two had brown hair as well, longer this time, but it curled the same way. She looked the same age and had the same narrow chin. Apart from a scrape on her cheekbone, her face was untouched, and she seemed professional and collected.

Running in front of a car wasn't uncommon, the Were equivalent of a human jumper. Most times they weren't successful, landing under a doctor's care, where they should have been in the first place.

I followed Glenn to a fourth drawer, finding out why Jenks was being so quiet when he gagged and flew to the trash can. "Train," Glenn said simply, his voice soft with regret.

Coffee and lack of sleep were warring in me, but I'd seen a demon slaughter, and this was like dying in your sleep compared to that. I think I was earning points with Glenn as I looked her over, trying not to breathe in the scent of decay the chill of the room couldn't stop. It appeared as if Jane Wolf number three was as tall as the first woman and possessed the same athletic body build. Brown hair to her shoulders. I couldn't tell if she had been pretty or not.

Seeing me nod, Glenn zipped up the bag and shut the drawer, closing all of them on his way back to Vanessa. Not entirely sure why he had wanted me to see this, I trailed behind him.

Jenks's wings were silent as he returned, and I gave him a sympathetic smile. "Don't tell Ivy I lost it," he asked, and I nodded. "They all smell the same," he said, and I felt him hold on to my ear for balance as he stood as close as he could to my perfumed neck.

"Jeez, Jenks, they all *look* the same to me." But I don't think he appreciated my attempt at humor.

Glenn's steps slowed to a halt, and we gazed at Mr. Ray's secretary.

"Those three women were suicides," he said, "the first one dying by self-mutilation, as Mr. Ray's secretary appears to have died. I think she was murdered, then doctored up to mimic suicide."

I glanced at him, wondering if he was looking for ghosts in the fog. Seeing my doubt, he ran a hand over his short, curly hair. "Look at this," he said, leaning over Vanessa and picking up a limp hand. "See?" he said, his dark fingers circling her thin wrist in sharp contrast to her pale skin. "That looks like a bruise caused by restraints. Soft restraints, but restraints. They aren't on the woman who made it to the hospital, and I *know* they had to tie her down."

Okay. Now I was interested. Maybe Vanessa had been into sex games and it went too far? Leaning forward, I agreed that the soft red ring could have resulted from a restraint, but it was her nails that caught my attention. They had been professionally manicured, but the tips were split and ragged. A woman considering suicide doesn't pay beaucoup bucks to get her nails done, then tear them up before she can end her life properly. "Where was she found?" I asked softly.

Glenn heard my interest and flicked me a grin that quickly sobered. "Under a dock in the Hollows. A tour group spotted her before she could get cold."

Not wanting to be left out, Jenks flew from my shoulder to hover over her. "*She* smells like a Were," he proclaimed. "And fish. And rubbing alcohol."

Glenn twitched the sheet with which she'd been covered in lieu of a bag all the way off. "Her ankles have pressure marks, too."

My brow furrowed. "So someone held her against her will and then killed her?"

Jenks's wings clattered. "There's a strand of medical tape caught in her teeth."

The breath Glenn had taken to answer me exploded out of him. "You're kidding."

Adrenaline pinged, and feeling woozy, I looked to see. "I'm not trained for this," I said when Glenn took a penlight from his pocket and motioned for me to hold her mouth open. Gingerly I took her jaw in my hands. "I'm *not* going to take a knife to her and poke around."

"Good." He trained the light on her teeth. "I don't have authorization for that."

The squeak of the double doors pulled my head up. Jenks swore as I let go of Vanessa's jaw, my swinging hand almost smacking him. Tension flashed to fear for an instant as I saw Denon, my old boss from the I.S., standing in the middle of the floor like the king of the dead.

"This is an Inderland matter. You don't have clearance to even look at her," he said, his honey-smooth voice rippling over my spine like water over rocks.

Damn it all to hell, I thought, jerking my fear back. He wasn't my boss anymore. He wasn't anything. But I was too deep underground to tap a line, and I didn't like it.

The low-blood living vampire smiled to show his human teeth, a startling white beside his oh-so-beautiful mahogany skin. Iceman was behind him along with a second living vampire, high-blood this time by his small but sharp canines. The scent of burgers and fries had come in with them, and it looked like Glenn's fifty dollars had bought less time than he'd hoped.

Jenks rose in a hum of wings. "Look what the cat dragged in and puked up," he snarled. "It smells like it used to be something, but I can't tell what, Rache. Fuzzy rat balls, maybe?"

Denon ignored him, as he ignored everyone he thought beneath his notice, but I caught a twitch of an eye as he kept smiling, trying to impress me with his mere presence.

Glenn clicked off his penlight and tucked it away, his jaw tensed, unrepentant. Denon wasn't anything to be afraid of. Not that he ever had been, and especially not now. He was probably the reason I had lost my license, though, and that ticked me off.

With a practiced swagger, the large muscular man came forward on cat-light feet. He was technically a ghoul, a rude term for a human bitten by an undead and intentionally infected with enough of the vamp virus to partially turn him. And whereas living high-blood vampires like Ivy were born to their status and envied for having a portion of the undead's strengths without the drawbacks, a low-blood vampire was little more than a source of blood as they tried to curry the favor of the one who had promised them immortality.

Denon clearly worked hard to build up his human strength, and though his biceps strained his polo shirt and his thighs were heavy with iron-pumping muscle, he still fell short of his brethren and would until he died and became a true undead. And *that* was contingent upon his "sponsor" remembering and/or bothering to finish the job. With Denon taking the blame for Ivy's leaving the I.S. with me, that likelihood was looking slim. His master had turned a blind eye, and Denon knew it. It made him unpredictable and dangerous, since he was trying to ingratiate himself back into his master's good graces. The fact that he was working the morning shift spoke volumes.

Though still beautiful, he had lost the ageless look of one who feeds upon the undead. It was likely they were still feeding on him, though. He had once overseen an entire floor of runners, but this was the second time I'd seen him working the streets since leaving.

"How's your car, Morgan?" his beautiful voice taunted, and I bristled.

"Fine." Anger overpowered my fatigue to make me stupid. The two techs slipped quietly out, and I heard a soft conversation and the metallic clinks of a gurney being set up.

Denon's pupil-black eyes rose from the dead secretary. "Come to see your handiwork?" he mocked, and Jenks lit us with a burst of light.

"Move off the corpse, Jenks," I muttered, coming out from behind the drawer to give myself room to move. "You're getting dust all over it."

Denon smirked, hiding his human-size teeth like the joke they were. I put my hands on my hips and tossed my hair. "Are you saying this isn't a suicide?" I taunted, seeing a chance to irritate him. " 'Cause if you say I'm responsible for her murder, I'm going to sue your little brown candy ass from here to the next Turn."

In a smooth motion, Glenn yanked the sheet over Vanessa. He hadn't said anything yet, which I thought was remarkable since it had been only a year ago that he thought he didn't owe vampires any respect at all. Leave the needling to those who might survive it.

"The evidence speaks for itself." Denon moved forward to force Glenn and Jenks back. "I'm releasing her to her next of kin for cremation. Move."

Damn it back to the Turn, in a few hours everything would be gone. Even the paper and computer files. That's why he was doing this at such an insane hour. By the time everyone was at work, it'd be too late. Eyes narrowing, I forced a laugh. It was bitter, and I didn't like the sound of it. "Is that what you're doing now?" I mocked. "You been bumped to *clerk*?"

Denon's eyes tried to go black. It was stupid pushing him like this, but I felt the lack of sleep keenly, and I did have Glenn beside me. What was Denon going to do?

The rattle of the gurney intruded, and Denon swaggered forward, trying to shove Glenn away with his presence. Glenn wasn't moving. "You can't take her," the FIB detective said, putting a possessive hand on the top of the door. "This has become a murder investigation."

Denon laughed, but the two guys with the gurney hesitated and exchanged knowing looks. "It's been ruled a suicide. You have no jurisdiction. The body is mine."

Crap. We didn't have anything yet, and if we didn't find it, we'd look like fools.

"Until it's been ruled a human didn't murder her, I have all the jurisdiction I need," Glenn said. "She has pressure marks on her wrists. She was held against her will."

"Circumstantial." Denon's brown fingers reached for the drawer handle. Glenn didn't back down, and the tension rose until Jenks's wings were making a high whine.

I shuffled around in my bag and brought out my cell phone. Not that I could actually reach a tower down here. "We can have a court order in four hours. Your enthusiasm to destroy the evidence will be on it. Still want to release her?"

Jenks landed on my shoulder. "You can't get a court order that fast," he whispered, and I broke out in a sweat. Yeah, I knew it would take a day, if I could get one at all, but I couldn't just let Denon walk out of here with the body.

Denon's jaw was gritted. "Pressure marks don't mean shit."

Jenks flew from me to hover over Vanessa. "How about needle marks?" he said.

"Where?" I blurted, crossing the room to look. "I don't see them."

The small pixy was smug. " 'Cause they're small. Pixy-size needles. Like fiber-optics. You can see the welt on the torn skin. Whoever drugged her tried to cover it up by tearing her arm as if it was a suicide. But they're there. You'll need a microscope to see them."

A grim smile twitched Glenn's lips, and together we turned to

Denon. The word of a pixy didn't mean squat in court, but knowingly destroying evidence did. The vampire looked ticked. Good. I'd hate to think I was the only one having a bad morning.

"Get her arm looked at," he said brusquely, muscles hard with tension. "I want the report before the ink dries."

Oh, God, I thought, rolling my eyes. *Could he have picked a more trite analogy?*

Glenn shoved the drawer closed, locking it before handing the key to Iceman. Jenks was hovering beside me, and I said nothing, smiling because I knew we were right and Denon was wrong, and the I.S. was going to come out looking like idiots.

But Denon chuckled, surprising me. "You keep pissing people off, Morgan, and before long the only people who will want to hire you are those homeless bridge trolls and miscreants dealing in black magic. It's your fault she died. No one else's."

The blood drained from my face, and Jenks snapped his wings aggressively. Not only did Denon know she had been murdered and was trying to cover it up, but he was blaming me for it. "You son of a bitch," Jenks seethed, and I moved my fingers to tell him to stay out of it. I couldn't catch a pixy, but maybe a ticked vampire could.

Giving me a beautiful smile, Denon turned, as confident and power-hungry as when he had come in. Jenks was a blur of wings and anger. "Don't listen to him, Rachel. This wasn't your fault. It couldn't have been."

I looked at the covered corpse. *Please, God. Let it have nothing to do with me.* "Yeah, I know," I said, hoping he was right. There was no way. My only connection to her was that fish, and that had been settled. She had been Mr. Ray's secretary, not responsible for it at all. And besides, the fish hadn't been Mr. Ray's to begin with.

Glenn put a comforting hand on my shoulder, and we walked slowly to the double doors to allow Denon time to leave. The reception room held only Iceman and a fading conversation filtering in from the hall. I waited while Glenn exchanged a few words with the orderly, promising to come back for the paperwork after escorting me home. Vanessa's body wouldn't be released now until murder had been ruled out, but I wasn't finding any satisfaction in it. The I.S. was going to be really ticked if I blew one of their cover-ups. Goody, goody.

Tugging my bag back up my shoulder, I waved to the edgy Iceman and headed out with Glenn. Jenks was silent. Glenn had my coffee in one hand, my elbow in the other. My thoughts were on Vanessa while he guided me unseeing through the upper levels of the building and back into the sun. I didn't say a word all the way home, and the conversation between Jenks and Glenn lagged. In their silence I thought I heard agreement that I might have been responsible in some way for the woman's death. But I couldn't. I just couldn't have been.

I didn't look up from the dash until I felt the soothing shade of my street. Jenks muttered something and slipped out the open window before Glenn brought the car to a stop. I glanced up then, finding the hazy morning slipping into the time of day I was usually just waking.

"Thanks for coming out with me," Glenn said, and I turned to him, surprised at the honest relief in his eyes. "Officer Denon gives me the creeps," he added, and I managed a smile.

"He's a pushover," I said, gathering my bag onto my lap.

Glenn pulled his eyebrows up. "If you say so. At least Vanessa's body won't be destroyed. And now I'll have access to any record I want until human involvement is ruled out. I think I can take it from here."

I huffed. "Then why did you have me come out, Mr. FIB Agent?"

He grinned to show his teeth. "Jenks found the needle marks, and you distracted Denon and got him to back down. A court order?" he said, chuckling. I shrugged, and Glenn added, "He's afraid of you, you know."

"Me? I don't think so." I fumbled for the door handle. Crap, I was tired. "I'm still sending you a bill," I said, checking the time on the dash's clock.

"Uh, Rachel," Glenn said before I got out, "I've another reason I came over."

I hesitated, and looking unhappy, Glenn reached under the seat and handed me a thick folder held closed with a rubber band.

"What is it?" I questioned, and he gestured at me to open it. Setting it atop my lap, I rolled the rubber band off and leafed through the file. It was mostly photocopied newspaper clippings and reports from the FIB and I.S. concerning theft crimes spanning the entire North American continent and a few overseas in the UK and Germany: rare books, magical artifacts, jewelry with historical significance . . . I felt myself go cold despite the July heat as I realized that this was Nick's file.

"Call me if he contacts you," Glenn said, his voice with a curious tightness to it. He didn't like asking me, but he was.

I swallowed, unable to look at him. "He went off the Mackinac Bridge," I said, feeling unreal. "You think he survived that?" I knew he had. He had called me when he realized he'd swiped the fake Were artifact from me and I had the real one.

A band fixed around my chest and squeezed. *Crap. That's what Newt was looking for. Shit, shit, shit—this was why Vanessa was murdered?* The I.S. knew I'd possessed the focus once, but they and everyone else thought it had gone over the bridge with Nick Sparagmos. Did someone know that it had survived and was now killing Weres to find out who had it? *Oh, God. David.*

"I want this one, Rachel," Glenn said, jerking me back to reality. "I know it's Nick."

I felt like I was wrapped in cotton, and I knew my eyes were too wide when I turned to him. "I guessed he was a thief. I didn't know until he left. I didn't want to believe it," I said.

Soft pity was in his eyes. "I know you didn't."

My pulse leapt, and I took a fast breath. Glenn touched my shoulder, probably thinking it was the shock of finding out for sure that Nick was a thief that had my hands shaking, not that I knew what Newt wanted and why Vanessa had been murdered. Damn it, she'd been drugged and then murdered because she hadn't known anything about it. Telling Glenn wouldn't do any good. This was an Inderland concern, and he would only get himself killed. I had to call David. Take it back before Newt tracked it to him. He couldn't fight a demon.

Like I can?

I reached for the door latch, my mind whirling. "Thanks for the ride, Glenn," I said, my manners on autopilot.

"Whoa, whoa, whoa," he said, putting a dark hand on my arm. "Are you going to be okay?"

I forced myself to meet his eyes. "Yeah, I'll be fine," I lied. "This threw me, is all."

His hand slipped away, and I slid the folder onto the seat between us and got out to stand unsteadily on the sidewalk. My eyes went to the house where Ceri lived. She was probably asleep, but as soon as she woke up, I was going to talk to her.

"Rachel . . ."

Maybe she knew a way to destroy the focus.

"Rachel?"

Sighing, I leaned to look back into the car. Glenn was extending the folder to me, shoulder muscles bunched from the weight of it. "Keep it," he said, and when I moved to protest, he added, "They're copies. You should know what he's done . . . in any case."

Hesitating, I took them, feeling its heavy bulk pulling me down into the sidewalk. "Thanks," I said, not caring. I shut the door and headed for the church.

"Rachel!" he called, and I jerked to a stop and turned. "The visitor tags?" he prompted.

Oh, yeah. I came back and set the file on the roof of the car while I removed the tags and handed them to him through the window.

"Promise me you won't drive until you finish your driver's ed," he said in parting.

"Sure thing," I muttered, retrieving the file and walking away. It was out again. The world knew the focus hadn't been lost, and as soon as someone realized I still had it, I was going to be in seriously deep shit.

FIVE

The hot morning had turned to rain by the time I'd gotten up again, and it felt odd rising so close to sunset. I'd gone to bed in a bad mood, and I awoke with the same, having been startled into consciousness by Skimmer ringing the front bell at about four in the afternoon. I'm sure Ivy had answered it as fast as she could, but going back to sleep was too much an effort. Besides, Ceri was coming over tonight, and she wasn't going to find me in my underwear again.

My arm ached as I stood at the sink in my shorts and camisole and polished the copper teakettle; Ceri's silent disgust at my kettle this morning had galvanized me into cleaning it. She was going to help me sketch out another calling circle. Maybe in chalk this time, so it wasn't as gross. I was starting to look forward to Minias's visit. He might destroy the focus in exchange for my finding Newt for him, and after watching Ceri bargain with Al, I wanted her help with Minias. That woman was more devious with her turns of phrase than Trent.

I had called David before falling asleep, and after a heated discussion that had emptied the church of every last pixy, he flatly told me that if the murderer hadn't tracked the focus to him by now, whoever it was probably wouldn't, and moving it out of his freezer would only draw attention to it. I wasn't convinced, but if he wouldn't bring it to me, I'd have to go get it. Meaning I'd be bringing it home on the bus or the back of Ivy's cycle. Neither of which was a good idea.

Blowing a red curl out of the way, I rinsed the kettle, dried it, and set it on the back burner. It wasn't gleaming, but it was better. The cloying scent of polish was thick in the close air, and since the rain had stopped, I shoved the window open with two gritty fingers.

Cool damp drifted in, and I looked out onto the dark, soggy garden as I washed my hands. A frown settled as I saw my nails, the polish ruined and green in the cuticles. *Crap. I just did them, too.*

Sighing, I set the dish towel aside and turned to the pantry. I was starved, and if I didn't eat something before Ceri got here, I'd look like a pig when I ate the entire bag of cookies intended for the occasion. I stood in the walk-in pantry, staring at the cans of fruit, bottles of ketchup, and cake mixes in the tidy rows into which Ivy organized our groceries. She'd probably label them if I let her. I reached for the elbow macaroni and an envelope of powdered sauce—quick, fast, full of carbs. Just what the witch doctor ordered.

From the sanctuary came a thump and a light laugh, reminding me I wasn't alone. Ivy had galvanized her old high-school roommate, Skimmer, into moving the living room furniture to the sanctuary, partly to make room for Three Guys and a Toolbox to put the paneling up, partly to put space between Skimmer and me. Though Skimmer was frustratingly nice, she was Piscary's lawyer—as if being a living vampire wasn't scary enough—and I wasn't keen on being nice back to her.

Dropping the saucepan on the stove, I dug around under the counter until I remembered that Jenks's kids were using the big pot as a fort in the garden. Bothered, I filled my largest spell pot with water and set it on the stove. Mixing food prep and spell prep wasn't a good idea, but I didn't use this one for spells anymore—now that it had a dent the size of Ivy's head in it.

I melted the butter for the sauce while the water warmed. There was a burst of noise from the sanctuary, and my shoulders eased at NIN's belligerent music. The volume dropped, and Skimmer's cheerful voice made a pleasant counterpoint to Ivy's soft response. It struck me that though a living vampire, Skimmer was a lot like me in that she was quick to laugh and didn't let bad things bother her on the outside—a quality Ivy seemed to need to balance herself out.

Skimmer had been in Cincinnati for a good six months, out from California and a sympathetic vampire camarilla to get Piscary out of prison. She and Ivy had met their last two years of high school on the West Coast, sharing blood and their bodies both, and that, not Piscary, was what had pulled Skimmer from her master vampire and family. I had met her last year, when she started our relationship off firmly on the wrong foot by mistaking me for Ivy's shadow and, as was polite, making a courteous bid for my blood.

My motions to push the pat of butter around the saucepan slowed, and I forced my hand from my neck, not liking that I'd tried to cover the scar hidden there under my perfect skin. The jolt of desire the woman had given me had been heady and shocking, surpassed only by the embarrassment that she had misunderstood the relationship Ivy and I had. Hell, I didn't understand it. Expecting Skimmer to in the first thirty seconds of meeting me was ridiculous.

I knew that Ivy and Skimmer had picked up where they'd left off, which I think was the reason Piscary agreed to take Skimmer into his own camarilla if the pretty vampire could win his case. And as I mixed the butter, milk, and sauce powder, I wondered if Piscary was starting to rue his leniency in letting Ivy maintain a friendship with me that was based not on blood but on respect. He probably expected Skimmer to lure Ivy back to a proper vampiric frame of mind.

Ivy, though, had been a lot easier to live with the last few months as she slaked her blood lust with someone she loved who could survive her attentions. She was happy. Guilty, but happy. I didn't think Ivy could be happy if she didn't slather it with guilt. And in the interim we could pretend that I wasn't feeling the first lure of blood ecstasy, not pushing the issue because Ivy was afraid. Our roles were reversed, and I didn't have as much practice as Ivy did at telling myself I couldn't have something I wanted.

The wooden spoon rattled against the pan as my hand trembled, the thrill of adrenaline zinging through me at the memory of her teeth sliding cleanly into me, fear and pleasure mixing in an unreal sensation, filling me with the rush of ecstasy.

As if the memory had called her, Ivy's lanky silhouette appeared in the hallway. Dressed in tight jeans and a shirt cut high to show her belly-button ring, she went to the fridge for a bottled water. Her motions to open it slowed as she scented the air, realizing I'd been thinking about her, or at least about something that would get my rush flowing and my pulse up. Pupils swelling, she eyed me from across the kitchen. "That perfume isn't working anymore," she said.

I hid my smile, thinking I should just stop wearing it, but pushing her into biting me again was a bad idea. "It's an old one," I said. "I didn't have anything else in the bathroom."

Much to my surprise, she shook her head and chuckled. She was in a good mood, and I wondered what she and Skimmer had been doing in there besides rearranging the furniture. *Not my business,* I thought, turning back to my sauce.

Ivy was silent as she took another swig, leaning against the counter with her ankles crossed. I felt her eyes rove the kitchen, landing on the kettle shining dully on a back burner. "Is Ceri coming over?" she asked.

Nodding, I looked into the damp garden, shadowed into an early dusk from the clouds. "She's going to help me with my calling glyph." I glanced at her, my spoon still circling. *Clockwise, clockwise . . . never widdershins.* "What's your schedule tonight?"

"I'm out and won't be back until almost sunup. I've got a run." In a motion of powerful grace, she used one hand to ease herself up to sit on the counter.

"You going to take Jenks?" I asked, wanting him here with me, but my scaredy-cat fears came in second after a real job.

"No." Ivy ran her fingers up through the downward spikes of her shorter hair in a show of nervousness, telling me she was doing something for Piscary, not her bank account. She was the master vampire's scion, and that came first—when it didn't involve me. "Do you think that ugly statue is what that demon was after?"

"The focus?" Running a finger over the spoon, I licked it and set it in the sink. "What else could it be? Ceri says if Newt knew that David had it, she would have shown up at his apartment, not here, but I'm going to bring it back anyway. Someone in Cincy knows it's surfaced again." My gaze went distant, and a nasty feeling of betrayal settled into my belly. Besides Ivy, Jenks, and Kisten, the only person who knew I still had the focus was Nick. I couldn't believe he would have betrayed me like that, but he *had* sold information about me to Big Al before. And now he was pissed at me.

The water was boiling, and I shook in enough macaroni for three.

Leaning, Ivy dragged the open box of pasta to her. "What did Glenn want?" she asked, crunching through a dry piece.

Breaking apart the clumps of macaroni, I turned the flame down. "My opinion of a Were murder. It was Mr. Ray's secretary. Whoever did it tried to make it look like a suicide."

Defined eyebrows high, Ivy's gaze went to the calendar pinned to the wall beside her computer. "A week from the full moon? No way was it a suicide, and the I.S. knows it."

I nodded. "I don't think they expected the FIB to take an interest. She had bruises from restraints and needle marks. Denon was covering it up."

Ivy hesitated as she reached into the box for another piece of pasta. "You think it has something to do with the focus?"

"Why not?" I said, exasperated. Damn it. I'd only had the ugly statue for two months, and already word was out that it hadn't been lost going over the Mackinac Bridge. Tucking a strand of hair out of the way, I stirred my pasta and tried to remember if I'd gone to see or even called David in all that time. Apart from the night I gave it to him, I didn't think I had. He was my alpha, but it wasn't like we were married or anything. Crap, this wasn't safe. I needed to get it back from him, like today.

"I can ask around if you want," Ivy said, swinging her boots up onto the counter to sit cross-legged with the box of pasta.

My thoughts jerked back to her. "Absolutely not," I said. "The less I dig, the safer I'll be. Besides, we'll never get paid for it if you do find something."

She laughed, and my mood eased. Ivy didn't laugh often, and I loved the sound of it.

"Is that why you're thinking about Nick?" she asked, shocking me. "You never make pasta in Alfredo sauce unless you are."

My mouth dropped open in protest, then snapped shut. *Crap. She's right.* "Mmmm," I said, peeved as I stirred the pasta. "Glenn gave me his file today. It's four inches thick."

"Really?" she drawled, and I frowned. She hadn't liked Nick from day one.

"Yes, really." I hesitated, watching the steam rise. "He's been at this a while."

"I'm sorry."

I forced my face into a bland expression. She hated Nick, but she was genuinely sorry he had cracked my heart. "I'm over it." And I was. Except for the part about feeling used. He'd been selling information to Al about me for favors *before* we broke up. Ass.

NIN's "Only" went soft, and I wasn't surprised when Skimmer came into the kitchen, probably wanting to know what we were up to. I felt more than saw Ivy's posture shift to a more closed mien when Skimmer's jeans-clad dancer's body breezed in.

Ivy was as open with me as she was with Skimmer, but she wasn't comfortable letting Skimmer know that. We three had an odd dynamic, one I wasn't keen on. Skimmer flatly loved Ivy, having moved here on the promise that if she got Piscary out of prison she'd be accepted into his camarilla and could stay. I was the one who had put him there, and the day he got out, I'd probably find my life not worth troll farts. Ivy was a large part of why I was still alive, which put her in a hard spot whose pressures slowly built with each court success.

Skimmer would do what she had to do to stay with Ivy. I would do what I had to do to keep my body and soul together. And Ivy was going to go quietly insane, wanting both of us to succeed. It would've helped if Skimmer weren't so darn nice.

The perceptive vampire clearly recognized that she'd interrupted something, and, tucking her long, blond, severely straight hair back behind an ear, she settled herself into Ivy's chair at the table. From the corner of my sight, I saw her features scrunch up for a moment when she and Ivy exchanged a look, but then she smoothed them, her small nose and chin easing into a pleasant expression. Beside Skimmer's delicate features, I thought my strong jaw and cheekbones looked Neanderthal. Though sharp as a cracked whip and at the top of her game, the woman looked innocent with her blue eyes and West Coast tan, a trait that probably stood her in good stead in her profession when the competition underestimated her.

"Lunch?" she said brightly, her pleasant voice showing a calculated hint of distress.

"Just white pasta," I said, going to drain the macaroni. "I've got enough for three if you're interested." I turned from the sink, finding that her vivid blue eyes had a shrinking iris of blue to make them even more striking. Her eyelashes were thick and long, accentuating her delicate features. I wondered what they'd been doing in the sanctuary. There was more than one place to bite someone—and most of them were covered by clothes.

"Count me in," she said, glancing at her watch with its diamond-chip numbers. "I've got an hour before I need to be back in the office, and if I'm not there, they can damn well wait for me."

That was cool—seeing as she was the boss—but my blood pressure started clicking upward when she went to the fridge, reaching above it for one of Ivy's Brimstone cookies. God, I hated those things, and I lived in worry that one day the I.S. would have an excuse to search my kitchen and I'd be dragged off.

"Why don't we make it a real meal?" the vampire said, clearly aware I was upset but determined to forge ahead. "Ivy has a run tonight, and I've got to get back to work. It won't take much to make it a sit-down lunch right now."

If my pasta isn't enough for you, then why did you say yes? I thought nastily, but I stifled my first reaction since I knew that the offer had been made out of a genuine attempt at camaraderie. I glanced at the clock, deciding there was plenty of time before Ceri came over, and when Ivy shrugged, I nodded. "Sure," I said. "Why not?"

Skimmer smiled. It was obvious she wasn't used to having anyone dislike her, and it wasn't that I hated her, but every time she came over, she did something that rubbed me the wrong way through no fault of her own. "I'll make garlic bread," she said brightly, hair swinging as she tugged open the cupboard door to the spices.

"Rachel's allergic to garlic," Ivy prompted, and the living vampire hesitated. Her eyes went to mine, and I could almost hear her berate herself.

"Oh. Herb toast, then." With a forced cheerfulness, she went to wash her hands.

I wasn't really allergic, just sensitive to it thanks to that same genetic aberration that would have killed me had Trent's father not intervened. Ivy slid off the counter, and after snapping the box of pasta shut, started gathering salad stuff. She was right next to Skimmer, and when their heads almost touched, I thought I heard soft encouragement.

Standing at the stove with my pasta, I found I was beginning to feel bad for the woman. She was really trying, recognizing that I was important to Ivy and making an effort to be gracious. Skimmer knew that Ivy had once set her sights on me, dropping her play for my blood after she'd finally gotten it, the encounter's ending bad enough to scare her into never doing it again. And it was no secret that I didn't give a flying flip that the two of them were sharing blood and a pillow both. I think that this had a lot to do with Skimmer's attitude. I was one of Ivy's few friends, and Skimmer knew that the quickest way to tick Ivy off was to be mean to me.

Vampires, I thought, shaking the pasta into the white sauce. I'd never understand them.

"How about some wine?" Skimmer asked, standing at the open fridge with a stick of butter in her hand. "Red goes with pasta. I brought some over today."

I couldn't drink red wine without risking migraines, and Ivy didn't drink much—not at all before a run. I opened my mouth to simply say none for me, but Ivy blurted, "Rachel can't tolerate red wine. She's sensitive to sulfur."

"Oh, God." Skimmer's pretty face was creased when she came out from behind the door. "I'm sorry. I didn't know. Is there anything else you can't tolerate?"

Just you. "You know what?" I said, dropping the lid on the finished pasta and turning the flame off. "I'm going to get some ice cream. Anyone else want ice cream?"

Not waiting for an answer, I snatched up my shoulder bag and one of Ivy's canvas sacks and walked out of the kitchen. "I'll be back before the bread's done!" I called over my shoulder.

The echo of my sandals was different in the sanctuary, and I slowed to see the cozy area Ivy and Skimmer had arranged in a front corner as a temporary living room. The TV would be lame, since we didn't have cable out here, but all I needed was the stereo. Skimmer must've brought the floor plants, since I hadn't seen them before. Damn vampire was just moving in.

And I'm having a problem with that? Irritated at myself now, I shoved one of the thick doors open, slipping out onto the wide stoop and shutting it hard. The light over the sign was on to make the damp pavement shine. Rain-soft air caressed my bare shoulder, but it didn't soothe me.

Was I bothered because I'd begun to think of the church as mine, or was it because Skimmer was taking some of Ivy's attention?

Do I really want to answer that?

My mood worsened when I passed my car in the carport. Couldn't drive my stupid car to the stupid corner store because of the stupid I.S.

I scanned the street for my pack-hopeful, not finding Brett. Maybe the rain had chased him off. The man did have to work sometime.

The thump of the church's front door shutting cut through the damp air, and I turned with an apologetic look on my face. But it wasn't Ivy.

"I'm coming with you," Skimmer said, shrugging into her lightweight cream-colored jacket and taking the steps two at a time.

Swell. I turned and started walking.

Silent, Skimmer held her purse tight to herself as she matched me step for step, a shade too close since the sidewalk wasn't that wide. Our feet splashed through a puddle, and I glanced at her white boots. Though inappropriate for a runner to work in, they looked great on her, showing off her little feet. *What in hell does she want?*

Skimmer took a slow breath. "Ivy and I met the day she moved into my dorm room."

Whoa. This is not what I had expected. "Skimmer . . ."

The cadence of her boots never slowed. "Let me finish," she said, her cheeks spotted red in the occasional streetlight. "My old roommate was expelled, and Ivy moved in. Piscary had screwed her mind royally, and her parents managed to get her out from under him for a few years so she could find an identity that didn't hinge on him. I think it saved her life. It damn well made her stronger. She needed someone, and I was there."

My pulse quickened, and my pace slowed. Maybe I should hear this.

Skimmer's posture eased at my response, her slight shoulders losing much of their tension. "We hit it off," she said, the black in her eyes swelling. "She was away from her master and parents with a year of master-vampire techniques at her fangtips. I was looking for trouble. My God, it was fantastic, but she scared me into settling down, and I gave her something to believe in." Skimmer fixed her eyes on me. "She was straight until she met me. Apart from a few latent tendencies. It took me two semesters to convince her that she could love me and Kisten both without betraying him."

My light steps seemed to jar me to my bones. *And that was a good thing?* Our pace had slowed, becoming less angry. Skimmer was at the top of her class, and I knew that anything she said would be slanted to scare me. Whatever. She couldn't scare me any more than Ivy had.

"It was a private school," Skimmer said. "Everyone lived on campus. It was expected that, as roommates, Ivy and I would share blood as a matter of convenience, but it wasn't insisted on. That we became lovers only meant . . . that's the way we were. I needed her to balance me out, and she needed me to feel good about herself after Piscary screwed her over."

The anger in her voice was shockingly hard. "You don't like him," I said.

Skimmer jerked the strap of her purse back up her shoulder as we walked. "I hate him. But I'll do whatever he asks if it means I can stay with Ivy." Her eyes met mine, the light from a nearby streetlamp glowing on her. "I'm going to get him out so I can stay with Ivy. If he kills you afterward, it's not my problem."

The threat was obvious, but we kept moving, her steps meeting mine solidly. That's why she was being nice to me. Why risk getting on Ivy's bad side if Piscary would take care of it?

I was shaking inside, but Skimmer wasn't done yet. Her pretty features knotted in an inner turmoil as she added bitterly, "She loves you. I know she's using me to try and make you jealous. I don't care." Flushed, her eyes dilated. "She wants to share everything with you, and you're kicking it in the dirt. Why do you live with her if you don't want her to touch you?"

Suddenly it was making a lot more sense. "Skimmer, you've got it wrong," I said softly, the night silent but for the wet hush of traffic a street over. "I *want* to find a blood balance with Ivy. She's the one balking, not me."

Her white boots scuffed to a halt, and I stopped. Skimmer stared at me. "She always mixes sex with her blood," she said. "Uses it to keep control. You won't do that. Ivy said so."

"I won't have sex with her, yeah. But that doesn't mean we can't . . ." I hesitated. *Why am I telling her this?*

Shock was clear on Skimmer's pale face, and her outline came into sharp relief as a car passed us, its lights throwing her into a stark reality that left the night darker when it passed. "You love her," Skimmer stammered.

My face flamed. Okay, I loved Ivy, but that didn't mean I wanted to sleep with her.

Skimmer hunched, becoming almost ugly. "Stay away from her," she hissed.

"Ivy's making the decisions here, not me," I said quickly.

"She's mine!" Skimmer shouted, lashing out.

I moved instinctively, without fear, blocking and stepping forward to land a side kick in her middle. She was a dancer, not a martial artist, and the kick landed. It wasn't much, but the vampire sat down hard on the wet sidewalk, eyes watering as she caught her breath.

"Oh, God," I apologized, reaching to help her up. "I'm so sorry."

Skimmer gripped my hand, yanking me off balance. Yelping, I fell, rolling across the wet grass and getting soaked. The living vampire beat me to my feet, but she was crying, tears silently slipping down her face. "Stay away from her!" she shouted. "She's mine!"

Nearby, a dog barked. Frightened, I tugged my shirt straight. "She isn't anyone's," I said, not caring if the neighbors were listening. "I don't care if you two are sleeping together, or sharing blood, or whatever, but I'm not leaving!"

"You selfish *bitch*!" she seethed, and I backed up as she came forward. "Staying without letting her touch you is cruel. Why do you live with her if you don't want her to touch you?"

Curtains were being pulled aside in the neighboring houses, and I started to worry that someone might call the I.S. "Because I'm her friend," I said, beginning to get mad. "She's just scared, okay? And a friend doesn't walk away when another friend is scared. I'm willing to wait until she isn't. God knows she waited for me. She needs me, and I need her—so back off!"

Skimmer stopped her advance, pulling herself up to look possessed, calm, and pissed. "You let her taste your blood. What could *you* do that would scare her?"

I was wet from hitting the grass, and I looked up from my damp legs. "I trusted her so much that I would've let her kill me if Jenks hadn't stopped her."

Skimmer went even whiter.

"Skimmer, I'm sorry," I said, gesturing helplessly. "I didn't plan this."

"But you're sleeping with Kisten," she protested. "I can smell him all over you."

This was as embarrassing as all hell. "You're the one who taught her she could love two people at the same time, not me."

With an abrupt motion, Skimmer turned on a heel and started back the way we came, blond hair swinging and steps sharp.

Actually, that I was sleeping with Kisten while wanting Ivy to bite me was a twinge on my conscience. But I figured between Ivy's fear and the vampiric mentality that multiple blood and bed partners were the norm, I could deal with the issue when it became an issue. I loved Kisten. I wanted Ivy to bite me. It made sense if I didn't think about it too hard.

Depressed, I scooped up my shoulder bag and Ivy's canvas sack. "If you jump me again, I'll freaking break your damn arm," I muttered as I trailed behind her, knowing she could hear me. I didn't know where we stood, but ice cream now sounded as appealing as eating a hot dog in the snow. Perhaps the encounter had been inevitable. It could have been worse. Ivy could have heard us.

"You okay?" I asked when I caught up to Skimmer on the church steps, the lights in the sanctuary making yellow swaths on the wet concrete.

Giving me a sideways glance, she felt her middle, her expression a mix of sullen mistrust and anger. "I love Ivy, and I'll do anything to protect her. You understand me?"

My eyes narrowed at the implication that I was a threat to Ivy. "I'm not endangering her."

"Yes you are." The woman's narrow chin lifted as she stood a step above me. "If she kills you by mistake because you goad her into something, she will never forgive herself. I know her. She'll end it all to escape the pain. I love Ivy, and I'm not going to let her kill herself."

"Neither am I," I said hotly.

Skimmer's face emptied of emotion, chilling me. A quiet vampire was a plotting vampire. Yanking the door open, she slipped in ahead of me. Great. I think I had just put myself on Skimmer's hit list.

While I leaned against the wall and wedged off my sandals, Skimmer muttered something about the bathroom. Wiping her boots, she clattered into Ivy's bathroom, making an obvious amount of noise, and slammed the door. I followed the scent of warm bread into the kitchen, my steps silent from being barefoot. I found Ivy at her computer buying music. "What flavor did you get?" she asked.

"Ah, it started to rain," I ad-libbed, "and we decided it wasn't worth the effort." It wasn't really a lie, just looking at it from an expanded point of view.

Ivy nodded, eyes on the screen. I had expected some sort of reaction, but then I noticed that her boots were wet, and I slumped. Crap, she'd seen the entire thing.

I took a breath to explain, but her brown eyes flicked to mine, halting me. Skimmer came in, her cell phone in hand. "Hey, the office called," she said, the lie coming from her as easily as breathing. "They want me back early, so I'm going to cut out on you. You two go ahead and have lunch. I'll take a rain check."

Ivy sat straighter. "You're headed into Cincy?" Skimmer nodded, and Ivy rose, stretching. "Mind if I get a ride from you?" she asked. "That's where my run is." Ivy glanced at me. "You don't mind, do you, Rachel?"

Like I could really say anything? "Go on," I told her, moving to the stove and stirring the cooling pasta. My eyes drifted to the opened bottle of white wine. "I'll give Ceri a call. Maybe she'll come over early."

Ten to one they were both going to see Piscary. Why didn't they just come out with it?

"See you later, Rachel," Skimmer said tightly, then headed to the front, her boots loud.

Ivy pulled her purse across the table. My gaze dropped to her boots, and when I brought them back up, I saw a wisp of guilt. "I won't do it," she said. "If I bite you, it'll blow everything we have into the ever-after."

I shrugged, thinking she was right, but only if we were stupid about it. If she had been listening, then she also knew I was willing to wait. Besides, to think that I could satisfy all of her blood lust was insane. I didn't even want to try. I only wanted to prove that I accepted her the way she was. I'd just have to wait until she was ready to believe that.

"You'd better get going," I said, not wanting her to be here when Minias showed up.

Ivy hesitated in the threshold. "Lunch was a good idea."

I shrugged without looking up, and after a moment's hesitation she walked out. My eyes followed her wet prints, and I frowned when I heard Ivy say defensively, "I told you she did. You're lucky she didn't hit you with anything other than her foot."

Tired, I slipped into my chair, the scent of cooked pasta, vinegar dressing, and grilled bread heavy in the air. I knew that Ivy wasn't going to move out of the church. Which meant the only way Skimmer was going to get Ivy all to herself was if I was dead.

How nice was that?

SIX

I thunked the sauce off the spoon when I heard the front door open and Ceri's voice, soft in conversation. Jenks had gone to get her, having come in when Ivy and Skimmer left. He didn't like the thin blond vampire and had made himself scarce. It was after sunset and time to call Minias. *I* didn't like the idea of kicking sleeping demons, but I needed to reduce the confusion in my life, and calling him was the easiest way to do that.

Damn it, what am I doing, calling a demon? And what kind of a life do I have when calling one is at the top of my to-do list?

Ceri's steps were soft in the hallway, and I turned to her smile when her pleasant laughter at something Jenks said filled the kitchen. She was wearing a summery linen dress in three shades of purple, a matching ribbon holding her long, almost-transparent hair up off her neck against the moist heat. Jenks was on her shoulder to look like he belonged there, and Rex, Jenks's cat, was in her arms. The orange kitten was purring, her eyes closed and her paws wet with rain.

"Hello, Rachel," the young-seeming woman said, her voice carrying the slow relaxation of a damp summer night. "Jenks said you needed some company. Mmmm, is that herb bread?"

"Ivy and Skimmer were going to have lunch with me," I said, turning to get two wineglasses. "Ah . . ." I hedged, suddenly embarrassed and wondering if she had heard Skimmer and me . . . discussing things. "It fell through, and now I've got a ton of food with only me to eat it."

Ceri's green eyes pinched in worry, telling me she had. "Nothing serious?"

I shook my head, thinking it could turn real serious real fast if Skimmer worked at it.

At that, the lithe elf smiled, sashaying to the cupboard for two plates as if it were her kitchen. "I'd love to eat lunch with you. Keasley would be happy with fish sandwiches every night, but honestly, the man wouldn't know fine food if I put it on his tongue and chewed it for him."

The chatter about nothing lured me into a better mood, and, relaxing, I fixed two plates of pasta in white sauce while Ceri made herself tea with the special leaf she kept over here. Jenks sat on her shoulder the entire time, and, watching them together, I remembered how Jih, his eldest daughter, had taken to Ceri. I couldn't help but wonder if elves and pixies had a history of coexistence. I'd always thought it odd that Trent went to such great lengths to keep pixies and fairies out of his personal gardens. Almost like an addict removing the source of temptation, rather than my first guess, that he simply feared they might literally smell him out as an elf.

It was with a restored calm that I followed Ceri to the sanctuary with my wineglass and plate to take advantage of the cooler space. Her tea was already on the coffee table between the suede couch and matching pair of armchairs in the corner. I didn't know how she could stand the stuff when it was hot, but, seeing her in her lightweight dress, I had to admit she looked cooler than I was in my shorts and chemise, even though I had more skin showing. Must be an elf thing. The cold didn't seem to bother her either. I was starting to think it grossly unfair.

Set to the side was my scrying mirror to etch the calling pentagram on, my last stick of magnetic chalk, more of that yew, a ceremonial knife, my silver snips, a little white bag of sea salt, and a rude sketch Ceri had drawn earlier using Ivy's colored pencils. Ceri had brought out the bucket from the pantry, too. I didn't want to know. I really didn't want to know. The circle was going to be different from the one she had drawn on the floor just this morning: a permanent connection I wouldn't have to invoke with my blood every time I wanted to answer it.

Most of the stuff on the table was meant to get the curse to stick to the glass.

The soft clatter of our plates was pleasant as we arranged ourselves, and I collapsed into one of the cushy chairs, wanting to pretend for a few moments longer that this was just three friends getting together for lunch on a rainy summer's night. Minias could wait. I slid my plate onto my lap and picked up my fork, enjoying the quiet.

Setting the entire bottle of untouched red wine on the table beside her, Ceri took her teacup in her bandaged fingers and sipped graciously. Nervousness started to tickle and wind its way through my spine, ruining my appetite. Jenks was heading to the honey Ceri had put in her tea, and the woman capped it, putting it firmly out of his reach. Grumbling, Jenks flitted to the plants on my desk to sulk.

"You sure this is safe?" I asked, gaze flicking to the paraphernalia. I didn't understand ley line magic and therefore distrusted it.

Ceri's eyebrows rose as she tore a chunk from her herbed bread—a strand of her hair drifting in the breeze from the open transom windows above the fixed stained glass, dark with night. "It's never safe to ask for a demon's attention, but you don't want this unsettled."

My head bobbed, and I wrangled another blob of pasta on my fork. It tasted flat, and I set my fork down. "You think Newt will come with him?"

A soft flush showed on her. "No. In all likelihood she doesn't remember you, and Minias won't allow anyone to remind her. He's reprimanded when she strays."

I wondered what Newt knew that was so terrible she had to forget it to stay halfway sane. "She took your circle. I didn't think that was possible."

Ceri delicately dabbed the corner of her mouth with a napkin to hide her fear. "Newt does what she wants because no one is strong enough to hold her accountable," she said. My anxiety must have shown, for she added, "It's skill in this case. Newt knows everything. It's just a matter of her remembering it long enough to teach someone."

Maybe that was why Minias stuck with her despite the dangers. He was picking things up, bit by bit.

Ceri reached for the remote and pointed it at the stereo. It was a very modern gesture for such an old personality, and I smiled. If you didn't know she'd spent a thousand years unaging as a demon's familiar, you might think she was a set-in-her-ways thirty-something.

The soft jazz lifting through the air cut off. "The sun is down. You should rescribe the calling circle before midnight," she said brightly, and my stomach twisted. "Do you remember the figures from this morning? They are the same."

I stared at her, trying not to look stupid. "Uh, no."

Ceri nodded, then made five distinct motions with her right hand. "Remember?"

"Uh, no," I repeated, having no idea what the connection was between the sketched figures and her hand motions. "And I thought you would do it. Scribe it, I mean."

Ceri's breath escaped her in a long sound of exasperation. "It's mostly ley line magic," she said. "Heavy on symbolism and intent. If you don't draw it from start to finish, then I'll be the one who gets all the incoming calls—and, Rachel, I like you, but I'm not going to do that."

I winced. "Sorry."

She smiled, but I caught a grimace when she didn't realize I was watching. Ceri was the nicest person I knew, giving treats to children and squirrels and being polite to door-to-door solicitors, but she had little patience when it came to teaching. Her abrupt temper didn't mix well with my scattered concentration and haphazard study habits.

Flushing, I set my plate aside and slid the cool, sinking-into-my-legs feeling of my scrying mirror onto my lap. I wasn't hungry anymore, and Ceri's impatience was making me feel stupid. I reached for my magnetic chalk, nervous. "I'm not very good at this," I muttered.

"Which is why you're doing it in chalk, then etching it in," she said. "Go on, let's see it."

I hesitated, looking at the big blank expanse of glass. *Crap.*

"Come on, Rache!" Jenks coaxed, dropping down to land on the mirror. "Just follow me." Wings going full tilt, he started to pace in a wide circle.

I arranged myself to follow his lead, and Ceri said, "Pentagram first."

I jerked my hand from the glass. "Right."

Jenks looked up at me as if in direction, and I felt a sinking sensation.

Ceri set her plate down, her disgust obvious. "You don't know a thing about this, do you?"

"Jeez, Ceri," I complained, watching Jenks flit furtively to steal the smear of honey on Ceri's spoon. "I haven't actually finished any ley line classes. I know my pentagrams suck dishwater, and I have no idea what those symbols mean or how to draw them." Feeling dumb, I grabbed my wineglass—the white wine, not the red Ceri had brought out and took a sip.

"You shouldn't drink when you work magic," Ceri said.

Frustrated, I set the glass down almost hard enough to spill. "Then why is it out here?" I said, a shade too loudly.

Jenks eyed me in warning, and I puffed my air out. I didn't like feeling stupid.

"Rachel," the woman said softly, and I grimaced at the chagrin in her voice. "I'm sorry. I shouldn't expect you to have the skills of a master when you're only starting out. It's just . . ."

". . . a stupid pentagram," I finished for her, trying to find the humor in it.

She reddened. "Actually, it's merely that I wanted to get this done tonight."

"Oh." Embarrassed, I looked at the blank mirror, my reflection a gray shadow peering back at me. It was going to look like crap. I knew it.

"The wine is a carrier for the invocation blood, also washing the salt off the mirror when you're done," Ceri said, and my gaze went to the bucket, now understanding why she'd brought it out. "The salt acts as a leveler, removing the excess intent in the lines you scribe in the glass as well as bringing the acidic content of the yew back to a neutral state."

"Yew is toxic, not acidic," I said, and she nodded apologetically.

"But it will etch the glass once you coat it in your aura."

Euwie. It was one of those curses. Great. "I'm sorry for barking at you," I said softly, my gaze flicking to her and away. "I don't know what I'm doing, and I don't like it."

She smiled and leaned across the table between us. "Would you like to know the meaning behind the symbols?"

I nodded, feeling my tension ease. If I was going to do this, I really ought to.

"They are pictorial representations of ley line gestures," she said, her hand moving as if signing in American Sign Language. "See?"

She made a fist, her thumb tight to her curled index finger, angling her hand so that her thumb pointed to the ceiling. "This is the first one," she added, then pointed to the first symbol on the cheat sheet lying on the table. It was a circle bisected by a vertical line. "The thumb's position is indicated by the line," she added.

I looked from the figure to my fist, turning my hand until they matched. *Okay.*

"This is the second one," she said, making the "okay" sign, angling her hand so the back of it was parallel with the floor.

I mimicked her, feeling a stirring of understanding as I looked at the circle with three lines coming out the right side. My thumb and index finger made a circle, my three fingers stretching out like the lines fanned out from the figure's right side. I glanced at the next figure of a circle with a horizontal line, and before she could shift her fingers, I made a fist, turning my hand so my thumb was parallel to the floor.

"Yes!" Ceri said, following the gesture with her own. "And the next would be . . . ?"

Thinking, I compressed my lips and stared at the symbol. It looked like the previous one, with a finger coming out one side. "Index finger?" I guessed, and when she nodded, I stuck a finger out, earning a smile.

"Exactly. Try making the gesture with your pinkie, and you can see how wrong it feels."

I tucked my index finger back and stuck out my pinkie. It did feel wrong, so I went back to the proper gesture. "And this one?" I asked as I looked at the figure in the last space. There was a circle, so I knew that something was touching my thumb, but which finger?

"Middle one," Ceri offered, and I made the gesture, grinning.

She leaned back, still smiling. "Let's see them."

More confident now, I made the five gestures, reading them as I traveled around the pentagram clockwise. This wasn't so hard.

"And this middle figure?" I asked, looking at the long baseline with three rays coming up from the center equidistant from each other. It was where my hand had been when I contacted Minias earlier, and by the looks of it, my fingertips would hit the ends of the lines.

"That's the symbol for an open connection," she said. "As if an open hand. The inner circle touching the pentagram is our reality, and the outer circle is the ever-after. You're bridging the gap with your open hand. There is an alternate pattern with a series of symbols scribed between the two circles that will hide your location and identity, but it's more difficult."

Jenks snickered, still trying to scrape honey off Ceri's spoon. "I bet it's harder, too," he said. "And we do want to finish before the sun comes up."

I ignored him, feeling like I might be starting to understand this.

"And the pentagram is simply to give structure to the curse," Ceri added, trashing my good mood. *Oh, yeah. I forgot it was a curse. Mmmm, goody.*

Seeing my grimace, Ceri leaned over the table and touched my arm. "It is a very small curse," she said, her attempt to console me making things worse. "It's not evil. You're disturbing reality, and it leaves a mark, but truly, Rachel, this is a small thing."

It's going to lead to worse, I thought, then forced a smile. Ceri didn't have to help me with this. I should be thankful. "Okay, pentagram first."

Wings clattering, Jenks landed on the glass, shivering once before he put his hands on his hips and peered up at me. "Start here," he said, walking away, "and just follow me."

I looked at Ceri to see if this was allowed, and she nodded. My shoulders eased, then tightened. The chalk felt almost slippery as it skated over the mirror, like a wax pencil on hot stone. I held my breath, waiting for a tingling of rising power, but there was nothing.

"Now over here," Jenks said when he lifted into the air and dropped down at a new spot.

I played connect the dots, my lip finding its way between my teeth until a pentagram took up nearly the entire mirror. My back was feeling the strain, and I straightened. "Thanks, Jenks," I said, and he lifted up, his complexion red.

"No prob," he said as he went to sit on Ceri's shoulder.

"Now the symbols," Ceri prompted, and I reached for the top triangle, being careful not to smear my other lines. "Not that one!" she exclaimed before the chalk could touch the glass, and I jumped. "The lower left," she added, smiling to soften her voice. "When you scribe, you want to rise clockwise." She made a fist, her eyes going to the cheat sheet. "This one first."

I glanced at the diagram, then the pentagram. Taking a breath, I held the chalk tighter.

"Just draw it, Rache," Jenks complained, and as the hush of cars shushing against wet pavement soothed me, I sketched them all, my hand becoming more sure with each figure.

"As good as I," Ceri praised, and I leaned back and let my breath slip from me.

Setting the chalk down, I shook out my hand. It was only a few figures, but my hand was starting to ache. I glanced at the yew, and Ceri nodded once. "It should etch the glass if you tap a line and let your aura slip into the glass," she said, and my face scrunched up.

"Do I have to?" I asked, remembering the sinking, uncomfortable feeling of my aura stripping away. Then I looked over the church. "Shouldn't I be in a circle?"

Ceri's hair floated when she leaned to stack our plates up. "No. The mirror isn't going to take it all, just a slip of it. No harm in that."

She seemed confident, but still . . . I didn't like losing any of my aura. And what if Minias showed up or called in the meantime?

"Oh, for the love of little green apples," Ceri said darkly. "If it will make this any faster."

I winced, feeling like a chicken, then jumped when she tapped the line out back and, with a word of muttered Latin, set a loose circle. Jenks's wings hit a still-higher pitch when the large bubble of black-coated ever-after shimmered into existence around us. Ceri was at the exact center, as was the way with undrawn circles, and I could feel the pressure of ever-after against my back. I scooted forward, and Jenks's wings hit a still-higher pitch. He finally settled himself on the table by the salt. I knew he didn't like being trapped, but after seeing Ceri's impatience, I decided Jenks was a big boy and could ask to be let out himself if it bothered him that much.

Ceri's circle was held with only her will, completely undrawn and entirely from her imagination. It wouldn't hold a demon, but all I wanted was something to keep nebulous influences out while my aura was not protecting my soul. Why ask for trouble? And with that in mind, I earned a huff of indignation when I picked up the phone and took out the batteries. An incoming call could open an opportunistic path.

"You're not going to lose all your aura," she said, moving our stacked plates aside.

Yeah, well, I felt better, and as much as I liked Ceri and respected her knowledge, I was going to fall back on my dad's admonishment never to practice high magic without a protection circle around you. Demon curses probably fell under that umbrella.

So it was with a lot more confidence that I plucked the makeshift stylus of yew from the table and tapped a line through Ceri's circle. The energy spilled in—warm, comforting, and a little too fast for my liking— and I tilted my head and cracked my neck to hide my unease. My chi seemed to hum, and my fingers about the yew cramped briefly. I flexed them, and a tingling ran from my center to my fingertips. I'd never felt anything like it before while spelling, but then I was drawing a curse.

"You okay?" Jenks asked, and I blinked, brushing my hair from my eyes and nodding.

"The line seems warm tonight," I said, and Ceri's face went empty.

"Warm?" she questioned, and I shrugged. Her eyes grew distant in thought for a moment, and then she gestured to the chalk-marked scrying mirror.

My eyes fixed on the chalk lines, and with no hesitation I reached for the pentagram.

The stick of yew touched the glass resting on my lap, and with a shudder my aura pooled out of me like icy water. I gasped at the sensation, my head jerking up, my eyes finding Ceri's.

"Ceri!" Jenks shouted. "She's losing it! The damn thing just left her!"

The elf caught her alarm fast, but not so fast I didn't see it. "She's fine," she said, getting up and fumbling for the chalk on the table. "Rachel, you're fine. Just sit tight. Don't move."

Frightened, I did exactly that, listening to my heart pound as she drew a circle inside her original one and invoked the more secure barrier immediately. My smut-damaged aura had colored my reflection, and I tried not to look at it. The click of the chalk hitting the table was loud, and Ceri sat across from me, her legs tucked under her and her back straight. "Continue," she said, and I hesitated.

"That wasn't supposed to happen," I said, and she met my eyes, a hint of shame in them.

"You're fine," she said, looking away. "When I did this so I might screen Al's calls, I wasn't making such a deep connection. I erred in not making a secure circle. I'm sorry."

It was hard for the proud elf to apologize, and, knowing that, I accepted it with no lingering feelings of "I told you so." I didn't know what in hell I was doing, so it wasn't as if I could expect her to get it all right. But I was glad I had insisted on a circle. Very glad.

I turned my gaze back to the mirror, trying to keep my focus shallow so I wouldn't look at my reflection. I felt dizzy without my aura, unreal, and my stomach was knotting. The scent of burnt amber rose to tickle my nose as I drew the lines of containment, and I squinted, seeing the faint haze of smoke on both sides of the glass where the yew was burning the mirror. "It's supposed to do that, right?" I asked, and Ceri murmured something positive-sounding.

The red curtain of my loose hair blocked my view, but I heard her whisper something to Jenks, and the pixy flew to her. I shivered, feeling naked without my aura. I kept trying not to glance into the mirror as I scribed, the haze of my aura looking like a mist or glow around my dark shadow of a reflection. The once-cheerful pure gold color of my aura had been tainted with an overlaying black of demon smut. *Actually,* I thought as I finished the pentagram and started on the first of the symbols, *the black gives it more depth, almost like an aged patina.* Yeah, sure.

A rising of tingles cramped my hand as I finished the last symbol. Exhaling, I started on the inner circle, relying on the points of the pentagram to guide me. The haze of burning glass grew thicker, distorting my vision, but I knew the instant my starting point and ending point met.

My shoulders twisted when I felt a vibration chime through me, first in my extended aura in the mirror and then in me. The inner circle had been set, and it seemed to have been etched onto my aura by way of marking the glass.

Pulse quickening, I started on the second circle. This one, too, resonated upon completion, and I shivered when my aura started to leave the scrying mirror, pulling the entire figure into me and carrying the curse with it.

"Salt it, Rachel. Before it burns you," Ceri said urgently, and the white drawstring bag of sea salt edged into my tunnel vision.

My fingers fumbled at the ties, and I finally closed my eyes to make better progress that way. I felt disconnected. My aura was coming back painfully slowly, seeming to crawl over my skin and soak in layer by layer, burning. I had a feeling that if I didn't finish this before my aura came entirely back, it was really going to hurt.

The salt made a soft hush as it hit the glass, and I flinched at the feeling of unseen cold sand rasping against my skin. Not bothering to trace the patterns, I dumped it all, my heart pounding as the weight of it hitting the mirror seemed to make my chest heavy.

The bucket appeared at my feet and the wine at my knee—silently, unobtrusively. Hands shaking, I scrabbled for my big-ass symbolic knife, pricking my thumb and dropping three plops of red into the wine as Ceri's voice hovered at the edge of my awareness and told me what to do: whispering, guiding, instructing me how to move my hands, how to finish this thing before I passed out from the sensations.

The wine cascaded over the mirror, and a moan of relief slipped from me. It was as if I could feel the salt dissolve into the glass, bonding to it, sealing the power of the curse and quieting it. My entire body hummed, the salt in my blood echoing with the power, settling into new channels and going somnolent.

My fingers and soul were cold from the wine, and I shifted them, feeling the last of the gritty salt wash away. *"Ita prorsus,"* I said, repeating the words of invocation as Ceri gave them to me, but it wasn't until I touched my wine-wet finger to my tongue that it actually invoked.

The wave of demon smut rose from my work. Hell, I could see it looking like a black haze. Bowing my head, I took it—I didn't fight it, I took it—accepting it with a feeling of inevitability. It was as if a part of me had died, accepting that I couldn't be who I wanted, so I had to work at making who I was someone I could live with. My pulse jumped, then settled.

The air pressure shifted, and I felt Ceri's bubbles go down. From above us came the hint of a bell resonating in the belfry. The unheard vibrations pressed against my skin, and it was as if I could feel the curse imprinting itself on me in smaller, gentler waves, pushed by sound waves so low they could only be felt. And then it was done, and the sensation was gone.

Inhaling, I focused on the wine-damp mirror in my hands. A glistening drop of red hung, then fell to echo in the salted wine inside the bucket. The mirror now reflected the world in a dark, wine-red hue, but that paled next to the double-circled pentagram before me, etched in a stunning crystalline perfection. It was absolutely beautiful, catching and reflecting the light in shades of crimson and silver, all glittery and faceted. "I did this?" I said in surprise, and looked up.

I blanched. Ceri was staring at me with her hands on her lap, Jenks on her shoulder. It wasn't that she looked scared, just really, really worried. I shifted my shoulders, feeling a light connection from my mind to my aura that hadn't been there before. Or perhaps I was more sensitive to it. "Does it get better?" I said, concerned by Ceri's lack of response.

"What?" she asked, and Jenks's wings blurred, sending a strand of her hair flying.

I glanced at the bucket of salted wine next to me—hardly remembering pouring it on the mirror—then set the glass on the table. My fingers parted from it, but it was as if I still felt it with me. "The feeling of connection?" I said uncomfortably.

"You can feel it?" Jenks squeaked, and Ceri shushed him, her eyebrows knitting together.

"I shouldn't?" I asked as I wiped my hands on a napkin, and Ceri looked away.

"I don't know," she said softly, clearly thinking of something else. "Al never said."

I was starting to feel more like myself. Jenks came forward, and I kept wiping my hands, dabbing the damp off. "You okay?" he asked, and I nodded, discarding the napkin and pulling my legs up to sit cross-legged. I tugged the mirror to sit atop my lap. It made me feel like I was in high school, playing with a Ouija board in someone's basement.

"I'm fine," I said, trying to ignore the fact that I thought the white crystalline pattern I had made on the glass was absolutely beautiful. "Let's do this. I want to be able to sleep tonight."

Ceri stirred, drawing my attention to her. Her angular features were drawn, and she looked frightened by a sudden thought. "Ah, Rachel," she stammered, standing up. "Would you mind if we waited? Just until tomorrow?"

Oh, God. I did it wrong. "What did I do?" I blurted, reddening.

"Nothing," she rushed, reaching out but not touching me. "You're fine. But you just readjusted your aura, and you probably ought to go through an entire sun cycle to settle yourself before trying to use it. The calling circle, I mean."

I looked at the mirror, then her. Ceri's face was unreadable. She was hiding her emotions, and doing a damn fine job of it. I'd done it wrong, and she was mad. She hadn't expected all my aura to slide off, but it had. "Crap," I said, disgusted. "I did it wrong, didn't I?"

She shook her head, but she was gathering her stuff up to leave. "You did it correctly. I have to go. I have to check on something."

I hurried to get up, knocking the table and almost spilling my glass of white wine when I set the mirror down. "Ceri, I'll do better next time. Really, I'm getting better at this. You've helped me so much already," I said, but she stepped out of my reach, disguising it as swooping forward for her slippers. I froze, scared. She didn't want me to touch her. "What did I do?"

Slowly she halted, still not looking at me. Jenks hovered between us. Outside, I could hear the neighbors yelling friendly good-byes and a horn beeping. Reluctantly her eyes met mine. "Nothing," she said. "I'm sure the reason your aura all spilled out was because your blood invoked it and not another demon's, as was in my case when I was bound to Al's account to field his calls for him. You need to let your aura settle in firmly before using the curse, is all. A day at least. Tomorrow night."

I took in Jenks's worry. He had heard the lie in her voice, too. Either she was making up the reason my aura pooled out or she was lying about the need to wait to call Minias. One scared the crap out of me, and the other was just bewildering. *She doesn't want to touch me?*

She turned to go, and I glanced at the calling circle, beautiful and innocent-looking on my coffee table, reflecting the world in a wine-stained hue. "Wait, Ceri. What if he calls tonight?"

Ceri stopped. Head bowed, she came back, put her hand atop the middle figure with fingers spread wide, and murmured a word of Latin. "There," she said, glancing hesitantly at me. "I've put a 'do not disturb' notation on it. It will expire at sunup." She took a deep breath, seeming to make a decision. "This was necessary," she said, as if convincing herself, but when I nodded agreement, her features pinched in what looked like fear.

"Thank you, Ceri," I said, bewildered, and she slipped out the front door and closed it without a sound. I heard her feet slap the wet pavement as she ran, then nothing. I turned to Jenks, still hovering. "What was that all about?" I asked, feeling very unsure.

"Maybe she can't admit she doesn't know why your aura pooled out," he said, coming to sit on my knee when I flopped back into the couch and propped my arches on the edge of the table. "Or maybe she's mad at herself for almost exposing you without your aura." He hesitated, then said, "You didn't get a hug good-bye."

I reached for my glass and took a sip, feeling a tingling rise up through my wine-stained aura, almost as if responding to what I'd just drank. Slowly the sensation faded. I thought back to Ceri's circle dropping and the feeling of the bell resonating through me when the curse had invoked. It had felt good. Satisfying. That was okay, wasn't it?

"Jenks," I said wearily, "I wish someone would tell me what in hell is going on."

SEVEN

The afternoon sun was warm on my shoulders, bare but for the straps of my chemise. Last night's rain had left the ground soft, and the moist heat hovering an inch or so over the disturbed earth was comforting. I was taking advantage of it by tending my yew plant, having an idea that I might make up some forget potions in case Newt showed again. All I needed now was the fermented lilac pressings. It wasn't illegal to *make* forget charms, just *use* them, and who would fault me for using one on a demon?

The soft plunk of a cut tip dropping into one of my smaller spell pots was loud, and with my face turned to the earth, I knelt before the tombstone it was growing out of and sent my fingers lightly among the branches, harvesting the ones growing inward to the center of the plant.

Ceri's reaction to my aura's pooling out last night had left me very uneasy, but the sun felt good, and I took strength from that. I might have made a strong connection to the ever-after, but nothing had changed. And Ceri was right. I needed a way for Minias to contact me without having to show up. This was safer. Easier.

A grimace crossed my face, and I turned my attention from pruning to pulling weeds to widen the circle of cleared earth. Easy like a wish. And wishes always came back to bite you.

Glancing at the angle of the sun, I decided I ought to call it good and get cleaned up before Kisten came over to take me to my driver's-ed class. I stood, slapping the dirt from my jeans and gathering my tools. My gaze expanded from the singular vision of the pollution-stained grave marker to the wider expanse of my walled graveyard, the domestic Hollows beyond that, and, even farther, the tallest buildings of Cincinnati across the river. I loved it here, a spot of stillness surrounded by life, humming like a thousand bees.

I headed for the church, smiling and touching the stones as I passed, recognizing them like old friends and wondering what the people they guarded had been like. There was a small flurry of pixies by the back door to the church, and I picked my way to it, curious as to what was up. My faint smile widened when the snap of dragonfly wings turned into Jenks. The pixy circled me, looking good in his casual gardening clothes.

"Hey, Rachel, are you done over there?" he said by way of greeting. "My kids are dying to check out your gardening."

Skirting the circle of blasphemed ground encompassing the grave marker of a weeping angel, I squinted at him. "Sure. Just tell them to watch the oozing tips. That stuff is toxic."

He nodded, his wings a gossamer blur as he went to my other side so I wasn't looking into the sun. "They know." He hesitated, then with a quickness that said he was embarrassed, blurted, "Are you going to need me today?"

I looked up from my uneven footing, then back down. "No. What's up?"

A smile full of parental pride came over him, and a faint sparkle of gold fell as he let some dust slip. "It's Jih," he said in satisfaction.

My pace faltered. Jih was his eldest daughter, now living across the street with Ceri to build up a garden to support her and a future family. Seeing my worry, Jenks laughed. "She's fine! But she's got three pixy bucks circling her and her garden and wants me to build something with them so she can see how they work, then make her decision from that."

"Three!" I adjusted my grip on my spell pot. "Good Lord. Matalina must be tickled."

Jenks dropped to my shoulder. "I suppose," he grumbled. "Jih is beside herself. She likes them all. I just stole Matalina and didn't bother with the traditional season-long supervised courtship. Jih wants to make a dragonfly hut. Poor guy who wins is going to need it."

I wanted to look at him, but he was too close. "You stole Matalina?"

"Yup. If we had jumped through all the hoops, we never would have gotten the front entryway gardens or the flower boxes."

My eyes went to my feet, and I picked my path so I wouldn't jar him. He had dropped tradition to gain a six-by-eight swath of garden and some flower boxes. Now he had a walled garden of four city lots. Jenks was doing well. Well enough that his children could take time from their life for the rituals that marked it. "It's nice that Jih has you to help her," I said.

"I suppose," he muttered, but I could tell he was eager for the chance to guide his daughter in making a good decision in who to spend her life with. *Maybe that's why I keep making such stellar decisions in my own love life,* I thought, smirking at the idea of Jenks coming out on a first date with me and grilling the poor guy. Then I blinked. He had warned Kisten to behave himself when I went out with him that first time. Damn, had Kisten gotten Jenks's stamp of approval?

The gust from Jenks's wings cooled the sweat on my neck. "Hey, I gotta go. She's waiting. I'll see you tonight."

"Sure," I said, and he rose up. "Tell her I said congrats!"

He gave me a salute and darted off. I watched him for a moment, then continued to the back door, imaging the grief he was going to put the three young pixy bucks through. The heavenly scent of baking muffins was slipping out the kitchen window, and, breathing deeply, I climbed up the few stairs. I checked the bottoms of my sneakers, stomped my feet, and entered the torn-apart living room. Three Guys and a Toolbox had yet to show up, and the smell of splintered wood mixed with the scent of baking. My stomach rumbled, so I headed into the kitchen. It was empty but for the muffins cooling on the stove, and after dropping my cuttings by the sink, I washed my hands and eyed the cooling bread. Apparently Ivy was up and in the mood to bake. Unusual, but I was going to take advantage of it.

Juggling a muffin and the fish food, I fed myself and Mr. Fish both, then pulled a dark green T-shirt on over my chemise and collapsed into my chair, happy with the world. I started at the sudden skittering of claws, and an orange ball of feline terror streaked into the kitchen and under my chair. Pixies spilled in, a swirling storm of high-pitched screeching and whistles that made my skull hurt.

"Out!" I shouted, standing. "Get out! The church is her safe place, so *get out!*"

Pixy dust thickened to make my eyes water, but after the loud complaints and muttered disappointment, the Disney nightmare subsided as quickly as it had come. Smirking, I peered under my chair. Rex was huddled, her eyes black and her tail fluffed, the picture of fear incarnate. Jenks must already be at Jih's, since his kids knew he'd bend their wings backward till they slipped dust if he caught them teasing his cat.

"What's the matter, sweet pea?" I crooned, knowing better than to try to pet her. "Did those nasty pixies bother you?"

Eyes averted, she hunched down, content to stay where she was. Snorting, I carefully settled back, feeling like the great protector. Rex never sought me out for attention, but when danger threatened, I was where she ended up. Ivy said it was a cat thing. Whatever.

I reached for my nail polish, taking careful bites of breakfast between touch-up swipes. A soft scuffing in the hallway brought my attention up as Ivy came in, and I smiled. She was dressed in her exercise tights and had a light sheen of sweat on her. "What was all that about?" she asked, going to the stove and wedging a muffin out of the tin.

Mouth full, I pointed under my chair.

"Oh, poor kitty," she said, sitting in her spot and dropping her hand to the floor.

Disgust puckered my brow when the stupid cat padded to her, head up and tail smoothed. My annoyance deepened when Rex jumped into her lap, settling down to stare at me. The cat suddenly turned to the hallway, and a sharp rapping of heels grew loud. Eyes wide, I looked at Ivy, but my question was answered when Skimmer breezed in, brushed, tidied, and looking as perfect as an uncut wedding cake in her stark white shirt and black slacks.

When did she get here? I thought, then flushed. *She never left last night.* I glanced at Ivy, deciding I was right when my roommate dumped Rex out of her lap and found great interest in her e-mails, opening them up and throwing out the spam—avoiding me. Hell, I didn't care what they did together. But apparently Ivy did.

"Hi, Rachel," the slight vampire said. Then, before I could answer, she bent to give Ivy a kiss. Ivy stiffened in surprise, and I blinked when Ivy pulled away before it could turn passionate—which was clearly where Skimmer had intended it to go. Recovering smoothly, Skimmer headed for the muffins. "I'll be done with work about ten tonight," she said, putting one on a plate and sitting carefully between us. "Do you want to meet for an early dinner?"

Ivy's face was creased in annoyance at the attempted kiss. Skimmer was doing it to bother me, maybe scare me off, and Ivy knew it. "No," she said, not looking up from her monitor. "I've got something planned."

Like what? I thought, deciding that Skimmer's and my relationship was probably going to nosedive like a brick with wings. This was really, *really* not anything I was prepared for.

Skimmer carefully broke her muffin in two, then got to her feet to find a knife and the butter. Leaving them by her plate, she moseyed to the coffeemaker, her steps carrying the presence and power of the courtroom. *Damn. I'm in trouble.*

"Coffee, Ivy?" she asked, the sun blinding on her shirt, crisp and pressed for the office.

"Sure. Thanks."

Feeling the tension, Rex slunk out. Wish I could.

"Here you go, sweets," the vamp said, bringing Ivy a cup. It wasn't the oversize mug with our Vampiric Charms logo on it that Ivy liked, but maybe she used them because I did.

Ivy jerked back when Skimmer tried to steal another kiss. Instead of being upset, the woman confidently sat down again to meticulously butter her muffin. She was pulling both Ivy's and my strings, fully in charge though Ivy was the more dominant of the two.

I wasn't going to leave because she was trying to make me uncomfortable. Feeling my blood pressure rise, I settled myself firmly in my chair. It was my kitchen, damn it.

"You're up early," the blond, blue-eyed vamp said to me as if it meant something.

I fought to keep my eyes from narrowing. "Did you make these?" I asked, raising what was left of my muffin.

Skimmer smiled to show her sharp canine teeth. "Yes, I did."

"They're good."

"You're welcome."

"I didn't say thank you," I shot back, and Ivy's hand on her mouse paused.

Skimmer ate her muffin, watching me with unblinking eyes and slowly widening pupils. My scar started tingling, and I stood. "I'm going to shower," I said, irate that she was giving me the creeps, but I did need to get cleaned up.

"I'll alert the media," Skimmer said, licking the butter suggestively from her finger.

I went to tell her to shove it up her ass and lay an egg with it, but the front doorbell rang, and my manners stayed intact. "That's Kisten," I said, then grabbed my shoulder bag. I was clean enough, and the last thing I wanted was three vampires in my kitchen and me naked in the shower. "I'm outta here."

Ivy broke from her computer, clearly surprised. "Where are you going?"

I glanced at Skimmer, feeling a blush rise. "Driver's ed. Kisten's taking me."

"Oh, how sweet!" Skimmer said, and I gritted my teeth. Refusing to respond, I headed for the hallway and the door, dirty knees or not. A sharp snap jerked me to a stop, and I turned, catching a blur of motion. Skimmer was red, clearly shocked and chagrined, but Ivy was smug. Something had happened, and Ivy arched an eyebrow at me in dry amusement.

The front doorbell clanked again, but I wasn't a good enough person to walk out of here now without saying something. "You going to be around tonight for dinner, Ivy?" I asked, cocking my hip. Maybe it was mean, but I was mean.

Ivy took a bite of her muffin, crossing her legs and leaning forward. "I'll be in and out," she said, wiping the corner of her mouth with a pinkie. "But I'll be here about midnight."

"Okay," I said lightly. "I'll see you later." I beamed at Skimmer, now sitting primly but obviously torn between seething and sulking. " 'Bye, Skimmer. Thanks for breakfast."

"You're welcome."

Translation: Choke on it, bitch.

The doorbell rang a third time, and I hustled down the hallway, my good mood restored. "Coming!" I shouted, fussing with my hair. I looked okay. It was only a bunch of teenagers.

I plucked Jenks's aviator jacket from the post in the foyer and shrugged into it just for looks. The coat was a remnant from his stint at being people-size. I'd gotten his jacket, Ivy had gotten his silk robe, and we'd thrown out his two dozen toothbrushes. Shoving the door open, I found Kisten waiting, his Corvette at the curb. He didn't work much until after sunset, and his usual trendy suit had been replaced with jeans and a black T-shirt, tucked in to show off his waist. Smiling with his mouth closed to hide his sharp canines, he rocked from heel to toe in his boots with his fingers jammed in his front pockets, tossing his dyed-blond hair out of his blue eyes with a practiced motion that said he was most assuredly "all that." What made it work was that he was.

"You look good," I said, my free hand slipping between his trim waist and his arm, using him for balance as I leaned up and in for an early-afternoon kiss hello right there at the threshold.

Eyes closing, I breathed deeply as his lips met mine, intentionally bringing in the scent of leather and the incense that clung to vampires as if it were a second skin. He was like a drug, throwing off pheromones to relax and soothe potential blood sources. We weren't sharing blood, but who was I not to take advantage of a thousand years of evolution?

"You look dirty," he said when our lips parted. I fell back to my heels, my smile growing to meet his when he added, "I like dirty. You've been in the garden." Eyebrows rising, he tugged me back into him, angling us into the darker foyer. "Am I early?" he said, the richness of his voice under my ear sending a shiver through me.

"Yes, thank God," I replied, enjoying the mild rush. I liked kissing vampires in the dark. The only thing better was being in an elevator descending to certain death.

I was blocking his way into the sanctuary, and when he realized I wasn't going to invite him in, his grip on my upper arms hesitated. "Your class isn't until one-thirty. You have time to take a shower," he said, clearly wanting to know why I was rushing out the door.

Maybe if you help me, I thought wickedly, unable to stop my grin. He caught my look, and as a spark of titillation zinged through me, his nostrils widened to take in my mood. He couldn't hear my thought, but he could read my pulse, my temperature, and considering the randy look I knew I had, it wasn't hard to figure out what was on my mind.

His fingers tightened, and from the hallway came Ivy's voice: "Hi, Kist."

Not dropping his gaze, Kisten answered, "Morning, love," not bothering to take out the heat rebounding between us.

She snorted, the soft sound of her bathroom door closing a clear indication that she was all right with the relationship Kisten and I had, despite their old boyfriend/girlfriend status. If he touched my blood, things would get nasty, which was why Kisten wore caps on his teeth when we slept together. But if I was going to be sharing my body with someone other than Ivy, she'd rather it be with Kisten. And that's . . . where we were.

Ivy and Kisten's relationship was more platonic these days, with a little blood thrown in to keep things close. Our situation had become a balancing act since she had tasted my blood and swore never to touch it again, but she didn't want Kisten touching it either, unable to give up the hope we could find a way to make it work, even as she denied it was possible. Defying his usual submissive role, Kisten had told Ivy he'd risk it if I succumbed to temptation and let him break my skin. But until then, we could all pretend that everything was normal. Or whatever passed for normal these days.

"Let's just go?" I said, my ardor cooling at the reminder that this screwed-up situation would hold steady as long as the status quo didn't change.

Chuckling, he let me push him to the door, but Skimmer's obvious throat clearing turned him from pliable vampire to immovable rock, and I slumped in defeat when her sultry voice echoed in the sanctuary. "Good morning, Kisten."

Kisten's smile widened as his gaze flicked between the two of us, clearly sensing my exasperation. "Can we go?" I whispered.

Eyebrows high, he turned me to the door. "Hi, Dorothy. You look nice today."

"Don't call me that, you S.O.B.," she said, her voice scathing across my back as I slipped out before Kisten. Apparently Skimmer felt about Kisten the same way she did about me. I wasn't surprised. We were both threats to her subordinate claim on Ivy. Neither of us was a true obstacle—me stymied by Ivy, and Kist because of their past—but try telling her that. Multiple blood and bed partners were the norm for vampires, but so was jealousy.

I took a deep breath as the door shut behind us, squinting in the sun and feeling my shoulders ease. It lasted all of three seconds until Kisten asked, "Skimmer sleep over?"

"I don't want to talk about it," I grumbled.

"That bad, eh?" he added, taking the steps lightly beside me.

I glanced longingly at my convertible, then back to his Corvette. "She's not being nice anymore," I complained, and Kisten picked up his pace to gallantly open the door before I could reach for the handle. Giving him a smile of thanks, I slipped in, settling myself in the familiar confines of his leather-scented, incense-rich car. God, it smelled good in here, and I closed my eyes and leaned back while Kisten went around to his side. I kept them shut even as he buckled himself in and started his car, willing myself to relax.

"Talk to me," he said when he started into motion and I was still silent.

A hundred thoughts sifted through me, but what came out was, "Skimmer . . ." I hesitated. "She found out that Ivy's the one not allowing a blood balance between us, not me."

His soft sigh drew my attention. The sun glinted on his stubble, and I stifled an urge to touch it. I watched his gaze flick behind us to the church through the rearview mirror. Depressed, I rolled my window down and let the morning breeze shift my hair.

"And?" he prompted as he gunned it, pulling out ahead of a blue Buick trailing smoke.

Holding my hair away from my eyes, I frowned. "She's gotten nasty. Trying to drive me away. I told her Ivy's just scared and that I'm waiting until she isn't, so Skimmer's gone from 'I want to be your friend because Ivy's your friend' to 'Suck my toes and die.' "

Kisten's grip on the wheel tightened, and he hit the brakes a little too hard at the stoplight. Realizing what I'd said, I flushed. I knew he'd rather have me lusting after a bite from him. But if I let him bite me, Ivy would snap. "I'm sorry, Kisten," I whispered.

He was silent, staring at the red light.

Reaching out, I touched his hand. "I love you," I whispered. "But letting you bite me would tear everything apart. Ivy couldn't take it." Jenks would say that my saying no to Kisten had more to do with the threat of his biting me being a bigger turn-on than the actual bite might be. Whatever. But if Kisten found a closer relationship with me when Ivy couldn't, it would hurt her, and he loved her, too, with the fanatical loyalty shared abuse often engenders; Piscary had warped them both.

From my bag came the trill of my phone, but I let it ring. This was more important. The light changed, and Kisten pulled into traffic, his grip more relaxed. Ivy had always been the dominant one in their relationship, but he was willing to fight for me if I was ever tempted enough to give him my blood. Trouble was, saying no had never been my strong suit. I courted disaster every time I slept with him, but it made for great sex. And I never said I was smart. Actually, it was pretty stupid. But we'd been over that before.

Depressed, I let my arm hang out the window and watched the Hollows turn from homes to businesses. The sun glinted dully on my bracelet and its distinctive pattern of links. Ivy had an anklet in the same pattern. I'd seen a few others around Cincy here and there, earning shrugs and smiles when I tried to hide mine. I knew they were probably Kisten's way to show the world his conquests, but I wore it nevertheless. So did Ivy.

"Skimmer won't hurt you," Kisten said softly, and I turned to him.

"Not physically," I agreed, relieved he was handling this as well as he was. "But you can be sure she's going to put extra love in her petition to get Piscary out."

He sobered at that, and quiet filled the car at the thought of what might happen if she succeeded. We'd both be up shit creek. Kisten had been Piscary's scion, betraying the master vampire the night I'd beaten Piscary into submission. Piscary was ignoring that right now, but if he got out, I was sure he'd have a thing or two to say to his ex-scion, even if Kisten had been the one keeping Piscary's business ventures intact, since Ivy wouldn't, her scion status aside.

My phone rang again. Digging it out, I looked to see that it was an unfamiliar number before I set it to vibrate. I was with Kisten, and taking the call would be rude. "You aren't mad?" I offered hesitantly, watching the emotion on his face shift from worry about his physical being to that of worry for his emotional state.

"Mad that you're attracted to Ivy?" he said, the sun flashing over him as we crossed the bridge. My face warmed, and he pulled his hand from mine to manage the thicker traffic. "No," he said, his eyes slightly dilating. "I love you, but Ivy . . . Since leaving the I.S. and you moving in with her, she's never been happier, more stable. Besides," he said, settling himself suggestively, "if this keeps up, I might have a chance at one hell of a threesome."

My mouth dropped open, and I swatted him. "No way!"

"Hey," he said, laughing, though his eyes were firmly on the traffic. "Don't knock it until you've tried it."

I crossed my arms before me and looked straight out the window. "Not going to happen, Kisten." But when I met his eyes, I could tell he had only been teasing me. *I think.*

"Don't make plans this Friday," he said as we stopped at yet another light.

I stifled a huge smile, but inside I was singing. *He remembered!* "Why?" I asked, feigning ignorance.

He smiled, and I lost my battle to remain unmoved. "I'm taking you out for your birthday," he said. "I've got reservations for the Carew Tower restaurant."

"Get out!" I exclaimed, my eyes darting to the top of the building in question. "I've never been up there to eat." I squirmed, my gaze going distant as I started to plan. "I don't know what to wear."

"Something that comes off easy?" he suggested.

A horn blew behind us, and, not looking, Kisten accelerated.

"All I've got is stuff with lots of snaps and buckles," I teased.

He went to say something, but his phone rang. I frowned when he reached to take it. I never took calls when we were together. Not that I got that many to begin with. But I wasn't trying to run Cincy's underworld for my boss either.

"Snaps and buckles?" he said as he flipped open the top. "That might work, too." Smile fading, he said into his phone. "This is Felps."

I settled back, feeling good just thinking about it.

"Hey, Ivy. What's up?" Kisten said, and I straightened. Then, remembering my phone, I pulled it out and looked. Crap, I'd missed four calls. But I didn't recognize the number.

"Right beside me," Kisten said, glancing at me, and a flicker of concern rose. "Sure," he added, then handed the phone to me.

Oh, God, now what? Feeling like I'd heard a shoe fall, I said, "Is it Jenks?"

"No," Ivy's irate voice said, and I relaxed. "It's your Were."

"David?" I stammered, and Kisten pulled into the driving school's parking lot.

"He's been trying to reach you," Ivy said, her tone both bothered and concerned. "He says—are you ready for this?—he says he's killing women and he doesn't remember. Look, will you call him? He's called here twice in the last three minutes."

I wanted to laugh but couldn't. The Were murder the I.S. was covering up. The demon tearing my living room apart for the focus. Shit.

"Okay," I said softly. "Thanks. 'Bye."

"Rachel?"

Her voice had changed. I was upset, and she knew it. I took a breath, trying to find a glimmer of calm. "Yes?"

I could tell by her hesitation that she wasn't fooled, but she knew that whatever it was, I wasn't running scared. Yet. "Watch yourself," she said tightly. "Call me if you need me."

My tension eased. It was good to have friends. "Thanks. I will."

I hung up, glanced at Kisten's expressive eyes waiting for an explanation, then jumped when my phone, sitting in my lap, vibrated. Taking a breath, I picked it up and looked at the number. It was David's. I recognized it now.

"You going to take that?" Kisten asked, his hands on the wheel though we were parked.

In the next spot over, I watched a girl slam the door to her mother's minivan. Ponytail bobbing and mouth going nonstop, she chatted as she headed to class with a friend. They disappeared past the glass doors, and the woman behind the wheel wiped at her eye and watched through her rearview mirror. Kisten leaned forward to get into my line of sight. The phone vibrated again, and a sour smile lifted the corners of my mouth as I flipped the phone open.

Somehow I didn't think I was going to make my class.

EIGHT

David's hand trembled almost imperceptibly as he accepted the glass of cold tap water. He held it to his forehead for a moment as he gathered his calm, then sipped it and set it on the solid ash coffee table before us. "Thank you," the small man said, then put his elbows on his knees and dropped his head into his hands.

I patted his shoulder and eased farther from him on his couch. Kisten was standing next to the TV, back to us as he looked over David's collection of Civil War sabers in a lighted, locked cabinet. The faint scent of Were tickled my nose, not unpleasant at all.

David was a wreck, and I alternated my attention between the shaken man dressed in his suit for the office and his tidy, clearly bachelor town house. It was the usual two stories, the entire complex about five to ten years old. The carpet probably hadn't ever been replaced, and I wondered if David rented or owned.

We were in the living room. To one side past the landscaped buffer was the parking lot. To the other through the kitchen and dining area was a large common courtyard, the other apartments far enough away that it granted a measure of privacy by pure distance. The walls were thick, hence the silence, and the classy wallpaper done in browns and tans said he had decorated it himself. *Owned,* I decided, remembering that as a field adjuster for Were Insurance he was paid very well for getting the true story from reluctant policy owners trying to hide the reason their

Christmas tree had spontaneously combusted and taken out their living room.

Though his apartment was a calm spot of peace, the Were himself looked ragged. David was a loner, having the personal power and charisma of an alpha without the responsibilities. Technically speaking, I was his pack, a mutually beneficial agreement on paper that helped prevent David from being fired and gave me the opportunity to get my insurance at a devastatingly cheap rate. That was the extent of our relationship, but I knew he used me to keep Were women from insinuating themselves into his life.

My gaze landed on the fat little black book beside his phone. *Apparently that didn't slow him down when it came to dating.* Dang, he needed a rubber band to keep the thing shut.

"Better?" I said, and David looked up. His beautifully deep brown eyes were wide with a slow fear, looking wrong on him. He had a wonderfully trim body made for running, disguised under the comfortable suit. Clearly he had been on his way to the office when whatever threw him into such a tizzy happened, and it worried me that something could shake him like this. David was the most stable person I knew.

His shoes under the coffee table shone, and he was clean-shaven, not even a hint of black stubble marring his sun-darkened, somewhat rough skin. I'd seen him in a floor-length duster and dilapidated hat once while he had been stalking me, and he had looked like Van Helsing; his luscious black hair was long and wavy, and his thick eyebrows made a nice statement. He had about the same amount of confidence as the fictional character, too, but right now it was tempered with worry and distraction.

"No," he said, his low voice penetrating. "I think I'm killing my girlfriends."

Kisten turned, and I held up a hand to forestall the vampire from saying anything stupid. David was nothing if not levelheaded, and as an insurance adjuster he was quick, savvy, and hard to surprise. If he thought he was killing his girlfriends, then there was a reason for it.

"I'm listening," I said from beside him, and David took a slow breath, forcing himself to sit upright, if still on the edge of the couch.

"I was trying to find a date for this weekend," he started, glancing at Kisten.

"For the full moon?" Kisten interrupted, earning both my and David's annoyance.

"The full moon isn't until Monday," the Were said. "And I'm not a college Werejockey high on bane crashing your bar. I have as much control over myself on a full moon as you do."

Obviously it was a sore spot, and Kisten raised a placating hand. "Sorry."

The tension in the room eased, and David's haunted eyes went to his address book by the phone. "Serena called me last night, asking me if I had the flu." He looked up at me, then away. "Which I thought strange since it's summer, but then I called Kally to see if she was free, and she asked me the same thing."

Kisten chuckled. "You dated two women in one weekend?"

David's brow creased. "No, they were a week apart. So I called a few other women, seeing as I hadn't heard from any of them in almost a month."

"In high demand are you, Mr. Peabody?"

"Kisten," I muttered, not liking the reference to the old cartoon. "Stop it." David's cat was peering at me from the top of the stairway. I didn't even try to coax it down, depressed.

David wasn't cowed at all by the living vampire. Not here in his own apartment. "Yes," he said belligerently. "I am, actually. You want to wait on the veranda?"

Kisten raised a hand in a gesture of "whatever," but I had no trouble believing that the attractive, mid-thirties Were had women calling him for dates. David and I were comfortable leaving our relationship at the business level, though I found it mildly irksome that he had issues with the different-species thing. But as long as he respected me as a person, I was willing to let him miss out on a good slice of the female population. His loss.

"Apart from Serena and Kally, I couldn't reach one." His eyes went to his black book as if it were possessed. "None of them."

"So you think they're dead?" I questioned, not seeing the reason for the jump of thought.

David's eyes were haunted. "I've been having really weird dreams about them," he said. "My girlfriends, I mean. I'm waking up in my own bed clean and rested, not mud-caked and naked in the park, so I never gave them much thought, but now . . ."

Kisten chuckled, and I started wishing I'd left him in the car. "They're avoiding you, wolfman," the vampire said, and David pulled himself straight, ire giving him strength.

"They're gone," he muttered.

I watched warily, knowing that Kisten was too savvy to push him too far, but David was erratic right now.

"Either they don't answer their phone or their roommates don't know where they are." His eyes slipped to mine, haunted. "Those are the ones that I'm worried about. The ones I couldn't reach."

"Six women," Kisten said, now standing at the window wall that looked out on a small patio. "That's not bad. Half of them probably moved."

"In a month and a half?" David said caustically. Then, as if galvanized by the admission, he went to the kitchen, his pace fast with nervous energy.

My eyebrows rose. *David dated six women in as many weeks?* Weres weren't any more randy than the rest of the population, but remembering his reluctance to settle down and start a pack, I decided it probably wasn't that he couldn't keep a girlfriend but rather that he was content playing the field. Playing the pro field. *Jeez, David.*

"They're missing," he said, standing in his kitchen as if having forgotten why he went in there. "I think . . . I think I'm blanking out and killing them."

My gut clenched at the lost sound of his voice. He really believed he was killing these women.

"Well, there you go," Kisten said. "Someone found out you're a player and called the rest. You've been stung, Mr. Peabody." He chuckled. "Time to start a new black book."

David looked insulted, and I thought Kisten was being unusually insensitive. Maybe he was jealous. "You know what?" I said, spinning to Kisten. "You need to shut up."

"Hey, I'm just saying—"

David jerked as if remembering why he had gone into the kitchen, popping open a tin of cat food and shaking it onto a plate before setting it on the floor. "Rachel, would you refuse to talk to a man you'd slept with, even if you were mad at him?"

My eyebrows rose. He hadn't just dated six women in six weeks, he'd slept with them, too? "Uh . . ." I stammered. "No. I'd want to give him a piece of my mind at the very least."

Head lowered, David nodded. "They're missing," he said. "I'm killing them. I know it."

"David," I protested, seeing a hint of concern on Kisten's face, "Weres don't black out and kill people. If they did, they would've been hunted into extinction hundreds of years ago by the rest of Inderland. There's got to be another reason they aren't talking to you."

"Because I killed them," David whispered, hunched over the counter.

My gaze drifted to the ticking wall clock. Two-fifteen. I'd missed my class. "It doesn't add up," I said, coming to sit at a barstool. "Do you want me to have Ivy track them down? She's good at finding people."

Looking relieved, he nodded. Ivy could find anyone, given time. She had been retrieving abducted vamps and humans from illegal blood houses and jealous exes since leaving the I.S. It made my familiar rescues look vapid, but we each had our own talents.

My motions shifting the stiff barstool back and forth slowed. Since I was here, I ought to see about taking the focus home with me. Anyone who cared to look it up would know that I belonged to David's pack. Being a loner and trained to react to violence, David was a hard target. Anyone he worked with, though . . .

"Oh, shit," I said, then put a hand to my mouth, realizing I'd said it aloud. Both Kisten and David stared at me. "Uh, David, did you tell your dates about the focus?"

His confusion turned to a soft anger. "No," he said forcefully.

Kisten glowered at the smaller man. "You mean to tell me you nipped six women in six weeks, and you never showed them the focus to impress them?"

David's jaw clenched. "I don't need to lure women to my bed. I ask them, and if they're willing, they come. Showing them wouldn't have impressed them anyway. They're human."

I pulled my elbows off the counter, my face warming in indignation. "You date *humans*? You won't date a witch because you don't believe in mixed-species parings, but you'll *sleep around with humans*? You big fat hypocrite!"

David pleaded with me with his eyes. "If I dated a Were woman, she'd want to be a part of my pack. We've been over this before. And since Weres originally came from humans—"

My eyes narrowed. "Yeah, I got it," I said, not liking it. Weres came from humans same as vamps, but, unlike becoming a vamp, the only way to become a Were was to be born one.

Usually.

My thoughts zinged back to yesterday morning and being woken by a demon tearing my church apart looking for the focus. *Oh-h-h-h, shit,* I thought, remembering to keep my mouth shut this time. Missing girlfriends. Three unidentified bodies in the morgue: athletic, professional, and all with a similar look. They were brought in as Weres, but if what I thought happened *had* happened, they wouldn't be in the Were database but the human. Suicides from last month's full moon.

"David, I'm so sorry," I whispered, and Kisten and David stared at me.

"What?" David said, wary, not distraught.

I looked helplessly at him. "It wasn't your fault. It was mine. I shouldn't have given it to you. I didn't know all you had to do was have it in your possession. I never would have given it to you if I did." He looked blank at me, and, feeling nauseous, I added, "I think I know where your girlfriends are. It's my fault, not yours."

David shook his head. "Give me what?"

"The focus," I said, my face wrinkled in pity. "I think . . . it turned your girlfriends."

His face went ashen, and he put a hand to the counter. "Where are they?" he breathed.

I swallowed hard. "The city morgue."

NINE

Two trips to the morgue in as many days, I thought, hoping I wasn't starting a pattern. My gardening sneakers were silent on the cement; David's steps beside and a little behind me were heavy with a deep depression. Kisten was behind him, and the vampire's obvious unease would have been funny if we weren't trooping down here to identify three Jane Wolfs.

The focus was in my bag now, silent and quiescent this far from the full moon. It still held the chill from David's freezer and made a cold spot against me. Experience said that next Monday it would have shifted from a bone statue of a woman's face to a silver-sheened wolf's muzzle, dripping saliva and making a high-pitched squeal only pixies could hear. *I have to get rid of this thing.* Maybe I could use it to pay off one of my demon marks. But if Newt or Al sold it in turn to someone else and it started an Inderland power struggle, I'd feel responsible.

We reached the end of the stairway, and with the two men trailing behind me I turned smartly to the right and followed the arrows to the double doors. "Hi, Iceman," I said, smacking the left side of the swinging door open and striding in as if I owned the place.

The young man sat up, pulling his feet from his desk. "Ms. Morgan," he said. "Holy cow, you gave me a start."

Kisten slunk in after me, eyes darting everywhere. "Come here often?" he asked when the kid behind the desk put down his handheld game and stood.

"All the time," I quipped, extending my hand to meet Iceman's grip. "Don't you?"

"No."

Iceman's attention flicked from me to Kisten, finally lingering on David, standing with his hands at his sides. His enthusiasm to see me dimmed as he realized we were here to identify someone. "Oh, uh, hey," he said, his hand slipping from mine, "it's great to see you, but I can't let you in there unless you have someone from the I.S. or the FIB with you." He winced. "Sorry."

"Detective Glenn is on his way," I said, feeling bouncy for some reason. Sure, I was here to identify a corpse or three, but I knew someone Kisten didn't, and that didn't happen often.

Relief turned him back into a young kid who should be serving smoothies at the mall, not morgue minding. "Good," he said. "You're welcome to sit on a gurney while you wait."

I glanced at the empty gurney against the wall. "Ah, I think I'll stand," I said. "This is Kisten Felps," I added, then turned to David. "And David Huc."

David pulled himself together and, finding a professional air, came forward with his hand extended. "Pleasure to meet you," he said, rocking back as soon as their handshake ended. "How . . . how many Jane Wolfs do you get on average a month?"

His voice carried a hint of panic, and Iceman went closed, sitting back behind his desk. "I'm sorry, Mr. Hue. I really shouldn't—"

David held up a hand and turned away, head bowed in worry. My good mood vanished. A sharp cadence of hard-soled shoes in the outer hallway brought our attentions up, and I puffed in relief when Glenn's powerfully built frame came through the door, his thick hand holding the heavy metal easy and his dark skin and pink fingernails standing out against the stark whiteness of the chipped paint. He was in his usual coat and tie, the butt of a pistol showing past his jacket. Angling himself, he slipped in almost sideways so he wouldn't have to open the door entirely.

"Rachel," he said as the door swung shut. His gaze lit on David and Kisten, eyebrows settling into a closed cast of FIB officialness. David's confidence had degraded into depression, and Kisten was nervous. I was getting the distinct impression he didn't like it down here.

"Hi, Glenn," I said, conscious of my less-than-professional appearance in sneakers, faded green T-shirt, and dirt-marked jeans. "Thanks for letting me get you out from behind your desk."

"You said it was about the Jane Wolfs. How could I refuse?"

David's jaw tightened. The reaction wasn't missed by Glenn, and his gaze softened, now that he understood why David was here. I could feel Kisten behind me, and I turned to him. "Glenn, this is Kisten Felps," I said, but Kisten had already pushed forward, smiling with his lips closed.

"We've met," Kisten said, grasping Glenn's hand and giving it a firm shake. "Well, in a manner of speaking. You were the one that downed the waitstaff at Piscary's last year."

"Using Rachel's splat gun," Glenn said, suddenly nervous. "I didn't . . ."

Kisten released his hand and stepped away. "No, you didn't tag me. But I saw you during the wrap-up. Good shooting. Accuracy is hard to find when your life is on the line."

Glenn smiled to show his flat, even teeth. He was the only FIB guy I knew besides his dad who could talk to a vamp without fear and knew to bring breakfast when knocking on a witch's door at noon. "No hard feelings?" Glenn asked.

Shrugging, Kisten turned to the double doors leading to the hallway. "We all do what we have to do. It's only on our days off we get to be ourselves."

You aren't kidding, I thought, wondering what kind of a mess Kisten was going to find himself in if Piscary got out. I wasn't the only one the master vampire had unfinished business with. And while Piscary *could* hurt Kisten while he was still in prison, I had a feeling that the undead vampire enjoyed drawing out the fear of the unknown. He might forgive Kisten for giving me Egyptian embalming fluid to incapacitate him, seeing the betrayal as the act of an unruly, rebellious child. Maybe. Me, he was just ticked at.

His shoes scuffing, David came forward. "David. David Hue," he said, eyes pinched. "Can we please get this over with?"

Glenn shook his hand, his expressive face turning to a professional detachment I knew he used so he could sleep at night. "Of course, Mr. Hue," he said. The FIB detective glanced at Iceman, and the college kid tossed him the Bite-Me-Betty doll with the key. As he caught it, the rims of the upright, meticulous FIB officer's ears darkened in embarrassment.

"Rachel?" Kisten murmured as we all headed that way. "Ah, if you can get a ride home with David, I need to fly on out of here."

I stopped. Glenn turned from holding the door open for me. Through it I could see the comfortable seating arrangement and Iceman's work partner puttering around with a clipboard, peering over his glasses at us. *Kisten is afraid of the dead?*

"Kisten . . ." I coaxed, not believing it. I had wanted to stop at The Big Cherry on the way home to pick up Glenn's tomato fix, at a charm shop for the lilac wine, and just about anywhere for a box of birthday candles for me in the hopes that a cake might be in my future. But Kisten backed up a step.

"Really," he said. "I have to go. There's some rare cheese coming in today, and if I'm not there to sign for it, I'll have to go to the post office and pick it up."

Rare cheese, my ass. And I hate not having my own car. Hip cocked, I took a breath to complain, but David interrupted with an easy, "I'll get you home, Rachel."

Kisten's eyes were pleading. Giving up, I muttered, "Go on. I'll call you later."

He jiggled on his feet, his usual poise gone to make him look charmingly vulnerable. Leaning in, he gave me a quick kiss on my neck. "Thanks, love," he whispered. His hand on my shoulder tightened, and with a quick hint of teeth he sent a spike of desire to my core.

"Stop that," I whispered, gently pushing him away and feeling myself flush.

Grinning, he retreated. With a self-assured nod to the rest of the men, he stuck his hands into his pockets and sauntered out.

Lord help me, I thought, pulling my hand down from my neck. I had the feeling he'd just used me to restore his confidence. Sure, he was afraid of the dead, but I was his girlfriend, and apparently proving it in front of three other guys had reaffirmed his masculinity. Whatever.

My face was still warm when Glenn cleared his throat. "What?" I muttered as I entered before him. "He's my boyfriend."

"Mmmm-hmm," he murmured back, shaking the Bite-Me-Betty

doll to make the key jingle. The living vamp intern checking tags left at Glenn's look. It was just us and whatever newly dead vamps were cooling their heels until dark.

David was cracking his knuckles when Glenn stopped beside a drawer, eyeing the Were. "You think you know these women?" he said, and I bristled. There had been more than a hint of distrust, his need to have someone to blame for their deaths, coming to the fore.

"Yes," I interjected before David could open his mouth. "He has a couple of girlfriends he can't reach, and since he was holding something for me that the right person would kill to get, we thought it better to check it out so we could sleep at night."

David seemed relieved at my explanation, but Glenn wasn't happy. "Rachel," he said as his short fingers worked the key, but he didn't open the drawer. "They are Weres. Technically this isn't a FIB matter. If someone calls foul, I could be in a lot of trouble."

I could sense David's rising fear and anticipation, and I wondered if that was why Kisten had left. Though not directed at him, it would have pushed his buttons. "Just open the drawer," I said, starting to get mad. "You really think I should bring Denon into this? He'd have David in the tower and under a spotlight. And besides," I said, praying I was wrong, "if I'm right, then this *is* a FIB matter."

Glenn's brown eyes narrowed, and with David's brow pinched, the FIB detective opened the drawer. I glanced down at the harsh sound of the bag opening, seeing the pretty woman in a new light, imagining her fear and the pain of turning into a wolf and not having a clue. God, she must have thought she'd been dying.

"That's Elaine," David breathed, and I took his arm as his balance wobbled. Glenn tripped into detective mode, his gaze bright and his stance stiffer, more threatening. I told him to be quiet with my eyes. His questions could wait. We had two more Pandora boxes to open.

"God, I'm sorry, David," I said softly, wishing Glenn would shut the drawer.

As if hearing my unspoken request, he slowly slid Elaine away.

David's face was pale, and I had to remind myself that though he could take care of himself and was no slouch when it came to confidence, these were women he had known intimately. "Show me the next one," he said, the scent of musk thickening in the closed air.

Glenn ripped a jotted note from his daily planner and tucked it in behind the ID card before going to the next. My stomach was in knots. This wasn't looking good. Not only was there the problem that David was involved in the accidental deaths of three women, but now I was going to have to explain to the FIB why they had human birth certificates.

Crap on toast. How in hell was I going to handle this? Every master vamp in the country, every alpha with delusions of grandeur, was going to be after me, the former to destroy the focus, the latter to possess it. Pretending to throw it off the Mackinac Bridge wasn't going to work a second time. Maybe . . . maybe it had been a fluke. Maybe Elaine had been a Were and she'd only told David she was human, knowing he wouldn't date a bitch.

Glenn unlocked the second drawer, and when we were arranged, he unzipped the bag. I watched David instead of Glenn. I knew the answer when his eyes closed and his hand trembled.

"Felicia," he whispered. "Felicia Borden." He reached to touch her, his trembling fingers brushing her brown hair. "I'm sorry, Felicia. I didn't know. I'm so sorry. What . . . what did you do to yourself?"

His voice cracked, and I darted a glance at Glenn. The FIB officer nodded. David was ready to lose it. We had better get the hard part over fast.

"Come on, David," I soothed, taking his arm and pulling him a step back. "One more."

David broke his gaze from her, and Glenn swiftly shut the drawer with the sound of scraping metal. The only one left was the woman who had been hit by a train. It probably hadn't been a suicide. Most likely she had snapped under the strain of a first transformation without pain relief or understanding, blindly fleeing in search of an answer. Or perhaps she had been lost in the glories of her newfound freedom and had misjudged her new capabilities. I almost hoped it was the latter, tragic though it would be. I didn't like the idea that she had gone insane. It would only mean that much more guilt for David.

I stood with David to the right of the last drawer. Realizing he was holding his breath, I slipped my hand into his. It was cool and dry. I think he was starting to go into shock.

Glenn opened the last drawer reluctantly, clearly not eager to show David the ruin of the woman's body.

"Oh, God," David moaned, turning away.

My eyes pricking with tears and feeling helpless, I put my arm over his shoulder and led him to the informal seating area where relatives waited for their kin to awaken. His back was hunched, and he moved without thought, grasping the back of a chair before falling into it.

He slipped out from under me, and I stood over him as he put his elbows on his knees and dropped his head into his hands. "I didn't mean for it to happen," he said, his voice sounding dead. "It's not supposed to happen. It's not supposed to happen!"

Glenn had shut the last drawer and was making his way to us with an aggressive FIB swagger. "Back off," I warned him. "I see where you're going, but he didn't kill those women."

"Then why is he convincing himself he didn't?"

"David is an insurance adjuster, not a killer. You said it yourself—they were suicides."

David made a harsh sound of inner pain. Turning to him, I touched on his shoulder. "Ah, hell. I'm sorry. I didn't mean it like that."

He didn't look up as he said flatly, "They were all alone. They had no one to help them, to tell them what to expect. That the pain would go away." His head rose, and he had tears in his eyes. "They went through that alone, and it was my fault. I could have helped them. They would have survived if I had been there."

"David . . ." I started, but his face abruptly lost its expression, and he rose.

"I have to go," he stammered. "I have to call Serena and Kally."

"A moment, Mr. Hue," Glenn said firmly, and I gave him a dirty look.

David's face was white, and his small but powerful build was tense. "I have to call Serena and Kally!" he exclaimed, and Iceman peeked in past the door.

My hands out in placation, I insinuated myself between Glenn and the distressed Were. "David," I soothed, gently resting my hand on his arm, "they'll be okay. It's a week before the full moon." I turned to Glenn, my voice hardening. "And I told you to back off."

His eyes narrowed at my harsh tone, but though he was the FIB's Inderland specialist, I was an Inderlander. "Back off!" I insisted, then lowered my voice lest I wake someone up. "This is my friend, and you will cut him some slack, or so help me, Glenn, I'll show you what a mean, mad witch is capable of."

Glenn clenched his jaw. I glared right back at him. I'd never pulled my magic on him before, but we had come down here to answer the question of whether the focus was turning humans into Weres, not submit to a homicide charge.

"David," I said, eyes on Glenn, "sit down. Detective Glenn has a few questions." *God, I hope I have some answers.*

Both men relaxed, and after Iceman let the door shut behind him, I sat as well and crossed my legs as if I were the hostess of this nice little party. David resumed his seat, but Glenn continued to stand and glower down at me. Fine. They were his wrinkles.

Then I started thinking. Crap, I wasn't smart enough to come up with a convincing lie. I'd have to tell him the truth. I hated that. Wincing, I pulled my gaze to Glenn's. "Hey . . . uh," I stammered. "Can you keep a secret?" I thought of the sleeping vamps, glad the drawers were soundproof. Too bad they weren't smellproof.

Glenn exhaled as if deflating, his attitude changing from that of an aggressive, stymied FIB officer to the neighborhood cop on the corner. "Since it's you, Rachel, I'll listen. For a while."

Okay, that was fair, since I had threatened to bop him with my magic. I glanced at David, and seeing him leaving it all to me, I clasped my hands in my lap. "The reason you can't find those women in the database is because they aren't in the Inderland files."

Glenn's eyebrows rose.

"They're in the human files," I said, almost able to hear the bolts sliding—my life shifting to a new, probably shorter, path.

The fabric of Glenn's suit made a soft sound as he turned. "Human? But—"

"They came in as Weres, yes," I finished. I pulled my shoulder bag to my front to sit on my lap, but I wasn't going to tell him I had the focus. He'd probably insist on taking it, and when I refused, he'd get all testosterone-laden and then I'd get all witchy. Best to avoid it. I liked Glenn, and every time I flexed my magic, I usually lost a friend.

From beside me came David's emotionless voice. "I turned them. I didn't mean to." His head came back up. "Believe me, I didn't want this to happen. I didn't think it *could* happen."

"It can't," Glenn said, anger coloring his confusion. "If this is your idea of a joke—"

He didn't believe me. "Don't you think I could come up with a better story if I was jerking your chain?" I said. "I have rent to make, and I'm not going to waste my day down here in the morgue." I glanced over the sterile surroundings. "As nice as it is down here."

The large man frowned. "Humans can't be turned into Weres. It's a fact."

"And forty years ago humans believed it was a fact that there were no vampires or pixies. What about fairy tales?" I said. "In the old ones, a bite could make a Were. Well, they're true, and the proof is that you will find those women in the human database."

But Glenn's face said he wasn't buying it.

Head drooping, I said to the floor, "See, there's this demon-cursed statue." *God, it sounds so lame.* "I gave it to David to hold for me because he's a Were and Jenks said it was giving him a headache. It's bad magic, Glenn. Whoever has it has the ability to turn a human into a Were. The Weres want it, and the vamps will kill anyone to destroy it to maintain the balance of Inderland power." I brought my gaze up, and though he was listening, I could tell he wasn't ready to give up his secure belief. "I had assumed there was some sort of additional ritual needed to turn a human." Feeling guilty, I touched David's arm. "Apparently not."

"You bit them?" Glenn accused.

"I slept with them." David's voice had a defensive edge. "I have to go. I have to call Serena and Kally."

Glenn's hand fell to rest on the butt of his weapon. I would have taken offense, but I didn't think he realized it.

"Look," I said, exasperated, "remember this May when the riots broke out in the mall between the vamps and the Weres?" Glenn nodded, and I scooted to the front of my chair, not liking his hand on his weapon. "Well, it was because three Were packs thought I *had* this Were artifact and they were trying to flush me out."

His eyes widened. He was starting to believe.

"And if it gets out that it didn't go over the Mackinac Bridge but is in Cincinnati turning women into Weres, I'm going to be a dead witch walking." I hesitated. "Again."

The FIB officer exhaled long and slow, but I couldn't tell what he was thinking. "That's why Mr. Ray's secretary was murdered, isn't it?" he said, gesturing behind him to the drawers.

"Probably," I said in a small voice. "But David didn't do it." Damn it. Denon was right. Her demise was sort of my fault. Miserable, I pulled my gaze from the drawer. It landed on David, slumped and struggling to come to grips with the deaths of three women. If this got out, we both were dead. My attention rose to Glenn.

"You're not going to tell anyone, right?" I asked. "You have to keep this quiet. Tell the next of kin they died in an accident."

Glenn shook his head. "I'll keep it as quiet as I can," he said, coming forward to stand in front of David. "But I'm going to get this on paper. Mr. Hue?" he said respectfully. "Would you come down with me to the office so we can fill out some paperwork?"

Crap. I slumped into the cushy chair, making a puff of incense-scented air billow around me. "You aren't arresting him, are you?" I asked, and David went whiter.

"No. Just taking a statement. For his protection. If you've told me the *truth*"—he stressed it as if I hadn't—"you don't have anything to worry about. You or Mr. Hue."

I'd told the truth, but somehow I wasn't reassured. I knew I wore a sour expression as I rose to stand beside David. "You want me to come with you?" I asked, wondering if I might trade my moving out of the church and away from Ivy for some pro bono lawyer work from Skimmer.

The Were nodded, looking shaken but okay in his suit and tie. "It's all right, Rachel. I know all about forms." Grimacing with a tired acceptance, he looked to Glenn. "If we stop at my house, I can give you the names and addresses of everyone I've slept with since taking possession of that . . . thing."

Thick lips pursed, Glenn ran a hand over his closely cut hair. "Just how many women have you had sex with in the last two months, Mr. Hue?"

David reddened. "Six, I think. I need my address book to be sure."

Glenn made a small noise, and I could almost see him grant the attractive man more respect. *God, men are pigs.*

"I'm going to take the bus home," I said, wanting to be alone—not to mention avoid a trip to the FIB. *Jeez, and they were just starting to like me, too.*

"It's no problem to drop you off," Glenn offered. "I can take the artifact into custody, too. No reason for you to be in danger."

My eyebrows rose, and I kept my eyes off my shoulder bag. "It's in the mail system," I lied, not wanting to go into why I wasn't going to give it to him. "Soon as it hits my mailbox, I'll call you." *Lie, lie, li-i-i-i-ie, lie lie.*

Glenn's brown eyes narrowed, and I felt myself warm. David said nothing, knowing where it was and apparently agreeing with my decision. Gathering myself, I adjusted the strap to my shoulder bag and headed for the door. This hadn't gone well at all. Maybe I could sell it online and donate the proceeds to the war relief fund, 'cause there was going to be a war.

"Thank you for your cooperation, Mr. Hue," Glenn was saying behind me. "I know this is hard, but the families of those women will be grateful to know what has happened."

"Don't tell them I turned their daughters," David whispered. "I'll do it. Give me that."

I glanced behind me as I pushed open the swinging doors. Glenn was hunched in sympathy as he walked beside the smaller man. I searched my feelings and decided it wasn't an act. "I'll do the best I can," Glenn said, his gaze rising to mine for a moment.

Yeah, I'd heard that before. What it meant was he'd do his best as long as it didn't mean bending his ruler-up-his-ass rules.

Stupid-ass, upright, uptight FIB detective, I thought. *What hurt would it do to bury this from the public?* Then I blew out my frustration. I was starting to think like Trent. This was a potential Inderland power struggle, though, not an illegal genetic lab. *But women had died, and I wanted him to lie to their families about how and why.*

We slowed when Glenn went to talk to Iceman, and David halted beside me. His few wrinkles were deepened by stress, and he looked terrible. "I'm so sorry, David," I whispered.

"It's not your fault," he said, but I felt like it was.

Glenn joined us and gestured David to walk out before us. The FIB officer took hold of my upper arm, keeping my steps slow until David was several paces ahead of us.

"Who did you get the statue from?" he asked as we started up the stairway.

I looked at his dark fingers encircling my arm, remembering that thick folder he had given me listing Nick's crimes. Shaky, I reached for the filthy banister and gripped it as I rose. "Tell me you'll do your damnedest to keep this locked in a drawer," I asked. "All of it."

"Tell me, Rachel," he threatened, not giving an inch.

Exhaling, I watched David's slumped back. "Nick," I said, seeing no point in not telling him. The thief was playing dead, so there was no reason for Glenn to go looking for him.

His entire posture easing, Glenn nodded. "Okay," he said. "Now I believe you."

TEN

It was hot at the bus stop, and I stood breathing in air flavored by pavement, gas fumes, and the nearby Skyline Chili. It was probably the only chain restaurant serving a tomato-based food that had survived the Turn and the tomato boycott that half the world's surviving population had adopted. I was hungry and tempted to get myself a cardboard bowl to go, but I knew that the moment I left the stop, the bus would show and I'd be waiting another half hour.

So I stood there in my jeans and green T-shirt, sweating in the sun beating down and watching the heavy traffic. The tidy Were beside me smelled nice, and the two warlocks monopolizing the shade of a newly planted tree chatted about nothing. I could tell they were warlocks because their characteristic redwood scent was almost hidden beneath the overdone perfume that was making the Were's eyes tear.

The more magic you practiced, the stronger your scent, though usually only another Inderlander could pick it up. The same went for vampires, the ones who indulged themselves the most having a more obvious incense smell. Jenks said I reeked of magic and Ivy stank of vampire. *And we all lived together in a little stinky church,* I sang in my head.

Uneasy, I ran a finger between me and the strap of my bag. Warlock was a designation of skill, not sex, warlocks simply being witches who hadn't gone through the trouble of learning how to stir a spell by heart.

They could invoke them, all right, but stirring them safely was out of their skill level. And as soon as humanity got their head wrapped around that, the entire demographic slice of educated male witches could take the chip off their shoulder and relax.

I had a two-year degree plus enough life experience to get the license to use my charms in my work. It wasn't skill holding me back from getting the license to sell my charms, but capital. Which might explain the incongruity of my riding the bus with an artifact that could start an Inderland power struggle. With my luck, I'd get mugged on the way home.

A sigh shifted me, and I plucked at my T-shirt, wondering if I should take it off and wear the chemise I had on under it home. It would be fun to watch the guy next to me react when I started stripping. A private grin curled up the corners of my mouth. Maybe I'd take off my sneakers and go barefoot. Muggers usually left dirty people with no shoes alone.

The Were next to me made a long whistle of appreciation, and I lifted my gaze up from my nasty sneakers, blinking at the Gray Ghost limo edging out of traffic and into the bus pull-off. My first reaction of surprise melted into annoyance. It had to be Trent. And here I was waiting for the bus with filthy knees and sweating. *Just peachy damn keen.*

I peered over my sunglasses when the tinted back window rolled down. Yup, it was Trent, the wealthy bastard looking good in his cream-colored linen suit and white shirt. His tan had deepened with summer, leading me to think he got out into his prizewinning gardens and nationally renowned stables more often than he let on. Smiling a confident, somewhat expectant smile, the elf in hiding arched his thin eyebrows at the dirt on my knees.

I didn't say a word, looking through his lowered window to the front seat to find Quen, his head of security, driving instead of his chief bootlicker, Jonathan. My pulse eased at the absence of the tall, sadistic man. I liked Quen, even if he occasionally tested my magic and martial-arts skills. He was honest, at least, unlike his employer.

Hand on my hip, I said snidely, "Where's Jon?" and the Were behind me had a conniption fit that I knew Trent well enough to be nasty to him. The two warlocks were busy taking photos with their phones, giggling and whispering. Maybe I ought to be nice lest I find my ugly scene plastered all over the Internet, and I relaxed my posture a smidgen.

Trent leaned to the window, green eyes squinting at the sun. His fair, neatly translucent hair moved in the breeze from the street, marring its carefully styled perfection. Much as I hated to admit it, his wind-mused hair pegged my attraction meter. Though his business prowess, expressed through his pristinely legal Kalamack Industries, was esteemed, his lean, well-proportioned body would look as good in a tight swimsuit perched on a lifeguard chair as it did in a suit in the boardroom. "Jonathan is occupied," he said, his practiced voice catching my attention and the hint of annoyance in it taking nothing from its mesmerizing grace.

"With *Ellasbeth?*" I mocked, and the Were beside me choked. *What, like I have to be nice to him because he supplied the East Coast's Brimstone trade and had half the world's leaders in his pocket through his illegal biomedicines?* After failing to buy my lifetime services, he had tried to scare me into it. It was a nice bit of blackmail that kept him off my back, but he refused to take the message that I wasn't going to work for him. 'Course, that might be my fault . . . since I seemed unable to say no when he waved enough money at me.

Trent sighed, visibly bothered at my admittedly childish behavior, but I was hot, damn it, and needed money, and therefore I was vulnerable to his bribes and his air-conditioned car.

"Get in," he said, and then, smiling and waving to the two warlocks, he slid back from the door and into the shadows.

I glanced at the Were beside me, guessing Trent wanted to talk to me about the RSVP I hadn't RSVP'ed to. "Think I should?" I said, and the man nodded like a bobblehead doll.

Trent leaned into the light. "Get in, Ms. Morgan. I'll drop you wherever you want."

I want to go to Vegas and win a car, I thought, but I stepped forward. "Do you have the air on in that thing?" I asked, and he arched his eyebrows. *Okay, that was probably a dumb question.* "I could use a ride home," I added.

Trent beckoned, and the two warlocks behind me almost swooned by the sound of it. "All I want is fifteen minutes," he said, his perfectly political smile starting to look forced.

He slid himself over so I could get in, and in a surge of defiance I grabbed the handle of the front passenger-side door and yanked it open. Quen jerked in surprise as I slipped in, slammed the door shut, and reached for the seat belt.

"Ah, Ms. Morgan . . ." Trent said from the backseat.

The air was on, but not nearly high enough, and after I put my shoulder bag at my feet, I started fiddling with the vent. "I'm not riding in the back," I said, angling my half of the vents to me and opening them full bore. "God, Trent. I feel like a kid back there."

"I know what you mean," he muttered, and Quen behind the wheel smiled.

That our dads had been friends and worked together to resurrect Trent's species didn't mean pigeon spots to me. After they had died a week apart, Trent was raised in privilege and I learned how to fight off teenage scumbuckets who saw me as an easy mark—being raised by a mother so thrown by her husband's death she almost forgot about my brother and me. Maybe I was jealous, but I wasn't going to let him think I'd sit beside him as if we were friends.

From behind us an industrial-size horn blew: the city bus trying to get into the pull-off. We were breaking the law by standing here, but who was going to give Trent Kalamack a ticket?

At Trent's gesture, Quen accelerated into the empty lane of traffic caused by the stopped bus. I felt like I'd won a few points, and I took off my glasses before settling into the plush leather to enjoy the cool air shifting the sweat-heavy curls hanging in my eyes. *This is nice.*

"The idea," Trent drawled, speaking louder than he clearly liked, "was that we'd talk."

"I want to talk to Quen." I turned to the heavily scarred man and smiled. He looked as old as my father would be if he were still alive, his dark skin marked by the damage with which the Turn had left even some Inderlanders. Quen was an elf, too, which made four that I'd ever met. Not bad for a species that was playing extinct. He must have a portion of human genes in him, or the T4 Angel virus that had offed a sizable portion of humanity wouldn't have affected him at all.

Though small, Quen was wiry and powerful, both in ley line magic and martial arts. I'd seen him use a black ley line charm once, though Trent probably didn't know he knew it. Sometimes it was better not to know how the people protecting you did their job.

He was wearing black, his outfit suggesting a uniform, but its design supple enough for ease of motion and comfort. He looked good, in a late-forties way, and if I ever needed a role model, Quen would do nicely. If he hadn't been working for Trent, that is.

"So how you doin'?" I asked Quen, and the usually stoic man let slip a glimmer of a smirk. Trent wouldn't be able to see it from his angle, and I wondered if Quen had a sense of humor I hadn't guessed at.

"I'm fine, Ms. Morgan," he said calmly, his voice as rough as his pock-marked skin. "You're looking . . ." He hesitated, taking a long glance at me as he slowed in bridge traffic. "What *have* you done to yourself? You look . . . glowing with health."

I flushed. He had noticed I'd lost my freckles along with every imperfection my soon-to-be-twenty-five years of living had bestowed on me, an unexpected benefit of shifting forms by way of a demon curse. "It's a long story," I said, not wanting to go into it.

"I'd be interested to hear," he prompted, his rough voice taking on a hint of accusation.

From the back came Trent's calculated sigh. Thinking I'd pushed him enough—and not wanting to continue this conversation with Quen—I pulled a dirt-stained knee up and twisted around so I could see Trent. "Look, Trent," I said dryly. "I know you want me to work security during your wedding, and the answer is no. I appreciate the ride home, but you're nuts if you think that's going to soften me up enough to get stupid. I'm not one of your fawning debutantes—"

"I never said you were," he interrupted. It was a soft protest, as if he liked the fact.

"And I'm not going to be a freaking *bridesmaid* in your wedding. You couldn't *pay* me enough." I hesitated, cursing my fate that he always seemed to show up when I needed large sums of money. *Is it luck, or does he wait until I'm short?* "Ah, it is a paying position, right? I mean, the dresses are generally god-awful, but you usually don't have to pay the bridesmaids to put them on."

Trent reclined in the back of the limo, relaxed and sure of himself, knees crossed and looking like he was at the top of his game. "It would be if you took it."

My jaw ached, and I worked to ease my tension as my thoughts returned to my church and the cost of resanctifying it. Trent had pockets so deep he wouldn't blink an eye. It wasn't fair to ask Ivy to shoulder so much of the financial burden when it had been my fault.

A smug smile, thoroughly irritating, came over Trent when he realized I wanted something badly enough to be tempted. This was one of the reasons I was in the front. The elf was a master at reading people, and we were enough alike that he had me down.

"I'm asking you to reconsider," he said, and then, his face losing all its smugness, he said, "Please. I could really use your help on this."

I blinked, scrambling to hide my shock. *Please? Since when does Trent say please?* Since I'd started treating him like a person? I mused, answering my own question. And why was that? Emotions sinking, I remembered not two months ago begging a suicidal vampire to consider drugs to ease his pain as an alternative to first-death, illegal drugs to which only Trent had access. God! It had been a mere twenty minutes ago that I'd asked Glenn to cover up how those women had died because it would make my life easier.

Ticked at myself, I started to see the reason behind Trent's murder and blackmail. I wasn't saying his methods were justified, just that I understood them. He was lazy like a wish, taking the easy way, not necessarily the lawful, harder way. But asking Glenn to hide information in order to prevent an Inderland power struggle wasn't on a par with killing your head geneticist to keep him from going to the authorities and turning you in. Was it?

Delaying my answer, I took off my T-shirt, the cool air hitting my flush hard as I shoved the soft cotton into my bag to help hide the focus. "Why?" I said flatly. "Quen's better than three of me."

Angular face showing a hint of strain, Trent handed me a returned invitation. I glanced at it, seeing the YES checked and a handwritten note under that saying whoever it was was looking forward to being his best man. "Yeah? So?" I said, handing it back.

"Look at who it's from," he said, extending it over the seats to me again.

Gut tightening, I glanced at the harmless, obscenely expensive linen paper between Trent's sun-darkened fingers. The rumble of going over a railroad track jarred me, and I took it, turning it over for an address. "Oh, crap," I whispered.

"That's nearly what I said," Trent muttered, his gaze on the small businesses and homes we were passing by.

Mouth dry, I looked from Trent to Quen, but they were silent, reading my reaction. Slowly I handed the invitation back. It was from Saladan, and it was dated four weeks ago.

"Lee can't be on this side of the ley lines," I said, then turned the air down.

Trent's fear of demons was well hidden, but clear to me. "Apparently he is," he said wryly.

My head moved back and forth. "He's Al's familiar. He can't be on this side of the lines."

"It's his handwriting." Trent tossed the invitation. With a soft hush, it landed on the rich leather where I would have been sitting.

Things started to click, and I stiffened. Okay, now I knew why Trent wanted me not only at the wedding but working up front, standing next to him every single stinking moment. "Oh, hell no," I said loudly. "I'm not standing up at your wedding if there's the chance that Al is going to show up as Lee's guest. I do *not* deal with demons, I do not like demons, and I won't put myself in a position where I have to defend myself or anyone else against one. No. Absolutely not."

"The wedding and rehearsal dinner are after sunset," Trent was saying, his voice far too calm. "That's where the most risk is. But I'd like you to come to the rehearsal as well, seeing that you're posing as a bridesmaid. The rehearsal and dinner are on Friday."

"This Friday?" I said, scrambling for an excuse. "That's my birthday. No way."

Trent's expression shifted. "You are responsible for Lee's being abducted, Ms. Morgan," he said coldly. "I'm sure the demon has an ulterior motive for allowing Lee to cross the lines for something as frivolous as a wedding. The least you can do is try to get him back."

"A rescue!" I yelped, spinning to see him face-on. "Do you know how hard it is to survive a demon, much less trick one's familiar from him?"

"No," Trent said, his dislike for me coming through very clearly. "Do you?"

Well, I did, but I wasn't going to tell Trent that there was another elf of pure descent living across the street from me. He'd use her badly in his biolabs.

Pulse fast, I braced myself when Quen stopped short at a light. We were almost to my neighborhood. *Thank God.* "Why should I help Lee?" I said angrily. "I don't know what you heard, but he took *me* into the ever-after, not the other way around. I tried to get us both out of there, but your *friend* wanted to give me to Al, and since I like where I live, I fought back. I warned him, and after Lee beat me to a pulp, Al took him instead—the better witch. I will not take the blame for that. Trying to give me to Al to pay off his debt was inhuman."

Trent's face lost none of its hard accusation. "Isn't that what you did to Lee?"

Teeth gritted, I held my arm out, palm up so he could see the demon scar still on my wrist. "No," I said flatly, shaking for showing it to him so plainly. "I'm sorry, Trent. He was going to give me to Al, and I fought back. I didn't give him to Al. Lee did that to himself through his own mistaken beliefs. I didn't gain anything but my freedom."

Trent's breath came out softly, the sound seeming to wash away all his tension. He believed me. How about that? "Freedom," he said. "That's all anyone wants, isn't it?"

I looked at Quen to figure out what he felt about all of this, but his expression gave no clue as he drove through the city's quiet residential area, eyes ranging over the small houses and tidy yards with blow-up pools in back and fallen bikes in front. Most humans were surprised at how normal an Inderland neighborhood was. Old habits of hiding die hard.

"I'm not judging you, Rachel," Trent said, pulling my attention back to him. "I'd be lying if I said I wasn't hoping you could free Lee from the demon—"

"There isn't enough money in the world for that," I muttered.

"I want you to be in my wedding in case there's an attack against me or my fiancée."

I flopped back around, feeling the cushions enfold me.

"Rachel . . ." the elf started.

"Stop your car and let me off right here," I said tightly. "I can walk the rest of the way."

The car kept going. After a moment Trent said slyly, "It would really grill Ellasbeth's tomatoes if she was forced to make you one of her bridesmaids."

A smile flickered over me as I remembered the tall, icily beautiful professional woman seething when she found Trent treating me to breakfast in his robe after I had pulled his freaking elf-ass out of the frozen Ohio River. They didn't even pretend to be in love, and their marriage was happening only because she was probably the purest-blooded elf out there for Trent to marry and have little baby elves with. I wondered if they'd been born with pointy ears and had them docked.

"It would cheese her off no end, wouldn't it?" I said, my mood lightening.

"Five thousand for two evenings."

I laughed, and beside me Quen's grip on the wheel tightened. "Not even if it was ten thousand for one event," I said. "And besides, it's too late to get the dress."

"They're in the trunk," Trent said quickly, and I cursed myself for even bringing it up as an excuse, since it implied that all he needed was to find my price.

Then I did a double take, turning to look at him. " 'They'?" I questioned.

Trent shrugged to shift from powerful drug lord to frustrated fiancé. "She hasn't decided between the two of them. You're an eight tall, right? Long in the sleeves?"

I was, and it was flattering he remembered. But then so was Ellasbeth. "What color are they?" I asked, curious.

"Ah, she's narrowed it down to a modest black shift and a full-length sea green," he said.

Unflattering flat black and cucumber-puke green. Grea-a-a-a-at. "No."

Quen gently applied the brakes and put the car in park. We were at the church. I grabbed my bag to look into it and make sure I still had the focus. They were elves. *I* didn't know what they could do. "Thanks for the ride, Trent." The tension rose as I unbuckled myself. "It was nice seeing you, Quen," I said, then hesitated, meeting his green eyes as he sat with his hands on the wheel and waited. "You . . . ah, aren't going to show up tonight to convince me, are you?"

Breaking his stoic expression, he met my gaze levelly. "No, Ms. Morgan. The danger is real this time, so I respect your decision."

Trent cleared his throat in a nonverbal rebuke, and I gave Quen a thankful nod. The security expert had enough clout to defy Trent if his reasonings were sound, and it made me feel good that someone could say no to him—though I doubted that it happened very often.

"Thanks," I said, but instead of feeling relieved I only found myself more worried. *"The danger is real this time"? Like it wasn't last time I worked for Trent?*

The moist heat and the sound of cicadas hit me when I got out, the old trees that blocked the sun serving to trap the moisture as well. I glanced across the street to Keasley's house, hoping Trent and Quen would just leave. I didn't like them being this close to Ceri. I didn't know anything about elves. Hell, they might be able to smell each other if they got close enough.

I pulled my attention back to Trent as I hitched my bag higher and started for the church. There was a van at the curb, and I frowned at the sign proudly proclaiming WE SPECIALIZE IN EXORCISM. Great. Ju-u-u-u-ust great. Now the entire street knew we had a problem.

I spun when the sound of a car door closing thumped through the muggy air. Trent was out and was circling to the limo's back. My blood pressure spiked. "I said no," I repeated loudly.

"Having a problem with your church?" he asked, lifting the trunk when it popped open.

My lips pressed together, and I stood so I could see him and Ceri's house both. I didn't like this at all. "We had an incident. Look. I'm not doing it, so just leave, okay?" I felt like I was talking to a dog who had followed me home. *Bad dog. Go home.*

I boldly turned my back on him and, feeling the hair on the back of my neck prickle, strode to the stairs. Not wanting him to follow me in, I paused two steps down from the landing.

"Ten thousand for two nights," Trent said, pulling two garment bags from the trunk.

"Your rehearsal is on my birthday. I have plans. Reservations at Carew Tower." A thrill went through me at the admission. It was going to be a date to remember.

But Trent squinted, looking as if the heat couldn't touch him. "Bring your date along." He gently pushed the trunk's lid down. The motor engaged and the trunk whined shut. Adjusting the garment bags over his arm, he came forward. The closer he got, the more nervous I became.

"You may have breakfast in the Carew Tower every Tuesday," I said, "but I've never been up there, and I'm looking forward to it. I'm not asking my date to change it."

"Thirty thousand. And I'll get your reservations changed to whatever night you want."

He was a step down, and his eyes were even with mine. "Everything is so easy for you, isn't it?" I said, disgusted.

A tired, haunted look showed in his green eyes, and his hair shifted in the breeze to ruin his professional carriage. "No. It only looks that way."

"Poor baby," I muttered, and his jaw tightened. Carefully arranging his hair, he returned to his callous self.

"Rachel, I need your help," he said with an irritated acceptance. "There're going to be too many people, and I don't want an ugly scene. Your being there might be enough to stop any trouble before it starts. You won't be doing this alone. Quen has his entire staff—"

"I don't work under anyone's direction," I said, my gut tightening as I looked past him to Ceri's house. I wanted him gone. If she came out, everything would go to hell.

"They'd work around you," he persuaded. "You're there if something slips by them."

"I don't play well with others, and I run with loaded guns," I said, taking a backward step up to distance myself from him. "Besides, Quen is better than me," I said shortly as the wind mussed his hair again. "There's no reason for me to be there."

His free hand smoothed his bangs as he saw me look at it. "You sat in the front. Why?"

"Because I knew it would bother you." The sound of unfamiliar voices in the sanctuary came out through the transom windows along the side of the church. I took another step up, and Trent stayed where he was, confident though I was now taller than him.

"That's why I want you there," he said. "You're unpredictable, and that can be the difference between success and failure. Most people make decisions in anger, fear, love, or obligation. You make decisions to irritate people."

"You're just chalking up the points here, Trent."

"I need that unpredictability," he continued, as if I hadn't said anything.

Agitated, I focused on him. "Forty thousand for a night of unpredictability is expensive."

His face shifted, and with sly delight he echoed, "Forty thousand?"

I cringed inside as I told him my price, then decided to go with it. "Or whatever it takes to get my church resanctified," I countered.

Trent took his eyes from me for the first time, sending his gaze up the length of the steeple, squinting at it. "Your church lost its sanctification? What happened?"

I took a breath, backing up on the landing. "We *had* an *incident,*" I said sharply. "I gave you my terms. Take it and leave, or just leave."

Eyes gleaming, Trent countered, "I'll pay five thousand if all three functions are incident-free, and forty thousand if you're required to intervene."

"Fine, I'll do it," I muttered, glancing across the street. "Just get your elf ass off my walk before I change my mind."

Then I froze, shocked when Trent lightly ascended the steps between us, the relief and genuine appreciation turning him from a successful, confident businessman into a normal, everyday guy, a little worried and unsure of his future. "Thank you, Rachel," he said while handing me the garment bags. "Jonathan will call when she finally chooses a dress."

The garment bags settled over my arm with the scent of perfume. Crap, they were made from silk, and I wondered what the dresses looked like. I felt odd having Trent thank me. He wasn't moving, though, and I prompted, "Well, good-bye."

He hesitated, eyeing me as he found the sidewalk. He went to say something, then turned away. Quen had the door for him, and, his steps quick despite the heat, Trent headed for the limo and slid in with a practiced grace. Quen gently shut the door. Watching me, he went to the front of the car and got in. Guilt pricked at me. Was I doing Ceri an injustice by not introducing her to Trent? I didn't want him using her, but she could take care of herself, and, if nothing more, she could find others of her kind. Trent probably had a Christmas card list.

I exhaled in relief when they pulled from the curb and accelerated down the street. "Thank God," I muttered, then frowned. I was going to be in Trent's wedding. Swell.

I turned to the door, and Ivy's voice echoed out. "That's not what your ad says!" she exclaimed, shortly followed by Jenks's voice, too faint to understand.

"It's not that I don't want to," an unfamiliar masculine voice protested, becoming louder. "I don't have the equipment or skill to fix it."

I hesitated, hand on the latch. The man had sounded embarrassed. The door swung open, and I jumped back, stumbling to catch my balance. A young man almost walked right into me, jerking to a halt at the last moment. His clean-shaven face reddened, and the purple sash of his faith draped around his neck and flowing down his front looked funny with his jeans and the casual polo shirt embroidered with his business name. An expensive-looking cell phone was clipped to his belt, and he carried a locked toolbox.

"Excuse me," he said in annoyance. Jiggling on his feet, he tried to get around me. I took a step to get into his way, and his eyes rose to meet mine.

Ivy was glowering behind him, Jenks hovering at head height with his wings clattering in anger. Her eyebrows went up when she saw the silk garment bags, then, catching her thought, she said dryly, "Rachel, this is Dr. Williams. He says he can't resanctify the church. Dr. Williams, this is my partner, Rachel Morgan."

Almost hiding his irritation, the man moved his toolbox to his left hand and extended his right. I shifted my garment bags and shook it. I felt a rise of stored ley line energy try to slip between us to equal out our balances, and I snatched the force back before it could make the jump. God, how embarrassing.

"Hi," I said, thinking he looked cute and had a nice grip. The heady scent of redwood flowed from him, stronger than I'd winded in a long time. He was a witch, and an educated one, and when his brown eyes widened, I knew he knew I was the same. "What's the problem?" I said, letting go of his hand. "If it's the financing, I just took care of it. I can have cash for you by Monday next."

It felt damn good saying that, but Jenks dropped three inches and groaned, and Ivy glanced at the garment bags in understanding. "Rachel, you didn't . . ." she said, and I flushed.

"I'm working a wedding and a reception," I said tightly. "How bad could it be?" *Really bad. Really, really bad.*

But Dr. Williams was squinting at his van and shaking his head.

"Your financing came through fine. I simply can't do it. I'm sorry. If you'll excuse me . . ."

Crap. The first guy to come out here hadn't been able to either.

The man tried to leave, but Ivy moved with a vampire quickness, surprising all of us. Giving me a tight-lipped look, she muttered to me, "We're going to talk about this," and then to Dr. Williams, blinking at her suddenly before him, "Your ad says—"

"I know what the ad says," he interrupted. "I wrote it. I told you, we don't have the experience for your situation."

He got another step down before Ivy was in front of him again, a dangerous thinning of brown around her pupil. He stopped, angry as he took off his purple ribbon. His disregard for the danger she represented surprised me, until I decided that if he could sanctify ground, he could probably take care of himself. I ran my eyes over him again, new thoughts sifting through me.

"Look," he said, dropping his head. When it came back up, there was an expression of warning in his gaze. "If it was just resanctifying it, I could do it, but your church has been blasphemed."

My lips parted, and Ivy crossed her arms over her chest in an unusual show of worry. *I twisted a demon curse on blasphemed ground without the protection of my aura? Great.*

"Blasphemed!" Jenks exclaimed, silver sparkles sifting from him. In the bushes there was a high-pitched call from a winged eavesdropper, quickly hushed.

The man looked from the bush to me. "From the bedrooms up to the front door," he said, clearly resigned he wasn't leaving until I was satisfied. "The entire church is contaminated. I'd have to get the demon smut off first, and I don't know how to do that."

His lack of fear seemed to give Ivy something to tie her emotions to and bring them back under control, but Jenks clattered his wings aggressively. He was getting ready to pix the man, and their attitudes were starting to tick me off. If Dr. Williams couldn't do it, he couldn't do it.

"Jenks," I admonished, "back off. If he can't do it, it's not his fault."

The doctor's grip on his tackle box tightened, his pride clearly feeling the sting. "It's usually the coroner who is called in to clean up failed demon summonings, not me."

Ivy stiffened, and before she could get all vampy, I interjected, "I didn't call the demon. She showed up on her own."

He laughed bitterly, as if he had caught me in a lie. "She?" he mocked. "Female demons can't cross the lines."

"Can't, or won't?"

That made him pause, his expression taking on a hint of respect. Then he shook his head and his expression became hard. "Demon practitioners have a life expectancy of months, Ms. Morgan. I suggest you change your profession. Before your state-of-aliveness does it for you."

Dr. Williams took a step down, and I shot after him, "I don't deal in demons. She showed up on her own."

"That's my point." His feet were on the sidewalk, and he stopped and turned. "I'm very sorry, Ms. Tamwood, Jenks . . ." His gaze lifted to me. ". . . Ms. Morgan, but this is outside my current abilities. If the ground hadn't been cursed, there would be no problem, but as it is . . . ?" Shaking his head again, he headed for his van.

I shifted the garment bags to my other arm. "What if we got the ground cleaned?"

He stopped at the back of his van to open it and set his toolbox in it. He slammed it shut, his purple ribbon still in his grip. "It would be cheaper to move the bodies out of the cemetery and build a new church on hallowed ground." He hesitated, his attention flitting to the copper sign above the church door, proudly stating VAMPIRIC CHARMS. "I'm sorry. But you should count yourself lucky you even survived."

Shoes scuffing the pavement, he disappeared around the side of the van. The sound of his driver's-side door shutting seemed loud in the quiet street, drawing attention to the tinkling of an ice cream truck. As his van drove away, Ivy sat on the second step down. Saying nothing, I sat beside her, draping the bags over my knees. After a moment of hesitation, Jenks landed on my shoulder. Together we watched the ice cream truck trundle closer, its merry tune sounding especially irritating.

In an eyeball-hurting, shrill cloud, Jenks's kids flocked over to it, diving in and out of the man's windows until he stopped. He had been coming down here every day since the first of July to sell a two-dollar snow cone to a family of pixies.

Jenks's wings shifted my hair in the breeze as he lifted off. "Hey, Ivy," he said confidently, "can you float me a couple of bucks?"

It was an old pattern by now, and, shoulders hunched, she got to her feet. Grumbling under her breath, she slipped into the church for her purse.

I knew I should be worried about the church and sleeping on blasphemed ground, but I was ticked about working for Trent for no reason—seeing as we couldn't resanctify the church. And on my birthday, too.

While Jenks yelled at his kids to decide on a flavor and get it over with, I dug my phone out of my bag and hit the speed dial. I had to call Kisten.

ELEVEN

The sound of heavy plastic was soothing as I hung up my new outfit beside my two bridesmaid dresses on the back of my closet door. The black plastic with the Poison Heart logo looked garish next to the silk garment bags, and I touched their smoothness just to prove that someone had actually spent money on something so extravagant.

Shaking my head, I ripped the plastic off my new purchase, wadded it up, and tossed it into a corner, where it slowly unfurled, the sound of it clear in the silence that held the church. I had just come from the mall by way of the bus, and I was eager to show somebody what I'd bought for Trent's wedding rehearsal and dinner, but Ivy was out and Jenks was in the garden. The Poison Heart was an exclusive shop, and I had thoroughly enjoyed my afternoon of guilt-free shopping. I *needed* this outfit for my run. It was tax-deductible.

The night was humid. My chemise was sticking to me, and since our central-air funds had become our resanctify-the-grounds funds, it looked as if the most we'd be doing this year would be a window unit somewhere. All the windows were open, and the shush of an occasional passing car mixed comfortably with the sound of Jenks's kids playing june-bug croquet.

It was as bad as it sounded, and Ivy and I had spent a hilarious evening last week watching his kids divide into two teams and, by the light of the porch lamp, take turns whacking the hapless beetles to very fat toads. The team whose toad hopped away first—stuffed to the gills—won.

My smile widened at the memory, and I brushed nonexistent lint from the snappy short black jacket, the beads sewn into it glinting in the overhead light. Smile fading, I looked the outfit over again—now that I was free of the clerk's enthusiasm. Maybe the beads were a little over the top, but they went well with the glitter on the stockings. And the shortness of the hip-hugger skirt was offset by its subdued black. It had come with a nice top that would show my midriff, and I had the jacket in case it got cold.

Shuffling in my closet, I pulled out a pair of flat sandals I could run in. Ellasbeth wouldn't be wearing jeans and a T-shirt. Why should I slum it to make her look good?

I dropped the sandals and stepped back in thought. Some jewelry would finish it nicely, but Ivy could help me with that.

"Hey, Jenks!" I shouted, knowing if he didn't hear me, his kids would go get him. "Come and see what I bought!"

Almost immediately there was a clatter of wings at my window. I had sewn up the pixy hole in the screen a few days previous, and I stifled my smile when Jenks ran into it.

"Hey!" he shouted, hovering with his hands on his hips and a soft glow of gold sifting from him. "What the hell is this?"

"A little privacy," I said, fluffing the lace about the skirt's hem. "Use the door. That's what it's for."

"You know what?" he snarled. "I oughta— Oh, for the love of Tink!"

I turned at his wonderstruck tone, but he was gone. In an instant he was in the hall, laughing as he drifted backward. "Is that it?" he said. "Is that the dress you bought to wear to Trent's wedding rehearsal and dinner? Damn, woman, you need some serious help."

Following his gaze, I looked at my outfit. "What?" I said, warming. My nose tickled, and I muffled a sneeze, the heat and humidity starting to get to me.

Jenks was still laughing. "It's a dinner, Rache. Not a dance club!"

Worried, I touched the jacket's sleeve. "You think it's too much?" I asked, working hard to keep my tone noncombative. I'd had this conversation with ex-roommates before.

Jenks landed on the hanger. "Not if you're going to play the part of the town whore."

"You know what?" I said, starting to get ticked. "Being sexy doesn't come naturally, and sometimes you have to go out on a limb."

"Limb?" he choked. "Rache, if that's the way you dress for a wedding rehearsal, it's no wonder you spent high school fighting off bad boyfriends. Image, girl! It's all about image! Who do you want to be?"

I went to flick him away, and he darted to the ceiling, a trail of silver dust drifting down like a ribbon of thought he'd left behind. At the window a cluster of his kids were giggling. Flustered, I closed my curtains. Rex, drawn by the sound of Jenks's voice, padded in from who knew where, settling herself in my threshold with her tail curled about her feet and her eyes on Jenks. The pixy had landed on Nick's file, now shoved in among my perfume bottles, and I hoped the idiotic cat wouldn't jump up there after him. I felt a slow buildup of a tickle in my nose, and I scrambled for a tissue, startling Rex into skittering out to the hall when I sneezed.

Looking over my tissue, I watched Jenks's head go back and forth. "It's a nice outfit," I protested. "And I didn't buy it for Trent, I bought it for my birthday date with Kisten." I touched the beaded sleeve again, feeling melancholy. So I liked to dress up. So what? But maybe . . . maybe my image could use a little more class and a little less party girl.

Snorting, Jenks gave me a long, knowing look. "Sure you did, Rache."

Bothered, I turned off the light and headed into the kitchen, scooping up the two bags of tomato stuff for Glenn that I had left in the hall. Still laughing, Jenks followed, landing on my shoulder in a show of apology.

"You know," he said, and I could hear the smile on his face in his tone, "I think you should wear that dress to the rehearsal. It will cheese off that witch of a woman."

"Sure," I said, starting to get depressed. I'd wait until Ivy came home, then ask her. What did Jenks know? He was a pixy, for God's sake.

I elbowed the rocker switch as I entered the kitchen, all but tripping on Rex when she darted between my feet. The ungraceful motion turned into a sneeze. I felt it coming but didn't have time to warn Jenks. He was catapulted off, and, swearing, he went to the window.

"Sorry," I said when he lit next to his sea monkeys. According to my mother, it was bad luck to sneeze between rooms, but it was Jenks's questioning look that had me worried.

Wincing, I looked at Rex, her cute little kitten face turned up as she sat before the sink and gazed lovingly up at her four-inch master. Jenks followed my attention to her, and when I set the bags down to wipe my nose, his wings stilled in understanding. I had been sneezing off and on since yesterday. *Crap, there are charms for it, but I don't want to be allergic to cats.*

"I'm not allergic to cats," I said, wrapping one arm around my middle. "Rex has been here for the past two months, and this is the first time it's been a problem."

"Okay," he said softly, but his wings weren't moving when he turned his back on me to wrestle with the vial of sea-monkey food.

It was too quiet in here. I wanted to turn on some music, but the stereo was in the sanctuary, and to crank it loud enough to be able to enjoy it in the kitchen would bother the neighbors. Working up a really good pity party, I pulled out one of my newest spell books and set it thumping on the center island counter. *Sneezing,* I thought, hunched as I thumbed through the index. I wasn't allergic to cats. My dad had been, but I wasn't.

The only spell in the book that had to do with sneezing was one for cat allergies, and as I debated trying it, I felt a tickle start. Eyes watering, I held my breath. It didn't do any good. I sneezed, accidentally tearing the page.

"Damn it!" I swore, looking up to see that I had startled Jenks into the air. "I'm not allergic to cats! It's a summer cold. That's all."

I felt the urge again. Exasperated, I closed my eyes and tried to stop it, making an ugly noise when I couldn't. I knew I had seen a spell for sneezing that didn't revolve around cats. Where the devil was it?

"Oh, yeah," I said softly, crouching down to get my old ley line textbook out from between *The Big Cookie Cookbook* and my copy of *Real Witches Eat Quiche.*

"Rache?" Jenks said, coming to stand on the counter when I opened it up to the index.

"What?" I snapped.

"You need any help?"

I stopped what I was doing and looked to find him standing miserably before me with his wings drooping. Rex was twining about my ankles, and if I thought it was anything other than misplaced affection, I would have been charmed. Slowly I exhaled. "I don't think so," I said, flipping to page 49. "Ley line charms are pretty easy. I'm getting better at them, and if it does the trick, then we're all set."

He nodded and flitted up to the ladle, his favorite spot in the kitchen, where he could see me, the door, and a good slice of the garden.

I quickly read over the instructions to grow more confident. I didn't particularly like ley line magic, having been classically trained in slower, but no less powerful, earth magic. Earth magic used potions and amulets, finding the energy to perform the spell in plants, who ultimately pulled it from the ley lines themselves. The energy was filtered and softened, making earth magic more forgiving and slower than ley line magic, but ultimately more far-reaching—the changes wrought with earth magic were generally real rather than illusion, as much of ley line magic was. I wouldn't just *look* shorter under the right earth charm, I would *be* shorter.

Ley line magic used incantation and ritual to pull the energy to change reality right off the line. It made this branch of magic faster and flashier, but there were ten times more black ley line witches than black earth witches. Apart from hitting someone with a hunk of ever-after to short out his or her neural network, changes were illusion and could be surmounted with willpower.

Before dying, my father had taken steps to direct me into earth magic. It was a decision I totally agreed with, but I had some skill in the ley line arts, and if it would stop me sneezing, where was the harm? And while going over the white charm before me, I decided the five-hundred-level spell was well within my grasp.

Pleased, I started to gather what I'd need. "White candle," I murmured, briefly considering the pack of birthday candles in my shoulder bag that I'd picked up along with the lilac wine. But then I pulled out a nicked taper from my silverware drawer where I kept it. It was blessed, and that was all the better. "Dandelion?" I questioned, looking up at Jenks.

"Got it," he said, cheerfully vaulting from the ladle and through the pixy hole in the kitchen window screen.

I had dried dandelions from last year, but I knew he'd appreciate the chance to harvest something for me. He was back almost immediately with a dew-wet, closed flower, and after shooing his kids from the window, he set it next to the lopsided pentagram I had sketched on my mobile chalkboard. It was the size of a laptop and had a cover to protect a design in transit.

"Thanks," I said, and he nodded, lifting briefly into the air to land on the textbook.

"You going to set a circle?" he asked, looking slightly nervous, and when I nodded, he added, "I'll . . . um, watch from the windowsill."

Hiding my smile, I moved all my stuff to the other side of the island counter so I could both work and see him. "It's a medicinal spell," I explained. "Why take chances?"

Jenks gave me a mild, "Ummm." I knew he didn't like seeing me under the influence of a line. He said it was because there was a shadow on my aura that wasn't there the rest of the time. I didn't like it because my hair got staticky, moving in the wind that always seemed to be blowing in the ever-after.

My pulse quickened in anticipation, and I glanced at the clock. It was way before midnight—lots of time. You could work white magic after midnight, but why push your luck? Grabbing a handful of salt, I sprinkled it over the line etched in the linoleum.

Jenks's wings shifted fitfully when I stretched out my awareness to touch the small, underused ley line running through the graveyard out back. My breath came in fast, but by the time I had exhaled, the energy flow was balanced. A faint tingling in my fingertips and a heavy sensation in my middle told me my chi was full, and I didn't pull more off the line to spindle in my head. I wouldn't need more than this to work the spell.

Uncomfortable, I wiggled my shoulders as if trying to fit into a new skin. It used to be that it took several moments for the strength to equalize. Practice had shaved it to almost nothing. My hair was floating already. I tried to flatten it, and my skin prickled where my muscles flexed. If I cared to, I could open my second sight and actually see the ever-after superimposed on reality, but it gave me the creeps.

"Whoops," I said, remembering I didn't have my candle lit yet, and went to the gas stove to get a burner going. Using a bamboo skewer, I lit the vanilla-scented candle I cleared the air with when I burned something. I shook the stick out and carefully carried the candle to the center counter, where it flickered in the muggy breeze coming in the window.

A last look at the instructions to be sure I had everything at the counter, and I kicked off a sandal. "Where's your cat, Jenks?" I said, not wanting to trap her in with me.

He took to the air. "Here, kitty, kitty, kitty . . ." he called, and with a chirping trill, her orange face appeared at the hall archway. She was licking her lips, but Jenks wasn't troubled.

"*Rhombus,*" I said softly, touching my toe to the salt circle. The single word of Latin invoked a hard-won series of mental exercises that condensed the five-minute prep and invocation of setting a circle into an instant. I stifled a jerk as the circle closed with a snap. Jenks's wings whirled as a molecule-thin sheet of ever-after rose up between us to keep any influences out while I worked the medicinal-class ley line charm. I was impulsive, not stupid.

Rex padded in, rubbing against the barrier as if it were covered in catnip. I'd take that as a sign that she might want to be my familiar—if she didn't run every time I tried to pick her up.

I grimaced at the ugly black sheen of demon smut crawling over my bubble, discoloring the usual cheerful gold of my aura. It was a visual display of the imbalance I carried on my soul, a reminder of the debt I owed for having twisted reality so far out of alignment that I could become a wolf and Jenks grew to human size. The discoloration was nothing compared to the thousand years of demon-curse imbalance that Ceri carried, but it bothered me.

All but the smallest amount of ever-after energy I had tapped had gone into maintaining the circle, but there was the tingle of a new buildup of force filtering in. It would continue to grow until I let go of the line completely. Many witches were said to have gone insane from trying to stretch what their chi could hold by allowing the pressure to build beyond what they could safely contain, but when my chi overflowed, I could spindle the line energy in my head. Demons could do the same, and their familiars. Ceri and I were the only two people this side of the lines who could spindle line energy. That we had survived Al with the knowledge intact hadn't been the demon's intent. Ceri had taught me the basics, but Al was the one who'd stretched my tolerances and made the skill second nature—by way of an excruciating amount of pain.

"Ah, Rachel?" Jenks said, green-tinted sparkles slipping from him to pool in the sink. "It's worse than usual."

My good mood vanished, and I frowned at the demon smut. "Yeah, well, I'm trying to get rid of it," I muttered, then pulled my sketched pentagram forward.

Taking up a stone crucible I had bought at a ley line shop up in Mackinaw, I set it in the lowest space between the bottom of the pentagram and the circle surrounding it. Fingers still touching it, I murmured, *"Adaequo,"* to set it in place and give its presence meaning.

I felt a small surge from the line and twitched. Oh, it was one of *those* spells. Great.

My nose tickled. I stiffened, realizing I hadn't brought any tissue in with me. "Oh, no," I said, my voice rising. Jenks looked panicked, and I sneezed. He was laughing when I brought my head up. Looking frantically for something to wipe my nose with, I settled on a scratchy paper towel, managing to tear off twice what I needed and getting it to my face just in time for the follow-up sneeze. Crap, I had to finish this spell fast.

The big-ass symbolic knife I had gotten at Findley Market from a cheerful woman went in the center space with the words *me auctore,* and a feather was given meaning when I placed it with the strength of *lenio* in the lower left-hand leg of the star. My nose was starting to tickle again, and I hurriedly checked the textbook.

"Iracundia," I said, holding my breath as I set Jenks's dandelion in the other leg of the star. All that was left was the candle.

The force in me had been building with every word, and with my eye twitching I set the blessed candle carefully in the topmost section of the star, hoping it wouldn't fall over and spill wax on my chalkboard so I'd be spending tomorrow cleaning it with toluene. This one wouldn't be set with a place-name until I lit it, and with that in mind, I plucked the bamboo skewer from where I had left it, setting it aflame again from the vanilla candle.

Wiping my free hand on my jeans, I shifted from foot to foot and transferred the flame to the blessed candle. *"Evulgo,"* I whispered, wincing as a surge came in from the line. My eyes widened. Oh, God, I was going to sneeze again. I didn't want to know what it might do to my spell if it wasn't cast yet.

I moved fast. Grabbing the feather, I dropped it into the crucible. I snatched up the knife, and before I could get uptight about the ugly symbolism, I pricked my thumb and squeezed out three drops of blood. I would rather have used one of my finger sticks, but ley line magic was based on symbolism, and it made a difference.

The knife went back into its little spot, and I peered at the text, thumb in my mouth so I didn't get blood all over the place. *"Non sum qualis eram,"* I said, remembering it from another spell. Must be a generic phrase for invocation.

My urge to sneeze vanished, and I jerked in surprise when the crucible was engulfed in flames. There was a whoosh, accompanied by a twang through me. The cheerful red-and-orange flames flashed to a weird gold and black that matched my damaged aura—and went out.

Wide-eyed, I pulled my gaze from the soot-blackened crucible to Jenks, hovering over the sink. There wasn't anything in the bowl but a smear of ash stinking of burnt vegetation.

"Was that what was supposed to happen?" he asked.

Like I know? "Uh, yeah," I said, pretending to look at the text. "See, I'm not sneezing."

I took a careful breath through my nose, then another, more relaxed one. My shoulders eased, and I let myself smile. I loved it when I learned something new.

"Good," Jenks grumbled, taking to the air to hover before the bubble, still up and running. " 'Cause I'm not getting rid of my cat."

With a small thought, I broke my connection with the ley line. The circle vanished, and Jenks flew in to land next to the crucible, his tiny features wrinkled in distaste. Content, I closed the textbook and started to clean up my mess before Ivy got home. "I told you I wasn't . . ." My words cut off as my nose started to tickle. "I'm not . . ." I started again, feeling my eyes widen. Jenks stared at me, horror in his expression.

Eyes watering, I waved helplessly. "Achoo!" I exclaimed, hunching over, my hair falling to hide my face. It was followed by another, then another. Ah, crap, I'd made things worse.

"The Turn take it," I gasped between sneezes. "I know I did it right!"

"Ivy's got some pills," Jenks said. I could hear his wings, but I was too busy trying to catch my breath to look at him. He sounded worried. I knew I was. "In her bathroom," he added. "Maybe they'll help."

I bobbed my head, then sneezed again. Ivy had caught a cold last spring when we'd come back from Michigan. She had moped around the church for three days, coughing and blowing her nose—snarling at me every time I suggested making her a charm. She had taken pills with her orange juice every afternoon.

My breath came in little pants, and my nose tickled. *Crap.* Lurching to the hallway, I sneezed again. "I'm *not* allergic to *cats,*" I said while I groped to turn the light on. My reflection looked terrible, my hair all over the place and my nose running. I opened the cupboard, uncomfortable rummaging in her things.

"This one!" Jenks said, tugging at a thin amber vial.

I sneezed three more times while I fumbled to get the stupid thing open, trying to read that I was to take two pills every four hours. Why in hell had I tried to use ley line magic? I should have known better than to self-administer a medicinal charm. The aides in Emergency were going to laugh their asses off if I had to go in for a counterspell.

I stared at Jenks. My eyes widened; another sneeze was coming, and it felt like a big one. Not using water, I took two pills, looking at the ceiling and trying to swallow them.

"Water, Rache!" Jenks said, hovering over the tap. "You gotta take them with water!"

Waving him out of my way, I swallowed them down dry, grimacing. And, like magic, the urge to sneeze vanished.

Not believing it, I took a breath, then another. Jenks was having a fit over the wax cups, so I filled one, dutifully swallowing the lukewarm water to feel the pills slide down. "Damn!" I swore in admiration. "Those are great. Caught it midsneeze." I set the cup down to pick up the vial, turning it over to read the label. "How much are these anyway?"

Jenks's wings clattered, he and his reflection slowly falling. "They don't work that fast."

I glanced at him. "Really?"

He looked worried, his feet gently touching the counter and his wings stilled. He took a breath to say something, but a soft *pop* jerked both our heads up. My pulse went into overdrive, and I felt someone tap the line out back. It startled me, and, gasping, I fell into Ivy's black porcelain toilet, slipping. I went down with a little shriek, and my butt met the tile. "Ow," I said, holding my elbow where it hit something.

"Witch!" a resonant voice echoed, and I tossed my hair aside, taking in the robed figure in the threshold. "Why, by Cormel's gonads, does my coffee taste like dandelions!"

Ah, crap, it was Minias.

TWELVE

"Get out, Jenks!" I shrieked, scrambling up.

Minias swooped into Ivy's bathroom, his smooth face creased in irritation. Panicking, I pressed into a fluffy black towel hanging between the commode and the tub. "Don't touch me!" I shouted, then flung the contents of Ivy's pill vial at him.

With a twang, I felt him set a circle. Jenks was at the ceiling shouting something, and the little white pills bounced harmlessly against Minias's black sheet of ever-after.

I had to get out! There were too many pipes and wires in here to set a demonproof circle.

"What the hell?" Minias said, his goat-slitted eyes confused as he picked up a pill and looked at it. He had broken his circle to do it, and, scrambling, I grabbed Ivy's hair spray.

"Get out of my church!" I shouted, spraying him.

Orange-scented detangler hit Minias square in the eyes. Yelping, he stumbled backward into the hall to hit the dark walls. Arms and legs askew, he slipped to the floor. I didn't wait to see if he was down. I'd seen enough movies to know better.

Pulse hammering, I lurched out over him. He grunted as my foot hit something, and I gasped when he went misty and my foot slipped through him and found the floor.

My hands touched the walls to pull me forward, and I ran for the kitchen. I had a circle there, still set with salt. Jenks was a blur of gold dust ahead of me.

"Look out!" he shouted, and I went down, my feet pulled from under me.

Memories of Al poured through me. I couldn't go back there. I couldn't be someone's plaything. I silently fought, kicking at anything, my years of martial arts forgotten.

"What is *wrong* with you?" Minias said, then grunted when my sandal hit something tender. He went misty, his grip falling away.

I pulled myself forward, almost crawling across the kitchen until the expanse of my circle was between us. Minias was close behind. *"Rhombus!"* I shouted, tapping the line and slapping my hand on the line etched in the linoleum.

Ever-after coursed in. Fear caused my control to slip, and more power than I liked raced through me, hurting. The circle went up, and Minias ran smack into the interior wall of it.

"Ow!" the demon exclaimed, purple robes furling as he fell back against the island counter. Hand over his nose, he looked at the smut crawling over my bubble. His hat had fallen off, and he glared at me from under his curls, turning almost choleric when he realized that his nose was bleeding. "You broke my nose!" he exclaimed, bright red demon blood pouring forth.

"So fix it," I said, shaking. He was in a circle. He was in my circle. I took a breath, then another. Slowly I pulled my legs under me and stood, cold despite the warmth of the night.

"What the *hell* is wrong with you?" he asked again, clearly furious as a sheet of ever-after slithered over him. He took his hand from his nose to show that the blood was gone.

"Me?" I said, burning off some angst. "You said you'd call first, not just barge in!"

"I did call!" Minias roughly adjusted his robes. "You never answered, and then," he shouted, flicking a finger under my expensive chalkboard to make it hit the floor, "instead of a simple 'I'm busy, could you call back again later,' you slam the door in my face! I want this mark between us settled. You are rude, ill-mannered, and as ignorant as a toad!"

"Hey!" Face warming, I leaned to look around the counter to find that my board had cracked. "You broke my chalkboard!" Then I hesitated, drawing back with my arms over my chest. "You were the one making me sneeze?" I said, and he nodded. "I'm not allergic to cats?" I looked at Jenks, elated. "Jenks! I'm not allergic to cats!"

Minias crossed his arms and leaned against the counter. "Ignorant as a toad. Rude as an unwanted guest. Al is a saint for putting up with you, the novelty of your blood aside."

Jenks was shooing his kids from the window, assuring them we were all right and to not tell their mother. "Me . . . rude?" I stammered, tugging my shirt back down where it belonged when Minias's gaze slid to my midriff. "I'm not the one just showing up!"

"I said I would call first." His demon eyes narrowed. "I didn't promise it. And I'm not the one flinging pills and mace," he added, scooping up his hat and jamming it on his head. His curls were sticking out all over, and damn me to hell if he didn't look good like that. Immediately I sobered. *No, no, Rachel. Bad girl.* And remembering what Ivy had told me this spring about my needing the threat of death to prove to myself that I was alive, I quickly shoved aside any idea that Minias was attractive. But he was.

Minias saw my anger fizzle, and, clearly used to dealing with volatile females, he dropped his gaze. When it returned to me, he was visibly calmer, though no less angry. "I apologize for startling you," he said formally. "Obviously you thought you had something to fear, and grabbing you probably wasn't the best idea."

"Damn right it wasn't," I said, jumping when Jenks landed on my shoulder. "And don't try to sell me any crap about the kindly demon. I know three of you now, and you are all evil, insane, or just plain nasty."

Minias smiled, but it didn't make me feel any better. His eyes drifted over the inside of my bubble. "I'm not kindly, and if I could get away with it, I'd drag you into the ever-after and have someone broker you off—but Newt would get involved. . . ." He shifted his eyes to focus on me. "She doesn't remember you right now. I would like to keep it that way."

"Tink's little red thong," Jenks whispered, grabbing my ear for balance. Stomach clenched, I retreated until I found the fridge, the stainless steel cold through my thin chemise.

"With this debt standing between us without even a mark to keep things tidy, taking you would be in bad taste." Minias tugged his sleeves down over his wrists. "Once I grant whatever stupid wish you want, I won't have to restrain myself, but until then you're *relatively* safe."

My chin lifted. Bastard. He had scared me on purpose. I didn't feel bad now at all for burning his eyes, or stomping on his privates, or for him running into my bubble. And I wasn't going to trust that until we settled this I was immune to him.

"Jenks," I said softly as Minias looked over my kitchen, "will you send one of your kids to get Ceri?" She was likely over her pique at my sorry-ass ley line skills. And I didn't want to do this without her.

"I'll go," he said. "They aren't allowed to leave the garden." My neck went cold from the breeze of his wings, and he hovered, his angular features pinched. "You'll be okay?"

I watched Minias touch the herbs drying on the overhanging rack, wanting to tell him to get his fingers off them. "I'll be fine," I said. "He's in a good circle."

Minias's eyes followed Jenks zipping out with an unusual amount of interest. Looking mildly annoyed, he scuffed his bare feet against the linoleum, and a pair of embroidered slippers appeared on them. Slowly his brow smoothed under his brown curls. I fixed on the alienness of his eyes, trying to see the sideways pupil beside the dark iris. His back against the counter, he crossed his ankles and waited. Beside him was my spell to stop sneezing, and I didn't like the patronizing look he had favored me with after giving the pentagram a cursory glance.

"You're vastly deficient in line etiquette," he said dryly, "but I'll admit that this is better than the moldy basements I'm always hearing about."

"I didn't know you were making me sneeze," I huffed. "You can't know what you haven't been told."

Minias brought his attention from the dark garden. One eyebrow rose. "Yes you can." Turning, he started messing in the remnants of my ley line spell. "So what's it going to be?" he said, holding the crucible in one hand and running a finger through the soot with the other. "Eternal life? Untold wealth? Unlimited knowledge?"

I didn't like the way he was rubbing his thumb and finger together, smelling the ash as if it had meaning. "Stop that," I said.

Eyeing me from under his brown curls, he set the crucible down.

The sight of his elegantly robed figure doing something as mundane as tearing a paper towel and cleaning his finger looked odd. I frowned, my tension rising when he crouched to see my spell books.

"Leave those alone," I muttered, wishing Ceri would hurry.

Swearing in Latin, Minias took his fingers off my books. When he rose, he had my nested set of copper spell pots, my splat gun sitting nice as could be in the smallest. I had a moment of worry that the charms in it, though expired, might have enough of my aura to break the circle. Minias, though, gave it only a quick glance, turning his attention to the largest pot. It was the one I had dented against Ivy's head, and I didn't like it when he held it up in disdainful disgust. "You don't actually use this?" he asked.

"Would you knock it off?" I protested. God, what was it with him? He was worse than Jenks when it came to inquisitiveness. His eyebrows high in amusement, Minias set the spell pot down and picked up the open spell book on the counter. My jaw clenched, but I said nothing this time. His lips curled up in amusement, Minias held the book splayed open in a single hand and, after adjusting his hat, levered himself up to sit on the counter beside my ley line charm. His curly head was almost among the pots and herbs.

Exhaling slowly, I took a step forward. "Look," I said, and he drew his alien-seeming gaze to mine. "I'm sorry. I didn't know you were trying to reach me. Can we just get this mark thing settled so we can all move on with our lives?"

Eyes returning to the book, Minias took off his hat and murmured, "That's what I'm here for. You've had time to think up a wish. It's been almost five hundred years since I dealt with temporals, and I don't want to start it up again now, so let's hear it."

My head dropped, and, suddenly nervous, I hiked myself up onto the counter beside the sink. *Temporals, huh?* Arms wrapped around knees drawn up to my chin, I thought of Jenks's shorter life span and how wishes always came back to bite you. Sure, the one I had made to get out of the I.S. had worked, but I was still trying to get out from under the demon marks that had come from it. If I wished for a longer life for Jenks, he might be in a state where he couldn't do anything. Or maybe he'd be the first vampire pixy, or something equally unpleasant. "I don't want a wish," I whispered, feeling like a coward.

"No?" Clearly surprised, the demon shifted his legs, letting them drape down the counter to hide my spell books. "You want a curse?" His clean-shaven features turned sour. "I've never taught a witch, but I could probably wedge something past your thick skull."

Interesting. "I don't want to know how to do a curse," I said. "Not from you anyway."

Minias brought his wandering gaze from my ycw cuttings drying in the corner. Cocking his head, he looked at me as if I'd only now caught his attention. "No?" he repeated. With one hand he made a gesture of question. "What do you want, then?"

Nervous, I slid from the counter. I didn't want to do anything without Ceri, but saying no seemed harmless enough. "I don't want anything."

Minias's smile went patronizing. "And I'll believe that when the two worlds collide."

"Well, yeah, I want stuff," I said bitterly, not fond of being offered everything when getting it would cause more trouble than not having it to begin with. "I want my partner to live longer than a stinking twenty years. I want my friend to find some peace in her life and her choices. I want my stinking church . . ." I slammed my hand on the counter to make my palm sting. ". . . resanctified so I don't have to worry about the undead while I sleep! And I want to get rid of that thing in my freezer before it (a) starts an Inderland power struggle or (b) brings Newt knocking on my door for a cup of sugar again. But you . . ." I pointed. ". . . would give me what I want in such a way that it would ruin any joy I found in it, so forget it!" Angry and wondering if I was making a mistake, I crossed my arms and sulked.

Minias closed the book with a snap. I jumped, and, his red eyes fixed on me with an unsettling intensity, he slipped from the counter and came two steps forward. "You know what she was here for? You have it?"

My pulse quickened, and I pulled myself straight in worry. "I think so."

Minias stood stock-still, only the hem of his robe moving. "Give it to me. I'll make sure Newt never bothers you again."

My mouth was dry. Seeing him want it so badly, I knew that giving it to him would be a *very* big mistake. He didn't even know what it was. "Right,"

I said. "Like how you kept track of her the other night? You can't control her, and you know it."

He took a breath to protest, and I arched my eyebrows. Head bowing in thought, Minias dropped back a step.

"You don't have anything I want, demon," I said. "You're going to have to owe me."

"You think I'm going to wear your *mark*?" he said, and my head came up at the incredulousness in his tone. "I am *not* going to wear your mark." His cheeks were pale, but there was a deep anger in his eyes.

"Why not?" I said, liking the idea if only because he didn't. I recalled Trent saying I made decisions on the basis of how much I could irritate people, and I frowned. Minias, though, didn't see it, since he had made a huff of noise and turned his back to me.

His shoulders were very broad, and with the robe he looked regal and elegant next to me in my sandals, jeans, and chemise. I was still connected to the line, and I could feel my hair starting to snarl. I ran a hand over my curls, thinking I was really stupid to be worrying about my hair when I had a demon in my kitchen.

Minias's head came up, and I heard the front door shut.

Ceri. Finally.

Ceri's light steps were soft in the hallway, her pleasant voice tight with worry when she called for me. She halted in the threshold, her wide eyes darting from Minias in my circle to me. She was still wearing the same summery, lightweight linen dress she'd had on earlier, and her toes were wet, telling me she had walked through the dew-wet grass barefoot. Jenks was sitting on her shoulder to look as if he belonged there, and I wasn't surprised to see Rex, Jenks's cat, in her arms. The orange kitten was purring, her eyes closed and her paws damp as well.

"God protect us," she said in relief. Jenks flew up in a sparkling of gold, and she let the cat slip to the floor. "Are you all right?" she asked, coming forward but not taking my hands as she used to.

"So far," I said, wondering if she was still mad about last night despite her assurances. I had set the calling circle properly—I just hadn't known it was ringing. Ceri was a hard taskmistress, but she wouldn't stay angry because I was slow on the uptake. Would she?

Rex stood in the middle of the kitchen, her tail twitching in bother as she found herself on the linoleum. She wouldn't let me touch her, but a demon standing three feet away didn't seem to bother her at all. *Stupid cat.*

"Good evening, Ceri," Minias said pleasantly, but she ignored him, the slight tightening of her lips and her fingers going to her crucifix the only sign she had heard him.

"Have you come to an agreement?" she asked me, worry obvious in her pinched features.

Jenks darted from the window, where he had been checking on his kids. "We were waiting for you."

My chest clenched. *We. He said we.* It was a small thing, but knowing he hadn't turned his back on me for dealing with demons meant a lot. *Damn it, I didn't ask for this!*

"Good." Ceri's thin shoulders relaxed. Only now did she turn to stand side by side with me and face Minias. "I'll help you make a contract that will be untwistable."

Minias's bark of laughter caught me off guard, and I frowned when he put his hands behind his back to make himself look immovable. "No," he said simply. "I heard what you did to Al. I bargain with her." His slitted eyes narrowed, and his gaze slid over me to make my skin crawl. "I do not bargain with you, nor will I allow you to act as her liaison."

Red spots appearing on her cheeks, Ceri stiffened. "You can't stipulate anything, you sophomoric . . . *leviter!*"

I didn't know what a *leviter* was, but Minias frowned.

Jenks landed on my shoulder. "She just told him he was a newbie at bargaining," he whispered, and I made a *hmmmm* of understanding, then wondered how he had known.

Minias looked positively ticked, and I didn't like the way he was tapping his slippers against the bottom of the circle as if looking for a way out. "Both of you knock it off," I said to get their attention. "It doesn't matter, Ceri. I don't want anything from him, so he's going to have to wear my mark."

That didn't sit well with Minias at all, and he smacked his hand into the barrier with a pained grunt. The scent of burnt amber became obvious, and my nose wrinkled. The demon turned his back on me, his robes furling as he inspected his fist, and Rex sauntered out. I heard the cat door squeak, and from the garden came a high-pitched cheer. Rex streaked in, her nails skittering in the hall as she ran to hide—under Ivy's bed, probably.

Jenks flitted to me, hovering so close my eyes almost crossed. "You can do that?"

"He seems to think so." I waved him away only to find Ceri watching me in worry.

"I'm not going to do this!" Minias interjected, and my gaze darted to him, then the clock. Damn it, Ivy would be home soon, and having those two meet was a really bad idea.

"You will," I said, hands on my hips and coming closer. "There is nothing you can give me, nothing you can teach me. Either you take Al's or Newt's mark off me in exchange for your own or you take my mark and get the hell out of my kitchen!"

"Easy," Ceri cautioned, and I jumped when her hand touched my arm.

My skin was tingling, and I felt a surge of incoming force from the line, my control of it slipping as my anger grew. I took a quick breath and narrowed the inflow before my chi overflowed and I'd have to spindle it. "I'm okay. I'm okay . . ." I said, pushing her hand off me. I felt uncomfortable, and even her light touch was too much.

She backed up uneasily, and Jenks landed on her shoulder. I turned from their twin worried looks. I was fine, damn it!

Ready to push the issue, I rounded on Minias, but the demon had dropped back to the center counter, his smooth face placid and a new glint in his goatlike eyes as he looked at me in speculation. Fear struck through me, and my anger vanished.

Seeing it, Minias smiled. "I'll take your mark, witch," he said. "I'll even teach you how to give one. For free," he added, and my breath hissed in.

"Rache," Jenks chimed. "This is a bad idea."

But Minias had pushed himself into motion, his robe's hem shifting to a halt as he came to stand within inches of the circle's barrier. He smiled, and I shivered. He had absolutely perfect teeth, and his skin was flawless. Just like mine.

Ceri was suddenly at my elbow. "I don't like this."

"Oh, Cerdiwen Merriam Dulciate doesn't like it." Minias arched his eyebrows and smirked. "She'll do it. Someday she's going to want something. She's going to want it bad. And I'm going to be the one she calls." He put his round hat back on. "I can hardly wait."

I was sure there were demons more dangerous than Minias, but his owing me a favor sounded like the back door into trouble, not the front door out of the same. My eyes went to the clock again. "Fine. Let's do this."

Ceri made a small noise, and Jenks's wings clattered. The two of them looked alone and unhappy. Minias, though, was pleased. Stepping back from the circle's edge, he gestured in invitation. "We can't do this through a circle," he said, inclining his head.

I cringed, and I wondered if I should just have made a stupid wish, like for a box of cookies or something. My thoughts went to Al and how he had given me my marks, and then Newt. "Newt didn't touch me," I said, feeling the mark heavy on the bottom of my foot.

"You know this . . . how?" he said, making me feel even better.

Oh, God. My stomach tightened at the idea of letting Minias out. Ceri could hold a circle bigger than my kitchen circle. She could make an airlock of sorts. "Ceri?"

"I can hold him, but to trust his word he won't hurt you? I . . . I don't like this."

It had been hardly a whisper, and I pulled my gaze from Minias's satisfied stance. Her eyes were worried, and she looked frightened. "There is nothing else I can do," I said. "And he won't hurt me." Sandals squeaking, I turned to him. "Will you?"

Flowing into a relaxed stance, he actually bowed. "I promise I won't hurt you. Until I leave, that is."

"Promise you'll go the instant the mark is made," I countered. "Alone and leaving me untouched."

He straightened and touched his hat to be sure it was in the right spot. "As you say."

Yeah. Right. I glanced at Ceri, who nodded, though she had yet to regain her color. Her motions subdued and unhappy, she took a piece of magnetic chalk from her waistband and, with a single unbroken line, sketched a circle a foot outside of mine. Jenks's wings hummed in agitation, and, steadying myself, I stepped over it. The demon watched it all in a bored satisfaction. *Why am I doing this again?*

k as I took the dagger from his long fingers. It was a
I thought, recalling that my demon marks had trans-
ith me when I'd been a wolf. Swallowing, I pulled my
rly hair and his eyes, so very wrong. "That's it?"
with no expression, and my tension rose another notch.
urse. To do it longhand would require some time and be

the dagger. It felt heavy and smooth in my grip, the ornate
ous against my fingers. "Who gets the imbalance?" I asked.
Iinias started. "You know about the cost?"
se she knows about that!" Jenks said. "You think you're
h a sophomoric *leviter*?"
vled, and I smiled, admittedly a sour one. Ceri moved so I
her. She was smug, pleased her student was holding her own.
s the smut?" I asked again.
s ran a finger down the embroidered edge of his sleeve. "The
f it. But unlike most curses, the smut vanishes along with the
nless the wearer dies before paying it."
nodded, saying he was telling the truth. My legs were shaking.
o get rid of my demon marks. I didn't know how much longer I
keep my body and soul together if demons kept showing up in my
h.
gger in my grip, I stared at him. I was going to have to cut him.
on magic sucked. "Tell me where you want it," I said.
Iinias drew back, his purple robes shifting about his ankles.
i're asking me?"
"Well, unless you want a big R on your forehead."
It almost looked like he wanted to smile. "Behind my ear, if you
uld."
I ran my gaze up his formidable height. "You're going to have to bend
ver."
Jenks snickered. "You want some lubricant? Rachel's going to screw
ou over good."
"Jenks!" I exclaimed, then stifled a shriek when Minias swooped
forward and, before Jenks could react, grabbed me about the wais
Twisting, he plunked my butt on the counter.
"Can you reach me now?" he said, his eyes happy that he had so

"I'm going in with yo[u]," [Jenks]
hovered beside me.

"No you aren't." I didn[...]

"Like you can stop me?'[...]

"Jenks . . ." But it was too[...]
circle went up, trapping him[...]

"You need someone to wat[...]
getic.

Oh, man . . . I thought, eyei[ng...]
between us. Once she got that ha[...]
useless. Jenks landed on my shoul[der...]
the oil he used to clean his garden s[...]
bared the lethal blade. "Let's kick t[he...]
the mood.

Kick the pig? How about kick the witch[...]
knocked into her. I turned to Minias. "You[...]
Taking a symbolic step backward, M[inias...]
through.

Steadying myself, I reached to touch the[...]
stiffened as the energy needed to hold the ba[...]
me, filling my chi before slipping back to the[...]
go of the line, wanting it in case I had to do s[...]
a relief to bring the levels coursing through m[...]
level. Jenks's wings fanned my neck, and my hai[r...]

Minias breathed deep as if cataloging my sce[nt...]
tainted by a sheet of ever-after, and my stomach [...]
sure, Rachel Mariana Morgan," he said.

My blood quickened at the new sound of his voi[ce...]
"Just Rachel, okay," I said, hoping I wasn't making as [...]
thought I was. Minias smiled. *Great. Another charming*[...]
prefer the insane ones. My eyes darted to the clock. I had [...]
before Ivy got back. I jerked when he moved, but all M[inias...]
pick up the knife I'd left on the counter behind him. *Oh, [...]*
to be sick.

Jenks took flight when Minias extended the blade to me[...]
"Cut me with it while saying *abyssus abyssum invocat*, and [...]
trigger the curse."

My hand sho[ok...]
curse? *Well, duh,*[...]
formed along w[...]
gaze up to his cu[...]

He nodded [...]
"It's a public c[...]
pointless."

I accepted [...]
carvings obv[...]

At that, M[...]
"Of cou[r...]
dealing wit[...]

He sco[...]
could see [...]
"Who get[s...]

Minia[s...]
wearer o[...]
mark. U[...]

Ceri[...]
I had t[o...]
could [...]
church[...]

Da[...]
Dem[...]
M[...]
"Yo[u...]

wo[...]

o[...]

me. Damn it, I wasn't safe in here, I don't care what he'd agreed to.

Ceri paced outside the circle, and Jenks was shedding white-hot sparkles. "Don't touch me," I said, my voice high as I sat frozen on the counter, shaking as I gripped my knife. "You touch me again, and I'll . . . I'll do something!"

"This is the most backward bargain I've ever made," Minias muttered sulkily, not impressed with my threat. He glanced at Jenks hovering out of his reach with his sword bared, then moved his attention to me. "Well?"

My hand was still shaking. He was at the right height, and nervous, I reached out with my free hand and brushed his curly hair aside to show the pale skin behind it. I could smell the ever-after on him, but combined with the herbs around me it sort of smelled nice. I let his soft hair slip through my fingers, then pulled his curls back once more, enjoying the sensation.

"Touch me like that again," Minias said in a low voice, "and I'll rip your fingers off."

I glanced at Ceri and remembered her twisted affections for her demon captor. "Sorry." Immediately I strengthened my hold on the line. Steeling myself, I felt my grip on the knife go slick with sweat. "I'm really sorry," I said, then made a quick downward cut.

Normal-looking blood flowed, and Jenks's wings hummed in agitation. Minias stiffened. "Invoke the curse, you idiot!" he snapped.

Ceri was standing helplessly outside her circle, and before I lost my nerve, I said the words. A curious sensation pulled through me, like when I had called Minias the first time. I was tapping in to a communal spell, and it gave me the willies. My lips parted, and Jenks swore as the cut mended right before me, a line of scar tissue showing when the smear of ever-after vanished.

"Holy crap!" Jenks blurted, and Minias jerked away. Three steps from me, he felt the skin behind his ear and frowned. Remembering the knife in my hand, I dropped it. The clatter of it hitting the counter was loud.

"You promised you'd leave," I reminded him. "Now."

His goat-slitted eyes fixed on me, and though I knew it was impossible, I felt as if he were seeing my past, or maybe my future. Face unreadable, Minias leaned close. The cloying odor of burnt amber mixed with the dry scent of his silk robes, and I refused to shrink away. "I can change my eyes if I work at it," he murmured, and I jerked back.

"It could be you didn't hear my voice because you're an unregistered user," he added, as if not having said his previous words. "You need to change that."

Ceri was pale, and feeling ill, I said, "I don't want to be in a demon registry. Go."

Minias touched the crucible, his fingers coming away with ash. "It's too late. You put yourself on it when you called me the first time. Either update your information so I can reach you, or I have every right to pop over here any time I think I have a way to remove my mark."

My head came up, and I stared, sick with dread. *Damn.* Was that why he had agreed to wear the mark in the first place? Minias's eyes glittered with success, and I dropped my head into my cupped hand. *Double damn.* "How do I register?" I said flatly, and he snickered.

"You need a password. Connect to your calling circle as if you're going to contact me, and while connected to a line, think your given name, and then follow it with your password. QED."

Simple enough. "Get a password," I said, feeling weary. "Okay. I can do that."

Minias was eyeing me from under some curls that had escaped from his hat. He was silent for a moment, and then, as if he didn't really want to, he crossed his arms over his chest and said, "You have a common name that everyone calls you and a password that you keep to yourself. Pick it carefully. That's how people pull demons over the lines."

Horrified, I looked from Jenks to Ceri, who was now holding her stomach. "A summoning name?" I stammered, figuring it out. "Your password is a summoning name?"

The demon grimaced. "If it gets out, yes, it can be used to force someone across the lines. That's why you pick a password that no one can piece together."

I backed up until I bumped into Ceri's circle. "I don't want a password."

"Fine with me," Minias said snidely. "But if I can't contact you, I'm going to come over when it's convenient for me, not you. And seeing as I don't care, it's going to be right before sunrise when you're trying to sleep, or making dinner, or screwing your boyfriend." His eyes drifted over the kitchen. "Or is it girlfriend?"

"Shut up!" I exclaimed, worried and embarrassed. But I was stuck, and stuck tight.

"Make it impossible to guess," Minias said. "Nonsense syllables."

My mouth opened in an O of realization. "That's why demon names are so weird," I said, and from behind him Ceri nodded. Her face was white, and she looked as shaky as I felt.

"Demon names aren't weird," Minias said indignantly. "They serve a purpose."

Jenks landed on my shoulder. "How about your name backward? Nagromanairamlehcar."

I felt my face twist. It sounded like a demon name.

"Terrible," Minias said, and I moved back when he picked up my chalkboard and set it on the counter. "Your names backward will be the first one Al tries, and if he figures it out, he can do untold mischief under your name. And nix on the birthdates, hobbies, favorite ice cream, movie stars, or old boyfriends. No numbers or weird characters that can't be pronounced. Stay away from the backward theme. It's too easy to run through the dictionary and find you."

"That would take forever," I scoffed, then blanched when Minias set his red eyes on me.

"Forever is just about what we have."

I felt something shift, and I watched him, ready to move if he did. But he turned away, glancing at my kitchen clock above the sink.

"You need to leave," I said, hearing my voice shake, and Jenks's wings clattered as he took flight to hover between us.

"Mmmm." Minias inclined his head. "I agree. We're done now, but with this mark between us to settle up, I will be talking to you. It's my God-given right to try to pay it off." Touching the side of his hat, he vanished in a cascading sheet of ever-after.

I tightened my grip on my line as I felt him use it to cross into the ever-after. Numb, I stared at where he had been. *What in hell have I just done?*

Immediately Ceri broke her circle, almost knocking me over as she gave me a hug to be sure I was still alive. "Rachel."

Crap. What have I done?

"Rachel!"

Ceri was shaking me, and I blearily looked at her. Seeing my awareness return, she sighed in relief, and her hands fell from my shoulders. "Rachel," she said again, softer. "I don't think you should do demon magic anymore."

Jenks lit on her shoulder where he could see me; he was scared. "You think?" I said bitterly, wiping a hand under my eye. It came away wet, but I wasn't crying. Not really.

"Actually . . ." Ceri dropped her head, clearly worried. "I don't think you should do any ley line magic either."

Sliding down from the counter, I looked past Ceri to the dark garden lit with the occasional flicker of pixy dust. My dad hadn't wanted me to have anything to do with ley line magic. Maybe . . . maybe I should have a talk with Trent as to why.

THIRTEEN

"Rachel, hand me the hammer, will you?" Ivy said, her voice raised so she could be heard over the pixies yammering in the corner loud enough to make my eyeballs ache. "I've got another popped nail," she added as I puffed to blow a curl that had escaped my ponytail out of my eyes.

Jamming the rolled insulation back between the two-by-four studs, I turned. The afternoon sun came through the high windows in the living room to make dusty beams that the pixies were playing in. They had just woken from their afternoon nap, and Jenks had them in here so Matalina could get a few extra winks. She'd been feeling poorly lately, but Jenks had assured us that she was doing fine. His kids were a bloody nuisance, but I wasn't going to suggest they leave. Matalina could get all the sleep she wanted.

Fumbling, I pulled the hammer from the sill. I had borrowed it from my mom this morning, having dodged her questions with the excuse that I was putting up a birdhouse, not fixing the damage of an insane demon who'd trashed our living room. That it was July and too late for nests had never occurred to her.

"Here," I said, smacking the ash handle into Ivy's bare hand with a soft and certain pop. She smiled before turning to pound in a nail that had pulled through the paneling Newt had ripped down. Pixies squealed, and Jenks's attention shot to them as he sat on a far sill with his youngest set of sextuplets, teaching them to tie their shoes.

Immediately his blurring wings stilled, and he resumed his lesson. It was a nice piece of pixy life we didn't get a chance to see often, a reminder that Jenks had an entire life outside of Ivy and me.

Ivy looked like a construction worker's calendar girl in her worn hip-hugger jeans and black T-shirt, her straight hair covered with one of those paper hats you get at paint stores. Body moving with a controlled grace, she pounded the stray nail into the paneling. Soon as she backed up, three pixies were there to inspect it, all helpfully pointing out the tear she had made in the paper veneer. Saying nothing, Ivy glued it back down and continued on.

Smiling, I turned away. Ivy wasn't pleased she had missed another one of my encounters with a demon. It was probably why she was hanging so tight today, needing to reassure herself that I was okay. And I could use her help. After seeing the estimate to replace a few sheets of paneling and carpet, we had decided to do it ourselves.

So far it had been easy. Just tidy the studs Newt had pulled the paneling off and put up new. There was no wall behind the thin sheets, and the insulation was the roll type, not the blown-in stuff we had put in the church's ceilings last fall. It didn't really look up to code, but that's what you get when you do it yourself. As for the carpet, it could stay out on the curb. There had been an oak floor under it. All it needed was a nice coat of shine.

"Thanks," Ivy said, handing the hammer back, and I slid it onto the mantel.

"No problem." I straightened my short-sleeved shirt to cover my midriff and pulled a handful of thin nails from the box beside the hammer and arranged them between my lips. "You wanna 'old 'is for 'e well I 'ammer it?" I asked as I tried to maneuver an unwieldy piece of paneling into place.

Bending, Ivy took it by the one edge and wedged it tight against the old paneling, her vampire strength making it look like she was holding a sheet of cardboard.

With a few quick whacks, I put a nail in the upper left corner, moved around her to put another in the lower right, then a third in the upper right. The rich scent of vampire incense mixed with the sawdust and my latest perfume in a pleasant fragrance of contentment. "Thanks," I said after I took the nails out of my mouth. "I can get it now."

Her smooth oval face showing nothing, she backed up, her hands rubbing against each other as if soothing herself. It was the first time we had done anything together since she had bitten me, and it felt good. Like we were back to normal.

"Hey, Rache," Jenks said loudly as the kids before him rose up and joined the others in a dusty sunbeam, "I've got one for you. How about Rumpelstiltskin?"

I didn't bother to write that one down on the legal pad sitting on the dusty mantel, simply lifting my eyebrows at him as he laughed at me. I'd been trying to think up a password since coming back from my mom's with the toolbox, and I wasn't having any luck.

"I'd go with an acronym," Ivy suggested. "One that isn't in the dictionary. Or your names backward?" Her eyes fixed on mine with an odd intensity as she intoned, "Nagromanairamlehcar."

That both Jenks and she had thought of the same thing proved Minias was right about the no-backward theme. "No," I said before Jenks did. "Minias nixed it. He said it's too easy to run through the dictionary backward and find you. No numbers, no spaces, no real words, and nothing backward." Grabbing a few more nails, I stretched to reach the top of the panel.

Ivy dropped back and watched me for a moment before starting to move quietly about and put the tools away. I could feel her attention on me as I worked down the stud line, aware she was there but not uncomfortable about it. It was noon, for criminy's sake, and she had probably slaked her blood lust with Skimmer last night. *And does that bother me?* I asked myself, smacking a nail with an extra amount of force. Not at all. Not one bit. But I couldn't stop the memory of her biting me from swimming up from my subconscious.

A soft tingle grew at my old demon scar, and I stayed still, simply tasting the feeling that warmed me from my skin inward and trying to decide if it had been born from my thoughts and Ivy's pheromones—or my desire for her to be happy. Did it matter?

Jenks flew up from the sill and moved to the mantel, his wings clearing the dust from where he landed. "How about something in Latin?" he said as he walked to my list and stared down at it. "Like 'kick-ass witch,' or 'royally screwed.'"

"*Raptus regaliter?*" I said, thinking it sounded too much like Rumpelstiltskin. "They all know Latin. I think that comes under using words in the dictionary."

His expression sly, Jenks glanced at Ivy as she put the drill away. "How about Iaasw," he said. "Which means 'I am a stupid witch'—or here's one." Grinning, he stood on my list with his hands on his hips. "Nuacsiepasn? That's a great name."

Ivy shook the thick contractor garbage bag down and dropped her paper hat in it. "What's that stand for?"

" 'Never under any circumstances should I ever pick a summoning name.' "

I pressed my lips together and hammered a nail.

Ivy snickered and took a sip of bottled water she had on the sill. "I think we should call her Spam, because her ass is going to be in a tin if she's not careful."

Ticked, I turned, hammer in hand. "You know what?" I said, waving it in a weak threat. "You can all just shut up. You can all shut up right now."

Capping her water, Ivy frowned. "I don't even know why you're doing this."

"Ivy—" I started, tired of it.

"It's asking for trouble," she said, setting the empty bottle back on the sill.

Jenks stood on my list, staring down at it with his hands on his hips. "She's doing it for the thrill," he said distantly.

"I am not!" I protested.

They both looked at me in disbelief. "Yes you are," Jenks said as if it didn't bother him. "It's textbook Rachel. Coming close to something lethal, but not quite there." He smiled. "And we lo-o-o-o-ove you for it," he crooned.

"Shut up," I muttered, turning my back on him and hammering. "I'm doing this so Minias doesn't have to pop over here to get that mark resolved." Leaning into the sun, I grabbed another handful of nails. "You liked Minias showing up that way?" I said.

His eyes on his kids clustered on the windowsill, Jenks shrugged. "I agree with what you're doing, but not why."

"I just told you why." Nervous, I tucked a wayward strand of hair behind my ear. "Look, if you don't want to help me pick out a password, that's fine. I can do it myself."

Ivy and Jenks glanced questioningly at each other—as if I were incapable of doing this on my own—and my blood pressure spiked.

"Dad!" came a high-pitched shriek from a desperate pixy. "Dad! Jariath and Jumoke glued my wings shut!"

Surprised, I felt my anger ping to nothing, and I turned to the window. Four streaks of gray raced out of the living room. There was a metallic crash from the kitchen, and I wondered what had hit the floor. Jenks stood frozen, his face a mix of fear of what would happen if Matalina found out and embarrassment that he had taken his eyes off them long enough for them to glue someone's wings together.

Instantly he recovered and was airborne. Darting to the shelf, he tucked the hysterical child under his arm and took off after the others. In a swirl of silk and dismay, the entire clan whirled into motion. "Jariathjackjunisjumoke!" Jenks shouted from the kitchen, and then even that was gone, to leave only a shimmering sifting of dust and an echo of memory in our thoughts.

"Damn!" Ivy said to break the silence, then started to laugh quietly. Taking up the glue, she glanced at the label and tossed it to me. *Water soluble,* I thought, then dropped it into the toolbox. I smiled ruefully, and though I hoped Jenks got his kid's wings unglued, I thought I had my summoning name right there. Jariathjackjunisjumoke. If I ever forgot it, all I'd have to do was ask any pixy kid who had gotten their backsides tanned for glueing someone's wings shut.

"Oh, hey," Ivy said after bending to the portable radio and clicking it on. "Have you heard Takata's latest?"

"Yup." Glad the pixies were gone, I grabbed more nails as the song in question belted out. "I can't wait until the winter solstice. Think he'll ask us to work security again?"

"God, I hope so."

She turned it up to sing with the refrain—her voice soft but clear. When I finished hammering in the last nail in the row, Ivy maneuvered the final piece of paneling in place, and I tacked in the corners without pause. We worked well together. We always had.

The sound of pixies laughing in the garden assured me everything was fine. Relaxing, I breathed in the distinctive scent of raw wood and insulation. It was a bright day. The heat wave had finally snapped. Jenks was doing dad stuff. Ivy and I were getting back to normal. And she was singing. It couldn't get much better than that.

My expression softened when I realized she was singing words to a verse that I couldn't hear. It was the vamp track that Takata put in his music, something special that only the undead and their scions could hear. Well, Trent had a pair of spelled headphones that let him hear it, but that didn't count. He had offered me a set once. I had turned him down because of what he would have attached to his "gift." Even so, while hearing Ivy harmonize to Takata's voice, both rough and smooth, I wished I had a pair. The one time I had listened in with Trent's headphones, the woman's tortured, pure voice had been exquisite.

Ivy grabbed the broom and started sweeping. I finished one line of nails, bent upside down for the last few, then started on the next column. Intent on trying to catch what Ivy was singing, I missed a nail, grazing my thumb. I jerked, yelping when the sharp pain zinged through me. My thumb was in my mouth almost before I knew I had nicked it.

"You okay?" Ivy asked, and I nodded, eyeing the red mark on my thumb, then checked out the wall. Crap, I had dented the paneling.

"Don't worry about it," Ivy said. "We can put the couch there."

Tired, I whacked the nail one more time. Tossing the hammer into the toolbox, I sat on the hearth, stretched out my legs, and eyed my thumbnail. It was going to turn purple. I knew it.

Ivy resumed sweeping, her motions slow and even—hypnotic, almost. The music changed from Takata to an obnoxious man screaming about cars, and I leaned to turn it off. My shoulders eased in the new silence. The hush of the broom was soothing, and the garden had gone silent, the pixies off doing pixy things at the far end of the graveyard, no doubt.

Bending sharply, Ivy swept the splinters and dust into the pan, her black hair flashing silver when it hit the sun. The rattle of plastic was soft as she dropped it into the contractor garbage bag. A wry smile came over my face when she began sweeping the entire floor again. I lurched to my feet and started rearranging the tools in the box so I could get the thing shut. I'd return them to my mom this Sunday when I went over for my post-birthday dinner. There was no getting out of it. I just hoped she hadn't invited anyone else with the intent to play matchmaker. Maybe I should call and tell her Ivy was coming. That would put the curl in her eyelashes. And then she would set an extra place for Ivy, just glad I was with someone.

"How's your thumb?" Ivy asked into the silence, and I started.

"Fine." I glanced at it as I came up from snapping the latches on the toolbox. "I hate it when I do stuff like that."

Ivy propped the broom against the wall by the door and came closer. "Let me see."

Eager for some sympathy, I held it out, and she took my hand.

A shiver went through me, and, feeling it, Ivy glanced from under her short bangs, iced in gold. "Stop it," she said darkly. Pissed almost.

"Why?" I said, pulling my hand away. "You did bite me. I know how it feels, and how it makes you feel. I want to find a blood balance. Why don't you?"

Ivy's face turned to a shocked surprise. Hell, I had surprised myself, and a stirring of adrenaline tingled under my skin as my pulse quickened.

"I bit you?" she said, anger coloring her words. "You practically seduced me. Played on every instinct I had."

"Well . . . you gave me the book," I shot back. "You expect me to believe you didn't want me to?"

For a moment she said nothing, eyes slowly dilating as she stood in the sun. I held my breath, not knowing what might happen. If she had to be mad to talk to me, then she had to be mad. But instead of coming back with more anger, she retreated a step. "I don't want to talk about it," she said. I started to protest, and she turned, vanishing past the archway.

"Hey!" I exclaimed, knowing it was a bad idea to follow a fleeing vampire, but when had I ever done the smart thing?

"Ivy," I complained, finding her at the kitchen sink, scrubbing furiously. The sharp scent of cleanser was thick, and a cloud of it hung over her, glittering in the sun. She must have dumped half the canister. "*I* want to talk about it," I said, and she shot me a look that struck me cold. "I know what to expect now," I added doggedly from the hallway. "It won't be as bad."

"You don't know what bad is," she said, then turned on the tap. Her motions were rough, edging into a vampire quickness. Realizing I was blocking her exit, I sidled into the kitchen and pretended to get a bottle of water. My pulse was fast, and I shut the fridge door, cracking the cap and taking a swig.

"How often do you need blood?" I asked, then jumped when she whipped around, her hands tangled in a dish towel.

"That's putting it ugly, Rachel," she accused, hurt showing in the slant of her eyebrows.

"It's not ugly," I protested. "That's the point. You need blood to feel good about yourself. Hell, I need sex at least once a week if I'm dating someone I care about, or I'm plagued with delusions that the guy doesn't love me, or he's cheating on me, or any number of stupid, groundless ideas. It doesn't make sense, but there it is. Why should you be any different? So how often do you need to share blood to feel secure and happy?"

Her face was scarlet beside her black hair. How about that? Under it all, Ivy was shy.

"Two or three times a week," she muttered. "It's not that I need a lot at any one time. It's the act, not the result." Then her roving eyes fixed on me, striking me to my core.

"I can do that," I said, heart pounding. *I can, right?*

Ivy stared. Abruptly she shifted into motion, and I was looking at an empty room.

"Ivy!" I exclaimed, setting the bottle on the table and following her out. "I'm not asking you to bite me. I simply want to talk!" I glanced into her room and bathroom in passing, then heard her footsteps in the sanctuary. She was leaving. Typical. "Ivy . . ." I cajoled, then caught my breath in a tiny gasp when I entered the sanctuary and she was suddenly before me.

I stumbled to a stop, taking in her wire-tight posture and her black eyes. I was pushing it, and we both knew it. My demon scar was tingling from the pheromones she was kicking out, and the memory of Jenks telling me I was an adrenaline junkie surfaced. But damn it, this was the most I'd gotten her to open up in months.

"You're following me," she said, the threat behind her voice making me stifle a shudder.

"I want to talk," I said. "Just talk. I know you're afraid—

"Hey!" I yelped when her arm shot out and pushed my shoulder. My back touched the wall, and I looked up. Ivy was right in front of me, eyes black as sin—and alive as the sun.

"I have good reason to be afraid," she said, her breath shifting my hair. "You think I don't want to bite you? You think I don't want to fill myself with you again? You love me, Rachel, whether you know what to do about it or not, and love without demands comes so seldom to a vampire. It drives me insane knowing you're right there and I can't have you!"

I stared, pulse racing, knees going weak. Maybe following her had been a mistake.

"I want it so bad that I hurt people to keep you safe and almost criminally innocent," Ivy said. "So if I don't bite you, trust me, there's a reason."

She pushed hard on my shoulder and turned around.

Shocked, I watched her walk away. The sun coming in through the stained-glass windows made spots of color on her as her arms swung stiffly. My resolve strengthened. I took a step after her. This pattern of her fleeing my questions was getting old.

"Talk to me," I demanded. "Why won't you at least try to find a way to make this work? You could be so happy, Ivy!"

Ivy halted just before the foyer, hand on her hip as she faced the door. For three heartbeats she stood before she slowly spun. Slim and tense, she made a picture of collected frustration. "You can't stop me," she said simply, and I took a protesting step forward. "You're too wrapped up in the ecstasy to keep conscious enough to stop me if things go wrong, and, Rachel, unless I mix sex with it, things *will* go wrong. It's how Piscary made me."

A glimmer of her self-disgust, her hatred of who she was, showed, and my heart ached to prove to her she was wrong. My breath came fast, and I held it. "I know what to expect now," I said softly. "It was the surprise. I can do better."

Hip cocked, she looked to her left as if searching for strength. Or maybe answers. "Better won't keep you alive," she said, and I went cold at the caustic sound. "You don't have it in you. You said yourself you don't want to hurt me. If I take your blood again without letting my feelings for you shackle my hunger, you're going to have to hurt me, because the hunger will take control, and I'm not capable of stopping then. Think you can do that?"

My mouth went dry, and my first words came out in a croak. "I . . ." I stammered, "I don't have to hurt you to stop you."

"Is that so?" she said, and as I stood frozen with my eyes wide, she dropped her purse. "Let's find out."

I jerked back as she leapt. Gasping, I dove toward her, pushing off the wall. My intent was to get past her. If she got a hold on me, I was dead meat. This wasn't passion. This was anger. Anger at herself, perhaps, but anger.

The thump of her hitting the wall where I had been brought my heart into my throat. I spun where I landed. She was coming back, and I grabbed her arm, wrenching it to lever her into falling. She twisted from me, rolled by the sound of it, and I spun.

But I was too slow, and I bit back a yelp when a white arm slipped around my neck. Her fingers pinched my hand, bending my wrist backward until it hurt. I went slack in her grip, caught and unable to best her vampire reactions. It was over that quickly. She had me.

"Hurt me, Rachel," she whispered, stirring my hair. "Show me you aren't afraid to hurt me. If you aren't brought up that it's the norm, it's harder than you think."

She wasn't masochistic. She was a realist, trying to get me to understand. Frightened, I struggled, pain ripping through my shoulder. Her grip was confining without being painful. It was my trying to get away that hurt. I went still, eyes wide and focused on the wall. I felt her warm against my back, and tension pulled my muscles tight one by one as the tingling started high in my neck and trickled lower.

"We can share blood without love if you hurt me," Ivy breathed, her breath brushing my ear. "We can share blood without hurt if you love me. There is no middle ground."

"I don't want to hurt you," I said, knowing that my magic was like a ball bat. I had no finesse. It would hurt her, and hurt her bad. "Let go," I demanded, shifting. She tightened her grip, and a thread of heat coiled in my center as my motion ended with more of our bodies touching. This had started as an object lesson to get me to leave her alone, but now . . . *Oh, God. What if she bites me again. Right now?*

"You're the one stopping us from finding a blood balance," she said. "Love is pain, Rachel. Figure it out. Get over it."

It wasn't. At least it didn't have to be. I wiggled again. "Ow, ow!" I said, feet scuffling. I was starting to sweat. Her scent poured over me, soothing, enticing, bringing the memory of her teeth sliding into me to the forefront of my thoughts as evolution had intended. And when my eyes closed at a surge of adrenaline pooling in me to set my blood rushing, I realized just what kind of trouble we were in. I didn't want her to let go. "Uh, Ivy?"

"Damn it," she whispered, and the heat in her voice hit me hard.

We were six kinds of stupid. I had only wanted to talk, and she had only wanted to prove how dangerous finding a blood balance would be. And now it was too late for thinking.

Her grip tightened, and I relaxed into it. "God, you smell good," she said, and my pulse thrummed. "I shouldn't have touched you. . . ."

Feeling unreal, I tried to move, finding she'd let me turn to face her. My heart jumped into my throat, and I swallowed as I gazed into her perfect face, flushed with the danger of where we were. Her eyes were black as absolute night, reflecting my image: lips parted, eyes wild. The darkness was colored by the blood lust shimmering in her eyes. And below that, deeper under it all, was her fragile vulnerability.

"I can't hurt you," I said, fear a faint whisper in me.

My neck throbbed with the memory of her lips on me, the glorious feeling of her pulling, drawing what she needed to fill the hurting chasm in her soul. Her eyes closed, and, breathing deeply, I felt myself relax against her as her forehead touched my shoulder. "I'm not going to bite you," she said, her teeth inches from me, and a pulse of need shocked though me. "I'm not going to bite you."

My soul seemed to darken with her words. The question of what she would do had been answered. She was going to walk away. She was going to let go, drop back, and walk away.

A feeling of loss rose to wind around my lungs, crushing my air from me.

"But I want to," she said, and the chained desire in her whisper sent a pulse through me.

I gasped as the unexpected sensation dove to my middle and set me alight, twice as potent since I had given up on it. It was followed by fear, and Ivy's grip clenched. I froze when she tilted her head, her lips brushing just shy of my scar. "Either bite me or let me go," I breathed, dizzy with need. *How did this happen? How did it happen so fast?*

"Close your eyes," she said, her gray voice holding the emotion she was trying to control.

My pulse hammered, and, lids fluttering, I felt her pull back. In my imagination I could see her black eyes, see the heat in them and the way she got off on self-denial followed by a savage fulfillment when it became too much for her to contain, the guilt coating her soul.

"Don't move," she said, and I trembled at her breath against my cheek. She was going to bite me. Oh, God, I'd do better this time. I wouldn't let her lose control. I could do this.

"Promise me," she said, running a finger across my neck to make my breath catch, "that this won't change anything. That you know it's a taste for you to try, and that I will do nothing to encourage you. I won't ever do it again unless you come to me. If you come to me. And don't come to me unless you want it all, Rachel. I can't do it any other way."

A taste. I had already tasted this, but I nodded, my eyelids closed. My breath came in a pant, and I held it, waiting. Aching for the feel of her teeth in me. "I promise."

"Keep your eyes shut," she breathed, and I almost moaned when her light touch upon my scar lit a path through me to my groin. I gasped, feeling the wall against my back and her grip on me tighten. My heart pounded, and anticipation coiled deeper, tighter.

The softness of her small lips on mine went almost unnoticed until her hand left my scar and crept to the back of my neck to hold me unmoving. I froze. *She's kissing me?*

My first reaction to jerk away rose and fell, everything confusing as my body still resonated with the wash of endorphins that her playing on my scar had started. A taste, she had said, and adrenaline pounded. She felt the lack of a violent response, and with her lips the barest whisper on mine, she shifted her hand, finding my scar again.

A groan escaped me. She had let up enough to be sure I knew what she was doing, and now she was going to let me have it all.

"Oh, God, Ivy," I moaned, the conflict between knowledge and emotion making me helpless, and she pressed me into the wall, her lips upon mine again becoming more sure, aggressive. The hint of her tongue brought a gasp from me, and I froze, not knowing what to do. It was too much. I couldn't think. Her light touch retreated, and with a suddenness that shocked through me, she pulled away.

Panting, I leaned against the wall, my eyes open and my hand pressing the throbbing pulse of my neck. Ivy stood four feet away, her eyes utterly black and her body clearly hurting from the effort she had exerted to let go.

"All or nothing, Rachel," she said, stumbling backward, looking afraid. "I'm not going to be the one to leave, and I won't ever kiss you again unless you start it. But if you try to manipulate me into biting you, I'm going to assume you're taking me up on my offer, and I'll meet you." Her eyes went frightened. "With all of me."

My pulse hammered and my knees wobbled. This was going to make our mornings alone a little more uncomfortable—or a hell of a lot more interesting.

"You promised you wouldn't leave," she said, her voice becoming vulnerable. And then she was gone, her steps sharp as she picked up her purse and fled the church and the confusion she had left me in.

My hand dropped, and I held myself as if trying to keep from falling apart. *What in hell have I done? Just stood there and let her do it?* I should have pushed her away, but I hadn't. I had started it, and she had used my scar to manipulate me into seeing what she offered without fear and holding all the passion it might entail. All or nothing, she had said, and now that I had tasted it all without fear, I knew what that meant.

The rumble of Ivy's cycle echoed in through the open transom windows, fading into the distant sound of traffic. I slowly let myself slide down the wall until I hit the floor, knees scrunched and trying to breathe. *Okay,* I thought, still feeling the promise of her resonating in me. *Now what am I going to do?*

FOURTEEN

The dry sifting of wings coming in the high windows drew my attention, and I stood, wiping the sweat from my neck. Jenks? Where had he been five minutes ago, and what in hell was I going to do now? Ivy had said she wouldn't do anything again unless I started it, but could I stay in the church with that kiss resonating between us? Every time she looked at me, I'd be wondering what she was thinking. *Maybe that was her intent?*

"Hey, Rache," Jenks called cheerfully as he dropped from the ceiling, "where's Ivy going?"

"I don't know." Numb, I headed to the kitchen before he could see my state. Clearly his kid's wings were okay. "Aren't you supposed to be sleeping?" I said, rubbing my sore wrist. Crap, if it bruised, it would look great with my bridesmaid's dress. At least I didn't have a new bite mark to go with it.

"Ah, hell," Jenks said, and I dropped my eyes when I saw his disapproving gaze. "It stinks in here. You pushed her again, didn't you?"

It wasn't a question, and I walked without pause into the kitchen.

"You stupid-ass witch," he said, shedding silver sparkles as he followed. "Is she coming back? You scare her off for good this time? What's wrong with you? Can't you leave it alone?"

"Jenks, shut up," I said flatly, grabbing my forgotten bottled water and heading into the living room. The radio was in there. If I turned it high enough, I wouldn't be able to hear him. "We talked, is all." *And she kissed me.* "I got a few questions answered." *And with her messing with my scar at the same time, it felt really good.* Shit. How was I supposed to figure this out? I thought I was straight. I was, wasn't I? Or did I have "latent tendencies"? And if I did, were they really a convenient excuse for thinking with my G-spot? Was that what I was all about? Had I no depth at all?

He followed me into the empty living room, and I sat on the raised hearth, trying to remember how to think. I clicked on the radio to find happy, bouncy music, and I turned it off.

"Well?" Jenks landed on my knee, looking almost hopeful. But then his wings stilled and drooped when I sighed.

"I asked about a blood balance, and she set some rules," I said, looking out the high windows at the undersides of the oak tree's leaves. "She's not going to make a move to touch my blood, but if I even hint that I want her to, it's with the understanding that I want everything."

He looked at me blankly, and I added, "She kissed me, Jenks."

His eyes widened, and a small part of me was reassured that he hadn't seen the entire thing and was hiding the fact. "Did you like it?" he asked bluntly, and I frowned, shifting my knee until he took off to land right where he had been.

"She was playing on my scar at the time," I muttered, blushing. "I got a real good idea what it would be like to let my hair down and go with it, but I don't know where the feelings are coming from anymore. She mixed them all up, then walked out the door."

"So . . ." Jenks hedged. "What are you going to do?"

I gave him a mirthless smile. His unconditional acceptance was a balm, and the tension eased. He didn't care what Ivy and I did, as long as we stayed together and didn't kill each other. "How should I know?" I said as I stood. "Can we talk about something else?"

"Hell, yes," Jenks said, rising up with me. "You just keep thinking whatever you need to think. As long as you don't leave."

Setting my water on the sill, I took up the broom and started to sweep our brand-new floor again. I wasn't going to leave because Ivy had kissed me. She'd said she wasn't going to do it again, and I believed her, knowing how she'd wanted this since our moving in together, and me being as dumb as a stone because of her ability to hide her desires the way she could. It had been a taste to show me what might be, then a return to the distance we kept to give me the time I needed to think about it. Figure things out. *The Turn take it.*

Jenks hovered for a moment, then landed on the sill and in the sun. "This is better," he said, scanning the bare walls. "I don't know why you didn't let the guys do it. It wasn't that much, and the amount you saved won't make a dent in what we need to resanctify the church." His face grew worried. "And we are going to resanctify it, right? I mean, we can't move."

Rising from sweeping the dust into the pan, I turned to him, hearing the worry he was trying to hide. It didn't matter how uncomfortable things got between Ivy and me. If the firm fell apart, Jenks would probably lose control of the garden. He had way too many kids, and Matalina wasn't up to staking out new territory. Jenks said she was okay, but I was worried.

"We aren't moving," I said flatly, and I dumped the pan in the black contractor bag. "We'll find a way to get the church resanctified." *Ivy and I will deal with the uncomfortable situation like we always have . . . by ignoring it.* It was something we were both good at.

Reassured, Jenks glanced into the garden, the sun glinting on his shock of bright yellow hair. "I still say you should've let the guys fix the walls," he said. "What did you save? A hundred bucks? Tink's knickers, that's nothing."

I set the broom aside and shook the trash down in the bag, looking for a twist tie. "I'll have a big chunk after Trent's wedding. Unless nothing happens, but what are the chances of that?"

Jenks snickered. "With your luck, nothing will."

I scanned the living room and tried to decide how to pick up the bag of trash without getting poked by a stray nail or jagged sliver. Though the space was empty and echoing, the walls were back together and the newly uncovered floor was clean. A quick trip to the store for a new piece of baseboard and we could move everything back. Actually, there was no reason to wait for the baseboard. I could move everything back in now, and finish it later. If I hustled, I could get it back before Ivy returned. It might be easier to do it myself than our doing it together.

"Phone's going to ring," Jenks said from atop the broom's handle, and I froze, jumping when it did.

"God, Jenks, that's creepy," I muttered as I dropped the bag and went to the hearth. I knew he probably heard the electronics click over, but it was still unnerving.

He was grinning as I plucked up the receiver. "Vampiric Charms," I said, adopting my most professional voice. I stuck my tongue out at Jenks, and he merrily flipped me off. "This is Morgan. We can help. Day or night, dead or alive." *Where are the freaking pen and paper?*

"Rachel? It's Glenn."

My breath puffed out, and I relaxed. "Hi, Glenn," I said, looking for something to sit on and finally moving to the kitchen. "What's up? You got another job for me? Maybe want to arrest another one of my friends?"

"I didn't arrest Mr. Hue, and it's the same job."

He sounded tense, and since the chance to get money out of the FIB didn't come very often, I dropped into my chair at the table. My gaze flicked to Jenks, the pixy having followed me in and clearly listening to both ends of the conversation.

"There's been another Were murder made up to look like a suicide," Glenn said around the noise of FIB scanners and birds, and I wondered if he was on site. "I'd like you and Jenks to give me your Inderlander opinion before they move the body. How soon can you get here?"

I glanced at my construction-dusty jeans and T-shirt, wondering just what he thought I could do that he couldn't. I wasn't a detective. I was a hired spell caster/bounty hunter. Jenks took to the air, darting out the pixy hole in the kitchen screen. "Ah," I hedged, "can't I just come to the morgue and look at the body?"

"You have something better to do?"

I thought about the living room and how I wanted our stuff back in it before Ivy got back. "Well, actually . . ."

"They're going to try to jerk it out from under me again," Glenn said, drawing my attention back to him, "and I want you to see it before the I.S. has a chance to doctor the body. Rachel . . ." His voice took on a hard edge. "It's Mrs. Sarong's accountant. You know . . . the Howlers? He was high in the pack, and no one is happy."

My eyebrows rose. Mrs. Sarong was the owner of Cincinnati's all-Inderland baseball team, the Howlers. It was their fish I had tried to recover from Mr. Ray—the same Mr. Ray whose secretary was already in the morgue. I had forced the woman to pay me for my time, actually meeting her in the process. That there had been two "suicides" from two of Cincinnati's most prominent packs in as many days was not good.

It was obvious someone knew that the focus was in Cincinnati and was trying to find out who had it. I had to get rid of it. The chaos would be astounding if an entire pack could turn humans. Vampires would start culling them. My fingers started to tap the table. Maybe that's what was already happening? Piscary was in jail, but that wouldn't stop him.

The sound of wings was a relief, and Jenks came back in dressed for work, a sword and belt in one hand, a red bandanna in the other. "The murdered Were is Mrs. Sarong's accountant," I said to him as I stood and looked for my shoulder bag.

"Oh." Jenks dropped several inches, a guilty look coming over him. "A-a-a-ah, that might explain the message on the machine."

I covered the phone receiver, unable to hide my exasperation. "Jenks . . ."

He made a face, leaking silver sparkles. "I forgot, okay?"

"Rachel?" came Glenn's tiny voice, pulling me back to him.

"Yeah . . ." I held a hand to my forehead. "Yes. Glenn, I can come out there. . . ." I hesitated. "Where are you?"

Glenn cleared his throat. "Spring Grove," he muttered.

A cemetery. Oooooh, how nice. "Okay," I said, standing up straight and scuffing into my sandals. "See you in a bit."

"Great. Thanks." He sounded preoccupied, as if he were trying to do two things at once.

I took a breath to say good-bye, but Glenn had hung up. Eyeing Jenks, I thumbed the phone off and cocked my hip. "I have a message?" I said dryly.

Jenks looked uncomfortable as he put the bandanna on, to look like an inner-city gang member in his black working clothes. "Mr. Ray wants to talk to you," he said softly.

I thought about his secretary having been murdered and the I.S. not only looking the other way but trying to cover it up. "I'll bet." Grabbing my bag, I looked to make sure I had all my usual spells. The thought occurred to me that Mr. Ray might be the one killing the Weres, but why would he kill his own secretary first? Maybe Mrs. Sarong had murdered the woman and the second killing had been in retaliation? I was getting a headache.

Remembering my suspended license, I hesitated, but what kind of image would I have if I arrived on a crime scene by bus, and I pulled out my keys. My gaze went to the shelves under the center island counter. Leaning, I smiled when the smooth, heavy weight of my splat-ball gun filled my palm. The metal parts clicked comfortingly as I checked the reservoir. Spells stored in amulets were good for a year, but unstored, invoked potions lasted only a week. These were three weeks old and useless, but waving my gun around made me feel good and ticked Glenn off. I dropped it into my bag as Jenks finished writing a note for Ivy. "Ready?" I asked him.

He flew to my shoulder, bringing the delicate scent of the soap Matalina washed his clothes in. "You want to take his ketchup?" he asked.

"Oh, yeah." I strode into the pantry, coming out with the gallon jar of super-duper belly-buster hot jalapeño salsa and the big red tomato I had gotten him as a surprise. Pulse fast, I headed for the hall, a gallon of salsa on my hip, a tomato in my hand, and a pixy on my shoulder.

Yeah, we bad.

FIFTEEN

The afternoon sun was hot, and easing my car door shut, I gave it a bump with my hip to latch it. My fingers were sticky from the pastry I'd eaten en route, and I scanned the sparrow-noisy grounds while I dug a tissue out of my bag. Wiping my fingers clean, I wondered if I should have taken five minutes to change into a more professional outfit than shorts and a top—professionalism being something I desperately needed, seeing as I was skulking around the mausoleum that I'd parked my car behind.

Jenks had run vanguard for me as I took the back roads to Spring Grove. If I had driven the interstate, the I.S. would have nailed my butt to a broomstick. It had made for slow travel—driving three blocks, parking, waiting for Jenks to do some recon, then moving forward another three blocks—but I couldn't stomach the idea of taking a cab. And as I hiked my shoulder bag higher and headed across the grass, I again thanked God I had friends.

"Thanks, Jenks," I said, stumbling when my sandal hit a dip the mower had hidden. His wings tickled my neck, and I added, "I appreciate you running rabbit for me with the I.S."

"Hey, it's my job."

There was more than a hint of annoyance to it, and, feeling guilty for having asked him to fly twice what I had driven, I said, "It's not your job to make sure my butt stays out of traffic court," then added softly, "I'll go to driver's-ed class tonight. I promise."

Jenks laughed. The tinkling sound brought out three pixies from the nearby bank of evergreens, but upon seeing Jenks's red bandanna, they vanished. The obvious color was his first line of defense against territorial pixies and fairies, a sign of good intentions and a promise not to poach. They'd watch us but wouldn't start catapulting thorns unless Jenks sampled the meager pollen or nectar sources. I'd rather have pixies watching me than fairies, though, and I liked the idea that pixies had Spring Grove. They must be well structured, since the grounds were huge.

The sprawling cemetery was said to have been originally developed to tastefully "rehouse" cholera victims in the late 1800s. It was one of the first garden cemeteries in the United States; the undead liked their parks as much as the next person did. It had been hard to keep your newly undead relatives out of the ground back then, and being unearthed in such peaceful settings must have been a small favor. I had to wonder if the large, hidden vampire population Cincy had in those days had much to do with how the Queen City gained the dubious distinction of being known for grave robbing. It wasn't so much that they were supplying the multitudes of teaching hospitals with cadavers but that they were pulling their relatives out of the earth and back where they belonged.

Scanning the quiet, parklike grounds, I wiped my mouth of the last of the frosting. The feel of my fingers across my lips brought Ivy to mind for obvious reasons, and I warmed. God, I should have done something, But no-o-o-o-o, I stood there like an idiot, too surprised to move. I hadn't reacted, and now I was going to have to think about how to handle this instead of settling it right then. *Stupid ass witch.*

"You okay?" Jenks asked, and I pulled my hand down.

"Peachy," I said sourly, and he laughed.

"You're thinking of Ivy," he needled, and my flush deepened.

"Well, duh," I said, stumbling on a marker set even with the ground. "You have your roommate kiss you, and you see if *you* can just forget it."

"Hell," Jenks said, flying just out of my reach with a grin on his face, "if one of you kissed me, I wouldn't have to think. Matalina would kill me. Relax. It was only a kiss."

I plodded over the grounds, following the sound of radios. This was just what I needed. As if an insane demon tearing apart my church weren't enough, I now had a four-inch man telling me to lighten up, go with the flow, live life—don't analyze it.

Jenks's wing clatter softened, and he lit on my shoulder. "Don't worry about it, Rache," he said, his voice unusually solemn. "You're you, and Ivy is Ivy. Nothing has changed."

"Yeah?" I muttered, not seeing it that clearly.

"Angle to the left," he said cheerfully. "I can smell dead Were down there."

"That's nice," I answered, continuing on past a marker and cutting a soft left. Downslope and through the trees were the flashing amber and blue lights of a multispecies ambulance. *I'm not too late,* I thought, arms swinging as we passed a huge stone marked WEIL. Beyond a row of cedars was an artificial pond, and between that and the evergreens was a cluster of people.

"Rache," Jenks said, his voice introspective. "You think this has anything to do with—"

"The bushes have ears," I warned.

"The thing I picked up for Matalina on our last vacation?" he amended, and my lips twitched in amusement. I had twisted a demon curse to move the curse in the focus to a knickknack. That it had slowly changed form to look like the original statue was just plain creepy.

Eyes on my feet, I murmured, "Mmmm-hmm. I'd be surprised if it wasn't."

"You think this is Trent looking for it?"

"I don't think Trent knows it exists," I said. "I'd be more inclined to think it's Mr. Ray or Mrs. Sarong, and they're killing each other as they try to find it."

Jenks's wings sent a cool breeze across my neck. "What about Piscary?"

"Maybe, but he wouldn't be having this much trouble covering it up," I said, glancing up when the men's tone of voice shifted, indicating that I'd been seen. I slowed at the hushed mutter of my name, but since everyone was looking at me, I didn't know who'd said it. There were two FIB vehicles, a black I.S. van, an I.S. cruiser, and an ambulance parked in the turnaround. Counting the third FIB vehicle at the cemetery's back entrance, the FIB presence was stronger than the I.S.'s, and I wondered if Glenn was pushing his luck. It *had* been a Were suicide.

The cluster of men surrounded a dark shadow at the foot of the cedars and a tall tombstone, and a second group in FIB uniforms and suits waited like cubs at a lion's kill. Glenn was with them, and while catching my eye he said a few words to the man next to him, touched the hilt of his weapon for reassurance, and headed over. People turned away, and I relaxed.

My feet scuffed the grass, and I cringed upon realizing I'd walked right on one of those markers set flush with the ground. Nervousness struck deep when a familiar bulk beside the tombstone straightened and Denon's brown eyes met mine. He was wearing a suit today instead of his usual slacks and polo shirt, and I wondered if he was trying to keep up with Glenn, who looked great in his suit. *I'm not afraid of Denon,* I thought, then gave in and sneered at him.

Denon's jaw clenched, ignoring the slight man in jeans and a lightweight short-sleeved shirt who had stepped forward to talk to him. I thought of my car and got worried. "Hey, Jenks," I said, lips barely moving, "why don't you flit around and see what you can overhear? Let me know if they find my car, huh?"

"You got it," he said, and with a sparkling of pixy dust he was gone.

Trying to look as if I'd been doing a reconnaissance of the surrounding area instead of hiking my way in, I angled to meet Glenn. He looked frustrated. The FIB was probably being pushed out of the investigation. I knew how bad that felt but had little sympathy, since he'd been the one pushing me out last time.

I took off my sunglasses as I stepped under the shade of the massive tree, tucking them to hang from the waistband of my shorts. "What's the matter, Glenn?" I said in greeting when he took my elbow and led me to an abandoned FIB cruiser. "Won't that nasty-wasty vampire let you play in the sandbox?"

"Thanks for coming out, Rachel," he grumbled. "Where's Jenks?"

"Around," I said, and he sourly gave me my temp tag. I pinned it on before I leaned against the FIB cruiser, crossed my arms over my stomach, and waited for the good news.

Running a hand across his smooth chin, Glenn sighed, turning so he could see me and the crime scene both. His dark eyes were tired, and there were faint worry lines at the corners, making him seem older than he was. His trim stature looked powerful even beside Denon, and his military background mixed well with his suit and loosened tie. Glenn had come a long way in a year as far as understanding Inderlanders, and while I knew he respected Denon's position, he didn't respect the man. He didn't mind telegraphing that either, which might be a problem. I had two big men with something to prove at a crime scene. Lucky me.

"How did you get out here?" he asked softly, his eyes envious as the I.S. collected their data. "I sent a car for you, but you'd left."

I put my arms to my side and fidgeted. Glenn slowly turned. "You drove?" he accused, and I flushed. "You promised me you wouldn't."

"No I didn't. I only *said* I wouldn't, not promised. I didn't know you were sending a car. And they don't have a bus run to the cemetery. There aren't enough pickups to warrant it."

He snorted, and both our postures eased. Glenn's weary gaze went to the body at the foot of the cedars, and I crossed my arms over my chest again. "You want to bull your way in there or wait until after they contaminate everything?" I asked.

Glenn rocked into motion, and I followed. "It's too late," he said. "I was waiting for you. Seeing as he's an Inderlander, I'm only going to get one look at him unless I can link him hard and fast to the murder of Mr. Ray's secretary."

I nodded, watching my feet so I wouldn't walk on any more markers. "I talked to Mr. Ray on the way over," I offered, and Glenn looked askance at me. "I have an appointment with him later today at his office." My hand went up when he took a breath. "You aren't coming with me, so don't ask—but I will tell you what we talked about if it touches on this." I couldn't bring a FIB detective to a client meeting. How lame was that?

Glenn looked ready to protest but then dropped his gaze. "Thank you."

The easing of my tension didn't last, and my blood pressure went higher the closer we got to the body. My nose started working, and over the scent of musk gone rank and excited vampire was the smell of redwood. I smoothed my expression into nothing, my gaze going to the tidy-looking guy in jeans and dress shirt standing a little apart from everyone. *They have a witch out here? Interesting.*

The circle of Inderlanders parted to show a Were corpse sprawled dramatically at the base of a large tombstone, the grass stained with black blood. A dead wolf the size of a pony was a lot less disturbing than a naked man, even one that had blood matting his fur and the eyes rolled back so far the whites showed. A hind leg had a clean tear to the bone, slicing the femoral artery open. The scent of blood was strong, and my gut tightened. *Suicide?* I thought, averting my gaze. I doubted it.

Denon was smiling at me with his lips closed to hide his human teeth. Beside him the witch's nostrils widened as he took in my scent hidden behind the orange spice perfume I used to muddle Ivy's instincts. His mouth quirked, and he touched his clean-shaven chin with the back of his hand. My skin prickled when he tapped a line, and I didn't know whether to be insulted or flattered that he thought I was a threat. What did he think I was going to do? Curse everyone? But upon remembering he could see my aura as easy as sneezing and that it was covered in black demon smut, I couldn't blame him.

Two men stood from their crouch over the corpse, leaving one to take core samples to determine how far the blood had soaked into the ground. I felt like we had interrupted punks tormenting a dog to death, and I forced myself not to back up when they turned their attention to us.

Glenn looked cool and casual in his suit and with his gun on his hip, but I knew by the strong scent of cologne coming off him that he was wired for action. Eyes fixed on Denon's, he said evenly, "Ms. Morgan and my team would like a moment with the body before you move it."

Someone snickered, and my face warmed.

"Whoring for the FIB, Morgan?" Denon said, ignoring Glenn. "I see the bus is picking you up again. Or did you need to use a disguise to get them to stop for you?"

I frowned, sensing Glenn's rising anger. Denon's honey-smooth voice made him sound like he should be hawking negligees on the women's channel. My God, it was beautiful, and I wondered if it was what had attracted his vampire master in the first place. That, and his deliciously dark skin now marked and scarred beyond belief. It hadn't been that way when he was my boss. Clearly things had changed.

"You seem upset, Denon," I taunted. "I bet you had some 'splainin' to do about almost releasing that murder victim." I smiled sweetly. "Be a prince and run the updated coroner's report over to me this afternoon? I'd be interested to see what you almost burned in the kilns."

The witch snickered, and the last Were rose, his gaze darting nervously. Denon's pupils widened to shrink the rim of brown about them. It wasn't as obvious as last year. He was losing status with whoever had promised to turn him when he died. A few more years like this and Denon wouldn't be much more than a shadow. And given his anger, I think he blamed me.

The Weres flanking him fell back at Denon's thick, casually moving fingers. The man eased closer with the same grace as before, but it lacked the threat it once had. That I wasn't trapped in a five-by-five cubicle probably helped.

"Leave," he said, his words smelling of baking soda toothpaste. "This is an I.S. matter."

Glenn stiffened, his hand nowhere near his gun. "Is that a refusal to let us examine the body?"

Denon moved his hard-muscled bulk gracefully in undeniable threat.

"Whoa, whoa, whoa!" I cried, then lurched back when Denon's arm shot out, his hand reaching for my raised arm.

Glenn moved, his squat stature stepping smoothly in front of me to grab Denon's hand. In a motion as sweet and smooth as melted chocolate, he twisted Denon's arm, levering the larger, muscle-bound man into submission. I blinked, watching with wide eyes. It was over already.

Bent at the waist, the living vampire shifted his weight. Glenn's grip tightened, and his feet scuffed for better traction. The Weres retreated, tense as Denon's neck reddened. Facing the ground and his arm held straight behind him, he was like a kitten being held by the scruff of his neck. Something popped, and Denon grunted.

Glenn leaned closer while holding the bigger man helpless. "You," the FIB detective said softly, "are a disgrace." He pushed on Denon's arm, and the man grunted again, sweat beading up on his shaved head. "Either crap or get off the pot, but this halfway nothing is giving the rest of us a bad name." Shoving him away, Glenn set his hand comfortably near the butt of his weapon.

Denon caught his balance and spun to face us. Hatred that Glenn had shown him up in front of his peons radiated from him. It was obvious his shoulder hurt, but he didn't touch it.

"I can handle my own battles, Glenn," I said dryly to distract Denon. I might survive one of Denon's retaliations, but Glenn was vulnerable without his gun and the element of surprise.

Glenn frowned. "He wasn't going to fight you fair," he said, handing me one of those zip-strips with a charmed core of silver that the I.S. used to keep ley line witches in custody.

My eyes went from the innocuous-seeming strip of plastic to the witch, then to Denon, scowling. "You little pissant," I said loudly. "What's the matter with you? All I want to do is look at the body. You got something to hide?" I took a step forward, and Glenn caught my arm. "If you've got a beef with me, let's do coffee and I'll explain things to you in little words," I said, jerking from Glenn. "Otherwise, get *out* of my way so we can do *our job*. Until murder has been ruled out, the FIB has as much right to look at the body as you do."

The little vein in Denon's forehead had popped, and the low-blood vamp gestured for everyone to fall back to the van. They moved slowly, hands in their pockets or fiddling with equipment. From out of sight, I heard the rustling of the FIB guys. The tension grew, not lessened, and I pressed my weight into the earth in case I had to move fast. Ceri's advice to avoid ley line magic flitted through me, but I sent a thought out for the nearest line anyway.

"You're a fool, Morgan," Denon said, his resonant voice vibrating in me though he stood ten feet away beside a tall tombstone. "Your search for the truth is going to kill you."

That sounded more like a threat than before, but he was walking away, I.S. personnel trailing behind him. At a loss, I tucked the zip-strip into my bag and looked for Jenks while Glenn organized the FIB personnel. Jenks was staying out of sight, though I'm sure he had seen the encounter. Slowly my pulse eased, soothed by the sounds of the insects and lapping water.

Glenn would have a hissy fit if I tried to look at the body before he was ready, and seeing the witch standing by himself, I smiled. It had been ages since I'd talked shop with anyone, and I missed it. He stared at me, and with that stellar response, I checked my impulse to go over.

"We're done here," Denon said loudly to the subordinate Weres.

"Leave the cleanup for the FIB." It was condescending, but Glenn made a pleased sound, making me think he didn't want to share his separate findings. Denon must have heard him, for when the officers headed for their vehicles, the living vampire grabbed the witch's arm and pulled him aside.

"I want you to stay," he said, and the man's eyes narrowed, the sun peeking through the leaves to make eerie shadows on him. "I want a report as to what the FIB does and finds."

"I'm not your lackey," the witch said, eyeing Denon's grip. "If you want my findings, submit a request at the Arcane's front desk like everyone else. Get your hand off me."

My eyebrows rose. *He works in the Arcane Division? My dad worked in the Arcane.* I looked him over with a new interest. Then I caught myself, cursing my idiotic attraction to the dangerous. God, I was a fool.

Denon let go of the witch's arm. Stiff and prideful, the big man headed for the van, gesturing to make the Were in the front passenger's seat move to the back. The door slammed shut, and shifting back and forth, the van worked its way onto the thin strip of pavement. The other I.S. vehicle followed, leaving us, the ambulance, and the witch—the latter having no way to get back to the I.S. tower that I could see. Man . . . I knew how he felt.

Sympathy rose high. Gathering my resolve, I headed over. *I'm being nice, not looking for a date,* I told myself, but he did have pretty blue eyes, and his hair was that soft curly brown that would feel oh so nice between my fingers.

From behind me came Glenn's hushed but impatient words, and the guys in lab coats descended on the Were like birds. Jenks dropped out of the oak tree, startling me with his harsh wing clatter when he landed on my shoulder. "Ah, Rache?"

"Can it wait?" I muttered. "I want to talk to this guy."

"You *have* a boyfriend," he warned. "And a girlfriend," he added, making me frown. "I know you. Don't overcompensate because of one lousy kiss."

"I'm just going to say hi," I said, stifling a swat at him. And it hadn't been a lousy kiss. It had been a pulse-pounding hell-of-a-kiss that had shocked me and left me breathless. I only had to figure out if the thrill had been an honest emotion stemming from Ivy or my shallowly reveling in the wicked thrill of being someone I really wasn't. My eyes dropped. *It matters. One will lead to hard questions about myself, the other will hurt Ivy. Leading her on just so I can find a thrill is really, really wrong, and I'm not going to do it.*

Forcing a smile, I halted before the guy. His I.S. badge said TOM BANSEN, and he used to have long hair, according to his picture. "I'm Rachel—" I started, extending my hand.

"I know. Excuse me."

It was terse, and, pushing past my extended hand, he went to stand over the FIB personnel and watch them take their data. Jenks snickered, and I stood there with my mouth hanging open. My eyes fell to my outfit. It wasn't *that* unprofessional. "I just wanted to say hi," I said, hurt.

"He doesn't smell as witchy as you do," Jenks said smugly. "But before your head swells up, if he works in the Arcane, he's classically trained and would flatten you. Remember Lee?"

My breath came and went, and I felt a stab of worry about this Friday. I had devoted my life to earth magic, and while not any less strong than ley line, it was slower. Ley line was flashy and dramatic, with a quick invocation and wider application. Demon magic mixed them both into something very fast, very powerful, and everlasting. Only a handful of people knew I could invoke demon magic, but the smut on my soul was easy to see. Perhaps that, along with my growing reputation that I dealt in demons, had him on edge.

I couldn't let the misunderstanding stand, so, ignoring Jenks's muttered dire predictions of hell and snowflakes, I sidled up alongside Tom. "Look, maybe we got off on the wrong foot," I said against the murmuring backdrop of the FIB conversation. "Do you need a ride anywhere when this is done?"

"No."

The denial was downright hostile, and the FIB guys crouched over the body looked up, eyes wide.

Tom turned and walked away. Pulse pounding, I took a step after him. "I don't deal with demons!" I said loudly, not caring what the FIB thought.

The young man retrieved a long coat hanging over a tombstone, draping it over his arm. "And you got that demon to testify how? That mark on your wrist is from what?"

I took a breath, then let it out. What could I say?

Looking justified, he walked off, leaving me surrounded by FIB personnel trying not to meet my eyes. *Damn it,* I thought, my jaw clenched and my stomach churning. I was used to fear and mistrust from humans, but from my own kind? Mood sour, I hitched up my shoulder bag. Tom had a cell phone pressed to his ear. He'd get a ride. Why had I even bothered?

Jenks cleared his throat, and I started, having forgotten he had been sitting on my shoulder the entire time. "Don't worry about it, Rache," he said in a small voice. "He was just scared."

"Thanks," I said. While I appreciated the thought, somehow it didn't make me feel much better. Tom hadn't looked scared. He had looked hostile.

From across the way, Glenn finished giving instructions to a young officer. Clapping him on the shoulder, he headed in my direction, the gleam back in his eyes and his posture holding a repressed excitement. "Ready to take a look?" he said, his thick hands rubbing together.

I glanced at the dead Were, nose wrinkling. "What about the footies?" I said dryly, remembering the last time I was at one of his precious crime scenes.

He shook his head, eyes on the body. "They fouled the site," he said, his disgust at the I.S.'s techniques clear. "Apart from throwing up on the victim, you can't make it any worse."

"Gee, thanks," I said, jumping when his hand hit my shoulder companionably. I smiled at him so he knew it wasn't unwelcome, just surprising, and he squinted.

"Don't let it get to you," the FIB detective said softly, his dark expressive eyes going to the witch's distant silhouette among the tombstones. "We know you're a good woman."

"Thanks," I said, exhaling to let the hurt go. *What do I care what one witch thinks anyway? Even if he is cute?*

From my ear Jenks snickered. "Awwww, you two are so sweet, I could fart fairy balls."

Tossing my hair to make him fly away, I turned my attention downward. The men at the body had finished their preliminary look and moved off, loudly discussing how long the corpse had been here. It couldn't have been more than since morning; the smell wasn't bad, and there was no tissue damage from decay or flies yet. And yesterday had been hot.

My thoughts flashed back to a gutted deer carcass I'd found in the woods this spring, and, steadying myself, I crouched beside Glenn. I was glad that my nose wasn't as sensitive as Jenks's. The pixy looked positively green. After letting him hover uncertainly for a moment, I swung my hair out of the way in invitation, and he immediately landed on my shoulder. His warm hands gripped my ear, and he took dramatic breath after noisy breath, complaining about the reek of alcohol that my perfume used to carry the orange scent. Glenn glanced at us as if wondering what the hell we were on about. I turned my attention downward.

Mrs. Sarong's personal aide made a very powerful wolf, and to think that the person in fur before me had committed suicide was ludicrous. He had the silky black hair most Weres did, his lips pulled back to show teeth whiter than a show dog's, now stained with his own blood. That his bowels had released somewhere else was proof to me that the body had been dumped. A bad feeling rose as Denon's words echoed in my memory. The I.S. was covering something up, and with me helping the FIB, it was coming out. Someone wasn't going to be happy about that.

Maybe I should just walk away.

"He didn't die here," I said softly, settling in more firmly where I crouched.

"I agree." Glenn shifted uncomfortably. "He was identified from an ear tattoo, and it's only been about twelve hours that he's not been accounted for. The first victim had been missing for twice that."

Damn, I thought, feeling a chill. Someone was getting serious.

Glenn picked up a foreleg and rubbed a thumb against the hair. "This has been cleaned."

Jenks flitted down, his tiny feet hovering just above the dull nails, almost as long as he was tall. "It smells like alcohol," he said, hands on his hips as he slowly rose. "I'd bet my back acres that he had medical tape on him like that secretary."

My eyes met Glenn's, and he set the Were's foot down. Without finding the tape, this speculation didn't mean squat. From the blood on his teeth, it looked likely that the leg wound he'd bled himself out from was self-inflicted, but now I wondered if "looked" was the key word. It had been given more succinctly than in Mrs. Sarong's secretary's case, as if someone were gaining experience. Blood matted his hindquarters and soaked the ground. It was probably Were blood, but I doubted the blood on his fur and the blood on the ground was from the same person.

"Jenks, any needle marks?" I questioned, and his wings hummed to life. He hovered over the ruined leg for a moment, then landed on Glenn's offered hand.

"I can't say. There's too much hair. I can go with you to the morgue if you want," he offered to Glenn, and the man grunted an affirmative.

Okay, it's only a matter of time before the two crimes are linked. "Think it's worth flossing his teeth?" I asked, remembering the medical tape in the woman's teeth.

It was Glenn's turn to shake his head. "No, I'm guessing the body was cleaned before it was dumped." A heavy sigh came from him, and he stood. Jenks took flight to land on the tombstone behind the Were. I tried to memorize the name on it, wondering if it might be important. Crap, I wasn't a detective. How would I know what was important or not?

"Proving he's been moved isn't a problem," Glenn said from above me. "It's tying this one to Mr. Ray's secretary that's the problem. Maybe after we get him turned back, he might have pressure or needle marks."

I rose as well, noticing that whoever had dumped the body had taken the time to press the Were's paws into the grass to get them dirty, but it was obviously surface dirt. His nails were as clean as if he'd been working at a desk the last twelve hours. Or strapped to a medical gurney.

"At the very least, you can get a proper necropsy," I offered. "The body has been moved. The I.S. has to admit that murder is a possibility. You'll find a link to Mr. Ray's secretary."

"And it might give the I.S. time to fabricate whatever evidence they want," Glenn said bitterly, pulling a pack of wipes out from a breast pocket and handing me one.

I hadn't touched the body, but I took it since Glenn obviously felt I should. "He'll have needle marks. Someone killed him. I mean, how do you tear yourself up enough to kill yourself but leave your feet clean and smelling of alcohol?"

Glenn's eyes were on the Were. "I have to prove it, Rachel."

I shrugged, wanting to get home and shower before my meeting with Mr. Ray. Prove it, shmove it. That wasn't my job. Just point me at someone to bring in and I'm there. "If we can find out who is doing it, we'll have a better idea how to find the proof," I said, but I wouldn't meet his eyes. I had a bad feeling the *why* they'd been killed was sitting in my freezer, and the *who* was a short list of Cincy's finest: Piscary, Trent, Mr. Ray, and Mrs. Sarong. I think I could cross Newt off the list. She wouldn't bother to cover anything up.

"Do you need me anymore?" I said, handing the used wipe back to him.

Glenn's eyes had lost their sparkle and were tired again. "No. Thank you."

"Why did you have me come out here, then?" I chided him. "I didn't do a flipping thing."

His dark neck reddened, and I followed him to the FIB vehicle. Behind us was the chatter of the ambulance guys getting to their feet to move the body to the city morgue. "I wanted to see Denon's reaction to you," he muttered.

"You got me out here because you wanted to see Denon's reaction?" I exclaimed, and several heads turned. The FIB officers were smiling like it was a joke—and I was the butt of it.

Inclining his head in amusement, Glenn took my arm. "Cut me some slack, Rachel," he said. "You saw him in the morgue. He didn't want you there and was afraid you'd see something us poor humans would miss. That points to obstruction of justice. Someone is looking for that statue you have, and you're damned lucky they aren't looking at you. Is it still in the mail system?"

I nodded, thinking it would be a mistake to do otherwise. Glenn's grip tightened as he walked us forward. "I could force you to give it to me," he said.

Ticked, I jerked away from him and stopped. "I brought that jar of salsa you wanted," I said, almost loud enough for the surrounding FIB officers to hear, and the man went gray. It wasn't my threat of withholding it but that I'd make public he liked tomatoes. Yeah, it was that bad.

"That's low," Glenn said, his eyes coming back to mine.

"Then find someone else to pimp your ketchup," I said, guilt making me flush.

Jenks dropped from the trees, startling the FIB officer. "Rache," the pixy said, giving no indication of what he thought of my blackmail, "I'll get you home, then go to the morgue. I want to see if the body has needle marks. I can be back before you go to talk to Mr. Ray."

I might have to be at the church alone with Ivy, was my first thought. "Sounds good," I said, then feeling bad, I whispered to Glenn, "I was serious about the salsa. You want it now?"

He tightened his jaw, clearly angry, and Jenks laughed. "Give it up, you lousy cookie," the pixy cajoled. "You have no right to the focus, and you know it."

"It's jalapeño," I coaxed. "Burn your freaking eyeballs out of their sockets."

Glenn's irate look faltered, and when Jenks nodded in encouragement, Glenn licked his lips. "Jalapeño?" he murmured, his focus blurring.

"A gallon," I said, feeling the thrill of the deal. "Do you have any zip-strips?"

Glenn's awareness abruptly cleared. "I'm working on them, but it's going to take some time. Do you want a pair of cuffs in the meanwhile?"

"Sure," I said, though they wouldn't stop a ley line witch. "I lost the first pair you gave me in the ever-after." Man . . . I missed my old cuffs with the charms and everything. Maybe I could put the right spells into the decorative charms Kisten had given me with my bracelet. I'd have to ask what kind of metal they were.

Glenn looked guilty as he scanned the people behind me collecting data. "I need a few days," he said, his lips barely moving as he slipped me his cuffs. "Can you hold on to it for me?"

I nodded as I tucked the sliding metal in my bag, then turned my attention to Jenks. "Ready?"

The pixy rose up. "See you at the car." His wings blurred, and then he was gone, heading across the cemetery at head height, dodging tombstones like a hummingbird on a mission.

Glenn's lips pressed, and, seeing a coming argument, I warmed. "Jenks is running vanguard for me," I said, tossing my hair behind my shoulder. "We got it covered." *I have to get to that class. This is really getting old.*

"Rachel?"

I halted my motion to leave, turning to arch my eyebrows at him.

"Take it easy," he said, a hand in the air in surrender. "Call me if you need bail."

My smile deepened. "Thanks, Glenn," I said, glad the ugly scene about the focus had been averted. "I'm going to class tonight. Really."

"Do that," he said, then turned back to his team, calling for some guy named Parker.

I felt funny walking across the grass between the grave markers to the car, plodding in Jenks's lightning-fast wake. My steps were small as I trudged up the hill, my head down to look for those flat markers. I swung my bag around and dug for my zebra-striped car key, but when I came around the corner of the large marker my car was behind, I stopped dead in my tracks.

Someone was messing with my backseat.

SIXTEEN

"Hey!" I said belligerently, and the jeans-clad man looked up from where he'd been leaning into the backseat, messing with Glenn's salsa. It was Tom, and my jaw dropped. "What are you doing?" I came forward, wobbling on one of those flush grave markers.

Tom stepped from the car, and I halted before him, puffing. There was a hint of anger and a lot of disdain in his blue eyes. I was looking into the sun to see him, and it ticked me off.

"I've been asked to talk to you," he said, and I snickered. *Now he wants to talk?* He was standing before my car, though, and didn't look like he was going to move without a little encouragement. But when I saw Jenks unconscious on the dash with his dragonfly wings splayed out in the sun, I was more than ready to apply said encouragement.

My pulse leapt, fueled by anger and fear. "What did you do to Jenks?"

The man started at the threat in my voice. Moving back a step, he almost got out of the way. "I didn't want him to overhear our conversation."

My stomach clenched in fear. "You knocked him out? You knocked Jenks out to get rid of him?" I took a step forward, and Tom retreated. "You son of a bastard."

Yeah, I was mixing my phrases, but I was really mad.

Eyes wide in surprise, Tom took another step back.

"He's a person, you know!" I said, my face hot. "He would have left if you asked." Worried, I leaned into my car and carefully edged Jenks into my palm before his wings burned from the hot dash. His small body was limp and felt far too light. I remembered him carrying me when I'd been weak from blood loss, and a panicked fear slid through me. Horror joined it when I saw that he was bleeding. "What did you do?" I exclaimed. "He's bleeding from his ears!"

The ley line witch stood before me, three feet back with his hands behind him. "Rachel Morgan, I would like to ask—"

Tension pulling tight through me, I held Jenks close. "What did you do to Jenks! Do you know how dangerous it is for a pixy to lose blood?"

"Ms. Morgan," Tom interrupted, "this is more important than your backup."

I couldn't seem to get enough air. "He is my friend!" I exclaimed. "He's not a tissue!"

I stepped forward, and Tom retreated. "Don't touch me," he warned.

But I got in his face, shouting, "I care more about this pixy's hang-nail than your whole stinking life, you sanctimonious little prick. What did you do to him?"

"Stay back," he said, backing away even farther with his hands in front of him.

"I'll touch my foot to your face if you don't take off that spell!" With Jenks held carefully to my middle in my cupped hand, I took another threatening step. The hair on my arms pricked when Tom tapped a line, and before he could say or do anything, I lunged forward, betting he was setting a circle. A circle can't form through a person coated in an aura but will slide to either the front or the back of him or her. I had a fifty-fifty chance. I would either make it into his circle or crack my nose open running into it as Minias had.

I jolted, the electric taste of tinfoil stabbing through my teeth. Gasping, I hunched over Jenks. Tom's power iced through me, and for an instant the world went black. My chi filled from him to me in an eerie sensation of wrongness. It overflowed, the excess running to spindle in my mind, rolling the power of the line into storage. I jerked, trying to break the connection.

It snapped with a twang that felt so sharp it had to be audible. I opened my eyes, finding Tom staring at me. I was inside his circle. It wasn't that big either.

The witch's eyes narrowed. His fingers moved, and I shot my fist out, smacking him in the gut. *Good going, Rachel,* I thought, seeing the breath explode from him as he fell, his butt landing on the grass and his back hitting the wall of the circle. He'd probably file charges for assault now, but he *had* threatened me with ley line magic first.

"You can tell Denon he can shove his falsics up his ass," I said, feeling that something was wrong but unable to stop and think about it. "He can't scare me off this case!" I remembered my splat gun in my bag—somehow still on my shoulder—but it would look really stupid if I hit him with blanks. Besides, it was hard to do anything with Jenks in my hand.

"Not Denon," the witch gasped, his face red as he tried to catch his breath.

I drew back, the strength of his circle humming over my head. He wasn't speaking for the I.S.? *What in hell is going on?*

I tugged my shirt to cover my middle, suddenly wary. Tom looked at me from the ground with his back pushed against the circle, his pained grimace making me retreat a step so he could stand. Looking shaken, stirred, and ticked, the witch got to his feet and brushed the grass clippings off. But then his face went still, and he looked at the arch of everafter over him. That sensation of *wrongness* in me strengthened, and I followed his gaze to the ugly blackness.

His circle hadn't fallen when I pushed him into it. That wasn't right.

"You took it," Tom whispered, his eyes tracking the come-and-go, knifelike slices of gold glimmering through the demon smut. "You took my circle!"

My gaze jerked to the arc of power over our heads in fearful recognition. It was my aura reflected there, not his. *I took his circle?* Newt had taken Ceri's, but it had required some effort. I'd simply walked into this one. That was it, I mused. It had been still forming and vulnerable.

Frightened, he backed up until he hit the slice of ever-after. "They told me you were an earth witch. Damn it, you took my circle. I never would have," he stammered, his cheeks pale. "I mean . . . God, you must think I'm an idiot for trying to best you."

Scared at how fast he had gone from cocky to frightened, I said, "Don't worry about it."

Tom's attention ran over the inside of the bubble. "I didn't mean to hurt your pixy," he said, watching Jenks, still cupped in my hand. "He's fine. I stunned him with a high frequency. He'll wake up in an hour. I didn't know he was important to you."

My pulse had yet to settle, and I didn't like how fast his attitude had changed. I'd be lying if I didn't admit that it was sort of flattering, though. At the very least, it had calmed my anger. I mean, how can you be angry at someone who thinks you're a stronger witch than he is?

"I didn't mean to take your circle, okay?" I said. Uneasy, I touched the circle I hadn't invoked, shivering when it broke and the energy someone else had tapped flowed through me and away. I was too distracted to unspindle the excess in my head, so I let it stay.

Tom swayed to catch his balance when the circle fell. He was clearly glad to be out of the circle, but he was still white under his brown hair.

"What did you want anyway?" I said, feeling Jenks's weight light in my palm.

"I . . ." Hesitating, he took a deep breath. "You have experience in summoning demons," he said, and I cringed. "My superiors would like me to extend an invitation to you."

Disgusted, I let my bag fall from my shoulder. Catching the strap in my hand, I threw it into the backseat. He had said he wasn't working under Denon, but I didn't want to be contracted out to the Arcane either. Reaching for the door handle, I muttered, "I don't work for the I.S. in any capacity, so forget it."

"This isn't from the I.S.—this is a private group."

My fingers slipped from the handle, and I stood with my back to him—thinking. The sun was hot—it would probably melt the birthday candles still in my shoulder bag—and I turned to put Jenks in the shade. Hip cocked, I sent my eyes over Tom's comfortable-looking shoes, his new jeans, his tucked-in dress shirt, and his hair drifting in the slight breeze. He was young, but not inexperienced. Powerful, but I had surprised him. He was working in the I.S. Arcane Division yet was speaking for someone else? That didn't sound good.

"This is about summoning demons, isn't it?" I said, and he nodded, too fresh-faced to look sage but trying for it anyway. I leaned against my car, amazed at how the brightest-looking people did the dumbest things. "Despite what you've heard, I don't summon demons. They just show up to irritate the hell out of me. I don't twist demon curses."

Anymore. "You couldn't pay me enough to twist one for you. So whatever problem your friends have, you can take it somewhere else."

"It's not illegal to summon demons," Tom said belligerently.

"No, but it's stupid." I reached for the door again, pulling when Tom stepped forward and put his hand on mine. I yanked out of his reach, ticked. Damn it, he was a demon practitioner.

"Rachel Morgan, wait. I can't tell them you didn't even listen."

I wasn't going to hit him again, but a yelling redhead could usually drive the most persistent person away. I took a breath, then hesitated. This wasn't about the focus, was it?

Exhaling, I eyed him. My gaze fell to Jenks, my hand starting to ache from holding that same stiff position, then back to Tom. "Are you the ones killing the Weres?" I asked flat out.

Tom's mouth dropped open in a surprise so genuine I had to believe it was real. "We thought you were," he said, and I didn't know which was more disturbing, that they thought I was capable of murder or that they thought I was capable of murder and wanted me to join them.

"Me?" I said, shifting my weight to my other foot. "What for? I've never killed anyone in my life!" *Let a demon take them instead of me but never killed them. Ah, except for Peter. But he wanted to die.* Feeling guilty, I searched the horizon.

The tips of Tom's ears went red in embarrassment. "The inner circle has extended an invitation," he said, struggling to regain my attention. "They request that you join them."

I'll just bet. "Excuse me," I said angrily. "Get your hand *off* my car."

Tom removed his hand, and I tugged the handle up. He backed up when I got in and settled into the sun-warmed leather seats. This was great. Just freaking great. A wacko fringe organization wanted me as a new recruit. Slamming the door shut, I held Jenks in my cupped palm and dug the box of tissues out of the console. I set it on my lap and carefully laid him in it. Seeing him there motionless, a feeling of panic slid through me and was gone. If he wasn't okay, Matalina would be devastated, and I would be really pissed.

The powerful practitioner of black ley line magic in jeans and sunglasses who could probably turn my blood to sludge wanted me in his little group. Even worse, he seemed to be an underling. Anger cresting,

I looked at Tom squinting in the sun, then with a small thought, willed my second sight into focus to check his aura. It was edged in a faint shimmer of black.

"Your aura is dirty," I said, my motions sharp as I buckled myself in and let my second sight drop before I saw something I didn't want to; I *was* in a graveyard.

Face red, he boldly said, "My position in the I.S. prohibits me from working with demons as much as I'd like. But I'm committed to the cause and am contributing in other ways."

Oh, my God. He's apologizing for not having more smut on his soul?

Tom misread my expression, his smooth brow tightening in anger. "My cloak may be light, but it serves a purpose. I can move unseen where those more versed in the dark arts can't." He stepped closer. "That's why we want you, Rachel Morgan. You openly consort with demons. Your cloak is as black as anyone's in the inner circle, and yet you're not afraid to walk proud and unrepentant. Even the I.S. can't touch you."

Stretching, I reached between the seats and got my bag. *Right. And that's why I don't have a license?* "And because of that, your little club thinks I'm worthy of them?" I said, digging for my keys. My fingers touched my splat gun, and I toyed with the idea of plugging him with a few defunct earth charms just to see him run away.

"It's not a club," Tom said, clearly insulted. "It's a tradition of witches that stretches back to the beginning of the crossing of the ley lines. A glorious lineage of secrecy and power, pushing the frontiers of our existence."

Yada-yada-yada . . . It had taken on the cadence of empty rhetoric. Wondering if the I.S. knew they had a cultist on their payroll, I jammed the key into the ignition. "You summon demons?"

Tom's stance became defensive. "We explore options that other witches are too timid to venture. And we think you are—"

"Let me guess. I've been found worthy to join your cause and be privy to the inner-sanctum secrets that have been passed down from master to student for two millennia."

Okay, maybe that had been a little sarcastic, but Jenks wasn't moving, and I was worried. Tom was trying to come up with something, and I started my car. The engine rumbled to life under me, the sound of security. Hot, I fiddled with the air conditioner though the top was open. The breeze from the vents turned cool, and I relished the tickling of the curls against my face.

Done with him, I jammed the car into first. Tom put his hand on the car, his fingers going white in their grip as his words stumbled over themselves. "Rachel Morgan, you have done great things, survived multiple demon attacks, but no one gives you your due. With us you can find the honor and respect you have earned."

His flattery meant nothing, and I angled a vent until Jenks's hair shifted. "I survived by luck and my friends. I shouldn't be honored. I ought to be committed for uncommon idiocy."

I reached for the gearshift, and he pressed closer. "You took my circle," he stated.

"Because I stepped into it while it was forming! It was a one-in-a-million shot of timing!" Worry pinched his eyes that I was leaving, and I hesitated. "Do yourself and your mother a favor," I said. "Run away. Tell your boss that I put a spell on you to make you unable to continue your great work. Forget you ever heard of them, or me, and run as fast and far away as you can, because if you play with demons, they will either kill you or take you as their familiar, and believe me, you want the former. And get your hands *off my car!*"

Tom took his hand away, but there was a new determination in his eyes. "You won't survive on your own," he warned. "Don't be greedy. Share what you've learned along with sharing the danger of summoning them. It takes a quorum of witches to control a demon."

"Then it's a good thing I'm not trying to."

"Rachel Morgan . . ."

A sound of exasperation came from me. "No!" I shouted. "And stop calling me Rachel Morgan. I'm Rachel, or Ms. Morgan. Only demons use every single damned name that a person is known by. My answer is no. No lifelines, no calling my best friend. That's my final answer. I do not deal with demons. I do not *want* to deal with demons. Go back and tell your architect that I am flattered for the offer but that I work alone."

His eyes slid to Jenks in my lap, and I scowled. "Jenks is family," I said darkly. "And if you ever hurt my family again, you and your little sorry-ass circle will find out there are worse things than demons to piss off."

"The I.S. won't help you," he said, backing up when I revved the engine and threatened to run over his foot. "They're a vamp-run institution controlled by self-minded individuals, not those seeking to elevate a closed mind."

Pulse pounding, I said, "For once we agree, but I wasn't talking about the I.S. I was talking about me." Foot letting up on the clutch, I pulled forward. I wanted to tear out of there like Ivy's last blind date, but in respect for the dead, I had to be content with a slow, careful crawl. I glanced at Jenks to be sure the jostling hadn't shifted him to snap a wing with his bodyweight.

Eyes flicking from him to the narrow road, I stewed, not just about Jenks but about Tom's request. It was never good to be offered a place in a wacko organization, especially when you tell them to shove their high ideals and their glorious work.

There was a soft pull on my chi, and my gaze hit the rearview mirror. My breath caught, and I almost drove right off the pavement when Tom turned his back on me and vanished.

Holy crap, he jumped to a line. Worried, I adjusted my grip on the wheel, alternating my focus from the road to where he had been as if it had been a mistake. He was good enough to use the lines to travel, and he was only a minor member?

Damn, who exactly had I just insulted?

SEVENTEEN

David's car windows were down, and the cool damp of the late afternoon felt good lifting through my hair. The complex scent of Were mixed with the smell of the riverfront, and I snuck a glance at David across the short width of his sports car. He had on his long leather duster and matching hat, and though he would probably be more comfortable with the air on, he hadn't suggested it—Jenks was on my big hoop earring, and quick temperature changes wreaked havoc with his small body mass. It was easier to sweat a little than listen to Jenks bitch about being cold. We were almost to Piscary's anyway.

Upon coming home from Spring Grove, I'd found a second message on the machine, the red light blinking like a ticking bomb. My first thought that it might be Ivy proved false. It was Mrs. Sarong's new aide. The owner of the Howlers wanted to meet with me, too. And seeing that the I.S. was blowing off the murder of her aide as a suicide, it was probable she wanted me to find out who had done it. Liking the idea of catching three paychecks with one job, I changed the location of my meeting with Mr. Simon Ray to a neutral place, then agreed to meet Mrs. Sarong at the same time. If nothing else, I'd find out if they were killing each other.

The tension in David's hands on the wheel increased as he made a right turn into the almost-deserted lot at Piscary's. The two-story bar/tavern was closed until five, when it opened for the Inderland lunch hour, and I thought it made the perfect neutral ground. Kisten had set new hours shortly after they'd lost their Mixed Public License—MPL for short—and went to an all-vamp clientele. The bar would be empty but for Kisten and a few waitstaff prepping for the day. Besides, doing this where Kisten could step in if needed was just good planning.

Nervous, I checked to see that I had my bag with my charms and splat gun, a fresh batch of sleepy-time potions in the hopper. David parked smoothly in an outer spot where he wouldn't have to back up to leave. Saying nothing, he popped the trunk and got out while I sat in the car and turned my phone to vibrate. It had been a very quiet ride over here; David's mind was clearly on his girlfriends, both living and dead.

I hadn't been keen on his coming with me, but he did have a car, and I was meeting with two alphas of Cincy's more prominent packs. Jenks said David had a right to be there as my alpha, and I trusted his judgment. Besides, I had worked with David before. Though distracted, he was better at reacting to violence than his easygoing looks would indicate.

"Ready, Jenks?" I whispered as David thunked the trunk shut.

"Soon as you get your lily-white witch ass outta this car," Jenks said sarcastically.

Ignoring that, I dropped my phone into my bag and got out. I scanned the lot, enjoying the cooler air off the river that set a few strands of my hair to drift. Kisten's boat was at the quay, and I started to the front door with a slow pace. David fell into step beside me, his eyes seeing everything from under his worn brown leather hat. "What was in the trunk?" I asked, and my eyes widened when he opened his coat and let me glimpse a big-ass rifle.

"I know these people," he said, his expression going hard. "We handle their insurance."

Oka-a-a-ay, I thought, hoping I wouldn't have to pull the little red splat gun tucked in my bag. They'd laugh themselves silly. Until the first of them dropped, that is.

There was an unfamiliar black Jag and an H2 pulled up to the front, clearly not belonging to the waitstaff. Someone had beaten us here, despite my efforts to be the first and take the high ground. Mr. Ray, I'd be willing to bet, as I credited Mrs. Sarong with more class than to cart her people around in a yellow Hummer—as cool as that appeared to be.

I glanced back at David's sports car, missing the freedom to jump into my red convertible and go. A sigh moved through me.

"Whatsa matter, Rache?" Jenks asked, still on my shoulder and remarkably quiet.

"I need to work on my image," I muttered, pulling up the waistband of my leather pants and trying to keep up with David's long strides. Leather was my fabric of choice when I was on a run; if I went sliding on the pavement, I didn't want to leave a skin graft. I had on a matching biker's cap with the Harley logo, and my vamp-made boots that kept my steps silent. My black leather jacket was too hot, and though it ruined the look, I removed it to leave only my chemise.

David had asked to take a few days off from work to sort himself out and had opted for jeans and a cotton tuck-in shirt instead of his business suit. The duster, the worn hat pulled over his brooding eyes, and his wavy black hair in a ponytail made him look like Van Helsing. His mood bordered on depressed—his few wrinkles deep and his brow etched with lines. His pace slow, he took almost a step and a half of mine to make it appear he was floating. He was clean-shaven, and his squinting eased when the sun turned to the cool shadow of the restaurant's canopy.

Maybe my image is just fine. . . .

I reached for the door handle, ignoring the city ordinance warning that the establishment had no MPL. It was before business hours, and even so, I didn't have to worry. I'd been over here lots of times with Kisten. No one had bothered me yet.

David's suntanned hand settled on mine atop the handle. "A female alpha doesn't open doors," he said, and realizing he was going to play this to the hilt, I let go. Effortlessly he opened the door and held it for me. Past him, the bar was quiet, the house lights down and everything gray and soothing. I took my glasses off as I entered and dropped them into my bag.

"Ms. Morgan!" a familiar voice called the instant my feet passed the threshold. It was Steve, Kisten's number-one guy, who ran the bar when he was out, and I smiled when the bear of a man did a single-armed vault over the bar to come and give me his traditional hug.

Jenks took off with a yelp, but my eyes closed as I returned Steve's embrace, pulling his luscious scent of incense and vamp pheromones deep into me. God, he smelled good. Almost as good as Kisten. "Hi, Steve," I said, feeling tingles at my vamp scar and putting space between us. "How ticked is Kisten that I asked to borrow the bar for a few hours?"

Kisten's assistant manager/bouncer gave me a final squeeze and let go. "Not at all," he said, a devious glint in his eyes. They were dilated more than the low light warranted, and his toothy smile probably owed to the fact that he knew I was enjoying breathing him in. "He's looking forward to taking the rental fee for the back room out of your hide."

"I'll bet," I said dryly, my hands falling to my sides. "Ah, this is David, my alpha," I said, remembering the man behind me. "And you know Jenks."

David leaned forward, his hand extended and the hem of his duster furling. "Hue," David said, his face melancholy. "David Hue. It's good to meet you."

Steve's gaze flicked from him to me and back again, silently remarking on David's depression. "It's a pleasure to meet you, Mr. Hue," the vampire said earnestly. "I heard that Rachel had taken up a pack. It's the rare man who can get her to let him put a claim on her."

"Hey!" I exclaimed, swatting Steve's shoulder with the back of my hand. But Steve caught it, his eyes flashing black as he kissed the tips of my fingers.

I forgot what I was going to yell at him when the hard coolness of his teeth grazed my skin. A shiver lifted through me, and I blinked, his eyes fixed on me from under his lowered brow. "Stop that," I said, and drew away.

Steve smiled at me like I was his little sister, and David pulled out of his funk to stare at me. "Mr. Ray is here already," the vamp said. "He's in the back with six men, waiting for you."

Six men? Why did he bring that many? He doesn't know Mrs. Sarong is coming, does he? "Thanks," I said, setting my coat on the bar when Steve started drifting away. "You mind if we wait here until Mrs. Sarong arrives?"

"Not at all." He pulled a stool out from the bar for me. "What can I get you and Mr. Hue?" He glanced at the melancholy Were. "I won't tell the I.S. if you don't."

David leaned against the bar. His brown eyes were everywhere, and he looked like a gunslinger coming in from the prairie. "Water, please," he said, not aware I was watching him. It must be tearing him apart, having caused those women's deaths, even if indirectly.

"Iced tea?" I said, hot in all my leather, then immediately regretted it. I was going to meet with two of Cincy's most powerful individuals, and I would be sucking down an iced tea when I did it? God! No wonder no one took me seriously.

I started to change it to a glass of wine, a beer, anything . . . but Steve was gone. The clatter of pixy wings brought my hand up in invitation, and Jenks landed on it, his wings shimmering with exertion. "The bar looks good," he said, tossing his bangs out of the way. "No charms but for the usual. I'm going to listen in on Mr. Ray if that's okay with you."

My head bobbed. "Thanks, Jenks. That'd be great."

Jenks touched his red cap in salute. "You got it. I'll be back when you need me."

The draft from his wings was a brief flash of cool, and he was gone.

From the far end of the bar, Steve headed our way, the two drinks in his big hands. He set them before us, then slipped into the kitchen, the double doors silently swinging closed.

David encircled his glass of water with one hand. Not drinking, he hunched over the bar and brooded. A murmur of conversation came from the kitchen, and my gaze went over the cool, dusky room, taking in the changes since Kisten had assumed a closer management.

The downstairs was now tight with a multitude of smaller tables where patrons could get a quick bite rather than a meal. Ah . . . no pun intended. Shortly after Piscary had been incarcerated, the kitchen made a shift from the gourmet cuisine for which Pizza Piscary's was known to bar food, but pizza was still served.

There was a large round table between the foot of the wide stairway and the kitchen. That was where Kisten spent most nights when he was working, somewhere he could keep an eye on everything without appearing to. The upstairs was a dance floor now, complete with a DJ nest, disco ball, and light display. I didn't go up there when they were in full swing; the pheromones of several hundred vampires would hit me as pleasantly and as fast as chugging a six-pack.

Against the odds, Kisten had turned losing their MPL into an asset;

Piscary's was the only reputable place in Cincy where a vampire could relax without having to live up to anyone else's ideas of reserved behavior and vampiric standards. Even shadows weren't allowed. I was the only nonvamp let past the door—seeing as I had downed Piscary, then let the bastard live—and I was honored they let me see them as they wanted to be. The living ones partied with frightening abandon, trying to forget that they were destined to lose their souls, and the undead tried to remember what it was like to have one, almost seeming to find it while surrounded by such an outpouring of energy. Anyone coming in looking for a quick blood fix was escorted out. Blood didn't have a place in the fantasy they sought.

My gaze ran over the pictures lining the walls just under the ceiling, and I started when I found the blurry shot of me, Nick, and Ivy on her bike. It was fuzzy, but you could still tell there were a rat and a mink standing on the gas tank. Warming, I lifted my iced tea to sprinkle some salt on my napkin.

"Is that a spell?" David asked, eyes going to the kitchen doors when someone laughed.

I shook my head. "It's so the paper doesn't stick to the bottom of the glass and make me look like more of a dork than I already am."

The Were pulled his head up from his melancholy hunch. "Rachel, you're wearing leather and sitting at a vamp bar. You could have a pink slushy with an umbrella in your hand and still impress the hell out of most people."

My exhalation was long and slow. "Yeah, but alphas aren't most people."

"You'll be fine. You're the alpha female for my pack, remember?" His gaze went behind me. "Afternoon, Kisten," he said, and I turned, smiling when I recognized the scent of incense and leather.

"Thanks, Mr. Peabody," the vampire said sourly, his attempt to startle me clearly ruined.

"Hi, Kist," I said, curving an arm about his waist and drawing him closer. He was wearing dark pants and a red silk shirt—his usual casual clothes. "Thanks for letting me borrow your club," I added, tugging at him suggestively. Damn, I could really have used some alone time with him this Friday. The memory of Ivy's kiss intruded, then vanished.

His eyes dilated, and my pulse increased despite my efforts. A smile hovered over his features, and his look became more intent. "You can borrow a back room anytime," he said, his hand finding my waist with a comfortable familiarity before he leaned in for a quick kiss hello.

He was aiming at my lips, but, conscious of David, I turned and he got the corner of my mouth instead. His low growl of bother sent a spike of desire unexpectedly through me. He wasn't truly upset—more like amused—and I wondered if playing hard to get one night might be extremely fun. Or deadly.

"I'm . . . ah, sorry for postponing our date," I said when he leaned back, becoming flustered when he'd lingered a moment too long. "Let me know when you have another night free, and I'll get the reservation changed."

David gave Kisten an up-and-down look, then took his drink and moseyed down the bar to stare at the pictures. Blue eyes gazing up at the ceiling, Kisten ran a hand through his hair to leave it attractively tousled. "Oh," he teased, leaning against the bar to look alluring and in control. "My witch has enough clout to snag a reservation at the Tower whenever she wants." He held a hand to his chest. "My masculine pride is wounded. I had to make mine three months ago."

"It's not me," I said, pushing at his shoulder, but not hard enough to move him. "Trent is doing it. It was part of the deal that I work his wedding."

"Doesn't matter," he said. "The point is that it's done, and it was done—for you."

Not knowing what to say, I drank my tea. The melting ice shifted, and I almost got a lapful of it. "I'm really sorry," I said again, shaking the glass to get the ice to move. "I wouldn't have said yes to Trent, but he waved enough money at me to get the church resanctified," I finished sourly. My gaze went distant as I wondered if I should tell him about my encounter with Ivy this morning, then decided against it. Maybe later, when we had more time.

Kisten bent to reach over the bar, and, realizing I was ogling him, I put my attention back on my drink and off his tight butt. Crap, the man knew how to dress to showcase himself.

"Forget it," he said when he settled himself on the stool beside me, a bowl of almonds in his hands. "Someday I'm going to have to cancel on you because of business, and then . . ." He popped a nut into his mouth and crunched through it. ". . . you're going to have to take it gracefully and not be a spastic girlfriend."

"Spastic girlfriend?" I huffed, realizing that his quick acceptance came from self-preservation, not understanding. Mildly ticked, I swiveled my stool, my fingers on my cold glass.

With a little hop as if having decided something, Kisten put a hand on my knee to stop my motion. "You want to come over tonight for dinner?" he said. As he leaned closer, his hair brushed against mine. "I've got to work tonight, but Steve can handle everything, and we can eat on my boat. No one will bother us unless it involves blood."

His shoulder was touching mine as I sat facing the bar, and his hand had curved around my back, his fingers playing with the hair over my left ear. My pulse quickened, and I was having a hard time remembering what I was upset about. His hand dropped lower, and his breath came and went upon my neck. The scar there didn't show anymore—lost under my perfect skin—but the vamp saliva the demon had pumped into me was still there.

"I've got something I'm dying to give you for your birthday," he said, his low voice heavy with intent. "If I'm not going to see you Friday, I want to give it to you . . . *now.*"

The last word was almost a demand, and I shivered at the tension that pinged through me. Straightening, I licked my lips, turning to tuck my head beside his. I couldn't help but remember Ivy's kiss, and then I quashed the thought. "God, that feels good," I whispered.

"Mmmm." Kisten's touch on my neck took on the hints of massage, promising more than dinner. My breath grew fast, and I intentionally pulled in his scent. I didn't care that he was throwing off pheromones to lure me into making myself vulnerable. It felt too damn good, and I trusted him to not break my skin, substituting sex in place of his need for blood.

Fingertips playing with the hair above his neck, my shoulders relaxed and my gut tightened in anticipation. My unclaimed scars were both a pleasure and a pain, making me vulnerable to any vampire who knew how to stimulate them, but when in the hands of an expert, it made for insanely good bedroom play, and Kisten knew it all.

Thoroughly lost, I went to swing my left leg over his to pull him to me, then stopped, remembering where I was. Gathering my will, I pushed back from him, and Kisten chuckled, desire heady in his gaze. "Damn it, look what you did to me," I said. My face was warm, and my hand rested atop my neck, hiding it. "Don't you have napkins to fold or something?"

His grin was cocky as he leaned back and ate another almond. My fluster worsened when he glanced at David with an infuriating, satisfied-male look on his face. So he had gotten me hot and bothered. It wasn't hard to do when you knew what buttons to push, and my demon bite was a huge button, easy to hit and hard to miss. Plus, I loved him. "See you tonight?" he had the nerve to ask.

"Yes," I snapped, but I was looking forward to it already despite my embarrassment that David had seen the entire incident. Okay, I was a witch with a vampire boyfriend. What did he think we did on our dates? Play tiddledywinks?

The hum of Jenks's wings caught my attention, and the pixy landed lightly atop the dessert menu. "What's up, Rache?" he asked, angular features concerned. "You're all red."

"Nothing." I sipped my tea, the ice sliding down the glass and smacking my nose again. "You want some sugar water or peanut butter?" I asked as I set it down.

Kisten subtly moved himself farther onto his stool and away from me. Jenks's wings increased their hum. "You sure you're okay? You're not sick, are you? You're throwing off heat like you've got a fever. Let me feel your forehead," he said, rising into the air.

"I'm fine," I said, waving him off. "It's all this leather. What's Mr. Ray doing?"

Jenks saw Kisten smirking as he ate his almonds, then my hand covering my scar. The pixy's attention went to David, who now had his back to us. "Oh!" Jenks sang out, laughing. "Kisten got you worked up? You tell him about Ivy kissing you, and he had to prove himself?"

"Jenks!" I shouted, and Kisten flinched, his face going white. From the end of the bar, David grunted, turning to look at me questioningly.

"Ivy kissed you?" Kisten said, and I could have just died.

"Look, it wasn't a big deal," I said, shooting evil glares at Jenks, who was now staring at me as if wondering why I was mad. "She was trying to prove to me that I couldn't control her when she lost herself to her blood lust, and things got out of hand. Can we talk about something else?" Jenks was spilling dust to make a sunbeam on the counter. "Jenks, what is Mr. Ray doing?" I said, flicking an almond at him. *Damn it, I don't have time to deal with this right now.*

Jenks stayed where he was as if nailed to the air, and the nut passed over his head to clatter behind the bar. "Bitchin'," he said, smirking. "He's been here for twenty minutes. And don't let her fool you, Kisten. She's been thinking about that kiss all afternoon."

I made a snatch at him, missing when he darted back. "It surprised me, is all." I snuck glances at Kisten as he tried to hide his worry. Behind him, David frowned and turned away. Remembering why I was here, I took Kisten's wrist and tilted it so I could see what time it was. "I want to go in with Mrs. Sarong, seeing as neither one of them know the other will be here. Where is she, anyway? She ought to be here by now."

By the end of the bar, David turned his attention to the door and tugged his coat straight. Kisten, too, sat up. "Speak of the devil," he said. "At least three cars by the sound of it."

His steps slow but seeming to eat the distance like magic, David came back, and I felt a wash of angst. Crap, I had magicked Mrs. Sarong's baseball field to convince her to pay me for my time when I'd stolen Mr. Ray's fish, thinking it had been hers. Yes, she'd asked for this meeting, and though it seemed likely she wanted to talk to me about her murdered aide, the possibility that she might still be on about that fish had me nervous.

"I'll be in the kitchen folding napkins," Kisten said softly, his hand trailing along my shoulder as he rose and slipped away.

The look on his face when Jenks told him Ivy had kissed me flashed before me. "I'm a coward," I said softly to Jenks as he landed on my earring.

"No you aren't," he started. "It's just—"

"Yes I am," I interrupted as I stood and made sure I didn't have spots of iced tea marring my pants. "I pick a place where I know someone will save my butt if I get in over my head."

David harrumphed and stood beside me, and I was thankful he didn't seem to think anything less of me. For whatever reason. "That's not being a coward," he said as the front door opened and light spilled in. "That's thinking ahead."

I said nothing. Nervous, I forced my features to find a confident slant as the light was eclipsed by what looked like eight people. Mrs. Sarong was first, a young woman close behind her. Her replacement aide, perhaps? Five men in identical suits flowed in after them to make a semicircle clearly protective in nature. Mrs. Sarong ignored them.

The very small woman smiled with her lips closed, taking off her gloves and handing them to her aide. Eyes on me, she reached up and removed her white hat, handing it and her white leather clutch purse to the woman as well. Heels clacking on the hardwood floor, she came forward. She was wearing a tasteful white suit that looked businesslike without hiding the curves of her small but well-proportioned body. Her feet were tiny. Though in her mid-fifties, I guessed, she clearly took care of herself, being trim and poised. Styled short and off her face, her blond hair had streaks of gray, but that only added to her professionalism. A string of pearls was about her neck, and she wore a diamond ring with enough sparkle to dance the Hustle by.

"Ms. Morgan," she said as she approached, her entourage fanning out to make me wary. "It's good to see you again. But honestly, dear, we could have met at my office or perhaps Carew Tower if you felt more comfortable in a neutral setting." She glanced quickly over the room, her nose wrinkling. "Though this has a certain rustic charm."

I didn't think she meant it as a slur, so I didn't take it that way. With David at my shoulder and Jenks sitting on it, I came forward to take her extended hand. My arm had been in a sling the last time we'd met, and I shook her hand, pleased to find her grip firm and sincere.

"Mrs. Sarong," I said, feeling tall and awkward in my leather since I stood almost eight inches over her. "I'd like you to meet David Hue, my alpha."

Her smile widened. "Pleasure," she said, inclining her head to David, who did the same in return. "Taking a witch as your alpha female to start a pack with?" Her eyebrows went up, and her eyes, untouched by age, glinted. "Wonderful way to play the rules, Mr. Hue. I have since plugged that particular gap in my employee handbook, but wonderful nonetheless."

"Thank you," he said gracefully, taking a step back and removing himself from the conversation, but not the meeting.

Mrs. Sarong held out her hand to her aide, and the woman took it, letting herself be drawn forward. "This is my daughter, Patricia," the older woman said, surprising me. "Since the unfortunate demise of my aide, she will be shadowing me for the next year to gain a better understanding of whom I deal with on a daily basis."

My eyebrows rose, and I stifled my surprise. *Aide?* The young woman before me wasn't Mrs. Sarong's aide but her freaking heir. "It is a true pleasure," I said earnestly, shaking her hand.

"Likewise," she said firmly, her brown eyes giving away her intelligence. Her voice was high but determined, and she was dressed with as much class as her mother, though admittedly showing a lot more skin. Now that I knew their relationship, the resemblance was obvious, but where Mrs. Sarong was aging beautifully, her daughter Patricia was just simply beautiful, long black hair softly curving about her face and her small delicate hands possessing a hard strength. Instead of pearls she had on a chain of gold, a brown stone at the nadir point. Her pack tattoo, a vine twining about barbed wire, circled her ankle.

Stumbling, I pulled David forward. "This is David," I said, almost hearing my unvoiced, He's single.

David started, but then, with a rueful smile that made him ten times more attractive, he shook her hand. "Hello, Ms. Sarong," he said. "It's a pleasure to meet you."

"Mr. Hue," the young woman said, her brown eyes amused.

Mrs. Sarong looked at me, her face questioning at my impertinence.

"Would you like something to drink?" I asked, thinking my rusty host skills were going to get a workout this afternoon while dealing with a woman so clearly raised on etiquette and form. *And what in hell am I doing introducing David to her daughter like he was on the market?* My lips tightened at Jenks's snort from my earring. "We can go to a private room," I added, not knowing if it would be easier to take her to Mr. Ray or bring him out here, but she interrupted with a wave of her hand.

"No," she said lightly, her businesslike air returning. "What I want will take only a moment." She looked at her daughter pointedly, and the young woman gestured for the men to back out of earshot. They went, sullen yet obedient, but when Mrs. Sarong glanced at David, I sent my gaze to her daughter, standing at her side.

"Fine," the older woman said in concession. "I simply want to contract your services."

Expecting this, I nodded, but a surge of morality tugged at me, and I found myself saying, "I'm already working with the FIB to find out who murdered your aide." I gestured for her to sit at one of the small tables. "There's no need for you to contract me as well."

She settled herself gracefully, and I took the seat across from her. David and Patricia remained standing. "Splendid," Mrs. Sarong said, clearly making an effort not to touch the top of the table. "But I want to contract your *other* services."

Confused, I stared at her blankly.

"Your older profession, dear," she added.

From my shoulder came a tinkling of pixy laughter, and my eyes widened.

"Mrs. Sarong . . ." I stammered, feeling my face flash red.

"Oh, for Cerberus's sake," the woman said in exasperation. "I want you to kill Mr. Ray for murdering my aide. And I'm prepared to pay handsomely."

Shock zinged through me as I finally got it. "I don't kill people," I protested, trying to keep my voice soft, but with a bar full of vampires and Weres, I was sure someone else heard me. "I'm a runner, not an assassin." *Has she heard about Peter?*

Mrs. Sarong patted my hand. "It's okay, dear. I understand. Shall we say seventy-five thousand? Place the appropriate bet the next game and let me know. I'll take it from there."

Seventy-five . . . I couldn't find enough air. "You don't understand," I said, starting to sweat. "I can't." *What if David finds out? Peter's death had been insurance fraud.*

The woman's eyes narrowed, and she pursed her lips, her gaze going to her daughter. "Has Simon Ray already hired you?" she asked, her voice vehement. "A hundred thousand, then. Damn, he's a bastard."

I looked at David, but he seemed as shocked as I was. "You misunderstand," I stammered. "What I meant is, I don't do that kind of thing."

"And yet," she said, each syllable clear and precise, "people who annoy you seem to die."

"They do not," I objected, leaning until my back hit the chair.

"Francis Percy?" she began, ticking names off on her fingers. "Stanley Saladan? That mouse of a man . . . ah, Nicholas Sparagmos, I believe?"

Her spread fingers closed elegantly, and alarm hit me. "I didn't kill

Francis," I said. "He managed that all by himself. And Lee was dragged off by a demon he summoned. Nick went over a bridge."

Mrs. Sarong's smile widened, and she patted my hand again. "Very well done on the last one," she said, glancing at her daughter. "Leaving an old boyfriend to clutter future relationships is investing in trouble."

For a moment I stared. She wanted me to kill Simon Ray? "I didn't kill them," I protested. "Really."

"But they are nevertheless gone." Mrs. Sarong gave me a perfect smile, as if I had done a fabulous trick. She suddenly straightened, the comfortable companionability that had wreathed her expression shifting to blank questioning. The hair on the back of my neck prickled, and I watched her pull the air deep into her. "Simon!" she barked, rising to her feet.

I jumped up when her entourage dived into motion, heading right for us. She knew. She knew Mr. Ray was here.

"Rache!" Jenks shrilled, leaving my shoulder in a sparkle of gold dust. I backed into David, but Mrs. Sarong's pack wasn't concerned with me.

A shout quickly followed by a muffled thump shook the air. Kisten lunged in from the kitchen, his steps holding that eerie vampire quickness. He was headed for the back room, but before he could get there, Mr. Ray stormed in.

Great, I thought when the rest of his thugs spilled out behind him with drawn weapons pointed at us. *Just freaking great.*

EIGHTEEN

"You pompous little *bitch*!" the infuriated Were shouted, red-faced and with his thugs backing him. "What are you doing here?"

Mrs. Sarong pushed past the men who had put themselves in front of her. "Arranging your removal," she said, her voice sharp and her eyes glaring.

Removal? As if he were an overgrown tree clogging the sewer line?

The short businessman seemed to choke on his own breath, becoming choleric. Mouth gaping to look like one of his prize fish, he struggled to respond. "Like hell you are!" he finally managed. "That's what I wanted to talk to her about!"

From my shoulder came a small, "Holy crap, Rache. How did you become Cincy's assassin of choice?"

I stared at the two packs separated by little round tables. *Mr. Ray wants to contract me to take Mrs. Sarong out?*

The clicks of cocking weapons startled me from my shock.

"Grab some air, Jenks!" I shouted, kicking over a table and filling the space it had been in.

Jenks left me in a dazzling burst of gold sparkles. A whiff of musk and David had my back, that freaking big-ass rifle in his grip making him look like a gunslinger out for revenge. Kisten leapt forward. Blond hair swinging, he stepped between the two packs, his arms up in placation but his expression hard. The air pressure shifted, and suddenly Steve was there, too.

Everyone froze. My pulse hammered, and my knees went watery. It was too much like the time I had stormed in here looking for Piscary after he had blood-raped Ivy. Except this time there were a lot of pointed guns.

Sweating, I watched Kisten force the visible tension from his face and stance until he was the casual, confident bar manager on the surface. "I don't give a rat's ass if you kill each other," he said, his voice carrying well. "But you'll take it out of my bar and into the lot, like everyone else."

David pressed into my back, and with his warmth grounding me, I took a deep breath. "No one is going to kill anyone," I said. "I called you here, and you are *all* going to sit down so we can settle this like Inderlanders, not animals. Got it?"

Mr. Ray took a step forward, a short finger pointing at Mrs. Sarong. "I'm going to rip—"

A burst of angst lit through me. "I said *shut up!*" I shouted. "What is wrong with you?" My bag was heavy on my shoulder, and though I could bring out my splat gun, I didn't know whom I'd aim it at. At this point no one was aiming at me. I think. And to tap a line and make a circle might just set them all off. No one was shooting—I'd work from there.

"I'm not going to kill Mrs. Sarong," I said to Mr. Ray.

To my left, Mrs. Sarong stiffened, but she looked pissed, not afraid.

"And I'm not going to go after Mr. Ray for you," I added.

Mr. Ray harrumphed, wiping his brow with a white handkerchief. "I don't need your help to pin the whiny bitch," he said, and the men surrounding him tensed as if to rush her.

That just ticked me off. This was my party, damn it. Weren't they listening? "Hey! *Hey!*" I shouted. "Excuse me, but I'm the one you both wanted to contract to kill each other. I *suggest*," I said sarcastically, "that we all sit at that big table over there, just you, and you, and me." I looked at the weapons still cocked and pointed. "Alone."

Mrs. Sarong nodded in a show of acquiescence, but Mr. Ray sneered. "You can say anything in front of my pack," he stated belligerently.

"Fine." I stepped from David, and he uncocked his weapon. "I'll talk to Mrs. Sarong."

The collected woman smiled cattily at the flustered man and turned to give her daughter a word of instruction. She was just as stymied as Mr. Ray, but by calmly capitulating rather than insisting we do it her way, she looked more in control. Intrigued, I filed the wisdom away for more thought later. *If I have a later.*

"You got this okay?" I murmured to David.

I could smell the musk coming off him, thick and heady from his tension. The depression was gone, leaving only a capable-looking man with a rifle that could blow a hole in an elephant. It was a vampire killer. It would work on Weres, easy.

"No problem, Rachel," he said, his brown eyes everywhere but on me. "I'll keep them right where they are."

"Thanks." I touched his upper arm. He flicked his gaze to mine, then backed up a step, his duster furling about the tops of his boots.

My breath came out in a long exhalation. Pulse slowing, I stepped between the two Were factions and those guns, headed for the table at the foot of the stairs. Kisten was still standing in the middle of the room, and he was pulled into my wake as I passed him. The hair on the back of my neck prickled, but it was from the Weres, not him.

"I've got this under control," I said softly, my lips barely moving. "Why don't you go fold more of those napkins?"

"I can see that," he said, smiling despite the tension in his soft voice. Jenks joined us from the ceiling, and under their twin scrutiny I rubbed my fingertips into my forehead. Crap, I was getting a headache. This wasn't the way I had planned it, but how was I supposed to know they both wanted to contract me to kill each other?

"I think she's doing great," Jenks said. "There are eighteen weapons in this place, and not one has gone off yet. Nineteen if you count the one in Patricia's thigh holster."

Exhausted, I glanced behind me to the slight Were. Yeah, with that slit skirt, a thigh holster would work really well.

Kisten touched my elbow. "I'm not leaving this room," he said, his blue eyes almost fully dilated. "But this is your run. Where do you want Steve and me?"

I slowed my steps, pleased to see that Mr. Ray had seated himself opposite Mrs. Sarong—a good five feet between them. "The door?" I asked. "One of them probably called in more people, and I don't want this to become a population contest."

"You got it," he said, and with a soft smile he slipped away. He spoke to Steve, and the large vampire went out to the parking lot, a cell phone in his thick hand and his fingers busy.

Satisfied, I headed to the table. *Nineteen guns?* I thought, gut clenching. Nice. Maybe I should put myself in a bubble and say "go." Call whoever's still standing in five minutes the winner.

"Jenks," I said as I neared the table, "stay back, will you? Work communication between us? It's only supposed to be me and them. No seconds."

Still hovering, he put his hands on his hips. His angular features seemed pinched, making him look older than he really was. "No one counts pixies as people!" he protested.

I met his eyes squarely. "I count you, and it wouldn't be fair."

His wings flashed a pleased embarrassment, and a sprinkling of dust slipped from him. Nodding, he zipped away in a clatter of dragonfly wings.

Alone, I took the chair with my back to the kitchen door, confident no one would be coming in that way with Steve outside. I could smell the odor of dough rising for pizza, and the tang of tomatoes. Pizza sounded really good for tonight.

Forcing the thought away, I settled myself, opening my bag as I set it on my lap. The heavy weight of my splat gun was comfortable, and I tried not to think about the weapons Mr. Ray and Mrs. Sarong probably had on them.

"First," I said, trembling inside from the adrenaline, "I'd like to extend my condolences to both of you on the loss of your pack members."

On my right, Mr. Ray pointed rudely at Mrs. Sarong. "I won't tolerate you harassing my pack," he stated, cheeks quivering. "The death of my secretary was an out-and-out declaration of war. Something I'm prepared to see through."

Mrs. Sarong sniffed, looking down her nose at him. "Murdering my aide was intolerable. I will not pretend that it wasn't you."

God! They were at it again! "Both of you stop it!" I exclaimed.

Ignoring me, Mr. Ray leaned across the table to Mrs. Sarong. "You don't have the balls to warn me off of what's mine by right. We will find the statue, and you will sit at my feet like the bitch you are."

Whoa! I thought, and a sudden wash of cold reasoning shocked through me. This was about the focus, not their respective dead. I glanced at David, and his lips pressed together. Case solved. They were murdering each other.

But Mrs. Sarong was inching her hand to her waistband and the one-bullet gun she probably had there. "I didn't kill your secretary," she said, keeping Ray's attention on her face and not her hands. "But I'd like to thank whoever did. Killing my aide to feign that you don't have the focus makes you a coward. If you can't hold it by strength and must rely on stealth, you don't deserve it. I have more control over Cincinnati than you do anyway."

"Me!" the incensed Were shouted, bringing Steve in for a quick look around. "I don't have it, but I damn well will get it. I haven't so much as sniffed the footprints of your dog-infested pack, but I will take every last member of it if you keep up this farce."

From the corner of my sight, I watched David take a threatening grip on his vamp killer of a weapon. The two factions were getting antsy.

"That's enough," I said, feeling like a playground monitor. "Both of you shut up!"

Mr. Ray turned to me. "You're a thieving, mewling bitch!" the pudgy Were exclaimed, his supremacy firmly entrenched in his mind.

David hefted his rifle, and the Weres brought for muscle started to shift on their feet. From my other side, Mrs. Sarong smiled like the devil and crossed her legs, saying the same thing as Mr. Ray without uttering a word. I was losing control. I had to do something.

Pissed, I drew myself up and tapped a line. Immediately my hair started to float, and from the middle of the room came an uneasy murmur. I focused on the two of them, unable to break eye contact after I took it. "I think you mean witch," I said softly, my fingers moving in nonsense as I pretended to set a ley line spell. But they didn't know that. "I suggest you relax. And that fish was a rescue, not a theft," I added, my face warming. Okay, maybe my conscience was still smarting.

"You're both idiots," I added, staring at Mr. Ray. "Killing each other for a stupid-ass statue when neither one of you has it. How lame is that?"

Mrs. Sarong cleared her throat. "You know he doesn't have it . . . how?" she drawled.

A good dozen answers fell through my brain, but the only one that they would believe would be the one that was the most impossible. "Because I have it," I said, praying it was the answer that would keep me breathing for another day.

Silence greeted my claim. Then Mr. Ray laughed. I jumped when his hand slapped down onto the table, but Mrs. Sarong's gaze was fixed on the Weres behind me, her face paling. "You!" the heavy Were said between guffaws. "If you have the focus, I'll eat my shorts."

My lips pressed together, but Mrs. Sarong spoke next. "You take ketchup with your silk, Simon?" she said sourly. "I think she's got it."

Mr. Ray stopped laughing. His brown eyes noted her ashen hue, and then he looked to me. "Her?" he said in disbelief.

My pulse quickened, and I wondered if I had made a mistake and they'd band together to take it from me before turning against each other once more.

"Look at her alpha," the slight woman said, pointing with her eyes.

We all looked. David was sitting half on a table with one foot on the floor, the other draped down and hanging. His duster was open to show his trim body, and his rifle was in his hands. Yes, it was a big gun, but there were—as Jenks said—nineteen other weapons in the place. Yet there he was holding two aggressive packs still and silent.

David had always been an impressive individual, having the standing of an alpha and the mystique of a loner. But even I could see the new expectation in his manner. He wasn't just capable of dominating another Were; he expected it to happen without a complaint. It was the focus's magic trickling through him. He had gained the power of creation, and though it had resulted in the deaths of innocents, it didn't lesson the magnitude of what that meant.

"My God," Mr. Ray said. Eyes wide, he turned to me. "You have it." He swallowed. "You really have it?"

Mrs. Sarong had taken her hands from the threat of her weapon and set them on the table. It was a submissive move, and a chill took me. *What have I done? Will I survive it?*

"You were there, at the bridge, weren't you? When the Mackinaw Weres found it?" she said coolly.

I leaned back to distance myself. What I wanted to do was run away. "I had it before that, actually," I admitted. "I was up there rescuing my boyfriend." I fixed on her eyes, wondering if they were a shade chagrined. "The one you think I killed," I added.

My pulse hammered when she dropped her eyes for an instant, then returned them to me. *God help me, what have I become?*

Mr. Ray wasn't convinced. "Give it to me," he demanded. "You can't hold it. You're a witch."

One down, one to go, I thought, scared, but to back down now would end my life more quickly than publicly claiming the stupid thing. "I'm his alpha," I said, nodding to David. "I say that says I can."

The man's eyes narrowed. Looking as if he had cracked a rotten egg, he said, "I'll make you part of my pack. That's my best offer. Take it."

"Take it or what?" I allowed a touch of sarcasm into my voice. "I have a pack, thank you. And why does everyone keep telling me I can't do things? I've got it. You don't. I'm not giving it to you. End of story. So you can stop killing each other trying to find out where it is."

"Simon," Mrs. Sarong said caustically, "shut your yap. She has it. Deal with it."

I would have tried to find a compliment in that but figured her support would only last until she found a way to kill me.

Mr. Ray met her gaze, and something I didn't understand passed between them. David felt it. So did every Were in the place. Like a wave, they all relaxed. I felt ill when both packs shifted and every weapon was put away. My worry tightened. *Damn and double damn. I can't afford to trust this.*

"I didn't target your aide," Mr. Ray said, his thick arms going to rest atop the table.

"I didn't touch your secretary," the woman said, taking out a compact and checking her makeup. It snapped shut, and she met his eyes squarely. "No one in my pack did either."

Just peachy damn keen. They were talking, but I didn't think I was in control. "Fine," I said. "Nobody is killing anybody, but we still have two murdered Weres." The two of them had given me their full attention, and my stomach knotted. "Look," I said, very uncomfortable, "someone besides us knows the focus is in Cincinnati and is looking for it. It might be the island Weres. Has either of you heard of a new pack in town?"

As I thought of Brett, they both shook their heads.

Okay. Swell. Back to square one. I wanted them to leave, so I leaned back as if in dismissal. I'd seen Trent do it a couple of times, and it seemed to work for him. "I'll keep looking for the murderer, then," I said, glancing at their thugs. "Until I figure out who's doing this, will you two let go of each other's throats?"

Mr. Ray sniffed loudly. "I will if she does."

Mrs. Sarong's smile was stilted and clearly false. "I can do the same. I need to make a few calls. Before sunset." A pointed look at her daughter and the young woman excused herself, cell phone in hand as she went outside. Mr. Ray gestured, and one of his men followed her.

I wondered what Mrs. Sarong had planned for sunset, then dismissed it. I didn't like the two of them fighting, but I liked this cooperation even less. Perhaps it was time for a little personal CYA. "The focus is hidden," I said. *Sort of.* "It's in the ever-after," I continued, and they stared at me, Mr. Ray's fingers twitching. *Liar,* I thought, not feeling a twinge of guilt. "Neither of you can find it, much less get it." *Lie, lie, li-i-i-ie.* "If I go missing, neither of you gets it. If any of my friends or family go missing, I'm going to destroy it."

Ever the one to test the limits in as crass a manner as possible, Mr. Ray harrumphed. "And I should take you seriously because . . . ?"

I stood, wanting them to leave. "Because you were ready to hire me to do something you couldn't. Kill Mrs. Sarong."

Mrs. Sarong smiled at him and shrugged.

Just a bit more, I thought, *and maybe I can sleep tonight.* "And because I have a demon who owes me a favor," I added, my pulse quickening.

No, a small part of my mind whispered, and I stifled a surge of fear for what I was doing. I was accepting that Minias owed me. I was accepting his bargain. I was dealing with demons. But the thought of these two people descending upon my life, setting fire to my church and burning it to the ground in search of that stupid statue filled me with a more immediate fear. Fear for myself, I could deal with. Fear for others, I couldn't.

"If something happens I don't like," I said, "he's going to come looking for you. And you know what?" My pulse pounded, and I held the table for balance as vertigo took me. "He likes killing things, so he might be a little overzealous about it. It wouldn't surprise me if he took you both out to be sure he gets the right person."

Mr. Ray's eyes dropped to my wrist, my demon mark clearly visible.

"Make your calls," I said, ready to dissolve into the shakes. "Calm your people. And keep your mouths shut. If the word gets out I've got it, it will decrease your chances that you'll find a way around my demon and get it yourself." I took a moment and captured their eyes. "Do we have an understanding?"

Mrs. Sarong stood, her purse in her tight grip before her. "Thank you for the drink, Ms. Morgan. It was a most enlightening conversation."

Kisten came out from behind the bar as she headed for the door, her entire entourage flowing into her wake. The sun entered in a flash as the door opened, and I squinted, feeling like I had been at the bottom of a hole for three weeks. Mr. Ray looked me up and down, his fleshy cheeks slack and unmoving. Giving me a nod, he made a gesture to his people and followed her out, their pace slow and provocative, weapons tucked away as they filed through the door.

I stood where I was until the last of them passed the threshold. I waited a bit longer until the door slipped shut and put me back in darkness. Only then did I give in and let my knees buckle. I could hear Kisten crossing the room, and I put my head on the table and sighed.

I had a reputation for dealing with demons. I didn't want it, but if it would keep those I loved safe, then I was going to use it.

NINETEEN

Kisten's boat was big enough that the wake from the tourist steamers just smacked into it, never making the sleek cruiser move. I'd been on it before, even spent a couple of weekends learning how well voices carry over dark, still water and to take my shoes off at the dock. It was three decks if you counted the highest where the controls were. Big enough to party on, as Kisten said, but small enough that he didn't feel like he had extended his reach.

Well, it's beyond my reach, I thought as I sopped up the last of the spaghetti sauce off the lightweight china with a corner of grilled bread. But if you were a vampire whose boss ran the uglier parts of Cincinnati's underground, appearances mattered.

The bread had been swiped from Piscary's kitchen nearby. I had a feeling the sauce had been, too. I didn't care if Kisten was trying to pass it off as his own cooking by warming it up on his tiny stove. The point was, we were having a relaxing dinner instead of arguing that I had put my job before his plans to take me out for my birthday.

I looked up and across the candlelit, sunken living room, my plate balanced on my lap. We could have eaten in the kitchen or out on the spacious veranda, but the kitchen was claustrophobic and the veranda too exposed. My encounter with Mr. Ray and Mrs. Sarong had me uneasy. Add on Tom's shunned invitation and you could color me paranoid.

Being surrounded by four walls was much better. The luxuriously appointed living room stretched from one side of the boat to the other, looking like a movie set, with wide windows showing the city lights and moon shining on water to one side, curtains closed on the other so I didn't have to look at Piscary's parking lot.

Technically Kisten was working—which was why we were here and not at a real restaurant—but when we had slipped into the kitchen to snatch a bottle of wine and the bread, I'd heard him tell Steve that he didn't want to be bothered unless blood was in someone's mouth.

It felt nice to sit that high in his priorities, and with my face still holding the pleasure from that thought, I lifted my eyes, finding Kisten watching me from across the low coffee table between us, the candlelight giving his blue eyes an artificial, dangerous darkness.

"What?" I asked, flushing since he obviously had been watching me for some time.

His contented smile deepened, and a thrill of emotion lifted through me. "Nothing." His voice was soft. "Every thought you have crosses your face. I like watching."

"Mmmm." Embarrassed, I set my plate atop his empty one and leaned into the couch, wineglass in hand. He stood and in a hunched motion shifted to sit beside me. Easing back, he exhaled in satisfaction when our shoulders touched. The stereo changed tracks, and light jazz came on. I wasn't going to say anything about the incongruity of mixing vampires and a soprano saxophone but sighed, enjoying the scent of leather and silk blending with his scent of incense and the lingering odor of pasta sauce. But my smile vanished when my nose started to tickle.

Crap. Minias? I don't have my scrying mirror. In a panic I sat up and out of Kisten's arms. My wineglass hit the coffee table just in time for a sneeze.

"Bless you," Kisten said softly, his hand curving about my waist to draw me back, but when I stiffened, he leaned forward. "You okay?" he added, real concern in his voice.

"I'll let you know in a minute." I took a careful breath, then another. My shoulders eased. Not wanting to worry Ivy or Jenks, I had shut myself in my room before sunset and set my password. Damn it, I should have scribed the glyph on a compact mirror.

Kisten was peering at me, and I said, "I'm fine," deciding it was only a sneeze. Exhaling slowly, I slumped into his warmth. His arm went behind my neck, and I pressed into him, glad he was here, and I was here, and neither of us had to be anywhere.

"You've been quiet tonight," Kisten said. "Are you sure you're okay?" His fingers began tracing a path along my neck, hunting for my demon scar, hidden under my perfect skin, and the light touch tickled.

He was asking after me, but I knew his thoughts were on Ivy's kiss. And with his fingers bringing my scar alight to mix the memory of it with the sensations he was pulling from me, I stifled a shudder of adrenaline. "I've a lot on my mind," I said, not liking how his touch and the memory of Ivy's kiss combined. I was confused enough already.

Turning in his arms to face him, I drew out of his reach, scrambling for something else to focus on. "I think I've gotten in over my head this time, is all. With the Weres?"

Kisten's blue eyes went soft. "After watching you curb two of Cincinnati's more influential packs, I would say that no, you aren't over your head." His smile widened, taking on a tinge of pride. "It was great watching you work, Rachel. You're good at this."

A puff of disbelief escaped me. It wasn't the Weres that had me worried, but how I'd gotten them to back off. Exasperated, I threw my head back against the top of the couch and closed my eyes. "Couldn't you see me shaking?"

My eyes flew open when Kisten's weight shifted, and I slid into him. Our hair mingled, and with his lips brushing my ear he said, "No." His breath came and went on my shoulder, and I didn't move but for sending my fingers to play with his torn earlobe. "I like a woman who can take care of herself," he added. "Watching you got me all hot."

I couldn't help my smile, but it faded distressingly fast. "Kisten?" I said, feeling vulnerable despite having his arms around me. "Really, I'm scared. But not about the Weres."

Kisten's searching fingers stopped. Removing his encircling arm, he leaned back and took my hands in his. "What is it?" he said, concern heavy in his gaze.

Embarrassed, I looked at our twined fingers and saw the differences. "I had to use the threat of a demon to get them to back off." I lifted my gaze, seeing the worry etching his brow. "It makes me feel like a demon practitioner," I finished. "I'm an idiot for using a demon as a bluff. Or a coward, maybe."

"Love . . ." Kisten drew my head to rest against his chest. "You aren't a coward or a practitioner. It's a bluff, and a damned good one."

"But what if it isn't a bluff?" I said into his shirt, thinking of all the people I had tagged for practicing black magic. They hadn't intended to become the fanatical, crazed people I threw in the back of a cab and hauled off to the I.S. "Some guy talked to me today," I said, fiddling with the top button of his shirt. "He invited me to join their demon cult."

"Mmmm." His voice rumbled through me. "And what did my bad-ass runner tell him?"

"That he could take his club and shove it." Kisten said nothing, and I added, "What if they call my bluff? If they hurt Ivy or Jenks . . ."

"Shhhh," he hushed, his hand gentle against my hair. "No one is going to hurt Ivy; she's a Tamwood vampire and Piscary's scion. And why would anyone hurt Jenks?"

"Because they know he's important to me." I lifted my head, taking a breath of the fresher air. "I might do it," I said, frightened. "If anyone hurts Jenks or his family, I might call Minias and trade in my mark."

"Minias." Kisten's surprise showed. "I thought you were supposed to keep their names secret."

There had been more than a hint of jealousy in it, and I felt the beginnings of a smile. "That's his casual name. He has red goat-slitted eyes, a funny purple hat, and a crazy girlfriend."

Kisten pulled me closer and settled his arms around me. "Maybe I should call this guy. Take him bowling so we can compare crazy-girlfriend notes."

"Stop it," I chided him, but he had managed to shift my mood. "You're jealous."

"Hell yes, I'm jealous." He was silent for a moment, then leaned forward. "I want to give you your present early," he said, reaching around the arm of the couch and to the floor.

Twisting, I put my back against the arm of the couch more firmly. Kisten set the obviously store-wrapped package in my hands, and I beamed. The ribbon about it was imprinted with VALERIA'S CRYPT, an exclusive supplier of clothing where the less fabric there was, the bigger the dent it would make in your checking account.

"What is it?" I asked, giving the shirt-size box a shake, and something thunked.

"Open it and see," he said, his eyes flicking from me to the box.

There was something odd in his behavior. Sort of an embarrassed eagerness. Not one to save paper, I ripped it off and tossed it, running a fingernail under the single piece of tape holding the box shut. Black tissue paper rustled, and I warmed when I saw what was under it.

"Oh, this is nice!" I said, lifting the teddy up. "Just in time for summer nights."

"It's edible," Kisten said, his eyes glinting.

"Whoa!" I exclaimed, hefting its light weight and wondering how we might explore this new option. Remembering the thing thunking around, I set the teddy aside. "What else is in here?" I questioned, rummaging. My fingers found a small, fuzzy box, and when I recognized its shape, my face lost all expression. It was a ring box. *Oh, my God.* "Kisten?" I breathed, eyes wide.

"Open it," he prompted, scooting closer.

Hands trembling, I turned it to find the opening. I didn't know what to do. I loved Kist, but I wasn't ready to be engaged. Hell, I was hardly ready to be anyone's girlfriend. What with two Were packs after my hide, demons showing up whenever, a master vampire itching to have at me. Not to mention a roommate who wanted to be more and me not knowing what to do about it. And how could I embark on a permanent relationship when I wouldn't let him bite me?

"But, Kisten . . ." I stammered, pulse racing.

"Just open it," he urged impatiently.

Holding my breath, I wedged it open. I blinked. It wasn't a ring. It was a pair of . . .

"Caps?" I questioned. Relief spilled through me. I looked up to see his fluster. They weren't his caps. No, these were sharp and pointy. *And they're for me?*

"If you don't like them, I'll take them back," he said, his usual confidence gone. "I thought it might be fun sometime. If you wanted to . . ."

My eyes closed. It wasn't a ring. It was a toy. I should have known after the edible teddy. "You bought me caps?"

"Well, yes. What did you think they were?"

I went to tell him, then closed my mouth. Flushing, I set the box aside and looked at the caps in their velvet cushion. Okay, it wasn't a ring, but where was this leading? "Kisten, I can't let you bite me." Closing the lid with a snap, I extended them to him. "I can't accept these."

But Kisten was smiling. "Rachel," he coaxed. "That's not why I bought them."

"Why, then?" I said, thinking he had put me in a very awkward position. I couldn't help but wonder if this had been a reaction to Ivy's kiss.

Placing the box back in my hands, he curved my fingers around it. "This isn't a backward way to wiggle my teeth into your neck. I'm not even looking for *you* to bite *me,* though that would be . . ." He took a breath. "Nice."

I could tell it was the truth, and my agitation eased.

Kisten dropped his gaze. "I wanted to see you with little pointy teeth," he said softly. "It's bedroom play. Like wearing a teddy. Sort of like . . . window dressing."

"You don't like my teeth?" I said, unhappy. Damn it, I wasn't a vampire, and he wanted more. This sucked royally.

But Kisten pulled me to him with a rueful chuckle. "Rachel, I adore your teeth," he said, his silk shirt against my cheek. "They nibble and pinch, and that you can't easily break my skin drives me fu—" He caught the next word, sensitive to my disapproval. "Crazy," he finished. "But with you wearing those caps and me knowing you *could* break my skin?" A sigh lifted through him. "I don't care if you bite me or not. It's the thought that you could that's exciting."

His hand against my hair was soothing, and the last of my confusion vanished. This I understood. I found a thrill in the same way. Knowing that Kisten could bite me but held back because of respect, will, and perhaps Ivy was enough to get my rush going full tilt. That someday his will might not be strong enough or he might be willing to stand down Ivy was the attraction.

"You . . . ah, want me to try them on?" I said.

His eyes were dilating. "If you want to."

Smiling, I shifted my body and opened the box again. "You just slip them on?"

He nodded. "They're coated with some miracle polymer. Put them on and clench your teeth, and they'll mold right to them. They'll come off with a little prying."

Cool. His eyes were on them, and I set the box on the table, the unfamiliar smoothness of bone under my fingers as I picked them up. Feeling like I was putting on contacts, I fumbled until I figured out which one went where and slipped the molded bone over my teeth. They felt odd as I gritted my teeth. Lips parted, I ran my tongue across the inside.

Kisten inhaled, and my attention went to him. "Damn, woman." The rim of blue about his pupils shrank. My smile widened, and, seeing it, his eyes flashed to black.

"What do they look like?" I said, jumping up.

"Where are you going?" he said, his voice holding a sudden urgency.

"I want to see what they look like." Laughing, I pulled away from him and headed for the bathroom down the hall. "Are you sure I won't cut my lip?" I asked when I found it. The overhead light flicked on, yellow and dim from the low voltage.

"You can't," Kisten said, his voice raised against the distance. "They're designed not to," he added from right behind me, and I jumped, smacking my elbow into the wall in the tight confines.

"God! I hate it when you do that!" I exclaimed.

"I want to see, too," he said, an arm curving around my waist and his head tucking into the hollow between my neck and shoulder.

His eyes weren't on my reflection. Trying to ignore the tingles his lips were creating, I looked in the mirror, my tongue feeling the backs of the caps. They had a delicate curve, and the backs were angular. I smiled and turned my head to get a good look, seeing how they fit into the concave space between my lower teeth. The memory of wearing wax fangs for Halloween when I was eight flitted through me and was gone.

"Stop flashing your teeth," Kisten growled.

I turned to face him, his hands tracing a delicious path about my waist. "Why?" I bumped into him suggestively. "Does it bother you?"

"No." His voice was terse, and his grip on me grew tight.

There wasn't much room in here, but when I tried to push him out, he stood firm. He was warm and solid, and I stayed where I was, putting my arms about his neck and using him to keep my balance. "Do you like them?" I whispered, inches from his ear.

"Yes."

His lips traced a path across my collarbone, and I shivered, feeling the stirrings of desire.

"Me, too," I said. Pulse hammering, I aggressively nuzzled his head away so he couldn't reach my neck, pulling myself up to run my new teeth teasingly across an old scar.

Kisten shuddered against me. "Oh, God. This is going to kill me," he whispered, his breath warm against my shoulder.

My blood pounded as I felt the new power I had. Kisten had gone still under my teeth, submissive without being docile. His hands drifted down to trace my curves, tugging my shirt from my jeans as they came up again.

Fingertips roughened from work traced lightly over me, rising until they cupped my breast. His other hand was at the small of my back, pressing me into him. Breath quickening, I gently bit an old scar at the base of his neck, sensations rising almost too fast to appreciate.

I turned my attention to a tiny scar I knew was sensitive. I breathed in his scent, a relaxed tension filling me. I hadn't come here looking for this, but why not? A small voice in my head wondered if I was letting Kisten sway my thoughts so easily on the teeth issue to reaffirm that he and I had something real already—and that accepting Ivy's offer, the surprise of it aside, would be cheating on him. If so, I would be the only one it would bother. Vampires considered multiple bed and blood partners the norm and monogamy the exception. And though I wasn't a vampire, to accept polyamorous relationships without a lot of soul-searching, all I could think right now was this felt damn good.

I grazed my teeth the length of his neck, feeling his muscles tighten. Kisten's hands trembled, and I wondered why I was trying to figure this out right now. His sigh flashed adrenaline through me, and it was all I could do not to bear down and dent his skin. A wicked feeling was beginning to grow, and I relished it. I *could* bite him. I *could* sink my teeth. And I knew exactly what it would do to him. I wasn't a vamp to set his scars alight, but he was, and one vampire was all it took.

His hands moved against me under my chemise, and in the gap between us I sent one of my hands downward, wanting to undo just one button. Just one.

Fingers awkward from the tight fabric, I managed it. Unable to resist, I fumbled for his zipper. Kisten shifted his weight, pressing me into the narrow slice of wall. His blue eyes were lost in black, and he pinned my hands above my head.

"You assume a lot, witch," he growled, and a spike of desire shot through me.

"You want me to stop?" I said, leaning forward and forcing a kiss.

Oh, God. His lips pushed aggressively against mine, tasting of wine. The thought of my teeth so close to his lips was thrilling. I knew Kisten could feel my need to find all of him building, and he played upon it. But as long as he had my hands pinned over my head, he couldn't stop me from tasting what I could reach.

A small shift forward and my lips found his neck. Kisten exhaled slowly. Enjoying being able to pull such a response from him, I explored, finding new reactions from old scars.

I should have done this before, I thought, hooking one foot behind his leg and pulling him closer. As soon as I got home, I would have to see what Cormel's guide to dating vampires said about this.

My arms dropped to encircle Kisten's neck lightly as he let go of my hands, and a sliver of thrill hit when he moved us into the unlit hallway. My back went up against the thin paneling with a thump, and he slid my camisole strap down my shoulder, bending to kiss the newly exposed, flawless skin that I knew was irresistible to vampires. The smoothness of his capped teeth across my unmarked skin sent a tremor through me. If his phone rang, I was going to kill somebody.

My eyes slipped shut in pure enjoyment, and I worked by feel to undo the buttons of his shirt. Jazz played, and the sound of a boat echoed over the flat water. I couldn't get the last of the buttons—Kisten kept nipping at my skin to send jolts that didn't have the chance to ebb before he added to them. Giving up, I gripped his shirt and pulled until the buttons snapped.

Kisten *mmm*'ed in annoyance. He shifted his weight, pinning me. Eyes flashing open, I reached for his belt. "Give me what I want," I whispered, feeling my new teeth. "And I won't have to get rough, vamp boy."

"That's my line," he said, his voice carrying a new edge to it.

The words were laced with blood hunger, and fear lanced through me, quickly stifled. Kisten's hands hesitated for an instant, to regain control, and then he continued. His restraint far stronger than mine, he took my shoulders, holding me unmoving as he found the base of my neck, wanting my blood but not taking it as he worked my old scar.

"Oh, God," I breathed. Unable to stop, I hoisted myself up, wrapping my legs around his waist and tightening my grip on his neck. He shifted again, adjusting for my weight. I could feel him heavy through his slacks, and my pulse quickened. Sensing it, his touch became aggressive, and silver threads of anticipation tightened to a hard ball in the pit of my being. This wasn't good. It was too much. I wasn't thinking anymore. It was too damn good.

I clutched at him, wanting the rush of feeling his teeth sink into me. If he knew how badly, he might ask, and I wouldn't be able to say no. *Ivy will kill him.*

As if sensing my confusion, his lips became gentle, tracing a cool-warm sensation from the base of my neck to rise slowly to behind my ear, where he stayed, pulling with a gentle pressure—hinting at more. "Can you stay through the morning?" he asked.

"Mmmm," I managed, making sure my willingness was obvious by sending my nails to trace the back of his neck.

"Good." Carrying me, he headed down the hall to the night-darkened bedroom. The lights from Cincinnati were a soft glow reflecting off the water, and I spared a thought that I wasn't going to have the chance to wear that teddy. At least not tonight. His bed was under the bank of windows, but he set me atop the dresser, my legs still wrapped around him.

I was at an excellent height that lent itself to all sorts of possibilities—and feeling surged when his hand sketched a heavy path to my breast, his thumb teasingly caressing. Kisten's lips left me, and with a deliberate slowness, he pulled back. The motions of his fingers against me stopped. Almost panting, I met his eyes.

They were black with a familiar, collected blood lust, glinting in the reflected light. Adrenaline zinged through me to mix anticipation and fear. Something was changing—I had become more with my sharp teeth. They weren't just bits of bone, they were a source of power, giving me control over him through the sensations I could invoke. And Kisten knew it; that had been his intention in giving them to me. With his teeth capped and mine sharp, he had elevated me above him. The thought was a definite turn-on for both of us.

Eyes never leaving mine, he took the hand that I had slipped between his open shirt and his back. He breathed deeply of my wrist, lids closing as he scented my blood. "You smell like my two favorite people all mixed up."

His words sent a tremor rippling through me. Ivy's scent coated me, a soft memory of what they once had. The two of them had banded together in their vulnerable youth to survive, and I knew he missed their past closeness. He ached with his need to find it again. His pain pulled on me, making me want to give him what he needed, soothing both his body and mind. I wasn't coming in second behind Ivy but first; I could give him something she couldn't—everything he had found with Ivy, but ignorant of what Piscary had put them both through. I knew that was why Ivy had left him. She couldn't live with the reminder.

The draw to submit and give him everything strengthened, and when he felt me lean into him, his grip tightened. Body meeting his suggestively, I pulled his scent deep into me. It swirled through my body, the pheromones flipping switches until I ached with need. My hands slipped to his back, feeling the tension there and wanting so badly to get lost in him. I exhaled, my breath shaking. "Come here," I whispered.

Tilting his head, Kisten held my shoulders and kissed my lower neck, gently, hesitantly, as if he had never touched me before. I lost my breath at the rush of feeling, the burning tracings of desire settling deep and low. I exhaled into it, calling it to me. The pause to gather our breath was over. *Oh, God. I have to do something.*

Fingers fumbling, I reached for his slacks. The top button was undone, and I unzipped them, pushing them down enough to give him freedom. His hands were at my lower back, and I clasped my arms around his neck, lowering myself off the dresser so he could pull my jeans down. My feet touched the floor long enough to shake off first one pant leg, then the other.

Impatient, I tightened my grip around his neck, lifting myself back up against him until I was on the dresser again. His hands ran over my curves to my waist, then higher. A groan of anticipation slipped from me when he bowed his head. Massaging my breast with one hand and sending his lips over the other, he tugged and teased—the hint of teeth telling me what he could do if I let him, almost promising.

If he hadn't had his caps, he would have bitten me. Adrenaline flashed deep, and I sent my hands down to find his taut, smooth skin. His motion against me grew rougher, and I responded. With a sharp tug, he leaned to find the base of my neck with his lips, his repressed need making him savage.

Feeling poured from my scar. I would have collapsed if he hadn't held me. My heart pounded as he eased up, and I could breathe again. Beneath my moving fingers, he was smooth and warm, a shocking contrast to his rough touch on my neck. His breathing deepened, and his teeth teased the skin about my scar, leaving me aching for him to find me fully. I squeezed my eyes shut, sensing the hint of coming ecstasy. I gasped, startled when he gave up his teasing and bit me without breaking the skin, hard and strong. Only his capped teeth stopped him.

Tension spiked through me, and I moaned. It hit Kisten like fear.

His fingers gripping my shoulders tightened. With a vamp quickness, he jerked me closer. I gasped again. Then, with my arms again about his neck, I shifted my body to make it easier for him, leaving the dresser entirely. He slid into me with an exquisite slowness that replaced reason with desperate need. I took a faltering breath. Lips parting, I brought the scent of him deep into me as he filled my mind and body both.

With him supporting my weight, we moved together. My arms were about his neck to keep myself to him, and I realized that apart from the obvious, I couldn't touch him with anything but my lips. The self-imposed restraint hit me, and with a frustrated desperation I went for his neck, tracing old scars and feeling a want grow headier with each shift of weight.

Kisten's breathing was fast, and he held me to him with a fervent need, moving toward climax. His mouth was on me, pulling. The thought of Ivy sinking her teeth flashed through me. Fear of the unknown dove to my groin, and Kisten moaned, sensing it.

I wanted Ivy to bite me, I wanted that feeling of utter bliss mixing with knowing the act was an affirmation of her being worth sacrificing for, all layered with the heady emotion of risk I craved. Even so, I trusted her to not bind me to her. But Kisten . . . Deep in my heart, he was still an unknown, the lure of the thrill of adrenaline driving me to risk everything. Ivy's protection was a crutch that allowed me to make myself vulnerable without risking his binding me to him. He couldn't bite me. But maybe . . . maybe I could bite him?

Adrenaline flared at the thought, and my hands upon him clenched even as I forced his lips to find mine. *Oh, God, I want to bite him,* I realized. I didn't want to bleed him or taste his blood. But I could fill him with that mind-shocking wave of ecstasy that waited just below his skin. The feeling of power over him was a rush almost as strong as fear. And I wasn't used to telling myself no.

"Kisten . . ." I panted as I pulled away. "Do you promise not to bite me if I bite you?"

His hands supporting me were shaking. "I promise," he whispered. "You've asked, and I've said yes. Oh, God, Rachel. You might . . . you might pick up an echo of my hunger. But it's not yours. Don't be afraid."

A surge of sensation struck through both of us. I felt the strength and satisfaction of power. Fear for tomorrow flashed through me and was gone. My hands went around the back of his neck, and I moved against him, feeling a new stirring of domination and desire.

My pulse thrummed. The scent of leather and wine drew on memories, pulling me to him. His lips parted, and with his drive singing in me to bring every cell awake, I silenced the part of me that rebelled against tasting another's blood and met his lips with my own.

Kisten exhaled in pained exhilaration. I eased into the kiss, tentatively tracing my tongue against his teeth as we moved together, doubly joined. My heart pounded, and I didn't care what might happen anymore. I couldn't move my hands to touch him or I'd fall, and I wanted to stay where I was, gripping him with my legs, feeling him inside me. Wild with need, our mouths moved together, and in an instant of abandonment, I found his lip. It didn't take much.

Blood flowed. My body shook in a spasm. Oh, God. It was all. It was everything.

Scintillating and alive, I tasted vampire blood. It struck through me, and I clutched at Kisten, unable to breathe, unable to pull away in sheer ecstasy. In a flash, hunger poured into me, and I knew what Ivy and Kisten fought to contain every day, and how good it felt to sate it. It was Kisten's hunger echoing in me, without fear.

This is not wrong, I thought as Kisten's hands clutched at me. The hunger demanded more, and I deepened the kiss we shared. There was only this. This was all. It was the spark of existence, pooled and collected, distilled to a feeling. And with Kisten's hunger echoing through me, I pulled his blood from him, taking it as my own. Vampire blood wouldn't make me stronger, or faster, or live forever. But it was a rush. A high like no other. And I could feel his aura mixing with mine, sharing the same space as I took him into me.

A surge of white-hot need ached, spinning from his blood. He moaned, and as I drew his blood into me again, I tightened my grip on him and wouldn't let go. I could feel us reaching for climax. It was there, dancing just out of my reach.

His arms shook. I breathed heavily, struggling for air. A savage sound came from him, and he clutched me close. His blood was liquid thought, racing to set me alight. I could feel him inside me, and I pressed into him, desperate.

And then we found it.

Eyes clamped shut, I flung my head back. I could do nothing as a wash of sensation spilled into me, into us. Every cell sang with the release, leaving a high so deep there was no thought but for its continued existence.

Kisten's grip shook, and he staggered. Unaware of anything, we hung, poised in the rapture that suffused us. "My God," he groaned, both satisfied and desperate as he reached out for the feeling. And with his words it slipped away. It was gone.

I took a gasping breath, slumping. My muscles wouldn't hold me, and I started to fall.

"Oh, God," he said again, this time in worry as he caught me and brought me to the bed. I felt myself ease down, and he peered close. "Rachel . . ." he said, his hands holding my head.

"I'm okay," I panted, trembling as I felt for the bed and put out an arm to keep myself upright. I shuddered, cold as my body tried to recover, and Kisten pulled me to him. Vampire blood and sex. Holy crap, they weren't kidding. It *was* good enough to kill a person.

Shifting himself back to the headboard, we found an almost-upright stance with his arms warm around me. "Are you okay?" he asked.

"Fine." I couldn't stand, but I was fine. I was better than fine. *I had been afraid of this?*

My hand was on his chest where his shirt hung open. Pulse slowing, I shifted my fingers across his skin, feeling the smoothness. I looked for my pants, finding them puddled before the dresser. Kisten was still in his. Mostly. Contentment rose high in me, and I smiled, worn out and exhausted. I could hear his heartbeat, and I listened to it as it slowed. "Kisten?"

"Mmmm-hmm?"

The sound rumbled up through his chest and into me. I could hear the peace in it, and I snuggled closer. Fingers fumbling, Kisten pulled the lightweight coverlet over us.

"That was incredible," I said, shivering at the comforter's smooth silk backing. "How do you . . . how do you go to work and live a normal life knowing that's there to find?"

Kisten's arms about me tightened. His one hand rose to find mine, stilling my motion against his skin. "You just do," he said softly. "And you're a good bite. Innocent and eager."

"Stop . . ." I moaned. "You make me sound like a . . . a . . ." I didn't know what to call myself, and "slut" sounded so nasty.

"Blood slut?"

"Shut up!" I exclaimed, and he grunted as my elbow jabbed him when I moved.

"Be still," he said, wrapping his arms around me, keeping me where I was against him. "You're not."

Forgiving him, I slumped back into his warmth. His hand moved against my hair, gentling me, and I watched the lights from the city reflected onto the low ceiling as a deep lassitude drifted into me. I ran my tongue across the insides of my caps to find the taste of him all the way to the back of my throat, and I couldn't concentrate well enough to decide if I liked finding it there or not. My pulse was slowing, taking my thoughts with it. I knew I should be worried about Ivy, but all I could manage was a sleepy, "Ivy . . ."

"Sh-h-h-h," he whispered, his hand ever moving, soothing me. "It's okay. I'll make sure she understands."

"I'm not leaving you, Kisten," I said, but it sounded like I was trying to convince myself.

"I know."

And in his silence that followed, I heard the echoes of the women before me who had said the same thing. "It wasn't a mistake," I whispered, eyes closing. I knew I was blood-sugared, his pheromones probably hitting me especially hard from my having taken his blood. "I didn't make a mistake."

His hand moving atop my head never slowed, never sped up. "Not a mistake," he agreed.

Reassured, I lay against him and inhaled his scent to find comfort. I wasn't going to abandon that feeling, no matter what. "So what do we do now?" I breathed as I started to fall into sleep.

"Whatever the hell we want," he answered. "Sh-h-h-h, go to sleep."

The last of my tension eased, and I wondered if I should take my caps off. "Anything?" I whispered, surprised at how natural they felt. I'd forgotten I had them on.

"Yeah, anything," he said. "Go to sleep. You haven't had a good sleep in days."

Safe in Kisten's arms, I closed my eyes, feeling more secure than I had since my dad had died. Only now did I feel the gentle movement of the boat, rocking me into oblivion. I was sated in mind and body and soul. Kisten's arm was over me. It was like the warmest comforter on the coldest morning. I exhaled, finding a peace I hadn't known I'd been missing.

And as I hovered in a curious mix of waking and sleep, I heard Kisten sigh, his fingers still gentling the hair about my forehead. "Don't leave us, Rachel," he whispered, clearly not aware I was still awake. "I don't think Ivy or I could survive it."

TWENTY

Standing at the church's door in the early-afternoon sun, I shifted the shiny paper sack of three-dollar pastries and wedged the foam container of brewed gourmet coffee into the crook of my elbow. One hand free, I managed the latch and pushed on the heavy door. The strap to my shoulder bag slipped to my elbow to throw me off balance, but my held breath eased out when it opened. Thank God it wasn't bolted. Ivy would hear me for sure if I had to come in the back.

Listening, I pushed the door wider. My stomach was upset. I'd like to say it was from lack of sleep, but I knew it was from how the next hour was going to play out. Kisten hadn't broken my skin, but Ivy was going to be pissed, especially after being so clear yesterday. One way or another, my life was going to change—in the next sixty minutes.

Letting Kisten face the fallout wasn't going to happen either. Ivy was my roommate; it had been my decision. And after I had quelled my minor panic attack in Kisten's bathroom this morning, I'd convinced him to let me tell her. She wanted a relationship with me, and if I came in unrepentant and matter-of-fact, she'd hide her feelings until she could deal with them. If he came to her meek and guilty, she'd get mad and do who knew what. Besides, Ivy had shown me what she could offer, then walked out the door. What did she expect me to do? Be celibate with Kisten while I figured it all out? Kisten had been my boyfriend first.

But she was my friend, and her feelings mattered.

The sack of Godiva chocolate and the thimble-size jar of dogwood-blossom honey that had set me back ten bucks swung from a pinkie as I eased the door shut and, in the darkness of the foyer, kicked off my shoes. So I wasn't above bribery. So sue me.

A thick silence gave me pause. It was eerie, and I padded in my sock feet through the sanctuary. Ivy had moved her stereo out, though the furniture was still clustered in the corner. I wondered if she was waiting for me to finish the living room together. The church felt different, the blasphemy seeming to grate heavily on my aura.

Head down, I hustled past her closed bedroom door, not wanting the scent of coffee to wake her until I was ready. I wasn't a fool to believe that coffee, pastries, chocolate, and honey would be enough to soothe Ivy's hurt emotions and Jenks's worry, but it might buy me time to explain before the shit hit the fan. Kisten wanted me to tell her I'd bitten him to understand her hunger better, but it would be a lie. I'd bitten him because I had known he'd enjoy it. That it had felt good to me had been an unexpected surprise—which I was embarrassed about now.

Safe in the kitchen, I set the pastries by the sink, wincing at the nine-by-thirteen pan of unfrosted chocolate cake and tub of white frosting. *She made me a cake while I was sleeping with Kisten?* Great.

"The nice plate," I said, quashing my guilt and rummaging for the plate Ivy had bought at a garage sale this spring after I'd said I liked the violets on the open-weave rim. Not finding it, I slid the top everyday black plate out, glancing at the empty hallway when the ceramic clinked. The sack crackled as I took out and arranged the pastries. The coffee was next, and my frown deepened when Ivy's Vampiric Charms mug wasn't in the cupboard. It wasn't like her to put it in the dishwasher, but the door creaked, so I poured the brew into a set of smaller cups.

"Now for Jenks," I muttered, getting a matching dessert plate and setting the single square of fudge on it, strategically placing the honey beside it. This was going to work. I'd talk to them both together, and it was going to be all right. It wasn't as if I had let him bite me.

Ready, I spun to the table. My face went cold. Ivy's computer was gone.

My thoughts flew to the sanctuary and her missing stereo. "Please, let us have been robbed," I whispered. Scared out of my mind, I hustled into the hallway. Had she found out and left? *Damn it! I wanted to be the one to tell her!*

Pulse pounding, I stopped before Ivy's door. I felt hot, then cold. Hesitating, I tapped the thick wood. "Ivy?" No answer. I took a deep breath, knocked again, and turned the handle. "Ivy? Are you awake?"

Heart in my throat, I looked in. Her bed was made and her room looked normal. But then I saw that her book was gone from her night-stand and the closet was empty.

"Oh . . . crap," I breathed. My eyes darted to the wall with her informal collage of pictures. They were all there from what I could tell, but then I wondered. The picture of Jenks and me standing before the Mackinac Bridge. Had there been an empty spot on the fridge?

Feeling unreal, I paced to the kitchen, my stomach caving as I entered. It was gone.

"Ah . . . shit," I swore, and a tiny harrumph pulled my attention to the sink.

"Shit?" Jenks said, standing on the windowsill between his sea monkeys and Mr. Fish. "Shit!" he shrilled, coming to hover before me. His face was tight in anger, and black pixy dust spilled from him. "Is that all you have to say? What did you do, Rachel?"

Mouth open, I took a stumbling step back. "Jenks . . ."

"She's gone!" he said, hands clenching. "Packed up and left. *What did you do!*"

"Jenks, I was—"

"She leaves, and you come home with bribes. Where were you?"

"I was with Kisten!" I shouted, then fell back two steps when he flew at me.

"I can smell him *in* you, Rachel!" the pixy shouted. "He bit you! You let him bite you when you knew Ivy couldn't! What the *hell* is wrong with you!"

"Jenks. It's not like that—"

"You stupid witch! If it's not one of you, it's the other. You women are all damned fools. She makes a pass at you, and you screw everything up by letting Kisten bite you so you can feel secure in your own sexual drives?" He darted at me, and I put the center island counter between us, but seeing as he could fly over it, that was kind of useless. "And then you try to buy me off with fudge and *honey*? You can stick my dragonfly's turds on a stick and roast them, because I can't take you two women screwing my life up anymore!"

"Hey!" I shouted, hands on my hips and leaning to put my nose inches from him. "He didn't bite me! She never said I couldn't bite him. She only said he couldn't bite me!"

Jenks pointed a finger at me. He took a breath, then hesitated. "He didn't bite you?"

"No!" I shouted, burning off some adrenaline. "You think I'm stupid?" He raised a hand, and I added, "Don't answer that."

He landed on the counter, arms crossed over his chest and his wings a blur of agitation. "That doesn't make it right," he said, sounding sullen. "You knew it would bother her."

Pissed, I slammed my hand on the counter to make him jump into the air. "I can't live my life by what bothers Ivy! Kist is my boyfriend! Ivy making a pass at me didn't change that, and I'll have sex with who I want and how I want, damn it!"

His feet touched the counter, and his wings went still. Guilt hit me hard as I looked at him standing there. I wished he were bigger so I could give him a hug and tell him it was going to be all right, anything to get that terrible look of betrayal and anger off him. But he just stared.

Sighing, I swung a chair around. I sat on it backward and put my folded arms on the counter, slumping to get my eyes on the same level as his. He wouldn't look at me. "Jenks," I said softly, and he sneered, wings coming alive. "It's going to be okay. I'll find her and explain." I reached out, letting my hand fall to curve protectively around him. "She'll understand," I said, gazing at the cake and hearing the guilt in my voice. "She has to."

He looked at me, his arms uncrossing. "But she left," he said plaintively.

My hand beside him moved in a motion of exasperation. "You know how she can be. She just needs to cool off. Maybe she went to spend the weekend at Skimmer's?"

"She took her computer."

Glancing at the empty space, I winced. "She couldn't have found out that fast. What time did she leave?"

"Right before midnight." He stopped pacing and looked at me

sideways. "It was really weird. Like that movie where the guy gets a call and it triggers a set of actions programmed into him years ago? What's the name of that movie?"

"I don't know," I muttered, glad he wasn't yelling at me anymore. She couldn't have left because of this. Kisten and I hadn't even had dinner yet by midnight.

"She wouldn't answer me," he said. He resumed pacing, and I watched, wondering how much of his outburst had been worry for Ivy finding an easy outlet in anger at me. "She just packed her clothes and her computer and her music and left."

My eyes went to the fridge and the empty tomato magnet. "She took our picture."

"Yeah."

I pulled myself up. Something had happened, but it was unlikely she knew about Kisten and me, and there was no way for her to find out until she got back. Jenks was the only one who knew; I had taken the bus home, so even Steve wouldn't smell Kisten's blood in me. "Who called? Skimmer?" I asked, wondering if it had simply been an emergency run. *An emergency run she hadn't taken Jenks on? Or even told him what it was?*

"I don't know," Jenks said. "I came in when I heard the whine of her computer shut off."

Lips pressed together, I thought about that.

"Why, Rachel?" Jenks asked, his voice tired.

I didn't move anything but my eyes. "My biting Kisten is not why she left."

His angular face pinched in distress. "Maybe someone found out and called her."

The thought of what Ivy was capable of in a fit of rage passed through me, and I reached for my shoulder bag. The timing was wrong, but still . . . "Maybe I should call Kisten."

He nodded in worry, coming closer as I punched the right buttons. I held the phone from my ear, and we both listened to it ring until it shunted me into voice mail. "Hey, Kisten," I said, eyes on Jenks, "give me a call when you get this. Ivy wasn't here when I got home. She took her computer and music. I don't think she knows, but I'm worried." I wanted to say more, but there wasn't more to say. " 'Bye," I whispered, and hit the "end" button. *'Bye? God, I sounded like a little lost girl.*

Jenks peered up at me, the color returning to his wings. "Call Ivy," he demanded, but I was already ahead of him. This time I was dumped right into voice mail, and I left a guilty-sounding message that I had to talk to her and not to do anything until I talked to her. I wanted to say I was sorry, but I closed the phone and looked at it sitting alone on the counter.

Suddenly the pastries arranged on their plate looked trite. I was an ass. "Jenks . . ."

The coaxing in my voice turned his worry into a cold anger. "I don't want to hear about it. You screwed everything up for one moment of blood passion. Even if that's not why she left, she will when she finds out. What's *wrong* with you? Can't you leave things alone?"

"No, I can't!" I exclaimed. "And it wasn't just a moment of blood passion, it was an affirmation of what I feel for Kisten, so you can shove it, you little twit. I know what I'm doing," I said. He opened his mouth to protest, and I threw my hands up in the air. "Okay, maybe I don't, but I'm *trying* to figure this out. It's all mixed up. The blood, the passion. It's all mixed up, and I don't know what to do!"

He was clearly taken aback, and I surged ahead, almost panicked. "I want Ivy to bite me," I said. "It feels too damn good, and it would do both of us good. But the only way to do it safely is to sleep with her. And I'm not going to sleep with her just for the blood passion until I know what's going on in my head. I never thought I'd like a girl—I mean, I'm straight, right? Is it the vamp scar that's turning me on, or her? Do I love Ivy or just the way she can make me feel? There's a difference, Jenks, and I'm not going to cheapen it if it's only about the blood." I knew my face was red, but he deserved to hear it all. "Ivy made a pass at me because she knows I make decisions by doing stuff and then thinking about it, not the other way around. Well, I'm doing different stuff, and look how messed up everything got. Isn't this nice?" I said sarcastically, gesturing behind me at Ivy's empty place.

Jenks's wings went still, and he sat down on edge of the fudge plate. "Maybe you should try it," he said, and a spike of adrenaline shot through me and was gone. "Just once," he coaxed. "Sometimes the quickest way to find out who you are is to be that person for a while."

I'd thought of that already, and it scared me. Slowly I brought my eyes to his. "Then why are you upset that I bit Kisten?" I said. "That's me trying to be someone new. You think I would've done that a year ago? Why is it wrong when I try things with Kisten and not Ivy?"

His gaze went to her empty spot at the table. "Because Ivy loves you."

My gut tightened. "So does Kisten."

Jenks brought his knees to his chin and clasped his hands around his shins. "Ivy would die for you, Rachel. Kisten won't. Put your emotions where they will keep you alive."

It was a hard truth. Ugly. I didn't want to choose who I loved by who could keep me alive. I wanted to make decisions on who I loved by who completed me, made me feel good about myself. Who I could love freely and help make a better person by just being there. God, I was confused. Tired, I pillowed my head on my folded arms and stared at the table, inches from my nose. I heard the soft sound of wings, and the draft from Jenks stirred my hair.

"It's all right, Rachel," he said, close and concerned. "She knows you love her."

My throat closed, and I sighed. Maybe I should try it Ivy's way. At least as far as I could without becoming uncomfortable or freaked out. Just once. A moment of embarrassment would be better than all this confusion. And awkwardness. And misery.

The small dinner bell at the front door rang, and I jumped. Jenks's face was full of hope when I brought my head up, then fear. If something had happened to Ivy, I wouldn't get a phone call but a stone-faced I.S. agent on my doorstep telling me my roommate was in the city morgue.

"I got it," I said, the chair scraping as I rose. I hustled into the sanctuary, hoping it was Ivy with her stuff and needing someone to open the door for her.

"I'm right behind you," Jenks said, sounding grim as he joined me in the hall.

TWENTY-ONE

My stomach was in knots when I pushed open the heavy oak doors to find Ceri. Forcing a smile, I felt both relief and disappointment when I saw her beaming in the sun, her long fair hair floating and a squishy wrapped present in her hands. She was wearing a summery, ankle-length linen dress and was barefoot—as usual. I wasn't surprised to see Rex, Jenks's cat, at her feet. The orange kitten was purring, rubbing her ankles.

"Happy birthday!" the young-seeming woman said cheerfully.

Jenks dropped three feet. "Crap, is that today?" he stammered, then zipped off.

My distress that it wasn't Ivy faded. "Hi, Ceri," I said, flattered she had remembered. "You didn't have to get me anything!"

She came inside and handed me the package. "It's from Keasley and me," she said in explanation, eager and flustered. "I've never gotten anyone a birthday present. Are you going to have a party?" Her face went solemn. "I wanted to have a party for Keasley, but he won't tell me when his birthday is, and I don't know what day I was born."

My smile went bemused. "You forgot?"

"My kin never celebrated a person's years, so the day I was born never meant anything. It was in the winter, though."

I found myself nodding as I followed her in. She was from the Dark Ages. They didn't celebrate birthdays then. I seemed to remember that from a class.

"Ivy made a cake," I said, feeling depressed. "But it's not frosted yet. Do you want some coffee and pastries instead?" *May as well. Ivy isn't going to eat them with me.*

Stopping in the middle of the sanctuary, she turned, anticipation brightening her expression. "So you're going to have a party later?" she asked.

"Probably not," I said, and when her shoulders slumped, I laughed. "Not everyone has a party, Ceri, unless they have stock in a card company."

Her lips pursed. "Now you're making fun of me. Go on. Open your present."

I could tell she wasn't really upset, so I opened the squishy package, tossing the paper into the trash basket under my desk. "Oh, thank you!" I exclaimed as I found a soft casual shirt made from brushed cotton. It was a vibrant red, almost glowing, and I could tell without trying it on that it would fit me perfectly.

"Jenks said you needed a new shirt," she said shyly. "Do you like it? Is it suitable?"

"It's beautiful. Thank you," I said, feeling the richness of the fabric. It was a simple style, but the cloth was scrumptious and the neckline would flatter my small chest. She must have spent a fortune. "I love it," I said as I gave her a quick hug, then rocked into motion. "I should hang it up. Do you want some coffee?"

"I'll make tea," she said, her gaze going to the empty spot where Ivy's stereo had been. Her steps soft behind mine, she hesitated at the door to my room upon catching sight of Trent's bridesmaid dresses and my newest party dress hanging from the back of the closet. "Oh!" she exclaimed. "When did you get *that*?"

I beamed, finding an empty hanger and wrangling her shirt onto it. "Yesterday. I needed something for a run, and since it's a party, I bought something appropriate."

Jenks's laugh rang out even before he was in sight. "Rache," he said as he landed on Ceri's shoulder, "you have some odd ideas of dress codes."

"What?" I fingered the stiff black lace at the hem of the skirt. "It's a nice dress."

"For a wedding rehearsal? It's in a church, right?" He screwed his face up in a pious look. "Spank me, Father, for I have sinned," he said in a falsetto.

My eyes narrowed, and I hung up Ceri's gift. It was in the Basilica, actually. The Hollows' cathedral. "It's the party afterward I want to look nice for."

Jenks snickered, and Ceri frowned. Her eyes were crinkled at the corners, but she didn't move, since Rex was twining about her feet, meowing for Jenks. "That's a nice dress," she said, and worry filled me at her forced tone. "It looks as if it will keep you cool and comfortable even if you are outside. And it's probably easy to run in."

"Tink's knickers, I hope it doesn't *rain*," Jenks said sarcastically. "*Everything* you got will be on display."

"Hush," Ceri admonished. "It's not going to rain."

Crap. I should have waited until Kisten could shop with me. Suddenly worried, I unzipped the two silk garment bags. "These are the brides-maids' dresses," I offered, wanting to get Jenks's attention off my new outfit before he saw the cherries painted on the jacket's snaps. "Ellasbeth hasn't picked which one yet," I said, touching the split skirt of the black lace dress. "I hope it's this one. The other is just ugly."

"And you *knows* ugly when you *sees* ugly, don't ya, sweet thang."

I glared at Jenks. "Shut up. What are you wearing tonight, pixy?"

Jenks's wings shifted into motion, and he rose from Ceri's shoulder. "My usual. Holy crap, tell me those aren't cherries?"

I snatched up the hanger and shoved it into my closet. Why was I worried about what I was going to wear? I should be worried about the focus and who was killing Weres to find it. I wasn't ready to believe that Mr. Ray and Mrs. Sarong weren't responsible. And, realistically, it was only a matter of time before they called my bluff and came after me.

Ceri was frowning at Jenks when I turned. Seeing my attention on her, she changed her severe, wordless admonishment to him to a worried smile for me. "I think it suits you," she said. "You will look . . . unique. And you are a unique person."

"She's going to look like a forty-dollar hooker."

"Jenks!" Ceri exclaimed, and he darted out of her reach to sit atop my dresser mirror.

Depressed, I looked at my closet. "You know what? I'm going to wear the shirt you just gave me. With some jeans. And if I'm underdressed, I'll just add some jewelry to it."

"Really? You want to wear the shirt I chose?" Ceri said, so brightly that I wondered if Jenks had coached her on what to buy to fit this situation. He looked far too smug, and Ceri's ears were as red as the shirt. My eyes narrowed in suspicion, and the slight woman turned her attention to the black lace bridesmaid gown, touching the fine fabric.

"This is beautiful," she said. "Do you get to keep it after the wedding?"

"Probably." I trailed my hands down the lace sleeves. They'd drape dramatically over my fingertips, and the built-in bodice would show off my waist. I'd never go to another function where I could wear anything so elegant, but just having it would be nice. It was slit up the side but cut so that it wouldn't give anything except brief glimpses.

"The bitch hasn't decided which dress yet," I said sourly. "If she picks the other, I'm going to double my fee. Call it hazard pay. Look at it." I gestured disparagingly at the lace-hemmed collar that dipped so low it would make my small chest look nonexistent. "There are no curves at all. Just a straight tube all the way from my shoulders to the floor. I won't be able to run if I need to, much less dance unless I hike the thing up past my knees. And the lace?" I touched the outer covering, trying to hide the ugly color of pea soup as if in shame, feeling the rough edges of the second-grade lace catch on my fingers. "It's going to catch on everything. I'll look like a freaking sea cucumber."

That didn't get the expected smile, and when I met Jenks's eyes, he glanced at Ceri's softly creased brow and shrugged. Rex sat at her feet as though she might get some attention if she stared hard enough. "He's marrying a Were woman?" Ceri said, her voice unusually soft.

"No. I was being rude." I shoved the green dress away, not wanting to talk about it.

Jenks moved to the closet's shelf. "I've never met Ellasbeth, but she sounds more prickly than a porcupine's scab."

Though icky, it was a pretty good description. "Nice visual, Jenks," I muttered.

Ceri's thin fingers were tracing the tiny stitches on the black sleeve. I don't think she had even heard me, so enamored of the dress was she.

"This one would be a pleasure to dance in. If she chooses the other, she is either an idiot or a sadist."

"Sadist," Jenks said, his feet swinging. "I wish they made cameras I could carry. I know the *Hollows Observer* would pay good money for a shot of Rachel and Trent dancing."

"Ha!" I barked, gently taking the pretty dress and putting it in my closet, newly organized thanks to Newt. "That will be the day."

"You have to," Jenks said, the sparkles sifting from him turning silver. "It's the rules."

I sighed. Yes, I was probably going to have to dance with him if I was in the wedding party. Ceri had a wicked smile on her face. "Well, I'm not going to enjoy it," I said, trying not to think about his tight ass and how he showed off a tux. My height looked good against his class, and it would be fun to get Ellasbeth's knickers in a knot. I shut my closet door, smiling. "Do you know how hard it is to slow-dance with a gun strapped to your thigh?"

"No." Jenks followed me out to the kitchen, Ceri and the cat trailing behind.

"Where's Ivy's computer?" Ceri asked when we entered, and I cringed.

"I don't know." My stomach tightened as I looked at her empty corner. "I spent the night at Kisten's, and she wasn't here when I came home."

Face still and empty, the elf looked up from the sink from where she was filling the copper kettle. Her gaze went from the pastries arranged on the plate to the store-bought coffee to the square of fudge. But it wasn't until she saw the honey that she figured it out. "She's gone," Ceri said, turning off the tap with excessive force. "What happened?"

"Nothing," I said, feeling guilty and defensive. "Well, sort of nothing," I amended. "God, Ceri, this isn't any of your business," I added, crossing my arms over my chest.

"She bit Kisten this morning," Jenks said helpfully. "While bumping uglies."

"Hey!" I said, embarrassed. "That is not why she left. We hadn't even finished dinner before she walked out." Taking a breath, I faced Ceri, surprised to find her jaw set in disapproval. "He's my boyfriend!" I exclaimed. "And he didn't bite me. And why in hell does everyone think I should live my life by what Ivy wants?"

"Because she loves you," Ceri said, standing beside the lit stove. "And you love her, as a friend if nothing else. She's afraid, and you're not. You're the stronger person in this situation and need to exert some restraint. You can't live your life by her wishes," she added, holding up a hand to forestall my protest. "But you know this is something she is aching to share with you."

Miserable, I glanced at Ivy's empty spot and then back to Ceri. "She can't separate blood passion from sex, and I don't think I can either," I whispered, wondering how my personal life had become everyone's favorite topic and why I was being so open about it. Apart from my being completely lost and trying to find anyone to help me.

"Then you have a problem," Ceri said, turning her back on me to open a cupboard.

I couldn't read her mood at all. "I never said I was good at this," I muttered. Getting up, I pulled a mug from the cupboard, but when I dropped a tea bag into it, her eyes narrowed.

"Go sit and drink your foul coffee," she said, her voice harsh. "I'll make my own tea."

Jenks snickered, and after I moved the plate with the honey and fudge to the table, I sat with my cold gourmet coffee. It had lost much of its appeal. Ceri's silent disapproval was obvious, but what was I supposed to do? I didn't like the idea that Ivy had left to move in with Skimmer without telling me, but it was the best explanation I had right now.

Ceri brought the ceramic teapot out from under the counter. Throwing my tea bag away, she measured out two spoonfuls of loose tea. Jenks flitted to his honey and wrestled with the top until I opened it for him. Some birthday this was turning out to be.

"Jenks?" I warned, my eyes going to Rex. The orange cat was sitting in the threshold of the kitchen, watching me with those creepy kitten eyes. I'd seen Jenks on honey; it got him drunker faster than a frat boy avoiding finals, and Rex liked little winged things too much for my comfort.

"What!" he said belligerently. "You bought it for me."

"Yes, but I was hoping you'd be sober this afternoon for our run."

Snorting, Jenks settled himself before the jar brimming with the sticky amber. "Like I've ever been drunk for longer than five minutes?" Clearly eager, he pulled what looked like a set of chopsticks from his back pocket. Manipulating them expertly, he spindled a wad of the honey into his mouth. His wings drooped and stilled when he swallowed, and a giggle slipped from him. "Crap, this is good stuff," he said around a gooey mouthful.

Five minutes. That was about right, but I was worried about Rex.

Ceri stood at the sink and warmed the teapot with hot tap water. I thought it a useless step that only served to make more dirty dishes, but Ceri was the expert when it came to tea. Her gaze went to Jenks, now holding the sticks high over his uptilted head and letting the honey dribble into him. It was going exactly where he wanted, even if he was starting to cant to one side.

"Can you take that into the overhead rack?" I said, worried.

Stiffening, Jenks gave me a wide-eyed, unfocused look. "I can fly, woman. I can fly better honey-drunk than you can fly stone sober." To prove his point, he lifted into the air, Making a whoop of exclamation, he lost altitude. Ceri's hand was under him in a flash, and he started giggling. "Listen, listen!" he coaxed while he slumped on her hand, then belched the first two lines to "You Are My Sunshine."

"Jenks . . ." I protested. "Get off Ceri. That's disgusting."

"Sorry, sorry," he slurred, almost falling. "Damn, that's good honey. Gotta take some of this to Matalina. Matalina would like it. Maybe help her sleep a little."

Clearly concentrating, he had sparkles sifting from him thick and furious as he wobbled down to the table. I sighed apologetically, and Ceri smiled, snagging Rex as the cat padded past her, headed for Jenks. The cat settled herself in Ceri's arms, purring.

"Kitty, kitty, kitty," Jenks slurred as he landed next to me and his honey. "Kitty wants some honey? S' good hu-honey?"

Yeah, my life was weird, but it had its moments.

Ceri leaned against the counter while she waited for her water to warm. "How have you been sleeping lately?" she asked as if she were my doctor. "Any more sneezing?"

I smiled, flattered she cared. "No. I didn't sleep much this morning, but that wasn't Minias's fault." Her eyebrows rose, and I added, "Do you think Newt will show up again?"

She shook her head solemnly. "No. He will watch her carefully for a time."

Fingers gripping my cold coffee, I thought that if Newt did show up, there wasn't much I could do about it, seeing as she had taken control of Ceri's triple circle with the ease of opening a letter. Remembering me taking Tom's circle. I went to ask her about it, then didn't. It had to be because I'd walked into its construction. That's all. I was sure I'd read somewhere that this was possible. And I didn't want to risk hearing her say it was unusual.

Singing the Rolling Stones' "Satisfaction," Jenks sat cross-legged before his one-ounce jar, ladling honey into himself. "I will protect you, Rache," he said, cutting his music short. "I'll give that demon a labiotomy, boobotomay, lob, lob, lobotomy if he shows up again!"

I made a wry face, watching him fall over, laughing merrily at himself, then sitting up with a loud "Ow." Depressed, I pulled a ribbon of dough from the pastry. It was dry, but I ate it anyway.

Ceri's water started to steam. Managing to fill her teapot with Rex still in her arms, she brought her brew to sit on the table. Jenks staggered to the teapot, wings a blur for balance as he put his back to it and slid down with a heavy sigh.

"May I ask you something?" Ceri asked, her eyes on her empty cup.

I didn't have anything to do until about six, when I would start getting ready for my run, so after putting the top back on Jenks's honey, I pulled a foot up onto my chair and clasped an arm around a knee. "Sure. What?"

A faint hint of pink on her cheeks, she asked, "Did it hurt when Ivy bit you?"

I stiffened, and Jenks—his eyes closed—started mumbling, "No, no, no. Damn vampire made it feel good. Ah, crap, I'm tired."

Swallowing, I met her eyes. "No. Why?"

Her lower lip turned in, and, biting it to look charming, Ceri grew solemn. "You should never be ashamed of loving someone."

My blood pressure spiked. "I'm not," I said defensively.

I was belligerent because I was afraid, but instead of responding with an equal amount of ire, she unexpectedly dropped her eyes. "I'm not finding fault with you," she said softly. "I . . . envy you. And you need to know that."

My fingers laced about my knee tightened. *Me? She envies my screwed-up life?*

"You say you don't trust people," Ceri rushed to explain, her vivid green eyes pleading for understanding. "But you do trust. You trust too much. You give everything even when you're afraid. And I envy that. I don't think I could ever love anyone without fear . . . now."

Jenks hiccupped. "Aw, Ceri. It's okay. I love you."

"Thank you, Jenks," Ceri said, sitting primly in her chair. "But it would never work. Your body is not as big as your heart, and much as I'd like to think I am a soul and a mind, I have a body that needs to be satisfied as well."

"The hell I'm not big enough!" he protested, lurching up. Only one wing was working, and it almost knocked him over. "You just ask Matalina." The pixy went pale. "Never mind."

Ceri poured out some tea, the amber liquid gurgling with the sound of contentment to stand at contrast with my unease. I slowly pulled my second knee up to my first. "Jenks, sit down," I murmured when his staggering path toward the honey went off track and he angled for the table's edge. Glad for the distraction, my thoughts drifted to Trent and Ellasbeth's marriage. I was reaching for Jenks when he collapsed into the napkins and pulled one over his head.

Why hadn't I told Trent about Ceri? Or Ceri about Trent? I was a lousy judge of character, but even I could tell that the two seemed made for each other. Trent wasn't that bad. Though he had kept me caged as a mink. And put me in the fights. And tricked me into trying to take Piscary down by myself, though some of that stupidity was my fault.

I pulled another ribbon of pastry from a roll. Trent *had* treated me with respect the night I'd been his paid bodyguard, then kept me alive during the aftermath. He'd trusted me to take care of Lee on my own instead of killing him like he wanted to. Though if I had let Trent kill his friend, I wouldn't be playing bodyguard at his wedding . . . probably.

This is a mess, I thought, washing the pastry down with a swallow of cold coffee. Ceri could decide what she wanted to do. And if Trent used her, I'd freaking kill him. And because I was gaining his trust, I could probably get close enough to do it. Which was a terrifying thought.

My heart beat faster, and I wiped my fingers on a napkin. "Ceri?" I said, and she looked up expectantly. Rex was still on her lap, and her fingers were gentling the animal. Taking a steadying breath, I said, "I've got someone I want you to meet."

Her green eyes met mine, and a smile grew. "Who?"

I looked at Jenks, but he was out of it, sleeping under the napkins. "Uh, Trent." My chest clenched, and I prayed I was doing the right thing. "See, he's an elf."

Beaming, Ceri pushed Rex to the floor so she could lean across the table. The cat stalked out of the room, and the scent of wine and cinnamon filled me when Ceri gave me a quick hug. "I know," she said as she leaned back and smiled at me. "Thank you, Rachel."

"You knew?" I said, warm from embarrassment. God, she must think me an insensitive boob, but she settled herself in her chair and smiled as if I had just given her a pony. And a puppy. And then the freaking moon. "Kalamack, right?" I stammered. "We're talking about the same Trent? Why didn't you say anything?"

"You gave me back my soul," she said, her hair drifting. "And with it the chance to redeem my sins. I look to you for guidance. Until you approved of him, it would have caused problems. You made no attempt to hide that you don't like him."

She smiled shyly, and I stared. "You knew he was an elf?" I asked, still not believing it. "How? He doesn't know about you!" *At least I don't think he does.*

Embarrassed, she pulled her feet up under her to sit cross-legged, looking both wise and innocent. "I saw him in a magazine last winter, but you didn't *like* him." Her eyes flicked to mine and then back down. "I knew he had hurt you. Keasley told me he controls the Brimstone trade, and, like anything in excess, it's damaging. But, Rachel, how can you condemn all the good for a little bad?" she said, not a hint of pleading in her voice. "It's been illegal for thirty-two years out of five thousand and is a blatant way for humans to try to control Inderland."

When you put it like that, Trent almost sounded respectable. Bothered, I leaned back. "Did Keasley tell you he blackmails people using illegal genetic research? That his Make-A-Wish camps are underground genetic labs where he helps children in order to blackmail their parents?"

"Yes. He also told me that Trent's father cured your blood disease because your father was his friend. Don't you think you owe him a debt of gratitude?"

Whoa. My breath caught, and I felt cold, not about the debt-of-gratitude thing, but that Keasley knew something I hadn't until last solstice. "Keasley told you that?"

Ceri watched me over her teacup. Her head went up and down, nodding sharply.

My worried gaze went to the blue-curtained window above the sink and the sunlit garden beyond. I was going to have to have a talk with Keasley. "Trent's father saved my life," I admitted, bringing my attention back to her. "My dad and his were friends and work partners. And they both died because of it, so I think that rubs out any gratitude I might have." *Stupid-ass elf thinks the world owes him everything.*

But Ceri only sipped at her tea. "Maybe Trent put you in the rat fights because he blames your father for his father's death."

I took a breath to protest, then slowly let it out. *Crap. Is Trent as insecure as the rest of us?* Smug, Ceri topped off her cup.

"Didn't you blame him for the loss of your father?" she asked, unnecessarily, I might add.

"Yes," I said, realizing that her putting it in past tense worked. I didn't blame him anymore. Piscary had killed him—in a roundabout way. Somehow. Maybe. And if I was a good little witch and kept Trent's little elf ass above the green, green grass during his wedding, he just might tell me the details. Giving myself a mental shake, I filed that away to think about later. "Do you want to meet him?" I asked tiredly, sounding oh so thrilled at the prospect.

Her remaining ire vanished, and she smiled from across the table. "Yes, please."

Yes, please. As if she needed my okay. "You don't need my permission."

My tone was almost sullen, but she dropped her eyes demurely. "I want it." She set her cup on the saucer with a clink. "I was raised with the expectation that someone would guide me in matters of the heart: a guardian and confidante. My mother and father are deceased. My kin has been diluted by time. You rescued my body, freed my soul. You are my Sa'han."

I straightened in my chair as if ice had washed over me. "Whoa! Wait up, Ceri. I'm not your guardian. You don't need one. You're your own person!" *Is she nuts?*

Ceri set her feet on the floor and leaned forward, her eyes asking for understanding. "Please, Rachel," she begged. "I need this. Being Al's familiar tore everything from me. Give this piece of my life back to me? I need to resume ties to my old life before I can cut them and move into this one."

I felt panicky. "I'm the last person you should seek advice from!" I stammered. "Look at me! I'm a mess!"

Smiling softly, Ceri dropped her eyes. "You're the most caring person I know, consistently risking your life for those who can't fight on their own. I see this in the people you love. Ivy, who is afraid she can't fight her battle alone anymore. Kisten, who struggles to stand in a system where he knows he's too weak. Jenks, who has the courage but not the strength to make a difference in a world that doesn't even see him."

"Aw, thanks, Ceri," the pixy mumbled from under his napkin.

"You often see the worst in people," she said, "but you *always* see the best. Eventually."

I gaped at her. Noting my unease, she hesitated. "Do you trust Trent?"

"No!" I blurted, then paused. But here I was broaching the subject of introducing Ceri to him. "Maybe in some things," I amended. "I trust your judgment, though."

Apparently it was the right thing to say, since Ceri smiled and put a cool hand upon mine. "You believe in him more than you realize, and though I may not know him, I trust your judgment, slow as it is in coming." Her smile turned wicked. "And I'm not a silly girl to be blinded by a tidy posterior and expansive landholdings."

Tidy posterior and expansive landholdings? Was that the Dark Ages equivalent of a tight ass and a lot of money? I chuckled, and her hand slipped away. "He's devious," I warned. "I don't want you to be taken advantage of. I know he's going to want a sample for his labs."

Ceri sipped her tea, her eyes focused on the sunlit garden. "He can have it. I want my species to recover as much as he does. I only wish I'd pre-dated the curse so the damage could be fixed completely instead of the bandage he has been slapping on our children."

My fingers curled around the cool porcelain, but I didn't bring the cup to my lips. Trent owed me big-time. Ceri was giving him one hell of a better bandage. "He's manipulative," I added, and she raised one eyebrow.

"And I'm not? Do you think I couldn't wind this man about my finger if I wanted?"

I looked away, worried. Yeah, she could.

Ceri laughed. "I don't want a husband," she said, green eyes twinkling. "I have to reinvent myself before I can share my life with anyone. Besides, he's getting married."

I couldn't help my snort. "To a really nasty woman," I muttered, starting to relax. I did *not* want Trent marrying Ceri. Even if Trent weren't such a dirtbag, I'd probably never see her again after she found his garden.

"I do believe," Ceri said wryly, "you think this wedding is just punishment for past sins."

Nodding, I glanced into the garden following a flash of motion. I stood up and went to the window to see that it was just Jenks's kids driving a hummingbird out of the yard. "You haven't met her," I said, marveling at their teamwork. Ceri came to stand beside me, the rich scent of cinnamon drifting off her to tickle my nose. "She's a terrible woman," I added softly.

Ceri's gaze followed mine into the garden. "So am I," she said, more softly still.

TWENTY-TWO

Slumped in the back of the cab, I watched the passing buildings and imagined Ellasbeth's disdain for the clearly lower-class shops. Though the Hollows' cathedral was world-renowned, it was in a somewhat depressed area of town. Unease trickled through me, and I straightened, pulling my bag with its charms and splat gun onto my lap. I should have worn something else. I was going to look like a slob in jeans.

Jenks was on my shoulder, rapping my hoop earring in time with the calypso beat on the cabbie's radio. It was way past annoying, and though I knew it would likely only encourage him, I murmured, "Stop it."

My neck went cold as he lifted off to land on my knee. "Relax, Rache," he said, standing with his legs spread wide for balance and his wings a blur. "This is a cakewalk. How many people? Five, counting her parents? And Quen will be there, so it's not like you're alone. It's the wedding you're going to have to worry about."

I took a deep breath, cracking the window to set my hair drifting. Looking down, I picked at the engineered hole in my knee. "Maybe I should have worn a dress suit."

"It's a wedding rehearsal, for Tink's panties!" Jenks burst out. "Don't you watch the soaps? The richer you are, the more you dress down. Trent will probably be in a swimsuit."

My eyebrows rose, picturing his trim physique wrapped in spandex. *Mmmm . . .*

Wings stilling, Jenks adopted a bored expression. "You look great. Now, if you had worn that *little thang* you picked out . . ."

I shifted my knee, and he took to the air. We were only a block away, and early.

"Excuse me," I said, leaning forward and into the cabbie's enthusiastic rendition of Madonna's "Material Girl." I'd never heard it done calypso before. "Could you circle the block?"

He met my gaze through the rearview mirror, and, though clearly thinking I was crazy, lurched into the left-turn lane and waited for the light. I rolled the window down all the way, and Jenks landed on the sill. "Why don't you check it out?" I said softly.

"Already ahead of you, babe," he said, reaching to see that his red bandanna was in place. "By the time you get around the block, I'll have met the locals and get the sitch."

"Babe?" I said tartly, but he had darted out and was among the gargoyles. I rolled up the window before the street breeze could make a mess of the intricate French braid his kids had put my hair in. I didn't let them go at my hair very often. Their work was fantastic, but they chatted like fifteen-year-olds at a concert—all at once and a hundred decibels louder than necessary.

The light changed, and the driver made the turn carefully, probably thinking I was a tourist getting an eyeful. The sharp-cornered, tidily mortared stones rose up as high as perhaps an eight-story building, to look massive and permanent compared to the low shops that surrounded it. The cathedral sat tight to the curb on two sides, shading the street. There were shade-loving plants tucked into the moist shelter of the flying buttresses. Expansive stained-glass windows were everywhere, shadowed and dull from the outside.

I squinted as I took it all in, surprised at the lack of welcome that I found in my church. It was like visiting your great-aunt who disapproved of dogs, loud music, and cookies before dinner; she was still family, but you had to be on your best behavior and you never felt at ease.

After a quick scan of the side of the cathedral, I dug in my bag for my cell phone and tried to call Ivy again. Still no answer. Kisten wasn't answering either, and there had been no response when I called Piscary's earlier today. I'd be worried, but it wasn't unusual. They didn't open until five, and no one manned the phone when they were closed.

The back of the cathedral was a narrow walled garden and cracked parking lot. At the corner I set my phone to vibrate and tucked it into my front jeans pocket, where I would know if it rang. More parking was on the third side, empty but for a dusty late-model black Saturn in the shade and a basketball court, the hoop bolted onto a light pole at NBA regulation height. Across the way was another, much taller one. Mixing species on the court wasn't a good idea.

I braced myself when the cabbie pulled up, running his left wheel over the low curb of the one-way street. Shoving the car into park, he started messing with a clipboard. "You want me to wait?" he asked, glancing at the dingy storefront across the street.

I dug a twenty out of my purse and handed it to him. "No. There's going to be a dinner afterward, and I'll bum a ride from someone. Can I have a receipt?"

At that, he looked at me over his paperwork, his deeply tanned face showing surprise. "You know someone who's getting married here?"

Jenks was hovering impatiently outside, but I hesitated, beaming. "Yes. I'm in the Kalamack wedding."

"You kidding me?" His brown eyes widened to show that the whites were almost yellow. The faint scent of musk tickled my nose. He was a Were. Most cabbies were. I had no idea why. "Hey." He fumbled for a card, handing it to me along with my blank receipt. "I have my limo license. If they need anyone, I'm available."

I took it, admiring his moxie. "You bet. Thanks for the ride."

"Anytime," he said as I got out. He leaned out after me through the window. "I've got access to a car and everything. This is only my day job until I finish getting my pilot's license."

Smiling, I nodded and turned to the multiple doors. *Pilot's license? That's a new one.*

The cab merged into the light traffic, and Jenks dropped down from wherever he had been. "I leave you alone for five minutes," he complained, "and you get hit on."

"He just wanted a job," I said, admiring the four strands of sculptured vines arching over the twin set of wooden doors. *Absolutely gorgeous . . .*

"That's what I'm saying," he grumbled. "Why are we here this early anyway?"

"Because it's a demon." I eyed the gargoyles and wished I could talk to them, but trying to wake a gargoyle before the sun was down was like trying to talk to a pet rock. There were a lot of them, though, so the cathedral was probably secure. I winced at the potted flowers on the sidewalk, wondering if I could get them moved. It would be too easy for fairy assassins to hide in them. Bringing my attention to Jenks, I added, "And as much as I'd like to see Trent taken down by a past jealous lover or a disgruntled demon, I want my forty thousand for babysitting."

He bobbed his head before landing on my shoulder. "Speak of the devil . . ."

I followed his attention to the street. Crap, they were early, too, and now, doubly glad for having gotten here when I had, I tucked in my new shirt and waited as two shiny cars approached, looking out of place among the flatbed trucks and salt-rusted Fords.

I had to jerk myself up and onto the shallow steps when the first one pulled out of traffic and up entirely onto the wide sidewalk. A gray Jaguar was behind it, also parking on the walk.

"You've got to be crapping in my daisies," Jenks said from my earring, and I took my sunglasses off to get a better look.

Ellasbeth was in the first car in the front seat, and while she collected herself, the uniformed driver opened the door for a pair of older people in the back. Mr. and Mrs. Withon, I assumed, since they were tall and elegant, darkly tanned and having the "trendy" look of the West Coast. They were in their sixties, I'd guess, but well-preserved sixties. Hell, they were elves—they could be three hundred for all I knew. Although they were dressed in casual slacks and tops, one could still tell that their shoes cost more than most people's car payments. They stood and smiled in the sun as if looking into the past and seeing the land without the buildings, cars, or urban apathy.

Ellasbeth stoically waited for the driver to open her door. Swooping out, she tugged the short jacket covering her white shirt straight and draped a matching purse over her shoulder. Sandals clicking, she rounded the back of the car, her ankles bare below trim capri pants. She was in hues of peach and cream, her yellow hair back in a braid similar to mine with green ribbons woven in. With red lips and shades firmly in place, she never looked at the church, clearly not pleased to be here.

Seeing her class, I was embarrassingly thankful that Jenks and Ceri had stepped in and bought me a clue.

Putting on my happy face, I came down the steps.

"Isn't this such a sweet little church, Mother?" the tall woman said, twining her arm in her mom's and gesturing at the basilica. "Trenton was right. This is the perfect place for an understated wedding."

"Understated?" Jenks muttered from my earring. "It's a friggin' cathedral."

"Hush," I said, liking her parents for some reason. They looked content together, and I found myself wanting to keep them that way, so when I woke at night alone, I'd know that somewhere there was someone who had found love and made it last. No wonder Ellasbeth was ticked at being asked to marry someone she didn't love when she had grown up seeing her parents' contentment. I'd be mad, too.

The hair on my arms prickled, and I turned to see Quen already out of the gleaming Jaguar. He was dressed in his usual black pants and shirt, a pair of soft shoes on his feet. A leather belt with a silver buckle was his only decoration. I wondered if it was charmed. The pox-scarred man raised his eyebrows at me in greeting, and I decided it probably was.

Quen was headed for Trent's door, but before he could get there, Trent had opened it himself. Blinking in the strong afternoon sun, he gazed at the sky, his eyes moving as he traced the lines of the front tower outlined against it. His jeans fit him nicely, properly faded and hitting his boots just right. A silk shirt of a deep green that matched Ellasbeth's ribbons gave him some flash, going well with his tan and fair hair. He looked good, but not happy.

Seeing the five elves together, I wondered at the differences. Ellasbeth's mother had Trent's same wispy hair, but her father's was closer to Ellasbeth's—rougher, almost looking like a poor attempt to match it. Beside them, Quen's dark features and ebony hair looked like the other side of the coin, but no less elven.

Ellasbeth brought her gaze from the scrollwork above the big doors when Trent and Quen approached. Her gaze lit upon me, and her expression froze. I smiled as she realized we had our hair up in the same way. Her face under her perfect makeup went stiff.

"Hello, Ellasbeth," I said, having been introduced to her by her first name the night she'd walked in on me soaking in her tub. Long story, but innocent enough.

"Ms. Morgan," she said, extending a pale hand. "How are you?"

"Fine, thank you." I took her hand in mine, surprised that it was warm. "I'm honored to be in the wedding party. Have you decided which dress yet?"

The woman's expression went even stiffer behind her shades. "Mother? Father?" she said, not answering me. "This is the woman Trenton arranged to work additional security."

As if they can't tell I'm not one of her friends? I thought, taking their hands as they were offered. "Pleasure to meet you," I said to each of them in turn. "This is Jenks, my partner. He'll be working the perimeter and communication."

Jenks's wings clattered to life, but before he could charm them with his sparkling personality, Ellasbeth's mother gasped. "He's real!" she stammered. "I thought he was a decoration on your earring."

Ellasbeth's father tensed. "A pixy?" he said, taking a wary step back. "Trent—"

A burst of dust spilled from Jenks to light my shoulder, and I all but snapped, "This is my team. I may be bringing on a vamp if I think it necessary. If you have a complaint, take it up with Trent. My backup can keep his mouth shut about your precious *secret identities,* but if you show up for the wedding dressed like extras for some ridiculous movie, it won't be my fault if someone figures it out."

Ellasbeth's mother was staring at Jenks in fascination, and the pixy had noticed. Red-faced, he zipped from one side of me to the other in agitation, finally landing on a shoulder. Clearly the pixy paranoia went from coast to coast, and she hadn't seen one in a while.

"I can't keep your butts above the grass without him," I continued, darting increasingly nervous glances at Ellasbeth's mom, whose green eyes were bright and captivated. "And this overdone media circus is likely going to bring the weirdos out of the woodwork."

I stopped, seeing as no one was listening. Mrs. Withon had blushed to look ten years younger, one hand on her husband's shoulder as she failed to hide her desire to talk to Jenks.

"Oh, the hell with it," I muttered under my breath. Then, louder, "Jenks, why don't you escort the ladies into the church where it's safer."

"Rache," he whined.

Mr. Withon pulled himself straighter. "Ellie," he warned, and I reddened.

Trent cleared his throat. Stepping forward, he took my elbow in restraint, disguising it as a companionable motion. "Ms. Morgan's commitment to her job is as obvious and up-front as her opinions," he said dryly. "I've used her in the past, and I trust her and her partners implicitly in sensitive matters."

Used me. That's about right.

"I can keep a secret," Jenks muttered, his fitfully moving wings shifting my hair.

Mrs. Elf beamed at him, and again I wondered at the possible species relationship elves and pixies might have had, broken when the elves went underground. Jenks's kids loved Ceri. 'Course, they loved Glenn, too, and I knew he was a human.

Ellasbeth caught her father's wary look, her red lips compressing at her mother's charmed smile. "Trenton, dear," the nasty woman said, looping her arm back into her mother's. "I'm going to show my parents the interior of the cathedral while you instruct the help on their duties. It's such a quaint little church. I honestly didn't know they made cathedrals this size."

I bit back my ire, proud of the Hollows' basilica. And I wasn't the "help." I was the person who was going to keep the rabble from taking potshots at them as they paraded their rich elf asses down main street.

"That sounds equitable, love," Trent said from beside me. "I'll meet you inside."

Ellasbeth leaned to give him a peck on the cheek, and though he trailed a hand along her cheek as she moved away, he didn't kiss her back.

Heels clacking on the sidewalk, she led her parents to the side door, since the front was clearly locked. "Send Caroline in when she arrives?" she said over her shoulder, effectively telling us to stay outside until the maid of honor got here. That was fine with me.

"I'll do that," Trent called after them, and the three elves turned the corner, Ellasbeth loudly telling her mother about the lovely little baptism pool. Her father was bent in conversation with her mother, clearly berating her for her interest in Jenks. She wasn't listening, almost walking sideways in her attempt to get a last look at Jenks.

Jenks was silent, clearly embarrassed. I thought it odd, since he charmed humans all the time. Why was it different when an elf liked him?

"Hey, uh, Rachel," he said, the hum of his wings loud as he lifted to hover before my eyes, "I'm going to take a look around. Back in five."

"Thanks, Jenks." But he was already gone, his tiny body a speck darting over the spires.

I brought my eyes back to find Quen waiting for me. "You expect me to believe a pixy is an effective backup?" he asked, eyebrows high. "Why do you have him out here? Are you trying to make the situation difficult?"

Somehow Quen's attitude didn't surprise me. Stifling my pique, I headed to the side parking lot. "He'll have the lowdown on the entire block in thirty seconds. I told you you're doing yourself a disservice by keeping pixies out of your garden. You should be begging for a clan to move in, not lacing sticky web in your canopy. They're better sentries than geese."

The older elf's wrinkles slid into each other as he frowned. He had come up on my left, and with Trent on my right I felt surrounded. "And you trust Jenks?" Quen asked.

I think it was the first time Quen had called Jenks by his name, and I glanced at him as we rounded the corner and the traffic noise dulled. "Implicitly."

No one said anything, and, embarrassed, I blurted, "I can't protect you if you aren't together. Or is this just a way to have someone pretty on your arm when you walk into a room?"

"No, Ms. Morgan," Trent said softly, his bangs drifting in the slight breeze. "But seeing as the sun is up, how much danger can we be in from a demon? I don't expect Lee to show, and if he does, it won't be until after dark." He hesitated. "With a demon pulling his strings."

We couldn't very well go in after Ellasbeth had told us to stay out, and I wasn't eager to spend more time than I had to with her. It seemed Trent wasn't either, so we settled to a stop by the side stairs and the less imposing secondary entrance off the parking lot. My sandals scuffed against the white lines of the painted-on basketball court, but Quen was silent in his soft shoes. I wanted a pair despite that they would leave me that much shorter.

"You . . . ah, trust me in sensitive matters?" I said to Trent. "What does that mean?"

Trent tracked a flock of pigeons, blinking as they crossed the sun. "It means I trust you to keep your mouth shut but not to keep your fingers out of my desk."

Quen shifted to stand almost out of my sight. I turned to keep him in it. "That bothered you, didn't it? That I could sneak into your office?" I asked.

Ears reddening, Trent glanced at me. "Yes."

Pleased, I shifted my shoulders. Casual looked good on him, and I wondered what he'd look like in a burger joint with his elbows on the table and his hands wrapped around a half pound of beef. He wasn't much older than me, forced to grow up fast when his parents died. I wanted to ask him if his kids would have pointed ears when they were born, but I didn't. "I won't do it again," I said suddenly, not knowing why.

At that, Trent turned to face me. "Break into my home? Is that a promise?"

"No. But I won't."

Quen cleared his throat to cover a chuckle. Green eyes fixed on mine, Trent nodded. He didn't look happy, and I was feeling sorry for him. "That," he said, "I'll believe."

Quen stiffened, but his attention was on the sky, not me. I put my hand up when I recognized Jenks's wings. "Rache," he panted, landing on my hand and grasping my thumb when he nearly fell off. "We got a problem . . . coming down the road . . . in a '67 Chevy."

"Better than a trip wire," I said dryly to Quen, wondering if I should move my new cuffs from my shoulder bag to my hip. Then I asked Jenks, "Who is it? Denon?"

The car in question came around the corner: a powder blue convertible with the top open. Engine racing, it pulled into the far end of the lot. Quen shifted from casual to protective. Pulse pounding, I tapped a line. The rush of power took me by surprise, and I staggered. "I'm fine," I said, pushing Trent's arm off me. "Stay behind me."

"It's Lee!" Trent said, his face alight. "My God, Lee!"

My mouth dropped open. The car lurched to a halt, parked ten feet away and cantwise to the lines. Trent stepped forward, and I yanked him back. *Lee escaped Al?*

The man turned off the car and pulled his head up, smiling at the three of us and squinting from the sun. Leaving the keys in the ignition, he opened the door and got out.

"Lee . . . ?" I stammered, not believing it. A rush of guilt swept me. Though I had tried to prevent it, I had been there when Al took Lee as his familiar instead of me. That he had escaped was impossible, but here he was, angling his trim surfer-boy body out of the car with an unconscious grace. His small nose and thin lips gave him casual good looks, and his Asian heritage was obvious in the straight, severely black hair cut short above his ears. Looking confident and cocky in a faintly frumpy black suit, he strode forward with hands outstretched.

"It's not Lee," Jenks said, having moved himself to my shoulder. "He doesn't smell right, and that's not a witch's aura. Rache, that isn't Lee!"

Shock became mistrust. "Stay back!" I said, jerking Trent behind me when he moved.

He stumbled, then caught his balance. Scowling, he tugged his shirt straight. "The sun is up, Morgan. I know a few rules about demons, and that one you can't break. Lee escaped. What did you expect? He's an expert at ley line magic. Deal with the jealousy."

"Jealous!" I barked, not believing this. "You want to bet your life on it?" Lee was still coming forward, and, putting out a hand, I shouted, "Stop right there! I'm telling you to stop!"

Lee obediently halted ten feet away, his black hair gleaming in the light. He drew a pair of round sunglasses from a pocket and perched them on his small nose, hiding his brown eyes. Hands spread wide in innocence wronged, he almost bowed. "Good afternoon, Rachel Mariana Morgan. You look eminently *ravishable* with the sun in your hair, love."

The blood drained from my face, and I took a faltering step backward. It wasn't Lee. It was Al. The voice had been Lee's, but the cadence and pronunciation were Algaliarept's. *How?*

"Holy crap! It's Al!" Jenks squeaked, and his grip on my ear tightened.

"Get him in the church," I hissed at Quen. Feeling betrayed, I almost panicked. The sun was up! This wasn't fair! There was scuffling behind me and Trent's indignant complaint. *Damn it,* I thought. *This isn't a committee decision.* "Get him out of here!" I yelled.

Al's smile widened. He stepped toward us.

There wasn't time. I lunged forward, my forearms hitting the pavement, my fingers brushing the white marking of the basketball court, and my toes taking the rest of my body weight. *"Rhombus!"* I shouted. Tears sprang up at the gravel cutting the soft part of my arms, but with a welcoming drop of power through me, the amber wash of ever-after flowed up from the earth, arching to a close over our heads.

Hurt, I let my knees touch the pavement, and I slowly got up, brushing my arms and palms free of grit. Damn it, I had ruined Ceri's present. I glanced first at Al—who looked mildly insulted—then Trent and Quen, safe inside my circle with me.

The older elf was stiff, clearly not liking being in my bubble—large as it was. Face tight, he eyed the black smears of demon smut crawling over my amber-tinted enclosure. It looked particularly ugly in the sun, and since Quen was skilled in ley line magic, he knew that the black was a reflection of what I had done to my soul—and the only way I could have gotten it that fast was by playing with demon magic.

Angry, I backed up, still rubbing my arms. "I got it twisting a demon curse to save my boyfriend's life," I said in explanation. "I didn't kill anything. I didn't hurt anyone."

Quen's face was empty of emotion. "You hurt yourself," he said.

"Yeah. I guess I did."

Trent scuffed his feet. "That's not Lee," he whispered, his face ashen.

Jenks landed on my shoulder—having flown off when I hit the ground. "Good God, the man is dumber than Tink's dildo. Didn't I say it wasn't him? Did my lips not move and say it wasn't him? I'm small, not blind!"

Recovering his earlier aplomb, Al smiled. Trent retreated into Quen's protection, away from me and Al both. Al had mauled Trent the same night the demon had first attacked me; Trent had a right to be afraid. But the sun was up. This could *not* be happening.

We all jumped when Al poked a finger at my bubble, and the black seemed to pool in the ripple he made. "No, not Lee," the demon said. "Yet it is him. One hundred percent."

"How?" I stammered. Had we been spelled into thinking it was daylight when it was really after sunset?

"The sun?" Al looked up, taking off his glasses and basking in it. "It is splendidly pretty without the red sheen. I quite like it." His gaze fell to me, and I shivered. "Think about it."

One hundred percent Lee, but not Lee? That left only one possibility. And whereas if someone had asked me Monday, I would have said it was impossible, I now found it remarkably easy to believe, after having shoved a demon out of my thoughts just three days ago.

"You're possessing him," I said, feeling my stomach clench.

Lee clapped his hands. He was wearing white gloves, and it looked wrong, so very wrong.

"You can't do that," Trent said from my elbow. "It's a—"

"Fairy tale?" Al brushed a piece of nonexistent dust from himself. "No, just *very* expensive and *normally* impossible. It's not supposed to last past sunup either. But your father?" Al looked from Trent to me and back to Trent. "He made Lee special."

It had been mockingly sincere, and I went cold. Lee's blood could kindle demon magic. So could mine. Ah, swell. Just peachy damn keen. But Lee was smarter than this. He knew that Al couldn't hurt me and get away with it. There was more. We hadn't heard it all.

I could smell the clean scent of crushed green leaves, and I realized Trent was sweating. "You tricked him," Trent said, the distress clear in his voice. I didn't think it was fear for himself. I think he was truly distressed that his childhood friend was alive and trapped in his own head by a demon.

Al put his shades on. "I got the better end of the deal, yes. But I'm following it to the letter. He wanted out. I gave him his freedom. In a manner of speaking."

"Lee," Trent said, moving forward, "fight it," he encouraged.

Al laughed, and I drew Trent back. "Lee's gone," I said, feeling ill. "Forget him."

"Yes, listen to the witch." Al wiped his eye with an elegant hankie drawn from a pocket. He wasn't using the ever-after. His sunglasses had been in a pocket, too. His abilities were diminished to Lee's. It went along with what Ceri had said about demons being no more powerful than a witch, apart from several thousand years of storing charms and curses inside themselves. If he was truly in Lee's body, then he was limited to what Lee could do until he brewed himself back to omnipotence.

Very expensive. Normally impossible. It added up to one person. One crazy person. "Newt did this, didn't she?"

Jenks swore softly, and Al spun, his anger looking wrong on Lee's face. "You are getting annoyingly perceptive," he said. "I could have figured it out on my own."

"Then why didn't you?" I said, fear tightening all my muscles. "You can't twist a curse complex enough to best the sun. You're a hack," I prodded, and Jenks's wings hummed.

"Rachel, shut up," he pleaded when Al reddened. But I forged ahead, wanting to know why he was here. My life might depend upon it.

"You had to *buy* a curse from her," I goaded. "How much did it cost, Al? What do you want that you're too dumb to get on your own?"

He stared at me through the shifting bands of color of my bubble, and I stifled a shudder. "You," the demon said, chilling me. "If it gives me a shot at you, then it's worth my everlasting soul," he intoned, his voice sliding through me to leave the taste of lightning on my tongue.

I refused to back up, almost numb. My breath came and went, and Quen's presence seemed to grow stronger. "You can't," I said, voice quavering. "You made a deal. You or your agents can't hurt me this side of the lines. Lee knows that. He'd never agree."

Al's smile widened, and when he tapped his dress shoes against the pavement in delight, I saw he had lace on his socks. "Which is why I will free him the instant before you expire, so he is the one actually doing it. He has reason enough on his own to want you dead, so the agent clause won't come into play. But killing you is the last thing I want to do." Gazing past me to where the sky met the basilica's towers, he breathed deeply. "The moment I leave Lee, I am susceptible to summonings and such. And much as I hate to miss the fall parties, this is so-o-o-o much more fun. Don't think that makes you safe, though." He brought his gaze down, and I shivered at the alienness hidden behind the normal brown orbs. "I can keep you alive through a tremendous amount of pain."

I swallowed. "Yeah, and you can't go misty to avoid my foot hitting your crotch either."

Tilting his head, Al stepped back. "There is that."

"Who is Newt?" Trent said, reminding me I wasn't alone, and I jumped when he touched my elbow. "Morgan. I want to know right now if you practice demonology!"

Jenks darted from my shoulder, anger hard on his tiny features. "Rachel is not a practitioner!" he said hotly, easily dodging Quen's attempts to get him away from Trent. Quen dropped his hand, probably only now realizing how dangerous a small flying thing with a sword could be.

Trent's eyes had never left mine, trusting that Jenks wouldn't hurt him. His question had been laced with an iron demand for an answer. Fear lay under it, but stronger than that was anger at me for dabbling in demons. My eyes returned to Al. "Newt is a very old, crazy demon. I bought a trip home from her when your *friend* dumped me there."

"Her?" Trent stammered, panic sliding behind his green eyes. "There are no more female demons. We killed the last few before leaving the ever-after."

"Well, you missed one," I said, but Trent wasn't listening, having been pulled aside by Quen. The older elf was very distressed and I wondered what was bothering him. Al? Being trapped in my circle? The threat of Jenks? Ellasbeth's wedding being crashed by a demon? All of the above?

But then my own fear started to tighten about my spine. I had shoved Newt out of my thoughts a few days ago. *She'd been looking for the focus. Shit. What if Al wants it to pay off his new debt to her?* He had said the curse to do this was expensive. Was he the one killing the Weres trying to find out who had it?

"Why are you really here?" I breathed. If he was after the focus, there wasn't much I could do to stop him once he realized I had it.

My question seemed to delight Al, and he simpered, adjusting the cuffs of his gloves. "I'm here for my best friend's wedding. I would have thought that was obvious."

Damn it. It was the focus. I had to call Minias. I'd rather get a mark removed for it, not hang on to it until the school bully took it from me and I got nothing. But if Al got it, it would hit the streets as soon as the sun went down, sold to the highest bidder, and there we would be with an Inderland power struggle, courtesy of me.

My pulse was fast, but standing in this circle wasn't doing anyone any good. "Ready, Jenks?" I said, and the pixy dropped to hover beside me. He nodded, features tight as he shifted his grip upon his sword. Eyes narrowing, I reached my hand out and broke the circle.

Quen exploded into motion, jerking Trent behind him. "Morgan!" he shouted, and I rounded on him.

"Relax!" I snapped, releasing some tension. "He isn't going to do anything. He's here for a wedding." I glanced at Al, seeming eminently controlled and still standing right where he had been. "If Al wanted us dead, we'd have been in the ground a week ago. He's been here since the invitation hit Lee's mailbox." Pulse hammering, I turned to Al. "Am I right?"

Eyes hidden behind his glasses, the demon nodded.

"He's harmless," I continued, as much to convince myself as Trent and Quen. "Well, not as lethal, maybe. If he's in Lee's body, he doesn't have access to all the curses he's stored in himself over the past millennia. He's only as good as Lee is—was. Until he spends some time in the kitchen anyway. And he's going to follow the rules of our society, or he's going to end up in jail, which won't be any fun." Forcing my jaw to relax, I arched my eyebrows, wishing I could do the one-eyebrow thingy. "Will it?" I said.

Al inclined his head, and Quen almost jumped him, catching his movement in a sharp motion. "How fast you learn," the demon said, scowling at Quen's mistrust. "We must sit together at dinner. We have so much to chat about."

"Go to hell," I said softly. This was a crappy birthday, forty thousand notwithstanding.

"Not until I kill you, and though I will, it's not going to happen today. I like your yellow sun." Tugging up the sleeve to his jacket, he glanced at his watch. "I'll see you inside. I do so want to meet your darling little-woman-to-be, Trenton. Congratulations. It is an honor to stand up with you." His smile widened to show perfect, simply dazzling teeth. "Fitting," he drawled.

I felt a chill as I remembered Ceri. Oh, man . . . I had to call her. Al was loose.

Steps jaunty, Al headed up the stairs to the door, oohing and aahing at the architecture and detail work. His body language looked wrong on Lee's body, and with the strength of the ley line running through me, I felt like I was going to throw up.

"Quen," Trent said, clearly alarmed. "He can't go in there, can he?"

I pulled out my phone, then put it away, since Keasley didn't have a phone and Ivy wasn't home to relay a message to them. "He can," I said, remembering how Newt had controlled me while I was on holy ground. "Besides, only the stage and altar are sanctified, remember?" The basilica hadn't been fully sanctified since the Turn to allow Cincy's more important denizens to partake of life's little ceremonies. The altars were still blessed, just not the entryway and the pews.

We all watched Al open the door. Turning, he waved to us, then passed the threshold. The door shut behind him. I waited for something to happen. Nothing did.

"This isn't good," Quen said.

I choked back my burst of laughter, knowing it would come out sounding hysterical. "We . . . ah, had better get in there before he does something to Ellasbeth," I said, wondering if we might all go out for a beer first. Or a six-pack. In the Bahamas.

Trent rocked into motion an instant before Quen, and with Jenks on my shoulder again, I fell into step beside him. Trent dropped his head for an instant, then pulled it up to me. "You aren't a demon practitioner?" he asked as we took the first steps up.

I put a hand to my stomach, wondering if this day could get any worse. "No, but they seem to practice me."

TWENTY-THREE

The twenty-four-piece band Ellasbeth had hired was taking a break, leaving the muted intensity of a single classical guitar as a pleasant background to the self-congratulatory conversation at the far end of the table. Having long since lost my upright posture, I had an elbow on the pristine linen tablecloth, my fingers rolling the stem of my wineglass back and forth, wondering if I could bill Trent for the forty thousand even if Al didn't do anything.

The rehearsal dinner had been way over the top. I could have lived for a week on what had been put in front of me, and the waste bothered me. But that paled in comparison to my discomfort during the dinner conversation. Ellasbeth had shoved me, Quen, and Al as far from herself as she could. I was sure if she could have gotten away with it, the prickly woman would have put us in a different room. Al had earned his spot because of fear, I out of spite, and Quen to keep an eye on both of us.

Everyone at our end of the table was long gone; the ring bearer and his parents, the three flower girls and their folks, the ushers, and the woman who was going to sing were all laughing in a fawning circle about Ellasbeth. Trent was sitting by her. He looked tired. Maybe he should have taken more interest in the wedding arrangements and made sure that some of his friends were invited to balance out Ellasbeth's. Maybe he didn't have any friends.

Right now Al's chair was vacant, he having excused himself to go to the little boys' room. Quen had gone with him, and I didn't have anything to do until they returned. I thought the idea of a demon using the facilities was odd, and I wondered if Al was a living being and used to it, or if going to the can was a new and exciting experience.

Jenks had spent the evening in the chandelier avoiding Mrs. Withon. I found myself hoping he might pix Ellasbeth so we could leave. Tired, I raised my glass and sipped my wine. I was going to pay for it tomorrow, but damn, it was one of the best red wines I'd ever tasted. I would've looked at the label, but I knew it was far out of my reach, even without the allergies.

My gaze slid to Ellasbeth, and I rolled the possibility around in my thoughts that she knew I was allergic to it and had served it intentionally. As if feeling my gaze, she turned to me, smug as she chatted with her friends. Her face shifted expression for an instant when I heard Al's voice in the hallway. The demon in Lee's body came in laughing with the band trailing behind him, and I worried until I saw Quen with him. From the chandelier came Jenks's soft wing chirp, letting me know he had seen them.

Quen met my eyes, and I relaxed, taking another sip of wine and setting it out of my reach. It had surprised me how easy it was to work with the elf. We complemented each other, seeming to have found a comfortable body language that usually took me several runs with a person to develop. I wasn't sure if that was good or not.

The band settled themselves—picking up seamlessly with soft forties jazz when the guitar ended—and I clapped with the rest when a woman in a sequined gown started singing "What's New?" I slumped back, then started when I felt someone's hand on my chair.

Heart in my throat, I spun, my alarm falling into self-disgust. It was Lee, or Al rather, and his normal-looking brown eyes glittered in amusement. Pulse still fast, I sent my gaze to Quen. The older man smiled, seemingly enjoying that I had been surprised.

"What do you want?" I said, shoving Al's gloved hand off the back of my chair.

His gaze lifted to touch upon the small dance floor as Trent and Ellasbeth moved to it. Great. They were dancing. I'd be here all night.

Smiling like . . . well, the devil, Al gestured as if inviting me to dance. My breath puffed out of me and I crossed my knees. "Right." No way was I going to dance with Al.

Lee's striking Asian features melted into a smile. "You have something better to do? I have a proposition concerning that nasty mark of mine you're wearing."

My heart gave a pound, then settled. I felt every muscle tighten. Getting rid of my demon marks was high on my to-do list. But I was sure whatever he had in mind wouldn't do me any favors. Still, talking to Al here was better than doing this on the bus ride home, or my kitchen, or my bedroom if he decided to follow me. I glanced up to Jenks in the chandelier, and the pixy shrugged, his wings a dull orange. "Why the hell not," I muttered, standing up.

"That's the spirit!" Al dropped back a step to elegantly offer his arm.

I thought about my splat gun, then left it in my bag under the table. No need to put it in Al's reach. "Jenks is up there," I said, edging past Al to reach the dance floor without his help. "You do anything funny and he'll pix you."

"Oh, I'm shivering in my little silk boxers," Al scoffed.

"You've never been pixed," I said, and a frown crossed his brow, making my guess that he couldn't go misty to avoid pain and discomfort seem likely. My feet were on the parquet floor, and he put out his hand, waiting for me to take it.

Suddenly I realized I was standing face-to-face with a demon—and he wanted to dance. *O-o-okay,* I thought, thinking my life couldn't get any more chancy. Al huffed impatiently, and I slid my hand onto his. The white cotton of his glove was soft, and I stifled a shudder when his free hand went to my waist. If he tried to get rid of the air between us, I was going to slug him.

"There," he said when my hand lightly touched him and he shifted us into motion. "Isn't this nice? Ceri danced very well. I miss that."

Nice? It was as nerve-racking as all hell. My pulse was pounding, and I was glad he had on the gloves, not only because I didn't want to touch him but because I was starting to sweat. He had said something about getting rid of my mark, though, so I'd listen. "What—" I croaked, then cleared my throat, embarrassed. "What do you want?"

"This is a rare opportunity," Al said, smiling at me with Lee's beautiful teeth. "How often does one have the chance to dance with her savior amid the glitter of elves?"

I sighed in impatience. At least I told myself it was impatience. The reality was, I was starting to get a little light-headed from not breathing. "I'm out here for one reason only," I said, moving stiffly with him in time with the music. "And if you don't start talking, I'm going back to arranging the sugar packets."

Al's hand tightened on mine, and he shifted my weight. I bobbled when he spiraled me out to a swoop of music. Tense and gasping, he yanked me back, and I hit him, a puff of burnt amber assailing me. I pushed, but he had me close. Eyes wide, I tensed to stomp on his foot, but my muscles went weak when he whispered, "I know you have the focus."

His breath moved my hair, and this time when I struggled, his grip loosened. Pulse hammering, I put air between us. His hand on mine pinched, and, conscious of people watching, I put my hand back atop his waist.

"I can smell it on you," he murmured. "Demon magic, older than you, older than me. It marked your hand where you grasped it. It stains everything you touch, a trail that the knowing can follow like the dusting of prints."

I swallowed, moving woodenly to the slow jazz. "I'm not giving it to you," I said, hardly breathing. If I did, it'd be on the streets by sunrise. "You kill me and you'll lose your lease on Lee's body and have to go back. You hurt me and Newt will put you in a bottle. Let go of me."

Charm flowed from Al, looking wrong coming from Lee's body. "Yes. Let's do that," he said, his voice wispy with distraction. "Let's call Newt. She will show up right here and put me in a bottle. You'd like that, wouldn't you?"

I fought to not twist my fingers from him, but I knew he wasn't going to call my bluff. He was scared of her, too. Besides, I didn't know how to call her. I'd have to go through Minias, and I knew he wouldn't agree to it, whether he owed me a favor or not.

"I want something," he whispered, his eyes finding mine. "And I'll pay you well for it, but it's not the focus. Wouldn't you like that? To be free of my mark? To be free of me?"

I stared at him as we danced. He wanted something from me? Not the focus? Feeling ill, I moved my hand to his shoulder. My unfocused gaze on Ellasbeth and Trent shifted as Al turned us. I felt disconnected, short of breath. Al leaned in, and I did nothing, numb.

"I don't want the focus," he breathed, his words ruffling my hair, "but since you brought it up, you are in a spot of trouble." He hesitated, coming even closer. "I can help you there."

Jerked out of my thoughts, I pulled back. His gloved fingers gripped harder, and his eyes were stern with the warning to stay where I was. "I don't think you can keep it a secret much longer," he cautioned. "And, you aren't strong enough to hold it on your own once the world knows you have it. What will you do, silly girl?"

"Don't call me that," I said, then went cold as I put it together. He didn't want anyone knowing I had it? Damn. He *was* the one killing the Weres.

Alarmed, my eyes widened and I twisted my hand, only to have his grip tighten until it hurt. "You're killing Weres to keep it quiet that I've got it?" I said, my dance movements going stiff. "You killed Mr. Ray's secretary and Mrs. Sarong's accountant to warn them off?"

Throwing back his head, Al laughed. Eyes were on us, but as in high school, where the football star gets away with whatever he wants, no one intervened, frightened.

"No," Al said, confidence flowing from him as he reveled in the power he had simply by what he was. "I'm not killing them to protect you. That is delightful. I know who is, though. If they should find it, they would have no qualms about killing you for it. And that would really piss me off."

My first impetus to get away from him faltered. "You know who's killing the Weres?"

As he moved us to the music, he nodded. His black bangs had fallen before his eyes, and I could tell it was bothering him, but he wouldn't let go of me. I didn't think he liked Lee's hair, and I wondered how long it would be until he invested some kitchen time in making a curse to change his looks.

"Do you want to know who?" he said, tossing his head to clear his vision. "I'll tell you. For an hour of your time."

First my mark, and now the name of the murderer? "An hour of my time," I said, imagining how that hour might go. "Thanks, but no," I said dryly. "I'll figure it out for myself."

"In time to do anything about the next death?" he mocked. "Is a life worth sixty minutes of your time?"

Tensing, I glared. "I won't feel guilty for that," I said. "And why do you care?"

"It might be someone close to you," he mocked, and fear spiked through me, even as the music changed and the singer started in with "Crazy He Calls Me." I couldn't think as the music swelled, and I moved without resistance when Al danced us away from Trent, who was trying to eavesdrop on our conversation.

"I need a favor," Al said, lips barely moving and his voice heavy with embarrassment. "Do this one thing and I'll take the focus off your hands. I'll even promise to keep it until after you die. You'll never have to see the wars, the pestilence." He smiled, sickening me. "It's a no-brainer."

A golden age of peace that would last as long as I lived. Right. As soon as he got it, he'd kill me. With Ceri's help I might be able to make an ironclad deal to keep myself alive, but it was a false hope, and it made my chest hurt. I wanted the simple answer so badly.

I managed to swallow as I danced with the demon of my future's past. He said he didn't want the focus but would take it as a favor? I moved woodenly as I thought. Something wasn't right. I was missing something. Al said he liked it here, but I could see that the loss of his omnipotence was chafing him. There had to be a reason he was lowering himself to this fraction of strength, and I didn't think it had to do with wanting a suntan. He wanted a favor. From me.

Pulse settling to a hard beat, I eyed him squarely, squeezing his hand until he noticed. "What aren't you telling me, Al?"

The demon grimaced.

Pulling my eyebrows high, I made a telling face. "You're over here for a reason, and it's not me. I'm not that big a pain, and nothing is stopping you from dragging me off . . ."

My words trailed to nothing as a thought trickled through me. *Why hasn't he just dragged me off?* A smile quirked my lips, and I aimed it at the suddenly unsure demon. "You're in trouble, aren't you?" I guessed, knowing I was right when his smooth pace bobbled. "You're up crap creek, and you're hiding on this side of the lines because they can't drag you back while you're possessing Lee."

"Don't be inane," Al said, but he was sweating. I could see a bead of moisture at his temple, and his hand gripping mine in its glove was getting damp. "I'm here to kill you. Slowly."

"Then do it," I said boldly. "If you do, you're back in the ever-after. You put yourself into a huge amount of debt to stay here when the sun is up. The only one who knows is an insane demon who probably forgot about you already." Al frowned. Knowing I was pressing my luck, I said, "What did you do? Forget to return a library book?"

Pain cramped my hand, and I tried to pull from him. "It's your fault," Al snarled, the hate in his eyes stopping my protest. "Newt found out Ceri is running around under a yellow sun knowing how to spindle line energy, and since Ceri was my familiar, I'm the one responsible."

"Let go," I said, twisting my fingers.

"If I go back, I'm going to be held accountable," he said darkly, squeezing.

"You are *hurting* me!" I said. "Let me go, or I'm going to kick you in the 'nads!"

Al's grip loosened. I pulled away, standing three feet from him and glaring as the band continued to play, the singer's voice becoming distracted and uneasy. For an instant we stared at each other. Then he snatched up my hand and got us moving again. "Forgive me," he said, not sounding at all apologetic. "I'm understandably upset. I have never been in such a position before." His eyes narrowed. "They don't know you know the same, and it's in your best interest to keep your mouth shut about it. But you were there when she and I struck the deal, and you're going to tell them that she's been bound to keep her mouth shut but for one child. That the damage is contained."

My pulse was fast, but his hold was again light. The song ended, and we seamlessly moved into the next one, the pace slowing. "I Don't Stand a Ghost of a Chance." Figures. Arching my eyebrows high, I eyed him warily. "You want me to verify your story?" I said caustically. "They don't trust you. Why should I?"

Bother flashed over him, and before I could react, he pulled me into him. My breath was a quick intake, and I lost my bravado in a wash of icy fear. "Oh," Al hissed threateningly, his words shifting my wispy curls, "no need to get nasty." He crushed me to him, his heavy hand landing on the back of my neck.

Adrenaline spiked. I was playing with a tiger. I was taunting a freaking demon!

Behind me the band continued, albeit shakily. Seeing my fear, Al split his lips in a nasty grin. Leaning into me, he tilted his head and whispered, "It doesn't have to be this way. . . ."

His hand caressed my neck, and I sucked in my breath. Hot need trilled through me, sparking from neuron to neuron, lighting a path to my core. My knees buckled, but I didn't move, held in his grip. He was playing upon my scar, and doing it really, really well.

My next breath was a harsh gasp. I couldn't think, it felt that good.

Al's breath mingled with mine, uniting us when his breath swirled in my lungs. The scent of burnt amber mixed with the delicious feeling he instilled, forever melding the two. "Did you think only vampires could play upon your scar?" Al murmured, and I shook when he rubbed his thumb against me. "We came first. They're only our shadows."

"S-stop it," I said, my eyes closing. My pulse was a fast thrum. I had to get away from this.

"Mmmm, such beautiful skin," he breathed, and I shuddered. "You've been dabbling in a little vanity curse, my dear. It suits you."

"Go to . . . hell," I panted.

"Come with me and testify that Ceri has agreed not to teach anyone but a daughter," he insisted. "I'll take away a mark. I'll give you a night of this. A hundred vanity curses. Whatever you want. Rachel . . . we don't have to be adversaries."

A moan, feather light, slipped from me. "You're crazier than Newt if you think I'm going to trust you."

"If you don't," he said, breath moist and hot on me, "I'll kill you."

"Then you'll never get what you want." His grip clenched, and finding strength in the knowledge that he was trying to dominate me, I opened my eyes. "Let go!" I demanded, my hand balling up and pushing.

"Excuse me, Lee?" came Trent's voice from behind me.

The passion flowing through me cut off so fast I staggered, groaning. It hurt, damn it, having it ripped away so suddenly. Dizzy, I turned. Though Trent looked calm and confident on the surface, I could tell he wasn't. Behind him Quen watched from across the room, tense but distant. It was obvious he didn't approve of his Sa'han interfering.

"You have monopolized Ms. Morgan long enough," Trent said, smiling. "May I cut in?"

Al's gloved hand slipped from my neck. I took a breath, trying to expunge the last of the ecstasy he had drawn through me. I stumbled, feeling both numb and alive—unreal.

"Of course, Trenton," the demon said, placing my hand in Trent's. "I will console myself with talking to your beautiful bride-to-be."

I wasn't breathing right, and I blinked at Trent as the warmth of his hand stole into mine. But Trent wasn't looking at me.

"Watch your step, demon," Trent said, his green eyes hardening with an ancient hatred. "We are not helpless."

Al's smile widened. "That's what makes it fun."

I jumped when Al put a gloved hand on my shoulder, and I cursed myself for it. "I'll be in touch, Rachel," he said, voice full and throaty when he leaned closer.

"I'll sharpen my stakes," I said, pulling myself out of my shock.

His hand fell away, and he walked off laughing, jaunty and sure of himself.

And through it all, the band played on.

I took a slow breath and brought my eyes to Trent's. I didn't know what to feel. I was frightened, relieved. Grateful. He hadn't needed to intervene. I was supposed to be protecting him. It was obvious he wanted to know what Al and I had been discussing, but there was no way in hell I was going to tell him. Still . . . "Thank you," I whispered.

A smile twitched at his lips. His head bobbed slightly with the music three times, and then he pulled me into motion. "Yes, well, it's not like I want to marry you," he said.

My free hand rose as we moved, and after a moment I placed it lightly on his shoulder. Trent didn't say anything, and I started to relax. My pulse slowed, and I began seeing things again. The scent of green leaves pushed out the stench of burnt amber, and I abruptly realized I was utterly pliant in his arms, letting him direct me about the floor without a thought in my head.

I met his eyes. Seeing my horror, he chuckled.

"You are a surprisingly fine dancer, Ms. Morgan," he said.

"Thanks. So are you. Did you take classes, or is it an elf thing?"

Okay, maybe that had been a little sharp, but Trent didn't take offense, inclining his head gracefully. "A little of both."

My eyes darted to Ellasbeth. Al was moving in on her, but the woman didn't know it yet, too intent on trying to kill me with her thoughts. Beside her, her mother was trying to coax Jenks down. Her husband was sitting sullenly beside her, clearly having given up on trying to stop her, and as I watched, Jenks left his post, coming to a light landing before her. Even from here I could see he was embarrassed at the attention, but he was slowly warming up.

Trent twirled us so my back was to them, and I looked at him. "I can't believe you didn't tell them about Jenks," I said.

His eyes flicked to mine and away. "I didn't think it mattered."

A chuckle escaped me, and I found it did more than anything else to wash away the remnants of adrenaline. "Your entire species has been shunning pixy contact for forty years, and you don't think it matters? I think you were afraid to tell them."

Trent returned his eyes to mine. "No. It was for the entertainment value."

I believed it. He must be bored out of his ever-loving mind. "Trent. Is there something about pixies that you like?"

His hand on my waist pinched in warning. "Excuse me?"

I felt a stir of confirmation. "I'm just curious if there's an interspecies bond or something that you've been neglecting—"

"No."

That had been way too fast, and I smiled. He liked pixies but wasn't going to admit it. "It just seems as if—"

"No."

His movements went stiff, and I backed off before he danced me over to Al. "Are you ready for Sunday?" I said, changing the subject. "Wow, married in the basilica. I never thought that would happen."

"Me neither." His voice was distant and emotionless. "It should be quite a day."

I ran my gaze down him. "I bet you wanted to get married outside, huh? Under the trees in the moonlight?"

Trent's ears reddened.

"Oh, my God," I said. "You do, don't you!"

His roving eyes never met mine. "It's her wedding, not mine."

Needling Trent was one of my favorite things, and thinking that Al's showing up qualified as trouble and a pay increase, I shrugged, pleased that the day would end with money in my pocket. "I don't think it's her wedding either."

We had made a full circuit, and I was looking at Ellasbeth again. Al had captured her attention, and knowing that Trent didn't like his back to them, I moved freely under his direction until he could see them. I wasn't fooling myself that he loved her, but he clearly took his duties as husband seriously. "Sure am glad I'm not royalty," I muttered. "I wouldn't want to have to bump uglies with someone I can't stand. On a regular basis. And no one else."

"Ow!" I exclaimed, trying to yank my fingers from Trent but finding them caught. Then I colored, realizing what I'd said. "Oh . . . sorry," I stammered, meaning it. "That was insensitive."

Trent's frown turned into a sly smirk. "Bump uglies?" he said, eyes on the table behind me. "You are a font of gutter slang, Rachel. We must do this again."

The song had ended, and I felt his hand start to slip from mine. I glanced at Ellasbeth, uptight and glaring at me as Al whispered in her ear. The thought of the unending indifference Trent would endure lay heavy on my mind, and I licked my lips in a sudden decision. I tightened my hold on his hand, and Trent eyed me suspiciously.

His attempt to rock away from me turned into a tug, and we seamlessly stepped into "Sophisticated Lady." He spun me, and I caught a glimpse of Ellasbeth, white-faced as she listened to Al. She was a big girl. She could take it.

It was obvious that Trent had felt my desire to keep dancing, and I wondered if he went along with it simply to bother Ellasbeth. My focus blurred, and as Trent kept silent with his own thoughts, I found myself imagining his life with her. I was sure they would be okay. They would learn to love each other. It would likely take only a few decades.

My gut tightened. Now or never. "Ah, Trent," I said, and his gaze sharpened on me. "I've got someone I want you to meet. Can you come over tomorrow about four or so?"

His eyebrows rose, and without a hint showing that I was about to complicate his life beyond reason, he chided me, saying, "Ms. Morgan. Your pulse has increased."

I licked my lips, my feet moving by rote. "Yeah. So can you make it?"

Disbelief shone in his green eyes. "Rachel," he said irately, "I'm a little busy."

The song was at the refrain, and I knew he wouldn't dance another with me. "You know that old card you have in your great room, framed on the wall?" I blurted.

That got his attention, and he took a slow breath. "The tarot cards?"

Nervous, I nodded. "Yes. I know someone who looks like the person on the devil card."

Trent's expression went cold, and his hand pressed heavy on my waist. "The devil card? Is this some sort of deal you've got going?"

"Jeez, Trent," I said, insulted. "Not the devil. The woman he's dragging away."

"Oh." His focus blurred as he thought that over, and then he frowned. "That is in really bad taste. Even for you."

He thinks it's a joke? "Her name is Ceri," I said, stumbling over my words. "She used to be Al's familiar before I rescued her. She was born in the Dark Ages. She's just started putting her life back together and is ready to meet what's left of her kin."

Trent stopped, and we stood unmoving on the dance floor. Shock showed in his eyes.

"And if you hurt her," I added, my hands leaving him, "I'll kill you. I swear I'll track you down like a dog and kill you."

His mouth snapped shut. "Why are you telling me this?" he said, his face pale and the scent of green leaves almost an assault. "I'm getting married in two days!"

I put my hands on my hips. "What does your getting married have to do with anything?" I said, not surprised he would consider himself first and foremost. "She's not a broodmare, she's a woman with her own agenda. And as much as it might surprise you . . ." I poked a finger at his chest. ". . . it doesn't include the great and desirable Trent Kalamack. She wants to meet you and give you whatever sample you need. That's it."

Emotions crossed his features too fast to be recognized. Then the wall came down, and I shivered at the icy control. Saying nothing, he turned on a heel and walked away.

I stared at him, blinking. "Hey, does that mean you aren't coming?"

Moving stiffly, he crossed the room to talk to his parents-in-law-to-be, clearly trying to escape.

A prickling at the back of my neck pulled my attention to Quen. His eyebrows were high in question, and I looked away before he decided to come over. Arms clasped about myself, I headed for a back table where I could sit out the rest of the evening. Jenks landed on my earring in a gliding slide of gold sparkles, his almost nonexistent weight comforting and familiar. "You told him about Ceri?" he asked.

I nodded as the music ended, the singer's voice rising beautiful and alone.

Jenks's wings fanned my neck. "What did he say?"

Sighing, I sat down and started fiddling with the sugar packets. "Nothing."

TWENTY-FOUR

My feet hurt, and as I walked the last few blocks from the bus stop to my church, I paused to lean against a maple to take my flats off. A car whizzed by going way too fast, and I scowled at it, listening to the brakes squeal as it turned the corner. Jenks yelped in surprise from my shoulder when I bent at the waist to remove my shoes, darting off in a clatter of wings.

"Hey!" he snapped, the pixy dust sifting from him. "How about some warning, witch!"

I glanced up. "Sorry," I said wearily. "You were so quiet I forgot you were there."

His wing noise dulled, and he returned to my shoulder. "That's because I was asleep," he admitted.

My shoes hooked over two fingers, I straightened. The party had broken up early so all good elves could get home for their midnight siesta. Pixies kept to the same clock—sleeping four hours around midnight and four again at noon. No wonder Jenks was tired.

The cracked sidewalk was warm against the soles of my feet, and we made our way in the streetlight-lit darkness toward the cheerful glow of the bulb illuminating the VAMPIRIC CHARMS sign above the door. In the distance a siren wailed. The full moon wasn't due for a few days, but the streets had been busy, even here in the Hollows.

Not that I'd been listening, but the gossip I caught on the bus was that The Warehouse on Vine had caught fire again. The route home hadn't taken us anywhere near it, but the number of I.S. cruisers I'd seen had been astounding. The few people on the bus had looked afraid, for lack of a better word, yet my thoughts were too full of my own troubles to strike up a conversation, and Jenks, apparently, had been asleep.

My feet were silent on the steps, and I yanked open the door, my gaze darting to the coat hooks in the hopes of seeing something of Ivy's hanging there. Nothing.

Jenks sighed from my shoulder.

"I'm calling her right now," I said, dropping my shoes by the door and swinging my shoulder bag around.

"Rache." The pixy left me to hover where he could see my face. "It's been a full day."

"That's why I'm calling her." The connection went through as I wandered into the sanctuary, flicking on lights as I headed for the kitchen. Guilt whispered at me. She couldn't have found out about Kisten and me, and even then I think she would have yelled at me before she left. I think.

The sound of crickets joined the hum of Jenks's dragonfly-like wings as I thunked on the kitchen light, squinting until my eyes adjusted to the glare. Ivy's missing computer was depressing, and I dropped my bag on the table to try to make it look less empty. My cell phone rang until Ivy's phone told me it was going to voice mail and I disconnected.

I closed the top with a dull snap. Jenks was sitting atop his brine shrimp, feet moving slightly as his wings hung still from worry. "If it's not one of you, it's the other," he said sourly.

"Hey, I'm not the one who left last winter," I said, padding to the fridge for one of Ivy's bottled waters.

"You really want to bring that up?" he snarled, and I shook my head, feeling guilty.

"Maybe she's with Kisten," I said, cracking the plastic top and taking a swig. I wasn't thirsty, but it made me feel better, as if Ivy might come storming in demanding to know what I was doing drinking her water.

Jenks rose into the air, slowly unfolding to stand on the lid of his brine shrimp. "Let me know if you hear something. I'm calling it a night. Jhan is in charge if something comes up. If you need me, let him know."

My eyes widened. He had his kid playing sentry? "Jenks?" I questioned, and he turned from the screen, hovering by the pixy hole.

His shoulders lifted and dropped. "I'm going to spend some time with Matalina," he said, and I worked hard to keep from smiling.

"Okay," I said. "You want tomorrow off?"

He shook his head, then vaulted through the hole in the screen. I stepped to the window, leaning over the sink to watch him trail a green shimmer of dust to the stump in the garden. Then he was gone. I was alone. My eyes drifted to the cake Ivy had made for me, still unfrosted. I'd put foil on it this afternoon so it wouldn't dry out.

God, this stinks.

Refusing to let this become a pity party, I yanked one of my spell books out from the shelf and headed into the sanctuary with my water and the tub of frosting. I wasn't hungry, but I needed something to do. I'd watch local TV, since the cable wouldn't stretch out here, pretend to do some research, then go to bed early. Jeez, some birthday this had been.

Is it my fault Ivy's gone? I thought as I shuffled into the sanctuary. Damn it, why did I let my emotions make my decisions? No one had forced me to bite Kisten. I could have given him the caps back. But Ivy had no right to be upset. He was my boyfriend! Besides, she had said her kiss was a taste so I could decide what I wanted. Well, I was trying to decide, and Kisten figured into that.

Depressed, I flopped into Ivy's cushy suede chair. Vampire incense puffed up, and I breathed it deeply, looking for solace. Far off, I heard the bang of a transformer go, and I waited for the lights to blink out. They stayed lit, happy for me but sad for the squirrel that had just bit the big one, thanks to a zillion volts of electricity. I opened my spell book and snatched up the remote. It was almost midnight. The news probably had something now about the fire.

The TV brightened, and as the commercials blared and I ate a spoonful of frosting, I called Kisten. Nothing. Pizza Piscary's was next, and I listened to the recorded message of their business hours wondering why no one was answering. They must really be busy.

My head tilted, and I looked at the dark foyer. I *could* just grab my keys and head over there, but the presence of so many cops on the street had me worried about my suspended license.

There was another bang from outside, closer this time, and the lights flickered.

Two squirrels? I thought, then frowned. It was dark. There wouldn't be any squirrels. Maybe someone was taking potshots at the street-lights again.

Curious, I set the frosting down and went to look out a window. The thumping at the door brought me spinning around, and Ceri blew in.

"Rachel?" she exclaimed, her heart-shaped face worried. "Rachel, thank God," she said, coming forward and taking my hands. "I have to get you out of here."

"What?" I said intelligently, then looked past her when Keasley trooped in, the older black man's steps painfully quick despite his arthritis. "Ceri, what's the matter?"

Keasley bobbed his head at me, then locked and barred the door.

"Hey!" I exclaimed. "Ivy isn't in yet."

"She's not coming," the old witch said, limping forward. "Do you have a sleeping bag?"

I stared at him. "No. I lost it in the great salt-dip of '06." There was a lot I had lost during my I.S. death threat, and replacing my sleeping bag was low on the list. "And how do you know Ivy's not coming in?" I added.

Ignoring that, the old man headed down the hall and into my room.

"Hey!" I said again, then turned to Ceri when she gripped my arm. "What's the matter?"

Ceri pointed at the TV, now a mishmash of noise and confusion. "He's out," she said, white-faced. "Al is walking this side of the lines. Free and under no one's compulsion—whether the sun is up or not."

Immediately my shoulders eased. "God, I'm sorry, Ceri. I meant to tell you. You really need to get a phone. I know. Al was at Trent's rehearsal and dinner."

The elf's eyes widened. "It's true?" she exclaimed, and I cringed.

"I was going to tell you as soon as I got home, but I forgot," I pleaded, wondering how she'd found out already. "But it's okay. He's not after anyone but me. He can do the sun thing because he made a deal with

Lee to possess his body until Lee kills me. And that's not going to happen until he's done with me." I couldn't tell her that the deal she'd made with Al was why he wanted me this time. It would prey on her.

Ceri hesitated. "Doesn't Lee killing you come under the 'him or his agents' clause?"

My stomach clenched, and I glanced at Keasley at the top of the hallway, waiting for us with my summer comforter in his arms. "Al's going to free Lee before he kills me, and since Lee has reason enough to want me dead, the agent clause won't come into effect."

Keasley dropped my pillow and comforter just inside the sanctuary before shuffling back down the hallway. Ceri took my arm and started to follow him. "We can discuss the intricacies of demon law later. You have to get to hallowed ground."

Exasperated, I pulled from Ceri's grip. "I'm fine!" I protested. "If Al was going to do anything, he would have done it already. He's not going to kill me. At least not right away."

I looked at the TV, mystified as to why everyone was freaking out. Then I looked closer. They weren't in front of The Warehouse, they were in front of a grocery store. Terrified people in vans and station wagons were looting the place. The announcer seemed scared as she told people not to panic, that the situation was under control. Uh-huh. It sure looked under control.

There was a boom of sound and a flash of light, and the pretty reporter swore, falling into a crouch. The camera panned to the gas station across the street. Another flash of light and I realized what had happened. A ley line witch had just blasted someone trying to cut in front of him at the gas station. The faint purple haze was still hanging in the air.

"Are you getting this?" the woman announcer cried out, and my stomach felt queasy when the picture dipped. "The city is going crazy!" she shouted, eyes wide. "The I.S. has declared a state of martial law, and all residents are told to remain inside. Buses will stop at midnight, and anyone on the street will be incarcerated.

"Jake!" she shouted, jumping when a loud bang shook her. "Are you getting this?!"

Jake was indeed getting it, and I stared at people frantically filling their gas tanks. I gasped when a frustrated driver rammed the car ahead of his to shove it forward. A fight started, and my mouth fell open when a ball of green-tinted ever-after blasted into the gas pump. It exploded in a shower of orange and red. The woman screamed, and the camera fell. My windows rattled, and I turned to the dark street. Damn, that had been close. What in hell was going on? So Al was walking around. I was the only one he wanted.

"I don't get it," I said, gesturing. "He can only do what Lee can. He's not any more dangerous than your average deranged, masochistic, black ley line witch." I hesitated, taking in the fear coming through the TV. "Okay," I amended. "Maybe a little screaming is in order, but he can be brought down."

"Someone tried." Ceri tugged at me, but I didn't budge, fixated on the chaos. "He caused trouble at a dance establishment tonight, and when the bouncers tried to get him out, he killed them. Incinerated them right where they stood and set the place to flame. Then he banished the six witches the I.S. sent to catch him into the ever-after. No one can stop him, Rachel, and he's not under anyone's control. People are scared. They want him gone."

"He incinerated them?" I said, my horror mixing with confusion. *All right, maybe he is more powerful than I thought.* "I'm the one he wants. Why is he doing this?"

She turned from the TV, her eyes wide, and tried to get me to move. "What did he ask of you?" she asked, and I licked my lips.

I hesitated, then said, "To testify that you promised to not teach anyone how to spindle line energy. I told him no, and if he goes back without me, they're going to put him in jail."

Ceri's eyes closed, her jaw clenching as she struggled to keep her fear and despair from showing. "I'm sorry," she whispered, her voice shaking. "He's trying to change your mind. I've seen him do this before. You and Piscary are the only two people who have demonstrated the ability to control him, and because you didn't circle him tonight, everyone will think he's doing this with your blessing. If you don't do what Al wants, he's going to turn the city against you."

"What!" I yelped as Keasley appeared in the hallway with three bottles of water and the dusty radio I had under the cupboards for when the power went out.

"Bring your phone," he said shortly. "Do you have extra batteries?"

I couldn't think. Seeing my confusion, he held up a twisted brown hand and went to look for himself. Ceri was tugging on me, and I let her drag me to the top of the hallway.

"This is not my problem," I said, starting to panic. "If I testify to get Al out of Cincy, then I'm a demon practitioner and he kills me that much sooner. And if I don't help him, then I'm responsible for everyone he hurts or sends to the ever-after?"

She picked up my comforter and, meeting my eyes, nodded.

"Swell." I couldn't win. I could not win for losing. Damn it, it wasn't fair!

"But that's not the worst of it," Ceri said, fear showing on her heart-shaped face. "It's all over the news that you had dinner with Al. You didn't take control of him, so they let Piscary out of jail to do it. He's the only other person in Cincy who can."

I stood for three seconds, taking that in. *Piscary is out? Oh . . . shit.*

"Jenks!" I shouted, heading into the hall. "Jenks! Is the backyard clear?" I had to get out of here. It was dark. The church was unsanctified. My security had become a trap.

Ceri followed me into the kitchen. She looked miserable at my fear, but I didn't care.

"Jenks!" I shouted again, and he buzzed in, his green robe furling.

"What the hell do you want?" he snarled. "Can't you spend one freaking night alone?"

I blinked, taken aback. "Cincinnati is panicking because Al is walking the streets with no one holding his leash," I said. "Six witches tried to circle him, and he sent them into the ever-after. Everyone's afraid he's here to harvest familiars, and because I didn't catch him, they let Piscary out to get control of him. Is the backyard clear? I'm going to be sleeping in the graveyard tonight." And tomorrow, and the day after. Hell, maybe I ought to put up a little cottage.

Jenks gaped at me, face pale. His mouth moved, and he said softly, "I'll check."

And he was gone.

"Good evening, Jenks," Ceri said to no one.

The back screen door slammed shut, and Keasley shuffled in. "Let's go."

I put a hand to my stomach. "I have to call my mother."

"Do it from the graveyard." Ceri took my elbow and led me to the back door. Keasley's bent shadow went before us, and I let them drag me out onto the wooden landing and into the night.

The back-porch light was on, and in its uncertain flicker I fumbled for my phone. Piscary's number glowed as the last line called, and in a wash of fear I realized where Ivy was. She hadn't heard about Kisten and me. Piscary had called her to him. This was a setup. Al and Piscary were working together as they had before. Piscary had called, and she had gone to prepare for him—like the scion she was.

"Oh, God," I whispered, my knees going weak as my bare feet found the cold grass. Ivy was with Piscary. Right now.

"Ivy!" I shouted, spinning to head back to the kitchen and my car keys.

"Rachel, no!" Keasley called. He reached for me, falling into a fit of coughing. I leapt to the stairs, jerking back when Ceri took my shoulder.

"She's a vampire," the elf said, eyes snapping in the dim light. "It's a trap. A lure. Al and Piscary are working together. You know it's a trap!"

"She's my friend!" I protested.

"Get into the graveyard," she demanded, pointing as if I were a dog. "We'll deal with this in an orderly fashion."

"Orderly fashion!" I shot at her. "You know what that monster can do to her? Who do you think you are!" I shouted, pushing her hand off me.

Ceri fell back a step. Then her jaw clenched, and I felt her tap a line.

I stiffened. *She's going to spell me?* "Don't you dare!" I exclaimed, shoving her like we were two girls on the playground fighting over a piece of chalk.

Ceri gasped, falling down on her butt, her eyes wide in shock as she looked up at me with her hair all over the place. My face went red in embarrassment. "I'm sorry, Ceri," I said. "She's my friend, and Piscary will screw her up. I don't care if it's a trap; she needs me."

The elf gaped at me, all her skills and magic forgotten in her confusion and affront that I had shoved her down. "Keasley," I said, spinning to find him. "I'll be back—"

My words cut off as I saw him with my cherry red splat gun in his hands. Adrenaline jerked through me, and I froze. "I can't let you knock me down," he said, the gun's alignment unwavering from my chest.

"I might break something," he said, then pulled the trigger, as smooth and unhurried as a waltz.

I tensed to run, but the puff of the escaping air shocked me. "Ow!" I yelped as the stinging sensation hit me square in the chest, and I looked down at the slivers of red plastic.

"Damn it, Keasley," I said, then collapsed, out before my head hit the soft garden soil.

TWENTY-FIVE

"Is it supposed to take this long?" came Jenks's voice, buzzing as if from behind my eyes. My shoulder hurt, and I shifted my arm, bringing my hand up to touch it. I was soaking wet, and surprise brought me awake.

Taking a lungful of air, I sat up, my eyes flashing open.

"Ho! There she is," Keasley said, worry in his brown eyes as he backed up and straightened. His leathery face was creased with wrinkles, and he looked cold in his faded cloth coat. The rising sun gave him a hazy glow, and Jenks hovered beside him. Both of them were watching me with concern as I slumped against a tombstone. We were surrounded by pixies, and their giggles sounded like wind chimes.

"You spelled me!" I shouted, and Jenks's kids scattered with squeals. I looked down, realizing it was salt water dripping from my hair, my nose, and my fingers, and pooling in my underwear. *I'm a freaking mess.*

Keasley's age-worn expression eased. "I saved your life." Dropping the plastic five-gallon bucket onto the grass, he extended a hand to help me up.

Avoiding it, I lurched to my feet before the water could seep farther. "Damn it, Keasley," I swore, shaking my dripping hands and disgusted with myself. "Thanks a helluva lot."

He snorted, and Jenks landed atop one of the nearby monuments, the sun glinting prettily through his wings. "'Thanks a helluva lot,'" he mocked. "What did I tell you? Oblivious, clueless, and bitchy. You should have left her there till noon."

I tried to wring salt water out of my hair, ticked off. It had been almost eight years since anyone had nailed me like this. My fingers froze, and my attention jerked to the rest of the graveyard, misty and golden in the rising sun. "Where's Ceri?"

Keasley bent painfully to tuck a folding chair under his arm. "At home. Crying."

Guilt hit me, and I looked at the graveyard's wall as if I could see his house through it. "I'm sorry," I said, remembering her shocked look when I had shoved her down. *Oh, God, Ivy.*

I stiffened as if to run, and Jenks got in my face, rocking me back. "No, Rachel!" he yelled. "This isn't some jackass movie. If you go after Piscary, you're going to be dead! You make one move to leave, I'm gonna pix you, then give you a lobotomy. I ought to pix you anyway, you stupid witch! What the hell is wrong with you?"

My urge to run to my car died. He was right. Keasley was watching me with his hand hidden suspiciously in the wide pocket of his jacket. My eyes rose from it to his face, wrinkled with intelligence. Ceri had once called him a retired warrior. I was way past believing her. He had pulled that trigger last night with too much familiarity. If I was going in to get Ivy away from Piscary, I was going to have to plan it.

Depressed, I crossed my arms and leaned against the grave marker. In the distance was a group of about ten people jumping the stone wall to get off the property. I bristled, then relaxed. It was holy ground, and I hadn't been the only one scared.

"Sorry about last night," I said. "I wasn't thinking. It's just . . ." My mind flashed back to Ivy last year, numb as she lay shaking under her covers, telling me how Piscary had raped her mind and body in an effort to convince her to kill me. My face went cold, and I swallowed my fear. "Is Ceri okay?" I managed. I had to get Ivy away from him.

Dark eyes sharp, Keasley harrumphed as if aware I was still teetering. "Yes," he said, his bent posture shifting to hold his chair more firmly. "She's okay. I've never seen her like this, though. Embarrassed that she tried to stop you using her magic."

"I shouldn't have shoved her." Stiffly I retrieved the radio and my pillow, wet from dew.

"Actually, that was one thing you did right."

The radio thunked into the empty bucket. "Huh?"

Smirking, Jenks took flight, rising forty feet straight up in the time it took my heart to beat. He was doing a surveillance check, bored with the conversation.

Keasley dropped a coffee-stained thermos into the bucket, groaning as he straightened his back. "You knocked her down because she was going to use magic to stop you. If you had reacted with your magic, too? Now, that would have been scary, but you didn't, showing a control she had forgotten to maintain. She's wallowing in shame right now, poor girl."

I stared, not having realized it.

"I'm glad you shoved her," he mused. "She's been getting uppity these last few weeks."

I tucked a strand of dripping hair behind an ear, cold. "It was still wrong," I said, and he patted my shoulder to send the scent of cheap coffee over me. My gaze fell to my new red shirt, the cotton holding the salt water like a sponge. Crap. I'd really ruined it now.

Plucking my comforter from where it hung over a tombstone, I gave it a good shake. Dirt and last week's grass clippings flew. It was still warm from having been wrapped about my body, and after draping it over me like a cloak, I squinted in the hazy glare and tried to remember what time the sun rose in July. I was usually asleep at this hour, but I'd been out since midnight. It was going to be a long day.

Yawning, Keasley started to shuffle away with his chair. "I called your mother," he said, reaching into a pocket and handing me my phone. "She's fine. Things should settle down. The radio said Piscary captured Al in a circle and banished him, freeing Mr. Saladan. The damned vampire is a city hero."

He shook his graying head, and I agreed. *Freed Lee from Al? Not likely.* I tucked my phone into a pocket, awkward because of the damp fabric. "Thanks," I said, then met his dubious expression. "They're working together, aren't they? Piscary and Al, I mean," I said, grabbing everything else and falling into place behind Keasley.

His silvering hair shone in the sun as he nodded. "Seems like a wise assumption."

A heavy sigh sifted through me. The two of them had a long association, both knowing that business was business and not caring that it had been Al's testimony that put Piscary away. So now Piscary was out of prison. The city was safe, but I was in trouble. Sounded about right.

I had my pillow under my arm, my blanket draped over my shoulder, and the bucket holding the radio and thermos in my hand. Catching my balance, I said softly, "Thank you for slowing me down last night." He said nothing, and I added, "I have to get her out of there."

Keasley set an arthritic hand atop a stone as we passed, halting. "You make one move toward Piscary and I'll plug you with another charm."

I scowled, and with a toothy grin Keasley handed me my splat gun.

"Ivy is a vampire, Rachel," the old man said, his mirth evaporating. "Unless you start taking some responsibility, you should accept that she is where she belongs and walk away."

My posture stiffened, and I tugged my blanket up when it slipped. "Just what in *hell* does that mean?" I snapped, dropping the gun in with the radio.

Keasley, though, smiled, his narrow chest moving as he caught his breath. "Either make your relationship official or let her go."

Surprised, I stared at him, squinting in the strong morning light. "Excuse me?"

"Vampires have an unbreakable mind-set," he said, putting an arm over my shoulder and starting us to the gate. "Apart from the master vampires, they physically need to look to someone stronger than them. It's hardwired in, like Weres and their alphas. Ivy looks powerful because there are so few people stronger than she. Piscary's one. You're another."

My steps, slow to match his, grew even slower. "I can't best him. Despite what I wanted to do last night." God, it was embarrassing. I deserved to have been downed by my own spell.

"I never said you could beat Piscary," the old witch said as we helped each other over the uncertain footing of the graveyard. "I said you were stronger than him. You can help Ivy be who she wants, but if she can't let go of her fear and make peace with her needs, she's going to fall back to Piscary. I don't think she's decided yet."

I felt odd. "How do you figure that?"

His wrinkles deepened. "Because she didn't try to kill you last night."

My stomach clenched. *How come he can see things so clearly and I'm thicker than a cement wall?* Must go along with the wise-old-man image. "We tried it once," I said softly, wanting to touch my neck. "She almost killed me. She says the only way she can control her blood lust is if we mixed it with sex. Otherwise she loses control, and I'd have to hurt her to get her to back off. I can't, Keasley. I won't mix the ecstasy of blood-letting with hurting her. It's wrong and sick."

My pulse had quickened from the foul thought that that's what Piscary did . . . and what he had turned her into. I knew that my face was red, but Keasley didn't seem shocked when brought his attention up. His brow pinched, he gave me a pitying look. "You're in a spot, aren't you?"

We passed the foot-high wall that divided the graveyard from the backyard. Pixies were everywhere, the sunlight flashing on their wings. This was really uncomfortable, but who else could I talk to? My mom? "So," I said softly, angling us to the tall gate that led to the street, "you think it's *my* fault she went running to Piscary? Because I can't bring myself to hurt her if she loses control and I won't sleep with her?"

Keasley grunted. "Ivy thinks like a vampire. You should start thinking like a witch."

"You mean like a charm?" I offered, recalling Ivy's aversion to them, then flushed at the eagerness in my voice. "Maybe one to mute her hunger or calm her without hurting her?"

His head went up and down, and I slowed our pace, seeing him start to labor. "So what are you going to do?" he asked, his hand landing on my shoulder. "I mean today."

"Plan something out and go get her," I admitted. I didn't know what to think anymore.

He was silent. Then, "If you try, he'll tighten his grip on her."

I went to protest, and he pulled me to a stop, facing me. His dark eyes were thick with warning. "You walk in there, and Piscary will make her kill you. Trust her to get herself out. Piscary is her master, but you are her friend, and she still has her soul."

"Trust her?" I said, shocked he thought I should do nothing. "I can't leave her there. He blood-raped her the last time she said no when he told her to kill me."

A soft hand on my shoulder pushed us into motion. "Trust her," he said simply. "She trusts you." His chest rose and fell in a sigh. "Rachel, if she walks away from Piscary without someone to assume his protection, the first undead vampire she runs into will use and abuse her."

"Like Piscary isn't abusing her?" I scoffed.

"She needs protection as much as you do," he chided. "And if you can't give her that, you shouldn't condemn her for sticking with the only person who can."

Put that way, it made sense. But I didn't like it. Especially when, if you thought about it, Piscary was protecting me through her. *Oh, swell* . . .

"Give her a reason for her to get herself out and she'll stand with you," Keasley said as we reached the wooden gate. "You know what that will make her?"

"No," I said, thinking it made me a coward.

He smiled at my sour expression, then took his thermos out of the bucket. "It will make her into someone no one can manipulate. It's who she wants to be."

"This is crap," I said as he lifted the latch and the gate opened. "She needs my help!"

Snorting, Keasley propped the folding chair against the wall and shuffled over the threshold. Past him, the street was quiet and damp with dew. "You've already helped her. You gave her a choice besides Piscary."

I dropped my eyes. It wasn't enough. *I* wasn't enough. I couldn't protect her against the undead. I couldn't protect myself—thinking I could protect her was ludicrous.

Keasley paused in the threshold. "I'll be honest with you," he said. "I don't like the idea of same-sex relationships. It doesn't seem right to me, and I'm too old to start thinking different. But I do know you're happy here. From what Jenks tells me, Ivy is, too. Which makes it hard for me to think you're making a mistake or that it's wrong. Whatever you do."

If I knew the charm to curl up and die, I would have used it. As it was, I watched my feet and moved forward to stand in the gate. Sort of like what I was doing in my life.

"Are you going after Piscary?" he asked suddenly.

Warm under my blanket, I jiggled on my feet. "I want to."

"Smart decisions, Rachel," he said with a sigh. "Make smart decisions."

Restlessness filled me as he headed to his tired-looking house a few homes up the street. "Keasley, tell Ceri I'm sorry for pushing her down," I called after him.

He raised a hand to acknowledge me. "I will."

Jenks dropped from the tree overhead to land atop the gate, making me think he'd been eavesdropping again. I glanced at him, then yelled to Keasley, "Can I come over later?"

Pausing at the curb to let the minivan belonging to the only human family on the street pass, Keasley smiled to show coffee-stained teeth. "I'll make lunch. Tuna sandwiches okay?"

The minivan beeped, and Keasley returned the driver's wave. I couldn't help my smile. The elderly witch carefully stepped off the curb and started home, head up and eyes scanning.

Jenks rose when the gate thumped shut, and with the splat gun rattling against the radio, I made for the back door. "And where were you when Keasley downed me?" I asked Jenks tartly.

"Right behind him, stupid. Who do you think told him what you stocked your splat gun with?"

There wasn't much I could say to that. "Sorry." I took the porch steps, juggling everything in my arms to manage the door. Jenks darted in to do a quick run-through of the premises, and, remembering him in his robe last night, I hollered, "Is Matalina okay?"

"She's fine," he said, swooping back in.

I wedged my soaked shoes and socks off, padding into the kitchen to leave wet prints as I dropped the bucket just inside it. Continuing on, I headed to my bathroom to wash my comforter. "Ceri's upset, huh?" I asked, fishing to find out what had happened while I was out.

"She's crushed," he said, landing on the raised lid as I punched buttons to get the washing machine going. "And you're going to have to wait. The power is out. Can't you tell?"

I hesitated, only now realizing it was eerily quiet in here, lacking the usual hum of computers, fridge fans, and everything else. "Not doing too well, am I?" I said, remembering Ceri gaping up at me, her hair in disarray and her eyes wide in shock at my having shoved her.

"Ah, we love you anyway," Jenks said, taking flight. "The church is clear. The front door is still bolted. I've got some things to do in the garden, just yell if you need me."

He lifted up, and I smiled at him. "Thanks, Jenks," I said, and he darted out, the buzz of his wings obvious in the power-outage-silenced air.

Shoving my comforter into the washer, I started to plan out my day: shower, eat, debase myself to Ceri, call the holy guy and offer to have his baby if he would find a way to remove the blasphemy and resanctify the church, prep some spells to storm the evil-vampire fortress. Typical Saturday stuff.

Barefoot, I wandered into the kitchen. I couldn't make coffee with the power out, but I could make tea. And by the time I changed into something dry, the water would be hot.

As I rattled around to get the kettle going, my thoughts kept returning to Piscary. I was in big trouble. I didn't think he had forgiven me for walloping him into unconsciousness with a chair leg, and I had an ugly feeling I was still alive so he could use me to bring Ivy in line when the timing was right. Even worse was my growing belief that he and Al were working together. This all was simply too convenient.

From what Al had said, I didn't think it was possible to summon and hold a demon in a circle if he was possessing someone. So Piscary had taken the credit for ridding Cincy of its newest Inderlander in what was probably a prearranged agreement. For services rendered, the master vampire had been pardoned for murdering those ley line witches last year. It was a con. The entire thing was a con. My only question now was who had helped arrange it, 'cause Piscary couldn't safely summon a demon in prison. Someone had helped him set it up.

It just wasn't fair.

The biting scent of sulfur rose as I lit a match and got the burner going. I held my breath as the smoke dissipated, thinking. If I didn't do something soon, I was going to be dead. Either Cincy would run me out on a rail for having dinner with Al and then letting him incinerate bouncers and toss six witches into the ever-after, or Mr. Ray and Mrs. Sarong would band together and kill me for the focus, or there was the yet-undiscovered faction still trying to find out who had the thing, according to Al. I had to get rid of it. I didn't know how vampires had kept it quiet for so long. Hell, they'd hidden it for half of forever before Nick found it.

My face blanked, and my motions slowed as I set the kettle on the flame. Vampires. Piscary. I needed protection from everyone and his brother, protection Piscary specialized in. What if I gave the focus to

Piscary in return for his freaking protection? Sure, Al and Piscary worked together, but vampire politics came before personal power plays. And even if Al did find out, so what? Al was hiding over here. Once the focus was safe, I could call Minias and rat out Al to get rid of him. I could turn in my favor for that, right? Then I'd be free of Al and Piscary both, and the damned focus would again be safely hidden.

I stood in my kitchen staring at nothing, elation and angst trickling through me. I'd have to trust Piscary to keep it in hiding. Not to mention giving up his desire to kill me. But he thought in terms of centuries, and I wasn't going to last that long. Vampires didn't want the status quo to change. Piscary had everything to gain if I gave it to him, and the only thing he had to lose was revenge.

Hell, if I did this right, I could get Lee free and Trent would owe me big-time.

"Oh," I whispered, my knees feeling funny, "I like this. . . ."

The front doorbell bonged, and I jerked. Rex was sitting in the kitchen's threshold—staring at me—and I brushed past her. If I was lucky, it was Ceri. I had tea already going.

"Rache!" Jenks said, zipping in from who knew where, his voice excited as I paced barefoot through the sanctuary. "You'll never guess who's on the front steps."

Ivy? I thought, my heart leaping, but she would have just walked in. I hesitated, drawing my hand back from the door, but Jenks looked wound up, glowing in the smothering darkness of the foyer with excitement, not fear. "Jenks," I said in exasperation, "cut the twenty questions and tell me who's out there."

"Open it!" he said, eyes bright and dust spilling from him. "You're clear. Tink's a Disney whore, this is great! I'm going to get Matalina. Hell, I'm getting my kids."

Rex had followed us—pulled by Jenks, not me—and with images of news cameras and vans, I reached for the locking bar, sliding it up and away. Nervous, I looked down at myself, fully aware of the disastrous image I made, with my salt-stained dripping hair, a pixy by my side, and a cat at my bare feet. God, I lived in a church!

But it wasn't a news crew on my front steps blinking at me in the sun; it was Trent.

TWENTY-SIX

Surprise flickered over Trent, then vanished under the cool confidence of his six-hundred-dollar suit and hundred-dollar haircut. Quen stood on the walk below like a chaperone. There was a fist-size pale blue package in Trent's hands, the lid fastened with a matching bow lined in gold. "Is this a bad time, Ms. Morgan?" Trent said, green eyes flicking from my bare feet to Rex, then back up to me.

It was friggin' seven o'clock. I should be in bed right now, and he knew it. Painfully conscious of my damp, rumpled state, I shook my stringy curls out of my eyes. My thoughts zinged back to my idea to get Lee free of Al, but he was here for Ceri. I had almost forgotten.

"Please tell me that's not for me?" I said, gaze dropping to the gift, and he flushed.

"It's for Ceri," he said, his gray-edged voice melting into the humid morning. "I wanted to give her something as a visible display of how pleased I am to find her."

Visible display . . . God, Trent had a crush on her before even meeting her. Lips pressed tight, I crossed my arms over my chest, but my tough-chick image was being ruined by Rex twining about my feet. She didn't fool me—I was a convenient rubbing post, that's all—and when she realized I was wet, she gave me an insulted look and stalked away. "You didn't find Ceri," I said tartly. "I did."

"Can I come in?" he asked wearily.

He took a step forward, but I didn't move and he stopped. My attention flicked behind him to Quen in his black outfit and shades. They had brought the Beemer instead of the limo. Good call; Ceri wouldn't be impressed. "Look," I said, not wanting him in my church unless there was a reason, "I didn't think you were coming, so I didn't say anything to her. This really isn't the best time." *Not with her crying the way she was.* "I'm usually asleep right now. Why are you here so early? I said four o'clock."

Trent took another step, and I stiffened, almost falling into a defensive stance. Quen twitched, and Trent rocked back. He glanced behind him, then rounded on me. "Damn it, Rachel, stop screwing with me," he said, jaw clenched. "I want to meet this woman. Call her."

My eyes widened. *Ooooooh, pushed a button, did I?* My gaze rose to Jenks sitting out of sight on the lintel inside, and he shrugged. "Jenks, you want to see if she can come over?"

He nodded, and surprise showed on both Trent and Quen when he dropped down. "You bet. She'll probably want a minute to get her hair brushed."

And her face washed, and put on a dress that doesn't have graveyard dirt on it.

"Quen," Trent ordered, and my warning flags went up.

"Just Jenks," I said, and Quen's soft-soled shoes scuffed to a halt on the damp sidewalk. The dark elf looked to Trent for direction, and I added, "Quen, park your little butt right here or nothing's happening." I didn't want Quen over there. Keasley would never speak to me again.

Jenks hovered, waiting, and Trent's eyebrows bunched, weighing his options.

"Oh, please, test me," I mocked, and Trent grimaced.

"Do it her way," he said softly, and Jenks darted off, gone in a flash of transparent wings.

"See?" I said, beaming. "That wasn't so hard." From behind me came a chorus of high-pitched giggles, and Trent blanched. Seeing him nervous, I stepped aside. "You want to come in? She might be a while. You know how those thousand-year-old princesses are."

Trent glanced past the dark foyer, abruptly reluctant. Quen took the steps two at a time, brushing past me in a whiff of oak leaves and aftershave.

"Hey!" I snapped, following him in. Trent pushed into motion and came in on my heels. He didn't shut the door, probably for a quick get-away, and as Trent drew to a halt in the middle of the sanctuary, I ducked back into the foyer and yanked the door shut.

Pixies squealed from the rafters, and Trent and Quen warily watched them. I plucked at my salt-stained shirt and tried to find an air of non-chalance as I prepared to introduce His Most Holy Pain in the Ass to Miss Elf Princess.

The hair on the back of my neck rose as I strolled past Quen and flopped into my rolling chair, parked beside my desk. "Have a seat," I said, shifting back and forth and gesturing to Ivy's furniture, still arranged in the inner corner of the church. "You're in luck. We usually don't have our living room out here, but we're doing some remodeling."

Trent looked at the gray suede couch and chairs and turned away, glancing at my desk before moving on to Ivy's piano, where interest pulled his eyebrows high. "I'll stand," he said.

Rex strolled in from the dark foyer and headed right for Quen. Much to my surprise, the older elf crouched, fondling the orange cat's ears to make her flop onto her back to show her white belly. Quen rose with Rex in his hands, and the cat's eyes slitted in pleasure as she purred.

Stupid cat.

Trent cleared his throat, and my gaze shot to him.

"Rachel," he said, setting his gift on top of the closed piano, "do you make a habit of showering in your clothes?"

My back-and-forth motion stopped. I tried to think up a lie, but that the power was out didn't lend itself for me to be damp. "I . . . uh, slept in the graveyard," I said, not wanting to tell him my neighbor had downed me with my own spell, hoping Trent might think it was dew.

A smirk came over him, and somehow he made it look good. He knew I was afraid of Piscary. "You should have killed Piscary when you had the opportunity," he said, his wonderful voice filling the open space of the sanctuary with the sound of grace and comfort. Damn, the man had a beautiful voice. I had almost forgotten. And yes, I could have killed Piscary and probably gotten off with a plea of self-defense, but if I had, the vampire wouldn't be around to hide the focus for me. So I said nothing. Trent, though, apparently wanted to talk.

"That doesn't explain why you're soaking wet," he prompted.

My jaw clenched, but then I forced myself to relax. Hell, if Ivy could do it, I could, too. "No," I said cheerfully. "It doesn't."

Carefully lowering himself to sit on the piano bench, he inclined his head. "Having trouble with your charms?" he said, fishing for an answer.

"Absolutely not."

Quen let Rex drop to the floor, and the cat shook herself, making the little bell Jenks had put on her jingle. I watched Trent fidget subtly, reading in his slightly elevated color and his crisp enunciation how nervous he was. My thoughts went to his anger when he had asked me to work security for his nuptials, his blaming me for Lee's capture and installation as a demon's familiar. A twinge of guilt took me, quickly suppressed. But if I got Lee free of Al, Trent would owe me a big debt of gratitude. One big enough that he might leave me alone?

"Ah," I said hesitantly into the pixy-giggle-laden air, and Trent looked at me, green eyes interested. Someone in the rafters shrieked when he or she got shoved off the beam, and Trent's eyelid twitched.

Feeling a smidgen of sympathy, I stood and clapped my hands at the ceiling. "Okay, you've all stared enough. Time to go. There's waxed paper behind the microwave. Go polish the steeple."

Quen started when Jenks's kids dropped down in a swirling maelstrom of silk and high-pitched complaints. It was Jhan who took control, and with his hands on his hips in a painful reminder of Jenks, he browbeat them all into the hallway.

"Thanks, Jhan," I said. "I heard blue jays earlier. Be sure to watch for them."

"Yes, Ms. Morgan," the pixy said seriously, then darted out, Rex trailing under him. There was a crash and a shriek from the kitchen, then nothing.

Wincing, I moved to lean against the back of Ivy's couch. Quen looked at me expectantly, and Trent said, "Aren't you going to see what they broke?"

My head shook. "I . . . uh, wanted to thank you again for interrupting Al yesterday," I said, and my face warmed. God! Al had practically pulled me into an orgasm, right in front of everybody.

Trent's attention flicked to the pixies in the side yard, blurs through the stained-glassed windows, and then his gaze came back to me. "No problem."

Uncomfortable, I crossed my arms over my chest. "Really. You didn't have to, and I appreciate it."

Quen shifted his weight and settled in, and, seeing his relaxed posture, Trent found a less-stiff position. He still looked like a male model, sitting at Ivy's baby grand. "I don't like bullies," he said simply, as if embarrassed.

I grimaced, wishing Ceri would hurry up. A beep came from the kitchen, and the whine of electronics hit my middle ear. The lights winked on, invisible in the bright sun, and from behind me the TV slowly blossomed into noise. Scrambling for the remote, I clicked it off.

Embarrassment sprang up from nowhere, and I got mad at myself. I could feel Trent evaluating me and my life—my little TV, Ivy's living room set, my plant-strewn desk, the two-bedroom, two-bath church we lived in—and it ticked me off that I was coming in so much shorter than his huge living room, his big-screen TV, and his stereo system that filled a wall.

"Excuse me," I muttered, hearing the washer start to fill. I bet Trent didn't have to entertain with the *chug chug* of a Whirlpool in the background.

Flicking off the overhead lights as I went, I stopped in my bathroom to open the washer's lid. It could soak. Then I did a quick check in Ivy's bathroom in case Trent wanted to rifle through her medicine cabinet under the excuse of using the can. It was neat and tidy, the incense-and-ashes scent of vampire a dim hint under the orange-perfumed soap she used. Depressed now, I headed to the kitchen to see if the lights were on.

My cell phone rang, the electronic music blaring out to startle me. Scrambling for it, I cursed Jenks. I usually had it on vibrate, but someone—aka Jenks—had monkeyed with it, changing my ring tones. Fumbling to the tune of "I've Got a Lovely Bunch of Coconuts," I finally wrestled the thing out of my damp pocket. *Real funny, Jenks. Ha-ha.*

It was Glenn's number, and after a moment's hesitation I leaned against the kitchen counter and flipped it open. I had a bug to put in his ear.

"Hi, Glenn," I said tightly; he knew I was usually sleeping right about now. "I hear Piscary's out. It would have been *nice* if *someone* had told me the undead vampire *I put in jail* was *free!*"

I could hear keyboards and a loud argument in the background. Glenn's sigh was heavy over it. "Sorry," he said by way of greeting. "I left a message on your phone when I heard."

"I never got it," I said, only slightly mollified. Then I grimaced. "Look, I didn't mean to bark at you. But I spent the night in my grave-yard, and I'm a little cranky."

"I would've called again," Glenn said, and I heard papers being shuffled. "But when your demon burned down The Warehouse using their bouncers as kindling, we got swamped."

"My demon!" I yelped, phone pressed tight to my ear. "Since when is Al *my* demon?" I said softly, remembering how well Trent and Quen could hear.

"Since you called him up to testify." The FIB officer covered the mouthpiece. I heard something muttered, and I stewed until he returned.

"That doesn't explain why Piscary is out," I snarled.

"What do you expect?" Glenn said, sounding annoyed. "Neither the I.S. nor the FIB is equipped to deal with a demon who can walk under the sun. You weren't doing anything. There was an emergency meeting of the City Council, and they let Piscary out to deal with it." He hesi-tated, then, "I'm sorry. They gave him a full pardon."

City Council? That meant Trent had known. Hell, he'd been in on it. What a total ass. I had risked my soul to put Piscary behind bars for killing ley line witches. Apparently that meant nothing. It made me wonder why I'd even bothered.

"This isn't why I called," Glenn said. "Another body has turned up."

My thoughts were still on Piscary, apparently free to do whatever he wanted to my roommate. "And you want me to come down?" I said, my hand to my forehead and my head bowed as I got angrier. "I told you. I'm not an investigator, I'm a haul-them-in person. Besides, I don't know whether I want to work for you anymore if you're just going to let mur-derers out when things get rough."

"Rough!" Glenn exclaimed. "We had sixteen major fires last night, five riots, and a near lynching of some guy in a dress reading Shake-speare in the park. I don't think they even know the number of fender benders and assault charges. It's a demon. You said yourself you spent the night hiding in your churchyard."

"Hey!" I snapped. *That was unfair.* "I was hiding from Piscary, not Al. Al's burning things up to get me to go to the ever-after with him. And don't you *dare* sit there and call me a coward because I don't want to."

I was furious—my anger fueled by guilt—and I fumed until Glenn muttered, "Sorry."

"All right, then," I huffed, wrapping an arm around my middle and turning away from the hall. *This isn't my fault. I'm not responsible for Al's actions.*

"At least he's gone," Glenn said, no emotion in his voice.

I laughed bitterly. "No, he isn't."

There was a moment of silence. "Piscary said—"

"Piscary and Al are working together. And you fell for it, letting him out so now you have two monsters with free run of Cincy, not one." My face twisted bitterly. "Don't ask me to take care of them for you this time, okay?"

The background office noise filled my ear. "Can you come down here anyway?" Glenn finally said. "I want you to identify someone."

My heart clenched. He had said there was another body. Suddenly Piscary was the last thing on my mind. "David?" I said, knees going weak, cold though the sun shone in strong on my back through the kitchen window. Someone had killed him. Someone was killing Weres looking for the focus, and lots of people knew that David was my alpha. *God help me, they've killed him.*

"No," Glenn said, and relief made my breath tremble in my lungs. "It's a Were by the name of Brett Markson. He had your card in his wallet. Do you know him?"

My brief elation that David was okay shifted to numb shock. Brett? The Were from Mackinaw? I slid to the floor, my back against the sink cupboard, my knees scrunching up.

"Rachel?" came Glenn's voice from far away. "You okay?"

"Yeah," I breathed. "No," I amended. "I'll come right down." *Ceri.* I licked my lips and tried to swallow. "Can you give me about an hour? *Shower and eat.* "Maybe two?"

"Ah, damn it, Rachel, did you really know this guy?" Glenn said, his voice guilty now. "I'm sorry, I should have come over."

I looked up, seeing Ivy's empty spot at the table. "No, I'm fine. He was . . . an acquaintance." I took a breath, remembering the last time I saw Brett, hanging at the outskirts of my life trying to ease his way into my pack, a powerful man looking for something to believe in.

"It's what? Seven-thirty?" Glen was saying. "I'll send a car at noon. Unless you have your license?"

I shook my head, though he couldn't see it. "A car would be nice."

"Rachel? Are you okay?"

There was a demon loose in the city. A master vamp was out to get me. My church was unsanctified. And Brett was dead. "I'm fine," I said, sounding wispy. "See you after noon."

Numb, I hung up the phone before he could say anything more. It felt heavy in my hand, and I stared at my spell books, at eye level. Damn it, this wasn't right. I wiped my eyes and got to my feet, feeling like everything had changed.

Bare feet squeaking, I headed into the sanctuary. I came to a halt just past the top of the hallway. Trent was examining the stained-glass artwork, and his shiny shoes caught the light when he turned. Quen was six feet away, looking ready for anything.

"Trent, I'm sorry," I said, thinking my face must be white when his eyebrows went high. "I can't do this right now. I don't think Ceri is going to come over anyway."

"Why?" he asked, spinning on a heel to face me fully.

Oh, God, they had killed Brett. "I shoved her down last night," I said, "and she's probably still upset about it." Brett was dead. He was military. How could someone kill him? He was damned good at staying alive.

Trent shook out the sleeves of his expensive suit and let out a disbelieving laugh. "You shoved her down? Do you know who she is?"

I took a quick breath, trying to hold myself together. Brett was dead. Because of me. "I know who she is, but when someone pushes me, I push back."

Trent glanced at Quen, his face going tight. My jaw clenched, and I kept my breathing shallow. I looked to the rafters for Jenks, trying not to cry. Someone had killed Brett. He had been only one step away from me. I was so damned vulnerable. All it would take was a sniper, but I couldn't live in a cave. This was crap. Purple fairy crap with green sparkles on it.

I trailed my hand along the wall as I went to sit in Ivy's chair. The scent of vampire incense made me feel even worse. I had to stop living my life as if it were a game. I had to start buying insurance, or I wouldn't live to hear my mother complain about the lack of grandchildren. Though it twisted my gut, I was going to give Piscary the focus to put into hiding, to bribe him into not killing me. Then I was going to rescue Lee to get Al back where he belonged and Trent off my case. *Might as well start there,* I thought, sitting up and taking a deep breath. Al, I could take care of later. After dark.

"Trent," I said, closing my eyes in a long blink as I felt my sense of right and wrong take a hit, "I think I might have a way to get Lee free of Al. It won't cost you a dime, but I want you to leave me alone." I looked at him, his face blank in wonder. "Think you can you do that?"

"You said you couldn't get a familiar free from a demon," he said, his velveteen voice holding a rough edge.

I shrugged, staring past him at the door and unfolding myself so I didn't look so miserable. "Where do you think Ceri came from?"

His expression empty, Trent glanced at Quen. The dark elf blinked once with meaning. "I'm listening," Trent said warily.

This was where it would get sticky. "I'm going to try to swing a deal with Piscary—"

"Careful," he mocked. "Someone might think your black-and-white outlook is going gray."

"Shut up!" I shouted at the billionaire, feeling the sting. "I'm not breaking the law. I have something he might want, and once he has it, I ought to be able to get rid of Al safely and in such a way that will free Lee. But I want your word that you'll leave me and the people I care about alone. And . . ." I took a deep breath, feeling like I was becoming one of them. ". . . I'll leave you and your business dealings alone."

I wanted to survive. I wanted to live. I had been playing in a sandbox with murderers and casual killers, with the arrogant innocence of a snowflake in hell. The FIB couldn't protect me. The I.S. wouldn't. Trent could kill me, and I had to respect that even if I didn't respect him. *God, who am I becoming?*

"You'd stop trying to tag me?" Trent said softly, and then went still an unvoiced thought. His lips parted, and he looked at Quen in wonder. "She has the focus," he said to him, then turned to me, amused. "That's what you're going to give Piscary. You have the focus," he said around his laugh. "I should have known it was you!"

My face went cold, and I felt my stomach drop. *Oh, shit.*

I stood upright when Quen shifted to stand between us—maneuvering.

"Stop!" I said, my hand outstretched, and he did. Heart pounding, I held him off with my fingers splayed, trying to figure it out. *Trent was the one killing the Weres?*

"You killed Brett?" I said, seeing him flush. "It was you!" I exclaimed, dropping my hand and warming in anger. Damn it, what had I almost done? What in hell was wrong with me? This couldn't be happening!

"I didn't kill him. He killed himself," Trent said, his jaw clenched. "Before he could tell me you had it," he finished, hands behind his back.

Quen was balanced with his weight on his toes, his arms loose at his side. As if in a dream, I said to him, "You killed Brett. And Mr. Ray's secretary. And Mrs. Sarong's aide."

Quen's face darkened with guilt, and his muscles tensed.

"You sons of bitches," I whispered, not wanting to believe it, cursing myself for wanting Trent to be better than he was, wanting both of them to be better than murderers and assassins. "I thought you had more honor than this, Quen."

The older elf's jaw clenched.

"We didn't kill them," Trent said, defending himself, and I snorted with derision. "They committed suicide," he insisted, the devil in his perfect suit and perfect hair. "Every last one of them. None of them had to die. They could have told me."

As if it made a difference. "They didn't know I had it!"

Trent took a step forward, finger pointing, and Quen pulled him back. "This is a war, Rachel," the younger man said tightly, shaking off Quen's grip. "There will be casualties."

I stared at him in disbelief. "This is not a war. This is you angling for more power. God, Trent, how much more do you need! Are you so insecure that you have to be king of the freaking world to feel safe?"

I thought of my church and my friends, and I lifted my chin. Yeah, they had killed people, but Ivy was trying to get out, and Jenks had to in order to ensure his and his children's survival. And seeing as I had pretty much sacrificed Lee in order to survive, I couldn't claim I was pristine and pure either. But I'd never killed for money or power—and neither had my friends.

My words hit Trent, and he reddened in shame or guilt. "How much do you want for it?" he said softly.

Shocked, I gaped at him. "You want . . . to buy it?" I stammered.

Trent licked his lips. "I'm a businessman."

"And a murderer by hobby?" I accused. "Or do you think the tenuous state of your species gives you the right to murder?"

Face showing his guilt and anger, Trent tugged his coat straight. If he had brought out a checkbook, I would have screamed. "Anything, Rachel. Enough to make you safe. You, your mother, Jenks, even Ivy. Enough to have anything you want."

It sounded so easy. But I didn't want to deal with him anymore. Piscary killed people, but he didn't have the concept of pity or remorse. It would be like telling a shark he was a bad fish and to stop eating people. But Trent? He knew he was doing wrong, and he did it anyway.

Trent never dropped his eyes, waiting. I hated him. I hated him to the bottom of my soul. He was attractive and powerful, and I had almost let that cloud my sense of right and wrong. So he could kill me. So what? Did that make it right to cut deals with him to keep myself safe? Why in hell should I trust him to honor his word? It was like making a deal with a demon or using a demon curse. Both were the easy way out, the lazy way.

I wasn't going to use demon curses. I wasn't going to make deals with demons. I wasn't going to trust Trent to honor his word. He was a casual murderer who put his species above all others. Screw him.

Quen knew what I was thinking, and I saw him tense. Trent, though, wasn't so perceptive. He was a businessman, not a warrior. A slimy little businessman. "I'll give you a quarter million for it," Trent said, disgusting me.

My face twisted. "You don't get it, pixy dust," I said. "It would start a war if it got out. I'm giving it to Piscary so he can put it back into hiding."

"He'll kill you once he has it," Trent said quickly, his beautiful voice thick with truth. "Don't be a fool this time. Give it to me. I'll keep you safe. I'm not going to start a war. Just bringing everything into balance."

"Balance?" I stepped forward, stopping when Quen mirrored me.

"Maybe the rest of Inderland likes how things are balanced right now. Maybe it's time for the elves to die out. If they're all like you and Ellasbeth, scrabbling for money and power, maybe you've gone so far from your roots, so far from grace and moral standing, that you're already dead as a species. Dead and gone and good riddance," I mocked while Trent reddened. "If you're the model of what you're going to build your species with, then we don't want you back."

"We were not the ones who abandoned the ever-after to the demons!" Trent shouted, anger pouring from him honest and raw, the source of his drive flowing from him in a wave of frustration. "You left! You left us to fight alone! We made sacrifices while you turned tail and ran! If I'm ruthless, it's because you made me that way!"

Son of a bitch . . . "You can't blame me for something my ancestors did!"

Trent grimaced. "Ten percent of my portfolio," he said, seething.

Sick bastard. "It's not for sale. Get out."

"Fifteen percent. That's a third of a billion."

"Get the *hell* out of my church!"

Trent gathered himself as if to speak, then looked at his watch. "I'm sorry you feel that way," he said, his steps loud as he quickly retreated to the piano. Pocketing his gift for Ceri, he asked, "Is it on the premises?" —pretending it was just an idle question.

Damn. I went wire-tight. "Jenks!" I shouted, finding my balance. "Jhan, get your dad!" But he was watching for blue jays, like I'd told him to. *Double damn.*

Quen was waiting for direction, and sweat broke out over me. Trent brought his head up with what I hoped was regret in his eyes. "Quen," he said softly, "secure Ms. Morgan. We'll talk to Ceri at a later date. Apparently she's not coming today. Do you have a memory potion?"

Oh, God.

"In the car, Sa'han."

It was not a happy voice, and I glanced at Quen, knowing what was going to happen.

"Good." Trent looked as unyielding as iron. "No memories means no loose ends. We'll leave her sleeping, and she'll wake when someone picks her up for her trip to the morgue."

"Son of a bitch," I whispered, then looked to the empty rafters. Damn it, why had I told them to leave? "Jenks!" I shouted, but there was no clatter of wings. Quen pulled a splat gun from the small of his back, and I swore under my breath.

"What is it?" I asked, thinking of mine in the bucket by the back door. If I moved, he'd shoot.

"A little different being on the other end of the weapon, isn't it?" Trent mocked, and it was all I could do to keep from screaming at him.

"Trent . . ." I backed up a step with my hands raised in placation.

Quen handed the gun to Trent. "You want her like that, you shoot her yourself," he said.

Trent hefted the gun, taking sight at me down its length. "I can do that," he said, then pulled the trigger.

"Hey!" I yelped when it hit me, stinging and painful. *Damn it, twice in one day.* But I didn't collapse. It wasn't a sleepy-time charm. Trent didn't seem surprised when I didn't fall but simply stumbled back, my impulse to flee coming far too late.

Trent handed the weapon back to Quen. "Honor is expensive, Quen. I don't pay you enough." Quen was not happy, and I stared at them, scared for what might happen next.

Voice cold, Trent enunciated clearly, "Rachel. Tell me where the focus is."

"Go to hell."

Trent's green eyes went wide. Quen looked me up and down in shock, then relaxed, almost laughing. "She's covered in salt water," he said. "She said she pushed Ceri down. The woman obviously spelled her, and Rachel's still wet from breaking the charm."

That wasn't quite what had happened, but I wasn't going to enlighten him. Standing in my bare feet, I started to get mad. From Trent's question I was forming the distinct impression that Trent had stocked his splat gun with subjugation charms. Illegal. Gray, seeing as you didn't need to kill anything to make it, but very, very illegal.

Trent made a puff of noise and tugged his sleeves down. "Fine. Subdue her your way. Try not to leave any bruises. No traces mean no reason to dig for missing memories."

Okay, not out of this yet . . . Pulse fast, I fell into a fighting stance, searching for the sound of pixy wings. Quen came forward, his earlier indecision apparently having stemmed from using magic, not force, to assert his right to dominate. Seemed if I couldn't best him physically, I deserved to be used and discarded.

"Quen, I don't want to have to do this," I warned, remembering our last fight. He would have creamed me if my roommates hadn't interfered. "Get out or I'll—"

"You'll what?" Trent said, standing sideways by the piano with an infuriating smile on him. "Turn us into butterflies? You don't do black magic."

Hands made into fists, I steadied myself.

"She doesn't," came Ceri's voice from behind me in the hall, and Trent's gaze shot over my shoulder. "But I do."

TWENTY-SEVEN

"Damn it," Trent swore softly, his eyes on Ceri as Quen halted.

The air seemed to crackle, but then I realized it was Jenks's wings. The pixy hovered beside me, waiting for direction. I could feel Ceri behind me, but I couldn't take my eyes off Quen, standing with his lips parted and his arms slack at his sides in his black uniform.

Slowly I straightened from my crouch. Ceri came forward, smelling of soap, in a fresh dress of purple and gold that hid her bare feet when she stopped beside me. Her crucifix rested easy against her, and her confidence was absolute. As was her anger.

"Uh, Ceri," I said, not knowing what else to do, "that man in the suit is Trenton Aloysius Kalamack, drug lord, murderer, and Fortune 20 member. That's Quen before him, his security officer. Trent, Quen, this is Cerdiwen Merriam Dulciate, originally from the Dark Ages of Europe." *Let's get this party started!*

Trent's face was white. "How long were you listening . . . ?"

Ceri's narrow chin lifted. "Long enough."

I blanched when I realized that the humming noise was coming from Ceri and the black haze edging her fingers with their little butterfly bandages was magic waiting for direction. *Oh, crap.*

"Uh, Rachel . . ." Jenks said, his voice high.

A shiver took me at her proud anger. "Let's hang back, Jenks. This might get nasty."

The warning slant to Trent's eyebrows told me he wanted to pretend nothing had happened so he could make Ceri's acquaintance without the ugly reality of his life intruding. *Ri-i-i-ight* . . .

Multicolored sun coming in through the stained-glass windows added a surreal look to the standoff. Quen was by the piano, and when the older elf stepped to join Trent, Ceri calmly turned her gaze to him. Quen stopped. Seeing his acquiescence, the black surrounding her hands vanished.

My shoulders eased when I felt her drop the ley line. I knew she probably had enough ever-after spindled in her head to blow the roof off the church, but Trent and Quen didn't.

"Now that I've found you, I see that Rachel is right," Ceri said as she gracefully took the middle of the room, her dress moving gently. "You're a demon."

"I beg your pardon?" Trent's beautiful voice held more ire than confusion.

I didn't have a clue how this was going to end, but I was glad to be out of the line of fire. Ceri noticed Quen moving to mirror my position, and she stiffened, pale hair shifting as she cocked her head regally. "Did Rachel tell you I was a demon's familiar before she rescued me?" she said to Trent. Seeing his understanding, she continued, "I know demons very well. And that's what they do. They offer you something that *looks* out of your reach in exchange for something they want that *is* out of theirs. They're called businessmen here. You're very good."

His face reddened. "This is not how I wanted to make your acquaintance."

"I'll bet," Ceri said. The modern phrase and the sarcasm with which she said it were shocking.

Proud and collected in his tailored suit, Trent fingered his gift and came closer, hiding his tension under a practiced calm learned in the boardroom. I couldn't help but be impressed with his determination to try to salvage something from this.

"I brought you a gift," he said, extending the wrapped box. "A show of thanks for your cellular sample."

Jenks landed on my shoulder. "The man has more balls than a prize bull," he muttered, and the rims of Ceri's ears colored. She didn't take it, and Trent finally set it atop the piano.

Ignoring him, Ceri turned to Quen. "You hesitated to attack Rachel at first. Why?"

Quen blinked, clearly not expecting this. "Rachel's strongest defensive abilities are in her physical skills, not her magic," he said, his gravelly voice blending beautifully with Ceri's smooth, perfect tones. "I'm proficient with both, and it wouldn't be honorable to defeat her using something she can't defend against when I can assert my will where she has a chance to meet me equally."

From my shoulder came Jenks's loud comment, "Piss on my daisies, I knew there was something I liked about the little cookie maker."

"That's important to you?" Ceri questioned regally, ignoring Jenks's comment.

Quen dropped his head, but his eyes were unrepentant from beneath his dark bangs. Trent shifted his feet. I knew it was a ploy to bring her attention to him, but Ceri smiled at Quen. "There is a spark of us left," she said, then took a breath as if readying herself for a difficult task.

Outside, pixies plastered themselves against the glass, and I felt a stab of nervousness when Ceri returned her focus to Trent. Seeing them together, I was struck by how much they looked alike. Their hair was that same fine, almost-transparent blond, their features both had the same delicate yet firm cast. Slim without losing strength. Strength without sacrificing beauty.

"I've been watching you for some time," Ceri said softly. "You're very confusing. Very confused. You have forgotten nothing, but you don't know how to use it."

Trent's expression almost hid his anger. Almost. "Mal Sa'han—"

Ceri's breath hissed, and she dropped back a step, dress furling to show her bare feet. "Don't," she said, complexion a delicate rose. "Not from you."

Quen twitched when she reached for her waistband, and she froze him with a look as she pulled a swab in a torn cellophane package from it. I recognized it as one of mine. "I came to give you this," she said, handing it to Trent. "But since I have your attention . . ."

Jenks's wings made spurts of cool wind on my neck, and the tension escalated. Ceri tapped a line, and her hair shifted in a breeze that touched only her. I thought I sensed a metallic taste on my tongue. My face cold, I looked over the sanctuary as if expecting a demon to melt into existence, but then my gaze fell upon Ceri, and I blanched.

"Holy crap . . ." Jenks breathed, his wings going absolutely motionless.

Ceri had gone deathly still, gathering intent and power about her as if supplementing her damaged aura. Her undeniable beauty was like that of a fairy, savage and pale, face hollow, hard, and unyielding. Quen didn't move as she closed in on Trent, near enough that her hair mingled with his. Near enough that she could pull his aura into her as she breathed.

"I am black," she said, and a shudder rippled through me. "I am foul with a thousand years of demon curses. Don't cross me or I will bring you and your house down. Rachel is the only clean thing I have, and you won't sully her to further your high ideas. Understand?"

A hard expression replaced Trent's shock, reminding me of who he was and what he was capable of. "You're not who I though you would be," he said, and Ceri let a cruel smile curve the corners of her mouth.

"I'm your worst nightmare come to walk this side of the lines. I'm an elf, Trent, something you've forgotten how to be. You're scared of black magic. I can see fear shimmering under your aura like sweat. I live and breathe black magic. I'm so tainted with it that I will use it without thought, without guilt, and without hesitation."

She stepped forward into his space, and Trent moved back. "Leave Rachel alone," she said, the words soft as rain and as commanding as a god's.

Ceri reached to touch him, and in a blinding fast motion, Quen bolted forward.

I took a breath to shout a warning, but Ceri spun, hurling a black ball of ever-after. *"Finire!"*

"Ceri!" I exclaimed, then cowered when it hit the circle Quen flung up and exploded into black sparkles.

Clearly ticked, Ceri strode to Quen, Latin spilling from her like black smoke. *"Quis custodiet ipsos custodies?"* she said wrathfully, then plunged a tiny white fist into his circle.

Quen stared in shock as his circle fell.

"Finire," Ceri said tightly, reaching for him, and when Quen grasped her wrist to do something, he froze, then dropped to the hardwood floor, out cold.

"Holy crap!" Jenks chirped from the rafters, and Ceri looked away from Quen. Anger made her pale beauty terrible.

"Ceri," I coaxed, then stopped when she rounded on me.

"Shut up!" she said, long hair flying. "I'm angry at you, too. No one has ever shoved me before in my entire life."

Mouth open, I looked at Trent. The shocked billionaire was backing to the door. "Excuse me," he said. "This was a mistake. If you will release Quen, I'll leave."

Ceri spun to him. "My apologies for keeping you from your next appointment. You're a very busy man," she said caustically, then turned her attention to Quen, slumped on the floor. "Is he a good person?" she asked abruptly.

Trent paused, and the metallic stench tickling my nose grew stronger. "Yes."

"You should listen to him more often," she said, crouching before him, her dress pooled like water turned to silk. "That's why we have others around us."

Jenks dropped down to me, and I wondered if Ceri thought of me like that. Sort of a servant with whom to talk things over.

Trent's eyes pinched in worry as Ceri muttered Latin, and a black shimmer of ever-after coated Quen. He snorted, the black splintering away to silver threads when his eyes opened. Scrambling up, he stood while Ceri found her feet with more grace. It was obvious by his chagrined expression that he was surprised and humbled. I couldn't help but feel bad for the man. Ceri was a handful, even when she wasn't pushing us around.

"Did you see what I did?" she asked him seriously, and Quen nodded, his green eyes fixed upon her as if seeing his salvation. "Can you do it?" she asked him next.

Glancing at Trent, he nodded. "I can now that I've seen you do it," he said guiltily.

But Ceri smiled in delight. "He didn't know you practice the dark arts, did he?"

Quen looked down, then blinked when he realized she was barefoot. "No, Mal Sa'han," he said softly, and Trent shifted uncomfortably.

Ceri laughed, the wonderful sound cascading over me like cool water. "Perhaps we are alive yet," she said, touching the top of his hand as if they were old friends. "Keep him safe if you can. He's an idiot."

Trent cleared his throat, but they were lost in each other's attention.

"It's what he was made into, Mal Sa'han," Quen said, kissing the top of her hand, the gesture full of grace. "He had no choice."

Ceri sniffed as she drew her hand from Quen. "Well, he does now," she said saucily. "See if you can't remind him of who and what he is."

With a respectful nod, Quen turned to me. I, too, was given that same head bob, but mine was accompanied by a smirk I couldn't decipher. Jenks sighed from my shoulder, and I found myself rocking back off the balls of my toes. It seemed to be over.

"Just a minute," I said, jiggling on my feet. "Don't leave yet. Ceri, don't let them leave."

Both men froze when Ceri smiled at them, and I jogged into my room. Snatching the two garment bags, I hustled back. I was alive—check. Still had the focus—check. Introduced Trent and Ceri—check. *I'm kind of hungry. Wonder what I've got in the fridge?* My eyes widened, now that I realized what that metallic stench was. Damn it, I had left the kettle over the flame, and it had gone dry.

"Here," I said, dumping the two dresses into Trent's arms. "I'm not working your lame-ass wedding. I'd refund your money, but you haven't given me any."

Trent's face was murderously furious, and he dropped them on the floor. Turning on a heel, he stiffly walked out the door, leaving it open behind him. I heard his feet on the sidewalk and the sound of a car door opening and shutting, then nothing.

Quen made an elegant bow to Ceri, who drew her dress up and curtsied back, shocking me. Hesitating, Quen bowed again to me, and I gave him a sloppy see-you-later salute. Like I could curtsy? His dark face smiling, Quen followed Trent out and quietly shut the door.

My exhaled breath seemed to be very loud.

"Holy crap," Jenks said, leaving my shoulder to make circles around Ceri. "That was the damnedest thing I've ever seen!"

As if it had been a signal, the sanctuary was abruptly pixy-filled. My head started to hurt, and though I was obviously happy with how this had ended, I was worried, too. I had to get rid of the focus as soon as possible. "Ceri," I said, waving pixy kids from my path as I flung the discarded dresses over the back of the couch and hotfooted it into the kitchen to turn off the burner, "just what am I to you anyway?"

She had followed me, and I was surprised to see Trent's gift in her hand when I glanced over my shoulder. "My friend," she said simply.

The stink was awful in the kitchen, and I wedged the window higher. See, this was why I liked coffee. You couldn't screw up making coffee. Even the bad stuff was good.

Using a hot pad, I moved the black kettle to the sink, the pops of superheated water startling me when the kettle hit the damp porcelain. "You want some coffee?" I said, at a loss for what to do. I knew she'd rather have tea, but not made in something so dirty on the outside.

"I like him," she said wistfully, and I spun, shocked at the shy tone.

"Quen?" I stammered, remembering him kissing her hand.

She was standing in the threshold to the kitchen, a dreamy look on her face where a powerful anger had just been. "No," she said, as if mystified at my confusion. "Trent. He's so deliciously innocent. And with all that power."

I stared at her as she took the lid off the gift box he had left and plucked an opal the size of a chicken's egg from it. Holding it up to the light, she sighed, "Trenton Aloysius Kalamack . . ."

TWENTY-EIGHT

The sun had shifted across to the far wall of the kitchen, and I sat at the table wearing one of Jenks's human-size shirts over a black chemise. I had it on for the comfort factor; I wasn't looking forward to going to the morgue again. To my left was that jar of jalapeño salsa and a tomato for Glenn. To my right a cup of long-cold coffee sat beside my cell and the land line. Neither one was ringing. It was a quarter after noon, and Glenn was late. I hated waiting.

Leaning closer to the table, I eased another coat of clear polish over my index fingernail. The odor of acetate mixed with the scent of the herbs hanging over the center island counter, and the sound of Jenks's kids was a balm as they played hide-and-seek in the garden. Three more pixies were braiding my hair, Jenks playing supervisor to prevent a repeat of "the snarl incident."

"No, not that way, Jeremy," Jenks said, and I stiffened. "You go under Jocelynn, then over Janice before you do the double back. There, that's it. Got the pattern?"

A weary chorus of "Yes, Dad," brought a smile to my face, and I tried not to move as I painted my thumbnail. I could hardly feel the tugs on my hair as they worked. Finished, I capped the bottle and held my hand up for inspection. A deep, almost maroon red.

I brought my hand closer, noticing that the faint scar on my knuckle was gone, undoubtedly erased along with my freckles after I'd used that demon curse to Were this spring. I'd gotten the scar from falling through the screen door when I had been ten. Robbie had pushed me, and after he dried my tears and put a bandage on it, I sucker-punched him in the gut. Which sort of left me wondering if Ceri would be landing one on me when I least expected it.

Robbie and I had come up with this wild story that the neighbor's dog had tried to jump through it. Looking back now, I was sure Mom and Dad knew that the black Lab had nothing to do with the broken screen, but they hadn't said anything, probably proud that we'd settled our differences, then hung together to escape punishment. I rubbed my thumb against the smooth skin of my finger, sad the scar was gone.

The draft from Jenks's wings brushed my hand. "What are you smiling about?"

My gaze fell upon my phone, and I wondered if Robbie would return my call if I left a message. I wasn't working for the I.S. anymore. "I was thinking about my brother."

"That is so weird," Jenks said. "One brother. I had twenty-four when I left."

Focus blurring, I tightened the cap on the polish, thinking that when he had left home, it had been as if they had died. He knew it was a one-way trip to Cincy. He was stronger than I.

"Ow!" I yelped when someone pulled too hard. My hand came up to my head, and I turned, sending them whirling up in silk and dust. The polish was still tacky, and I froze.

"Okay, get out!" Jenks said authoritatively. "All of you. You're just playing now. Go on. Jeremy, check on your mother. I can finish Ms. Morgan's hair. Go on!"

The three of them rose up in complaint, and he pointed. Still protesting, they flew backward to the screen, all talking at once, apologizing and pleading, wringing their hands and twisting their pretty little faces into sad expressions that tugged on my heart.

"Out!" Jenks demanded, and one by one they slipped into the garden. Someone giggled, and they were gone. "Sorry, Rache," he said, flitting behind me. "Hold still."

"Jenks, it's fine. I'll just take it out."

"Get your hands out of your hair," he muttered. "Your polish isn't dry, and you aren't going out with a half-assed braid. You don't think I know how to braid hair? Tink's little red shoes, I'm old enough to be your father."

He wasn't, but I set my hand on the table and settled back, feeling soft tugs as he finished what his children had started. A heavy sigh shifted me, and Jenks asked, "Now what?" his tone unusually gruff to cover his embarrassment over messing with my hair. The sound of his wings was pleasant, and I could smell oak leaves and Queen Anne's lace.

My gaze went to Ivy's empty space, and the sound of his wings dropped in pitch. "You going to get her out?" he asked softly.

He had reached the ends of my hair, and I slowly leaned forward, pillowing my head on my folded arms. "I'm worried, Jenks."

Jenks harrumphed. "At least she didn't leave because you bit Kisten."

"I suppose," I said, the warmth of my breath coming back to me from the old wood.

There was a final tug, and Jenks flew to land on the table before me. I sat upright to feel the heavy weight of my braid. His tiny features pinched. "She may not want to leave Piscary."

My hand rose and fell in a gesture of frustration. "So I'm supposed to leave her there?"

Looking tired, Jenks sat cross-legged beside my abandoned coffee mug. "I don't like it either, but he's her master vampire—the one that protects her."

"And screws with her mind." Bothered, I rubbed at a nail, smoothing out a nick before the polish finished setting.

"You think you're strong enough to protect her? Against an undead master vampire?" Jenks asked.

I thought back to my conversation with Keasley in the garden. "No," I whispered, glancing at the clock. *Where the devil is Glenn?*

Jenks's wings blurred, and he rose four inches, still sitting cross-legged. "Then let her get herself out. She'll be all right."

"Damn it, Jenks!" He started to laugh, which ticked me off. "There is nothing funny about this," I said, and, smirking, Jenks landed on the table.

"I had this same conversation with Ivy about you up in Mackinaw. She'll be all right."

My eyes went to the clock. "If she isn't, I'll kill him."

"No you won't," Jenks said, and I flicked my gaze to him. No, I wouldn't. Piscary kept Ivy safe from predation. When she came home, I'd make her a cup of cocoa, listen to her cry, and this time, damn it, I'd hold her and tell her it was going to be okay. *Vampire culture sucks.*

My eyes blurred, and I jumped when the front bell rang. "There he is," I said, chair scraping as I stood and yanked the waistband of my jeans up.

Jenks's wings were a subdued hum as I grabbed my phone and dropped it into my bag. My thoughts went to Piscary, and I added my splat gun. Then I thought about Trent, and I dropped the focus in there, too. Checking to see if I'd marred my nails, I slid the jar into my arms and picked up the tomato. "Ready, Jenks?" I said with a forced cheerfulness.

"Yup," he said, then shouted, "Jhan!"

The serious-minded pixy came in so fast I was sure he'd been on the gutters outside the window. "Watch your mother," Jenks said. "You know how to use my phone?"

"Yes, Dad," the eight-year-old said, and Jenks put a hand on his shoulder.

"Call Ms. Morgan if you need to reach me. Don't look for me, use the phone. Got it?"

"Yes, Da-a-a-a-ad." This time it carried a heavy exasperation, and I smiled, though I was dying inside. Jhan was assuming more responsibility to take his dad's place in the next few years. *Pixy life spans suck.*

"Jenks," I said as I shifted the jar of sauce to my hip, "it's noon. If you want to sit this one out, that's fine. I know you nap this time of day."

"I'm fine, Rachel," he said darkly. "Let's go."

To insist would only tick him off, so we headed out. My vamp-made boots clumped on the hardwood floor of the sanctuary, and after setting the jar on the table by the door, I fumbled in my bag for my sunglasses. I wrangled them on one-handed and pulled the door open.

"I got that sauce you wanted, Glenn," I said, then looked up. I was getting tired of finding unexpected people on my stoop. Maybe I ought to spend an afternoon with a drill and put in one of those peepholes. How expensive could they be?

"Hey, David, what's up?" I said, taking him in. He was out of his usual suit, wearing a soft gray suede tuck-in shirt and pair of jeans instead. His face was absolutely clean-shaven, and a long, dull scratch marked his cheek and neck. Behind him at the curb, his gray sports car idled.

"Rachel." His quick gaze darted to Jenks. "Jenks," he added. Standing a step back, the usually collected Were took a steadying breath, reaching to straighten his missing jacket. His hand clenched as if reaching for the handle of his briefcase. My worry intensified.

"What?" I said, expecting the worst.

David looked behind him at his car. "I need your help. Serena, my girlfriend, needs a heavy painkiller." His eyes were pinched when they met mine. "I would have phoned, but I think the FIB has tapped my line. She Wered, Rachel. My God, she actually Wered."

"Holy crap," Jenks said.

Tense, I took my shades off and set the tomato down beside the sauce. "The full moon isn't until Monday. That's when the others first Wered."

His head bobbing, David fidgeted. "I told her about the women in the morgue. I told her I was sorry, and that she probably wouldn't be able to stop from Wereing on Monday unless she gained some control over it between now and then." Brown eyes pleading for forgiveness, he added, "So I walked her through it, or I tried. She's not built for it," he said, his voice cracking. "Weres came from humans, but we've evolved apart from them for too long. It's not supposed to hurt this bad. She is in too much pain. Do you have a charm? A potion? Anything."

Lately I'd begun carrying pain amulets in my bag, like some people have breath mints. "I have three with me right now," I said, reaching behind me to shut the door. "Let's go."

David took the steps two at a time. Jenks was a flash of wings, and I brought up the rear, slipping into the passenger's side as David slammed his door shut. I thought that a curse that turned humans into Weres was stupid if it hurt too much to be of any use, but then again the focus enabled alphas to pack together to eliminate the pain of shifting, so maybe there was some sense to it.

"Hey!" I protested when the car started moving before I had my door shut. Ignoring me, David scanned the street as I buckled myself in, bracing against the dash when he took a corner too fast. Weres had excellent reflexes, but this was pushing it. "David. Slow down."

"I've doped her up on bane," he said, managing the wheel with one hand as he fastened his seat belt with the other. "I can't let her wake up and find me gone. The pain is killing her. I don't think it's going to stop until she turns back. This was a mistake. God, what have I done?"

My fingers felt the outline of the focus in its lead-lined bag. I didn't think the artifact was going to help. The dulling of pain happened when Were packs combined into a round. The focus only allowed them to do it more efficiently.

"David, slow down!" I repeated, when he came out onto a one-way, driving like he was in the Indy 500. Jenks hugged the stem of the rear-view mirror. He looked a little green. "The I.S. is watching for me," I added. "They usually have a cruiser in the church up on the right."

David slowed, a shaky hand on the wheel. The lot was empty, and he picked up speed.

"What do you mean, the FIB has tapped your line?" I asked as we got on the interstate to cross the river from the Hollows to Cincinnati. "They can't do that."

"They did," David said grimly. "Officer Glenn thinks I'm responsible for the Were deaths. Not just the suicides, but all of them. Thinks I'm a Jack the Ripper meets Mr. Hyde."

I made a scoffing bark of laughter, then tensed when he darted across the path of a semi. "It's Trent," I said in the fading adrenaline. "He told me himself. And watch what you're doing. God! You're a worse driver than Ivy!"

David gave me a quick look. "Trent Kalamack? What for?"

Jenks's wings were an odd shade of green. "He's after the focus," the ill pixy said. "He found out this morning that Rachel has it."

"Damn me back to my mother's bitch," David swore softly. "Do you have it? Is it safe?"

My head bobbed. "I'm going to give it to Piscary to put it back into hiding."

"Rachel!" David exclaimed, and I pointed to the truck stopped at the red light just off the bridge.

"I can't keep it safe," I said as he hit the brakes. "What am I supposed to do with it? I don't have enough magic to hide it once someone knows I've got it. At least Piscary has enough clout to keep people from drugging him into telling where it is."

David's eyes were worried. "But it belongs to the Weres."

The light changed, and I held my breath until I was sure David wasn't going to dart around the truck ahead of us, but the usually über-safety-conscious Were just fumed at the slow acceleration. "Believe me," I said softly, "if there was a way I could give it to the Weres, I would, but it's demon-crafted, and all it's going to do is cause problems. Change is needed, but slow, not fast. Otherwise . . ." I thought of his girlfriend's pain.

"A Were should hide it, then," he offered.

"Who, David?" I demanded, frustrated, and Jenks's wings shifted nervously. "You? We tried that. Mr. Ray? Mrs. Sarong? How about Vincent? He had three packs bound to him, and they were savage. Every one of them channeling the power of an alpha but lacking the restraint that evolved with the alpha position."

Silently his jaw clenched, and I continued. "You don't become an alpha, you're born that way. They couldn't handle it. Change has to come slow. It's like your girlfriend trying to Were without the mental and physical cushion a thousand years of evolution gave you."

David's grip on the wheel eased, and I relaxed. "Maybe it's not time yet?" I said softly, bracing myself as he made a quick right into his apartment complex.

"Ah, that doesn't look good," Jenks said, and David's face went empty of emotion. I followed their gazes to the parking lot, and my stomach sank. There were two I.S. cruisers, three from the FIB, and a multispecies ambulance.

"It's okay," I said, reaching for my seat belt. "I don't think they're at your apartment."

Saying nothing, David pulled up as close as he could get, fumbling with his seat belt, swearing until it released. "It's my apartment. My curtains were closed. They're open now. And Serena couldn't be awake yet." Leaving the keys in the ignition, he lurched out of the car, steps crisp and intent as he headed for his door.

I slowly got out to stand wedged between the car and the open door, my arms on the roof. Jenks landed on my shoulder, and we said nothing when an I.S. officer stopped David on the threshold. They spoke briefly, and I felt sick as the man cuffed him. David looked broken but offered no resistance, knowing that to fight would give them a reason to throw him in a cell and forget about him to the limit of the law.

Someone moved past the upstairs window, and I gripped my bag tighter, glad I had the focus, since the I.S. was taking the opportunity to search David's apartment. His cat was watching me from a second window, and it skittered away before a dark figure passed by it. "What are we going to do, Jenks?" I whispered.

Jenks's wings cooled my neck, and I squinted in the glare as they bundled David into a cruiser. "Jenks?" I said, and the pitch of the pixy's wings shifted.

"See you back at the church," he said, darting off to eavesdrop on them.

I held my breath as he hovered over the lot, dropping like a stone to dart inside the cruiser with David when no one was looking. I wished him well as the cruiser eased forward, hesitating briefly before pulling into traffic. *'Bye, David.*

My breath slipped from me, long and slow. Leaning into the car, I retrieved David's keys and dropped them in my bag. I'd find another way home, but I'd need his keys to get in to feed his cat. Damn it. I'd seen this before, and it hadn't ended well.

I shut David's car door with a thump, and my blood pressure spiked when I spotted Glenn's trim silhouette headed for me from across the lot. "Well, at least I know now why you didn't show for our date at the morgue!" I shouted across the distance between us.

His pace was purposeful, but his head was bowed in what I hoped was guilt. "I'm sorry, Rachel," the ex–military officer said as he halted beside me.

"Sorry!" I exclaimed, more than a little upset at Glenn's overzealous Boy Scout mentality. "Whatever David's been arrested for, he didn't do it! I was with Trent this morning, and he flat-out told me he was the one murdering the Weres to find that stupid-ass statue."

Glenn didn't look any happier, his stud earrings making an odd statement next to his otherwise eminently professional mien. "I'm really glad to hear you say that," he said, putting his hands behind his back and all but pinning me to the car with his too-close presence.

Taken aback, I felt my anger slow. "So . . . you're going to let him go?"

Head shaking, he squinted to look worried. "No, but if Mr. Kalamack can verify that you were with him this morning, I can keep the I.S. from arresting you right now."

I felt myself pale. "Me?" I stammered. "What for?"

"For aiding and abetting the murder of Brett Markson." His gaze went to my bag. "You got anything in there I need to know about?"

Adrenaline surged, and I felt like I'd been kicked in the stomach. "I've got my splat gun, but I don't need a permit for it. And this is crap, Glenn. I just told you Trent murdered them. All of them. The three Jane Wolves were accidents and have nothing to do with the murders."

Glenn pulled himself straighter, his hands still laced behind his back. "Rachel, could you step away from the car and come with me, please? And give me your purse."

My mouth dropped open. "Am I under arrest?" I said loudly, clutching my bag closer. Crap, I had the focus in there.

"No one is arresting you—yet," he said, his expression pained. "Please, Rachel. If you don't cooperate, the I.S. will handle your questioning. I'm trying to jump ahead of them here."

That was all the encouragement I needed. Feeling very alone for the lack of Jenks, I handed him my bag. It looked funny in his grip, and he gestured with a free hand for me to accompany him. Shaking inside, I fell into step beside him. We were moving steadily to the FIB van—the one with the metal mesh in the windows. "Talk to me, Glenn."

"Mr. David Hue was seen talking to Mr. Markson last night," he said unhappily. "Today the victim was found dead in Mr. Hue's apartment Dumpster with your card in his wallet. Mr. Hue admits to having relations with the three Jane Wolves now in the morgue, and when officers came to question him, they found a heavily sedated Were woman showing signs of assault."

My knees went watery. This looked really bad, and I was glad I'd told Glenn about the focus earlier. "Serena was human, Glenn. The focus turned her. David was helping her to learn to control it before the full moon so she would know what was coming and be able to deal with it. He doped her up in bane so he could get me to help with her pain. That's all that it is!"

Glenn glared at me, his brown eyes full of warning. "Lower your voice."

Eyes dropping, I frowned, listening to the distinctive radio chatter. "Sorry," I said, then scuffed to a halt before we got much closer to that open van. "David did not kill Brett," I said firmly. "The three women in the morgue were tragic accidents. Serena is trying to deal with what happened, and David is doing the best he can. You should be arresting Trent, not David."

"Rachel, stop."

"He told me he did it!" I exclaimed. "Why does no one believe me?"

Glenn leaned close, and I stiffened, using every ounce of will to not break his hold when he took my shoulder. "Shut. Up," he said tightly, so close I could smell the sweat under his aftershave. "Everyone with a badge knows you hate Kalamack. I can't ask for a warrant to arrest him because you said he told you he did it."

I made a scoffing noise, then yelped when he yanked me closer.

"I believe you, Rachel," Glenn said, almost whispering into my ear. "That man is slime. And I'm going to look into it."

"Look into it," I taunted, then winced when Glenn pinched my shoulder.

"I said I'm going to look into it, and if I find something, I'll let you know." He let go of me. "Just hang tight. You're no help to me if you're in jail."

Dropping back a step, I watched the ambulance crew bring Serena out. They had used a witch spell to trigger her return to her human shape. From what I could see, she looked like the women in the morgue, a trim outline showing under the stretcher's sheet, her long brown hair in disarray. David clearly had a preferred look to his women. Though she was unconscious, pain had drawn her face into lines.

"David didn't hurt her," I whispered as the ambulance crew loaded her in the back.

"Then he'll be released when she regains consciousness and tells us that," Glenn said.

I turned to Glenn, tears of frustration blurring my vision. "If we lived in a perfect world."

My nose tickled with the scent of incense, and I spun. Denon was behind me, clearly amused that he had startled me. He looked better, almost his old self and dressed in his usual polo shirt and slacks that showed off his narrow waist and his muscular legs. Obviously some dead vamp had been at him, giving a little back to boost his morale. It was in his attitude. My pulse quickened at the reminder of the I.S. officers bundling David into cuffs, and I backed up into Glenn. "Denon," I said stiffly, telling myself I wasn't afraid of him but of what he could do to me under the flag of I.S. justice.

"Morgan," the big man said, his deep, beautiful voice sounding like chocolate milk given sound. His gaze slid to Glenn behind me. "Detective Glenn."

I shivered, his voice creeping up my spine with the subtlety of velvet. Damn, someone had been playing with him, all right. Glenn seemed to have noticed, too, for all he did was nod.

Denon smiled to show his flat teeth. "Morgan, it gives me great pleasure to take you in for questioning in conjunction with the murder of Brett Markson."

My breath caught when he reached for me, and I fell back into Glenn's solid weight. Flustered, I pulled myself straight. "I have an alibi, Denon. Back off."

People were watching, and Denon arched his eyebrows. "The time of Markson's death was put at seven. You were asleep, and I know no one was with you. Seeing as both your boyfriend *and* your roommate were with Piscary at the time." He leered.

I didn't want to think about it. I couldn't think about it. "I was having an early-morning meeting with Mr. Kalamack," I said, keeping my voice soft so he wouldn't hear it shake.

Denon's eyes widened, cracking his cocky attitude and giving me a measure of strength.

"You know how humans are," I added, sliding sideways so if I had to move, I wouldn't bump Glenn, but Glenn shifted with me. "The way they insist everyone keep to their time clock. No respect for other cultures."

Brown eyes narrowing, Denon drew an obscenely thin cell phone out of a belt holster. His brown fingers hitting the buttons carefully, he appeared to scroll through a list of numbers. "You won't mind if I verify that."

I froze, not knowing if Trent would tell the truth. "Be my guest," I said boldly.

People were closing in around us. I could feel them. Glenn edged closer. "Rachel . . ."

My gaze flicked to his, and I felt small between the two black men. "Trent was with me," I insisted. *But will he admit to that?* I thought, cringing when I remembered how we had parted. *Probably not.*

"Mr. Kalamack, please," Denon said pleasantly, and I heard a woman's voice. "Of course, ma'am. This is Officer Denon from the I.S." Denon smiled at me as the call was put through. "Mr. Kalamack," he said cheerfully. "I apologize for interrupting your afternoon. I know you're busy, and this will only take a moment. I need you to verify that you were with Ms. Rachel Morgan this morning between seven and seven-thirty."

I swallowed hard, wanting my splat gun, tucked away in my bag. It was probably a good thing that Glenn had it.

Denon's eyes flicked to me. "No, sir," he said into the tiny phone. "Yes, sir. Thank you. You have a good day, too." Face empty of emotion, Denon snapped the phone shut.

"Well?" I asked. I was sweating. Even a human could see it.

"You act as if you don't know the answer," he said smoothly.

From behind me Glenn shifted. "Officer Denon, are you arresting Ms. Morgan or not?"

I held my breath. Denon's big hands clenched and released. "Not today," he said, forcing a smile. Exhaling, I tossed a strand of hair that had escaped Jenks's braid and tried to look confident.

"You're lucky, witch," Denon said as he rocked back a graceful step. "I don't know what star you're wishing on, but it's about to fall." And with that, he spun and walked away.

"Yeah, and angels cry when good men die," I said, wishing he would find a new book of clichés to memorize. Relieved, I reached for my shoulder bag, still in Glenn's possession. "Give me that," I said, yanking it to me.

The car Denon had gotten into drove away with a tiny squeak of tires.

Head down in thought, Glenn pointed me to an unmarked FIB car: big, black, and sporting blocky lines. "I'll get you home," he said, and I obediently headed for it.

"Trent told the truth," I said, our steps matching perfectly. "I don't get it. He could have gotten me in jail, then searched the church for the focus at his leisure."

Glenn opened the door for me, and I slipped inside, enjoying the courtesy.

"Maybe he's worried someone saw him," Glenn mused aloud, then shut my door.

"Maybe he was using Ceri and me as his alibi," I muttered as Glenn went around the front and got in. I grimaced, thinking, *How sick is that?* Using meeting a beautiful woman like Ceri as an alibi while one of your peons was shoving someone into a Dumpster for you. Glenn started the car, and we waited for the ambulance to leave before us, the lights off and moving slow.

"David won't be taking the blame for this," I said in determination, clutching my bag on my lap. Maybe Trent told the truth because he knew I had the focus with me, and if the I.S. got it, it would make his task to retrieve it a lot harder?

"I hope you're right." Glenn's voice was distant as he looked both ways before pulling out. "I really hope you're right. Because if Mr. Hue is officially charged with the murders, the I.S. is going to come after you for aiding and abetting, even with that alibi. David asking you for help looks really bad."

Settling myself into the leather seats, I put an elbow on the open window and stared at nothing. "Swell," I whispered to no one. *My life sucks.*

TWENTY-NINE

My eyes fluttered open when Glenn eased to a stop at a stoplight. Blinking, I realized I was almost home, and I sat up from my slouch. The day had gotten warm, and apparently I'd nodded off. Clearly, being knocked out for eight hours wasn't the same as sleep. Embarrassed, I glanced at Glenn, flushing when he smiled at me, his teeth a startling white against his dark skin.

"Please tell me I wasn't snoring," I muttered, never imagining I would have fallen asleep. I had only closed my eyes to gather my thoughts. Or maybe to escape from everything.

"You snore cute," he said, giving his unused ashtray a tap. "You two are funny."

Jenks rose from it in a puff of gold glitters. "I'm awake!" he exclaimed, tugging his clothes straight and looking charmingly wide-eyed as he arranged his shock of blond hair. He, at least, had an excuse, seeing as he was usually asleep this time of day.

The clock on the dash said it was a shade after two. After leaving David's, Glenn had first taken me to the FIB to make an official statement before the I.S. could choose the most inopportune time to get one from me. From there we went to pick Jenks up at the I.S. and physically drop off a copy of my paperwork, all nice and legal. We fitted the morgue in there, too, which had left me depressed. I was sure Glenn had more to do than cart us around, but since I didn't have a valid license, I appreciated it.

David was still in custody. Jenks had overheard his interrogation, and apparently Brett had met with David yesterday to talk about Brett joining our pack. It was supposed to have been a surprise, which had me in tears when I found out. That's why Trent had targeted him. Trent was slime, and I cursed myself for letting some of the good things he did—like admit he spent the morning with me, for instance—cloud the fact that he was a murderer and drug lord. He only did something decent if it might be of some use to him, such as giving himself an alibi for seven to seven-thirty. Ceri had it right. The man was a demon in all but species.

Under some made-up point of law, the I.S. was detaining David without any formal charges. It was illegal, but someone in the basement had probably realized that the focus was out, seeing as a loner was turning human women into Weres. David was knee-deep in it. It would only be a matter of time before I joined him. Maybe if he was in I.S. custody, Trent couldn't kill him. Maybe.

I'm sorry, David. I never expected this to happen.

The cool shade of my street fell over me, and I gathered my bag onto my lap, feeling for the heavy outlines of the focus. Squinting, I realized there was a black van parked in front of the church—and someone was tacking a note on my door.

"Jenks. Look at that," I whispered, and he followed my gaze.

Glenn eased to a stop several car lengths back, and when I cracked the window, Jenks darted out, saying, "I'll see what it is."

The man with the hammer caught sight of us, and with a worrisome quickness he hustled down the stairs and into his vehicle.

"You want me to stay?" Glenn asked, shoving the car into park. He had a pencil in his grip and was writing down the plate number as the black van drove away.

The dust spilling from Jenks as he hovered before the note shifted from gold to red. "I don't know," I murmured. Getting out, I stomped up the stairs.

"Evicted!" Jenks said, his face white when he spun in the air. "Rachel, Piscary evicted us. He evicted us!"

My stomach going light, I ripped the paper from the nail. "No freaking way," I said, skimming the official document. It was blurry from being the second copy, but clear enough. We had thirty days to vacate.

They were going to tear the church down now that it wasn't sanctified, but the impetus behind it was Piscary.

Glenn leaned out the window. "Everything okay?"

"Rache," Jenks exclaimed, clearly terrified. "I can't move my family. Matalina isn't well! They're going to bulldoze the garden!"

"Jenks!" I said, hands upraised though I couldn't touch him. "It's going to be okay. I promise. We'll work something out. Matalina will be fine!"

Jenks stared at me, his eyes wide. "I . . . I," he stammered, then with a little moan, he darted up and around to the back of the church.

My hands fell to my sides. I felt so helpless.

"Rachel?" Glenn called from the street, and I turned.

"We've been evicted," I said, moving the paper in explanation. "Thirty days." Anger trickled into me.

Glenn's eyes narrowed. "Don't do it, witch," he warned as he looked at my fists, clenched at my sides.

I gazed down the street at nothing, getting madder. "I'm not going to kill him," I said. "Give me some credit. This is an invitation. If I don't go see him, he'll do something worse." *Shit. My mother.*

Glenn ducked back in the window. His door opened, and he got out. My blood pressure rose. "Get your little brown-sugar candy ass back in your ugly Crown Victoria," I said. "I know what I'm doing."

My fingers felt the outlines of the focus in my bag as Glenn came to the bottom of the steps and looked up at me, pistol on his hip and attitude all over him like icing on a cake. "Give me your car keys."

"Don't think so."

His eyes narrowed. "Give them to me or I'm going to arrest you myself."

"On what grounds?" I asked belligerently, looking down at him.

"Your boots. They're breaking every unwritten fashion law."

Huffing, I looked at them, tilting one onto the toe to see them better. "I'm just going to talk to him, nice and friendly."

Eyebrows high, Glenn put his hand out. "I've seen how you talk to Piscary. Keys?"

My jaw clenched. "Put a car at my mother's house," I demanded, and when he nodded, I shoved the eviction paper into my bag, found my keys, and threw them at him. "Bastard," I muttered as they hit his hand.

"That's my girl," he said as he looked at the zebra-striped car key. "You get them back when you go to class."

I opened the door to the church and put my hand on my hip. "You call me your girl one more time and I'm going to turn your gonads into plums and make jam out of them."

Chuckling, Glenn got into his car.

Entering the dark foyer, I pulled the heavy door shut hard enough to make the upper transom windows rattle. My bag held tight to me, I stomped into the sanctuary and headed for my desk. Yanking open drawers, I slammed and banged around until I found my spare set of keys. It had everything the first had plus the key that opened Ivy's safe and one from Nick's apartment, never thrown away. God knows why.

A smug satisfaction tugged the corners of my mouth up into a wicked smile as I dropped the keys into my bag, and I went to the side window to watch Glenn turn the corner at the end of the street. The red of the stained glass gave everything outside an unreal look, like the ever-after.

"Jenks!" I shouted as his car vanished. "If you can hear me, get your best suit on. We have some major ass-kissing to do."

THIRTY

This isn't the same, I told myself, my two-handed grip tightening on the wheel of my convertible and the wind from the cracked window tugging a few strands from my braid. This wasn't anything like the night I had tried to tag Piscary last year. For one, Jenks was with me this time. I wasn't mad either—not blind mad anyway. It was daylight for at least a few more hours—not that that made a difference. Jenks was with me. I had a nice peace offering to buy my life with, and, lastly, Jenks was with me.

Signaling, I made a quick left turn, heading to the riverfront and going against the predominant flow of traffic. I had friends at Pizza Piscary's, but Piscary was back, and they wouldn't help me. Jenks was my confidence now that the focus really was at the post office, lost in the human bureaucracy so deep and jealously guarded that even the I.S. couldn't reach it. His presence meant more to me than my splat gun, fully stocked and tucked into my bag. I had an invoked pain charm around my neck, hanging outside my shirt so it wouldn't affect me until I needed it. And I had a feeling I was going to need it.

Other than that, I was going in pretty much naked of earth charms. I had a hefty amount of ley line energy spindled in my head, though, and in my pocket a pair of heavy-duty toenail clippers you might use on an elephant, which I hoped would be strong enough to cut an anti–ley line zip-strip. But it was Jenks I was counting on to be the difference between my walking out with a new lease on life or spending an eternity of hell with Piscary or Al.

This was my best option. Trent knew I had the focus. The I.S. wasn't so dense that they hadn't realized it was still in my possession. I wanted Piscary's protection from all of them.

My God. How did I get to this place?

The breeze from my window shifted Jenks's wings. He was sitting on the rearview mirror, facing backward as he gazed vacantly into the past. His features were lined and worried. There wasn't a scrap of red on him—a symbol of his intent. If we lost the garden, the stress might tip Matalina into a downward spiral. I'd be hard-pressed to keep him from trying to kill Piscary if push came to shove. But if push came to shove, killing Piscary might be the only way to survive.

I didn't want to do that. The undead vampire was the only person I knew who could keep the focus safe until it could be hidden again.

Seeing Jenks's misery, I took a breath to ask him about his outfit. I'd never seen it before, sort of a combination of Quen's black uniform with the free-flowing folds of a desert sheik's robes. But Jenks's gaze flicked to mine, making me pause.

"Thanks, Rachel," he said, wings utterly still. "For everything. I want to tell you in case we both don't make it through this."

"Jenks . . ." I started, and he cut me off with a sharp wing chirp.

"Shut your mouth, witch!" he snapped, though I could tell he wasn't mad. "I want to thank you—this past year has been the best in my life. And not just for me. That sterility wish I got from you is probably why Matalina made it through last winter. The garden and everything that came with working with you?" Jenks's gaze went distant. "Even if they bulldoze everything, I want you to know that it was worth it. My kids know you can make it if you take risks and work hard. That we can work in the system you lunkers set up. That's all a parent really needs to give his kids. That, and how to love someone with all your soul."

This was sounding like a last confession, and I flicked my gaze from the car braking in front of me to him. "Jeez, Jenks. We're going to be fine. I'll give Piscary the focus, and he'll rescind the eviction. And once everyone knows he has the thing, life will go back to normal. Matalina will be fine."

He didn't say anything. Matalina wasn't going to be fine no matter what happened in the next twenty-four hours. But I'd be damned if I wouldn't do what I could to get her through the coming winter. She was *not* going to hibernate and risk not waking up, that was for sure.

Jenks's wings drooped, and he pulled a fold of fabric up and polished his sword. Just as well. I wasn't enjoying the conversation, and Jenks's misery was making my stomach hurt. I wished he were bigger again, just so I could give him a hug.

Understanding hit me, and I stiffened. This inability to touch was what Ivy lived with every day. She couldn't touch anyone she cared about without her blood lust asserting itself.

We are so screwed up.

I forced myself back from the bumper of the guy in front of me. Piscary's was just ahead, and I wanted to get off the street before the I.S. found me. They were suspiciously absent, and I wondered if they were watching me from a distance to see if I had left to get the focus from someone. I suppose mailing it hadn't been the smartest thing, but I couldn't put it into a bus locker, and giving it to Ceri would've been a mistake. Humanity had steadfastly kept control of the mail system, and even Piscary would think twice about leaning on an overworked employee who might snap and go postal. There were some things even a vampire wouldn't mess with.

The jitters started, and Jenks's wings shifted fitfully as we pulled into Piscary's parking lot. Yeah, the plan looked good on paper, but Piscary might be more ticked than I thought about my putting him in jail. That I'd just been doing my job probably wouldn't go very far with him.

Nervous, I scanned the area. There were a few cars clustered about the kitchen entrance that were clearly not patrons'. I didn't see Ivy's cycle, but there was a huge mound of stuff piled at the curb. Sheets of paneling that once covered the upstairs windows and the tall, trendy tables and stools that Kisten had put in were now carelessly piled to make a five-foot wall between the lot and the street, waiting for pickup. Apparently Piscary was doing a little remodeling.

My eyes widened, and I took my foot off the gas when I realized Kisten's light show was among it, the metal scaffolding bent and twisted as if it had been pulled from the ceiling without regard. The colored lights were smashed, and his pool table was leaning atop it.

"Rache," Jenks said, chilling me, "that pile of trash just moved."

Fear slid through me, and my heart jumped. It was Kisten sitting on the curb between the mounds of debris. Sun glinting on his blond hair, he threw something into the pile with a metallic ting. He looked rumpled in his red silk shirt and black linen slacks. Discarded.

"Oh, my God," I whispered. His head came up as I swung the car around to point my nose to the exit, parking sideways against the faded lines. There was anger in his absolutely black eyes—utter hatred blending with betrayal and frustration.

"Ah, Rachel, maybe you should stay in the car."

Heart pounding, I fumbled for the door, and Jenks zipped out before me, aggressive and wary. Kisten stood, and, leaving the car running, I glanced at the dark restaurant and the upper windows overlooking the parking lot. Nothing moved but a scrap of paper taped to the door. Worried, I paced to him, my kick-butt boots tapping. "Kisten?"

"What are you doing here?" he barked, and I jerked to a stop, confused.

I stood there for a moment with the nearby cars whooshing past, trying to realign my thinking. "Piscary evicted us," I said, Jenks's wings clattering as he hovered. "What happened?" I said, gesturing to his club, now on the curb.

"What do you think happened!" he shouted, looking at the silent restaurant. "The son of a bitch kicked me out! He kicked me out and gave my last blood to someone."

God help us. His last blood? As in "Here he is, have fun draining him to death"?

Pulse quickening, I dropped back when Kisten swooped down to the fragments of his dance club. With vampiric strength he flung a chair at the front door, the metal tumbling and clanking to a stop short of the entryway. The wind from the nearby river tugged at my braid, and I felt cold despite the two shirts I had on. "Kisten," I said, frightened, "it's going to be okay."

But my confidence trickled away when he turned to me, his shoulders hunched and dark fear and hatred in his eyes. "No," he rasped. "It isn't. He gave me to someone as a thank-you. To kill. For their enjoyment. And no one will stop him because he's a *fucking god!*"

The draft from Jenks's wings tickled my neck, and an iron-cold band of fear slithered through my heart. There was death in Kisten's eyes.

There in the sunshine, death waited. Backing up another step, I felt my mouth go dry.

Kisten dipped a hand into a leather pocket of the pool table to come up with the five ball. "When Ivy says no, she gets praised for her strength of will," he said bitterly, hefting it experimentally for weight. "When I say no, I get fucking *kicked out!*" With a grunt he threw the ball. It sped over the parking lot, almost unseen. "*Fuck you, you bastard!*" he shouted, and a window broke in the upper story.

I jumped when Jenks landed on my shoulder. "Ah . . . Rachel?" he said, and gold dust spilled over me. "Leave. Please just get in the car and leave."

Swallowing, I took a hesitant step forward while Kisten found another pool ball. "Kisten?" I whispered, frightened at his show of temper. Never had I seen him this bad. "Come on," I said, reaching out to take his arm. "We have to go."

Jenks left me, and Kisten froze when I tugged on him. Face empty, he turned, his black eyes freezing me as they glinted from behind his blond-dyed bangs. Feeling like I'd made a mistake, I let go. "We have to leave," I said, worried someone would come out.

"Go where?" he said around a harsh laugh that didn't sound like him at all. "I'm dead, Rachel. Soon as the sun goes down, someone's going to kill me. As slowly as their anticipation can stand. I gave everything to that bastard, and now he won't—" His words broke off, and fear and pain crossed his face. "I did everything for him," he said, betrayal staining his anger. "Made a shitload of *profit* off his bar when it lost its MPL, and now he fucking won't *touch me!*"

His rage and desperation finding a release in a movement of controlled anguish, Kisten threw another pool ball. I fell back, almost tripping on the wreckage of his light show.

"I made more on his damned business after he lost his MPL than he did all of last year!" he shouted, and the ball thunked low and to the left of a wide plate-glass window.

"He never even looked at the books!" Kisten threw a third, and my pulse raced when it went through the wall. "He doesn't *fucking care!*" he raged, and the eight ball hit the window.

I gasped when it shattered completely and a shadow came forward to investigate.

Kisten turned away, palm on the pool table sitting at a forty-five-degree cant atop a stacked pile of little round tables. Beyond the rubble, cars passed, oblivious. "He never looked at the books," he said softly, as if trying to figure it out. "I thought that would mean something."

The creak of the restaurant's door opening sent alarm spiking through me. Fear for what was coming beat the fear of Kisten's having lost it, and I pulled on his arm, the scent of old blood mixing with his usual scent of leather. "Get in the car. Kisten, get in my car!"

"He never looked at the books," Kisten said again, in shock. "Just put down an ultimatum, then gave my last blood to the vampire who set up the deal between him and that demon to get him out. Someone who doesn't care about me. I . . . I wanted him to have it."

This was just too sick. "Kisten, we have to go!" I exclaimed, my gaze darting to the five big men walking toward us, their pace slow and their wide shoulders swinging. One hesitated at the chair Kisten had thrown, twisting a metal leg free before falling back into step. *Ah, shit.*

Kisten's head came up at the sound of metal tearing. My face went cold. He was dead inside. Though he breathed and his heart beat, Kisten was dead, killed by an anger and betrayal that I'd never comprehend. He'd known Piscary his entire life. Bound his life to him. Was given power and authority over others through him. Found and relished the power of living above the law because of him. And Piscary had ripped all the promises away and thrown him to the curb without pity or thought. Discarded. Given to someone as a gift to take pleasure in killing him. *This is who I wanted to buy protection from?*

"Please," I whispered, both wanting and fearing Kist's turning his black eyes to me. My hand was on his shoulder, and the muscles of his arm tightened as he made a fist. I saw his determination before he voiced it.

"I need to hurt someone, Rachel," he said, brushing my hand from him. "Don't stop this until I can't move." He pulled a pool cue from the wreckage and hefted it.

"Kisten!" I pleaded, but he shoved me backward. I stumbled to catch my balance, frightened, and Kisten went to meet them, never looking back. Panicking, I shifted my weight to follow, but Jenks dropped down to block my way.

"Let him go," he said, his hands on his hips and a grim determination on his face.

"They're going to kill him!" I said, pointing to the advancing vampires as Kisten took up a stance between me and my car, but Jenks shook his head.

"No they won't," he said, eyes never leaving them. "He belongs to someone else." His eyes went to me, filled with deep fear. "After they finish beating him up, you've got to get him out of Cincy before whoever that is finds him."

"That's what I'm trying to do!" I shouted, almost stamping my foot. Stupid, asinine men. How could I give Piscary the focus now? But then a thought hit me, painful and hard. If the focus was as important as I thought, then maybe I could buy Kisten's safety as well as mine? I had to let Ivy find her own way out, but Kisten . . .

My panic rose anew, and I shifted from foot to foot out of helplessness as the men closed on Kisten. One of the vampires slid across the hood of my car while four more continued forward to trap him against the trash. The one in the lead was familiar. I recognized the slant to his cruel smile. It was the guy Kisten had beat up last year before taking me down to see Piscary. Sam.

"Jenks . . ." I said nervously. My bag with my splat gun was out of reach in my car.

"It'll be okay," he said, his voice high, but I didn't believe him. "Stay out of it."

"Jenks?" I said louder, then jumped when Kisten shifted his grip and swung his pool stick at Sam. Sam blocked it without slowing down. Smiling to show fangs, he followed it with a hop-step and a side kick to Kisten's middle.

Kisten took it, turning his body into a roundhouse. His face was ugly with hatred: I'd never seen it raw in him before, and I backed up, a fist to my chest. *Do they really expect me to just stand here and let them beat him up?*

Almost too fast to see, Kisten and Sam exchanged blows, the other vampires ringing them. No one was paying any attention to me, but I couldn't get to my car.

"Kisten, behind you!" I shouted when one of them grabbed Kisten as he rocked back.

Teeth bared, Kisten took the second vampire's arm. A soft pull and a savage twist, and a scream of pain ripped from the vampire's throat.

Kisten licked his lips before smacking the butt end of the pool cue into the vamp's throat. Black eyes intent, he snarled and shoved the downed vampire to the pavement, kicking the writhing man as he tried to breathe.

Sam charged him, and Kisten swung his broken cue like a knife. Sam danced back, taunting until Kisten followed, coming away from the downed vampire. I didn't think he was breathing yet, still convulsing on the pavement.

A third vampire wearing a backward cap came forward, hunched and cautious with that chair leg in his grip. Lost in battle lust, Kisten jumped at him, fangs bared.

The vampire sprang sideways, and Kisten shifted, falling to the ground for a leg sweep.

The metal chair leg pinged as it hit the ground right before the vampire holding it. I gasped when Kisten moved too fast to see, covering the man for the span of a breath. His cry of pain cut off with a frightening quickness, and Kisten rolled away, the metal leg in his hands now. It was aimed at Sam, and the vampire cautiously backed up. Howling like a mad thing, Kisten attacked, his movements blurred and fast.

The twitching of the vampire Kisten had left on the pavement stopped. His eyes stared unseeing at the faultlessly blue sky. His hair shifted in the wind. But the man was dead. I could tell. And I hadn't even seen what Kisten had done to him.

"Kisten, stop!" I shouted, then leapt to the side when the fourth vampire smashed into the pool table beside me. He hit it hard, his eyes going blank and his limbs spread-eagle for a breathless moment until he slid to hit the pavement.

I turned to Kisten, my heart pounding. I wanted it to stop, but he was out of control and I was afraid to interfere. His face was twisted and ugly. His motions were sharp and aggressive. And when Sam came at him with the same look, I could do nothing.

Grunting, Sam spun, his hair flaring as he smashed a roundhouse into Kisten's head.

Kisten stumbled back, a hand coming up to touch the blood leaking from a cut under his eye. As if not feeling it, he took a back kick, then another, each one moving him closer to me.

The third one, Kisten caught. Sam's face went still, and with a savage smile, Kisten wrenched his ankle. Sam cried out in anger to drop back in a controlled fall and keep Kisten from snapping it. Kisten moved to follow up with a deathblow, and Sam spun on his back for momentum, flinging his unhurt foot at Kisten's knee in a sweep.

Kisten went down, his foot knocked out from under him. I reached out, then gasped when two of the other vampires he had previously downed fell on him. Grunts of pain and silent thuds of fists into flesh turned my stomach as they attacked Kisten. One vampire, Kisten could hold his own against, but two? It had turned into a mauling.

Sam staggered to his feet, wiping a ribbon of blood from his chin. "Get him up," he breathed heavily, and Jenks got in my way, stopping me from interfering. Frustrated, I jerked back. This was enough. He'd had enough!

But when Sam looked at me and pointed for me to stay, I did, frightened by the dark depth of hatred in him. "Don't worry, chicky witch," he said, breathing heavy. "We're almost done. Piscary gave him to someone else to kill, or he'd be dead already."

He laughed then, chilling me to my soul. He knew who it was. He knew who Piscary had given Kisten to. I wondered if it was whoever had summoned Al to arrange the entire con to get Piscary out of jail. "Who is it!" I shouted, but he only laughed harder.

Using the support of my car, the vampire with the broken arm and the one stunned by hitting the pool table struggled to drag Kisten upright. Blood leaked from Kisten's mouth, and there was a cut under his eye, which was swollen almost closed. His blond hair glinted in the sunlight as his head hung. Sam limped closer, grabbing his hair and jerking his head up.

Kisten squinted to see him. Anger simmered in him still, and Sam smiled tauntingly. "Thought you were such a bad-ass," he said, then punched him in the gut.

I lurched forward as Kisten sagged, almost pulling down the vampires who held him. "You're nothing!" Sam shouted, furious. "You never were! Everything was Piscary!"

Balance bobbling, Sam punched him again, and Kisten groaned.

"That's enough!" I shouted, ignored, and Jenks's wings hummed.

The angry vampire wiped the blood from his nose, marking Kisten's hair when he yanked his head up again. Kisten's eyes were shut, and I could see the breath passing his bloodied lip and his chest moving as he breathed. "You were never anything, Felps. Remember that when you die. You were nothing alive, and you'll be less when you're dead."

"I said that's enough!" I shouted, hearing the wail of distant sirens.

Sam glanced at me and smiled to show his teeth. "Come see me when you need a little something, chicky witch. I'd love to give it to you."

I took a breath to tell him to shove it, but the two vampires let Kisten go, and he slid down the side of my car. Balancing to keep the weight off his broken ankle, Sam leaned toward Kisten. Kisten jerked, and horror hit me when Sam straightened with the diamond stud earring from Kisten's ear.

"Piscary says you're going to be dead twice by sunup," Sam said, head tilted as he put the earring in his own lobe. "He doesn't think you've got the guts to see it through and redeem yourself. Says you've gone soft. Me? I think you never had it in you to be undead."

The other two vampires started to hobble away, and after giving Kisten a last look, Sam headed after them, leaving the last of them to stare at the sun.

Kisten barely moved, curling in on himself. Pulse fast, I went to him. This had been stupid. God! How stupid could men be? Beating each other up had done a *helluva* lot of good. "Kisten," I said, kneeling beside him. I glanced behind me at the road, wondering why no one had stopped. Kisten was a mess, his head hanging, bleeding all over from scrapes and contusions. His expensive slacks were scuffed, and his silk shirt was torn. Fingers fumbling, I got my pain amulet off my neck and around his, hearing him take a clean breath when I tucked it behind his shirt and it connected with his skin.

"It's going to be okay," I said, wishing I could see the restaurant, but my car was in the way. "Come on, Kisten. Help me get you up." At least I wouldn't have to drag him to the car.

He pushed me off him, then leaned back and used his legs to push himself against my car to get himself upright. "I'm okay," he said, squinting at my worried face, then spitting blood onto the gravel. "Give me . . . my . . . lucky stick."

His eyes were on the broken cue, and my lips pressed together. "Just get in the damn car," I swore. "We have to get out of here. It sounds like the I.S. is coming." I fumbled for the door, Jenks getting in the way as he tried to help, dusting Kisten's cuts.

"I want my stick," Kisten said again as he fell into the passenger seat, his bloodied hair smearing the window. "I'm going to . . . shove it . . . up Piscary's ass."

Yeah, that sounds likely. But after I put both of his feet into the car and yanked him upright, I scooped up the broken cue and set it next to him. I slammed the door shut, only now glancing at the restaurant. Fear hit me, and I held my arms around myself, feeling the wind tug at my hair. Ivy was down there, lost in the madness that was Piscary. And I was going to have to deal with him for Kisten as well as myself. My gaze went to Kisten, slumped in the front seat. I had to get Ivy out of there. This was insane. Stuff like this shouldn't happen.

The howl of sirens lifted through me, and as traffic passed at a hurried forty-five miles per hour, I paced to my side of the car. "Rachel," Jenks said, getting in my way, "this isn't safe."

"Gee, you think?" I said bitterly, reaching for the handle, but he got in my way again.

"No," he said, hovering so close I was almost cross-eyed. "I mean I don't think you're safe. With Kisten."

I looked at Kisten slumped against the blood-smeared window, then yanked open my door. "This isn't the time for pixy paranoia," I said tightly.

Shedding a bright coppery dust that landed on my hand to make it tingle, he refused to move. "I think Piscary told him to kill you," he pleaded softly so Kisten couldn't hear. "And when Kisten refused, he threw him out. You heard what Kisten said about Ivy saying no and getting praised and him getting kicked out."

I stopped, my hand on the open door. I felt cold. Jenks landed on the window before me, his wings never slowing. "Think, Rachel," he said, gesturing. "He's been dependent upon Piscary for his entire life. Ivy isn't the only one Piscary's been screwing over, but Kisten has always been pliant, so it doesn't show. Killing you is the only way he might get back in with Piscary. Rache, this isn't safe. Don't trust this."

Jenks's face was pinched in fear. The sound of sirens grew closer. I remembered what Keasley had said about vampires needing someone stronger than they were to protect them against the undead, and my resolve strengthened. I couldn't just walk away. "Watch my back, okay?"

At that, Jenks nodded as if expecting it. "Like you were my last seedling in the garden," he said, then swooped into the car. Taking a last look at the restaurant, I gathered my resolve. I got in, feeling light and unreal. Beside me Kisten groaned.

"Where's my stick?" he breathed, and I jumped when the starter ground as I tried to turn the already-running car over again.

"It's at your feet," I muttered, frustrated. I jammed it into first and lurched forward. I reached the exit before I remembered my seat belt, and I screeched to a halt at the entrance to fasten it. Sitting there watching the traffic pass, I felt my chest clench. I didn't have anywhere to go. In a sudden decision, I pulled out to go the opposite way from the church.

"Where are we going?" Jenks asked, dropping to land on my shoulder as the car settled into its new direction.

I glanced at my keys and Nick's apartment key. Nick had said he'd paid rent through August, and I was willing to bet the place was empty. "To Nick's. I can't take him home," I said, lips barely moving. "Everyone knows that's where I'd take him."

I snuck a glance at Kisten, his eyes swollen shut as he mumbled, "I shouldn't have put in the light display. I should have left the kitchen menu alone."

Jenks was silent. Then in a very small, panicked voice, he said, "I have to go home."

My breath caught, and I exhaled in understanding. Matalina was there alone. If someone showed up at the church looking for Kisten, Jenks's family might be in danger. "Go," I said.

"I can't leave you."

Twisting, I grabbed my bag from the back and fumbled until I had my splat gun on my lap. Eyeing Jenks's expression, torn with indecision, I pulled to the curb and hit the brakes. Kisten weakly braced himself as he shifted forward and back. Horns blew, and I ignored them.

"Get your little pixy ass out of the car and get home," I said, voice even and level as I rolled the window down. "Take care of your family."

"But you're my family, too," he said.

My throat tightened. Every time I screwed up big-time, Jenks was gone. "I'll be fine."

"Rache—"

"I'll be fine!" I shouted, frustrated, and Kisten turned to us, squinting and breathing hard. "I'm a witch, damn it! I'm not helpless. I can handle this. Go!"

Jenks lifted into the air. "Call me if you need me. I'll have my phone on."

I managed a smile. "Deal."

He nodded, his face looking old and young all at the same time, and I froze when he flew close, his wings brushing my cheek for an instant. "Thank you," he said.

And then he was gone.

THIRTY-ONE

As expected, I had found Nick's place empty. I didn't think anyone had noticed me helping Kisten inside and up the steps to the one-bedroom apartment. Kisten had revived somewhat on the way, and he had gotten himself into a warm tub of water without my help. There was no shower curtain, and I thought a soak would be better anyway. He was still in there, and if I didn't hear some water draining soon, I was going to go check on him.

The sound of the street noise coming through the open windows was nice. It had smelled musty when I hesitantly opened the door to find empty walls and barren carpet. Clearly, Nick had packed up everything on the solstice, leaving very little to return to if he ever found himself in Cincy again. Where all his stuff was now, I didn't know or care. His mom's, maybe?

I couldn't help but feel betrayed all over again, though there was nothing here to trigger the memories but worn carpet and empty shelves. I tried not to feel bitter as I drank the coffee Nick had left along with a sleeping bag, three cans of stew, and the pan to heat it up in. There was one plate, one bowl, and one set of silverware—nothing he would miss if he never came back, but there if he found himself on the run and needed somewhere to hide for a night or two.

"Bastard," I mumbled, not putting much emotion behind it. If he had just been a thief, I might have been able to see past it, what with my *new and improved outlook on life,* but he had been buying demon favors from Al with pieces of me. Innocent things, he'd said, worthless. But if they were worthless, why had Al agreed to it?

So I sat at the metal and Formica table that came with the apartment, drinking stale coffee and staring at the stains on the matted carpet. The traffic sounds were both soothing and unfamiliar. Nick's apartment wasn't in a residential area but what passed for downtown Hollows. There was no scent of Nick in the air, yet I could almost feel the stale magic.

I looked at the scratched linoleum for the circle Nick had said was there, scribed with a black-light marker. The memory of standing in Nick's closet to summon Al lifted through me. God, I should've walked away right then, even if calling up Al for information had been my idea. But I hadn't thought anyone who claimed to love me could willingly betray me like that.

The water in the bathroom sloshed, and the gurgle as it left the tub intruded into my thoughts. I sat up. Feeling bitter and stupid, I scooted my chair back and went to warm up a can of stew. The can opener was one of those cheap, flimsy things, and I was still fighting it when a soft breath and hesitant steps turned me around.

I smiled when I saw Kisten, wearing a towel, his hair damp. He had his torn and scuffed clothes in his hands, as if he didn't want to put them back on. Ugly bruises brought out by the warm water splotched his torso, and his eye was swollen bigger than before. Red-rimmed scratches marked his arms and face. His hair had been washed, and despite his beating, he still looked good—standing there in the kitchen wrapped in a towel, the definition of his muscles all damp and glistening. . . .

"Rachel," he said, looking relieved as he set his wad of clothes on a vacant chair, "you're still here. Um, don't take this the wrong way, but where are we?"

"Nick's old apartment." The can's lid finally popped off. Angst spiked though me at Jenks's warning, but I had to trust Kisten. Otherwise what was the point of loving him?

Kisten's blue eyes widened, and I licked a spot of cold gravy off my thumb. "Your old boyfriend's?" he said, turning to the empty living room with only the curtains moving in the slight breeze. "Kind of spartan with the decorating, wasn't he?"

Snorting, I dumped the stew into the pot and set the dial to warm. "I'm guessing he hasn't been here since the solstice, but he's paid up to August and I had a key, so here we are. No one knows but Jenks. You're safe," I said hesitantly. *For the moment.*

Exhaling, Kisten sat and put an elbow on the table. "Thank you," he said fervently. "I have to get out of Cincinnati."

I had my back to him as I stirred the stew, and a shiver rose through me. "Maybe not." The soft hush of the cotton towel as he straightened brought me around, and, seeing his wonder, I said, "I'm going to give Piscary the focus to put into hiding, if he will leave me alone and keep anyone else from knocking me or you off."

Kisten's lips parted, and I wished his towel would slip a little more. God! What was wrong with me? We were both teetering on death, and I was looking at his legs?

"You want to buy protection from Piscary?" Kisten said in disbelief. "After what he did to me? He gave my last blood to someone outside the camarilla! Do you know what that means? He's abandoning me, Rachel! It's not so much the dying I'm worried about, but being shunned. No one will risk his anger to keep me undead now except maybe Ivy, and if she's his scion, that's not going to happen."

He was scared. I didn't like seeing him like that. Taking a miserable breath, I leaned against the stove and crossed my arms. "It's going to be okay. No one is going to kill you, so you'll be fine. Besides, I've been getting protection from him by way of Ivy," I said, thinking I would cheerfully be a hypocrite if it meant we both would survive. "This is just making it more official. I'm going to ask that he leave you alone, too. Take you back. It will be okay."

Hope lit his blue eyes, then died. "He won't," he said in a flat tone.

"Sure he will," I coaxed, coming to sit beside him.

"No he won't." Kisten looked worse for having seen hope for an instant. "He can't. It's done. You'd have to make arrangements with whoever he gave me to, and I don't know who that is. I won't until they show up. It's part of the mind game."

His eyes darted nervously, and I drew back. It wasn't that cut-and-dried. I knew how vamps worked. Until the coffin was nailed shut, there were options. "Then *I'll* find out who he gave you to," I said.

Kisten took my hands, his eyebrows furrowing over lost chances. "Rachel . . . it's too late."

"I can't believe you're giving up!" I said, angry as I pulled from him.

He took my hand and kissed the top of it. "I'm not giving up. I'm accepting it. Even if you could find out who it was, or if you were here when they came for me—which you won't be—that would leave you with nothing to buy protection from Piscary with." His hand rose to touch my jawline. "I won't do that to you."

"Damn it, it isn't too late!" I exclaimed, standing up and going to stir the stew before it burned. I couldn't look at him anymore. The pot slopped over in my agitation, and I got mad. "All you have to do is lay low until I get this sorted out. Can you do that for me, Kisten?" I turned, angry. "Just hide and do nothing for a day or two?"

His sigh was heavy, and I wasn't certain I believed him when he nodded. Sure that I'd be able to buy both our safeties with a five-thousand-year-old artifact, I kept stirring the stew. There were a couple of packets of hot chocolate in Nick's emergency store, and my jaw clenched. I was *not* going to make hot chocolate. "Is Ivy okay?" I asked, reminded.

His feet squeaked against the floor. "Of course she is," he said flatly. "He loves her."

I couldn't tell if he was angry. I set the spoon aside and turned down the burner, spinning to find he had dropped his forehead into his cupped hand. Worry went through me, then pity. "Piscary was ticked about the embalming fluid, huh?" I said, trying to be light.

"I have no idea," he said in a monotone. "It never came up. He was angry about what I did to the restaurant." His blue eyes held the pain of memory when he lifted them to me. "He was . . . like an animal," he said, fear and betrayal staining his voice. "He ripped out my chairs and tables, unshuttered the windows, burned the new menus, and punished my waitstaff. He almost killed Steve." His eyes closed, and the faint wrinkles on his face deepened as if a lifetime of pain had fallen on him in an instant. "I couldn't stop him. I thought he was going to kill me, too. I would have been happy if he had, but he threw me out with everything else."

As if he were an old menu or a used napkin. "Why, Kisten?" I whispered. I had to hear it. It hadn't been what Kisten did to the bar that caused Piscary to do what he did. Afraid, I stayed where I was, hands holding my elbows. I needed to hear it. I needed to hear Kisten tell me the truth so I could trust him. "Why did he kick you out?" I asked again.

His free hand rubbing at a sore rib, Kisten looked at me. He hesitated as if waiting for me to guess it before saying it. "He told me to kill you," he said, and fear pinged through me. "He said it was the only way I could prove that I loved him. He didn't ask *Ivy* to prove herself," he said, his voice cracking and his need for my forgiveness pouring from him. "I said no. I told him anything but that . . . and he laughed."

The heat from the burner against my back wasn't enough to stop a shudder rippling through me. Kisten's expression shifted to fear, but it was the terror of realization, not madness. "I'm sorry, Rachel. I couldn't do it," he rushed. "I'm going to die. He gave my last blood to someone as a gift. They're going to kill me—and no one will hold them accountable. They're going to get away with it. I could handle that," he said, his quickening breath giving away his fear. "But he kicked me out of the camarilla, and no one will cross Piscary to keep me undead. It's a double death sentence. One done quickly by a stranger who will suck me dry for his or her pleasure, the other slow by madness."

His gaze met mine, and I froze at the controlled panic in his gradually widening pupils.

"It's not a good way to die, Rachel," he whispered, chilling me. "I don't want to go insane."

Tension pulled through me. Blood. He was talking about blood. He wasn't afraid of dying, he was afraid of not having anyone to keep him undead afterward. And he was looking for me to help him. *Damn it all to the Turn and back. I can't do this.*

Fear lay deep in his eyes, the rim of blue shrinking as he sat at the table in an empty apartment and saw his life fall apart and no one willing to risk Piscary's anger to help him. I shifted forward and sat before him, taking his hands on my lap. "Look at me, Kisten," I demanded, scared. *I can't become his source of blood. I have to keep him alive.* "Look at me!" I repeated, and his darting gaze met mine in agitation. "I am here," I said slowly, to try to ground him. "They won't find you. I'll work something out with Piscary. The thing is five thousand years old. It's got to be worth both of us."

The water from his bath glistened on his shoulders, his expression slack in fear as he looked at me as if I stood between himself and insanity. Perhaps at that moment, I was. "I'm okay," he said huskily, and he took his hands from mine, visibly trying to divorce himself from his emotions. "Where is Jenks?" he asked, changing the subject.

A hint of unease stained my senses. Not knowing why, I leaned back. Jenks's warning resounded in me. "Home," I said simply. "He went to check on his kids." But my heart beat hard, and the hair on the back of my neck rose. "Hey . . . uh, I should probably head home and make sure he's okay," I said lightly, not knowing why all my instincts said to leave, and leave now. If only for a moment. I had to think. Something told me I had to think.

Kisten's head swung up, panic clear in his eyes. "You're leaving?"

A shiver rose through me and died. "We have two hours before sunset," I said as I stood, not liking him between me and the door all of a sudden. I loved him, but he was pulled to the breaking point, and I didn't want to have to say no if he asked me to be his scion. "No one knows you're here. I won't be long." Drawing away from him, I scooped up his clothes. "Besides, you don't want to put these on until they're clean. I'll wash them and be back before sunset. Promise. It will get me some time to make up some spells, too."

I had to get out. I had to give him time to realize he was going to make it. Otherwise he would assume he wasn't and would ask me something I didn't want to answer.

Kisten's shoulders eased, and he exhaled. "Thanks, love," he said, making me feel guilty. "I wasn't looking forward to putting them back on. Not in that condition."

I leaned forward and gave him a kiss from behind, my lips touching his cheek while his hand rose to caress my jawline. "Do you want Jenks's shirt meantime?" I asked, slipping from him when he shook his head. "You want me to stop and pick up anything while I'm out?"

"No," he repeated, looking worried.

"Kisten, it's going to be okay," I said, almost pleading. I wished he would stand up so I could give him a proper kiss good-bye.

Hearing my misery, he smiled and stood. We moved to the door together, his scent rising from the armload of limp clothes in my hands. Wet from the bath, he had almost no scent at all. I hesitated at the door and shifted my splat-gun-heavy shoulder bag up onto my shoulder.

His arms went around me, and I exhaled, letting my entire body meld into him, relaxing and just taking him in. Under the smell of soap was the hint of incense, and my eyes closed as I encircled him, holding him tightly.

For a long moment, we stood there, and I wouldn't let him go when he tried to rock back.

His eyes met mine, and his brow rose at my naked fear for him.

"It's going to be okay," he said, seeing my doubt.

"Kisten—"

And then he pulled me closer, angling his head to kiss me. I felt the hint of tears prickle as our lips met. My pulse jumped, not from lust but heartache. Kisten's grip on me tightened, and my throat closed in misery. He was going to be okay. He had to be.

But in his kiss I could feel his fear through his tense muscles pressing against mine and his hold on me, a shade too tight. He said it was going to be okay, but he didn't believe it. Though he said he wasn't afraid to die, I could tell he was terrified of being helpless. And he was. A faceless stranger was going to try to end his life, and there would be no pity, no caring, no gentleness. Any sense of belonging or family, however warped, was going to be absent. Kisten would be less than a dog to whoever was coming. It would turn what might be a rite of passage into an ugly act of self-serving murder. It was not the way Kisten should die. But it was how he lived.

I couldn't take it anymore. I pulled from him. Our lips parted, and I met his eyes, heavy with unshed tears. He didn't believe. I was going to make him believe. I was going to prove him wrong.

"I have to go," I whispered, and his hands fell from mine reluctantly.

"Hurry back," he pleaded, and I dropped my head, unable to look at him. "I love you," he said as I opened the door. "Never forget that."

Almost in tears, I blinked fast. "I can't. I won't. I love you, too," I said, then fled, slipping through the door and into the hall before I changed my mind.

I hardly remembered going down the cool stairs, dark from old paint and faded carpet. I looked up before I got into my car, seeing

Kisten's shadowy silhouette hovering by the filmy curtains. A shiver went through me, rattling my keys when I didn't stifle it. I hadn't known that the depth of control the undead had on their underlings was so strong that they would willingly submit to planned murder, and I again thanked God that I had never let any vampires, even Ivy, bind me to them. Though he was seemingly independent and confident, Kisten's mental well-being hung upon the whim of someone who really didn't give a damn. And now he had nothing. Except my trying to keep a faceless vampire from killing him for sport.

Never, I thought. I loved Kisten, but never would I let a vampire bind me. I'd die first.

THIRTY-TWO

The soothing scent of vampire and pixy sifted through the upper levels of my thoughts, skimming through the hazy dream state I was slowly pulling out of. I was warm and comfortable, and as my mind moved from sleep to awareness, I realized I was curled up in Ivy's chair in the sanctuary with Jenks's black silk shirt draped over me. I didn't care to analyze my motives for falling asleep in Ivy's chair. Maybe I just needed some comfort, knowing she was going through hell and there wasn't a damned thing I could do about it.

Wait a moment. I'm sleeping in Ivy's chair? That would mean I was . . .

"Jenks!" I shouted, realizing what had happened and jerking upright. I'd come home to wash Kisten's clothes and had apparently fallen asleep, eight hours of spelled unconsciousness finally running thin. "Damn it, Jenks! Why didn't you wake me up!"

God help me—Kisten. I had left him alone, then fallen asleep.

I jumped up to call Kisten on his cell, jolting to a surprised halt when my body protested at the sudden movement, aching from having slept in a chair. It was chilly, and I glanced at the mantel clock atop the TV in passing as I slipped my arms into coolness of Jenks's shirt. My shoulders stretched painfully, hurting all the way to my lower back. I was fastening the first button as I entered the kitchen. It smelled like lilac in here, and candle wax, and the clock over the sink said the same thing.

Five-thirty? How could I have just fallen asleep? I hadn't gotten much sleep yesterday, but zonking out for an entire night? I hadn't made any charms or anything. Damn it, I was going to kill somebody if Kisten wasn't all right.

"Jenks!" I shouted again as I found the phone and hit it to dial. There was no answer, and I hung up before I was dumped into voice mail. A pang of fear shot through me, and I tried to collect myself before I went and did something stupid.

Taking a deep breath, I turned to get my car keys, hesitating in confusion. *Where did I leave my bag?*

"Jenks, where in hell are you!" I shouted, rubbing my aching upper arm. My wrist, too, was sore, and I shook it as I darted into the living room to see if my bag was in there, cataloging a myriad of aches and pains from my stiff neck to my aching foot. *Why am I limping? I'm not that old.* Unease went through me at the silence, and one hand was still holding my upper arm as I looked at the barren room in confusion.

"Rachel," came Jenks's worried, muffled voice an instant before he zipped in through the chimney, a thin trail of silver marking his path. "You're awake."

I stared at the vacant space, ticked—not because I had come in here searching for my bag and forgetting that the room was empty but because he looked scared. He ought to be. "Why didn't you wake me up?" I exclaimed, tucking my shirt in as he spilled dust coated with chimney soot. "Kisten was alone all night, and he's not answering his phone!"

"Are you okay?" he asked, coming too close, and I pulled back, my neck protesting.

"Apart from falling asleep in the middle of my bloody day and leaving Kisten alone, yeah," I said sarcastically, weight on one foot. "Why didn't you wake me?"

Jenks's wings dropped in pitch, and he landed on the mantel. "He called. After you fell asleep. Said he was moving underground to lessen the chance that anyone would hurt you to get to him. You needed the sleep," he said, sounding eerily relieved. "And besides, Piscary might not think the focus is worth you and Kisten both." His features tightened, and he couldn't seem to keep his wings from moving.

My urge to race to Nick's apartment slid into a general worry, and I focused on Jenks standing nervously on the fireplace. *Kisten went underground without telling me?* "He called before sundown?" I asked. I didn't want to feel guilty that my not being there forced him out into the open. Jenks shrugged, and I muttered, "Why didn't you wake me up?"

Jenks reached to clean the soot from his wings like a tiny cat. His distress clear, he said, "You needed the sleep. Kisten going underground was the best thing for everyone."

"Yeah?" I shot back sourly. "If he's not careful, he's going to be permanently underground." Frowning, I headed back to the kitchen and some coffee. *He went into hiding? In what? A towel and a smile?* And what was it with this human time clock I was on anyway?

Jenks took to the air to follow me. "Rache, Kisten was right. I wouldn't want you there either whenever whoever Piscary gave Kisten to finds him."

"Why? Because I might save his ass?" I exclaimed, frustrated as I stood in the sun and dumped out yesterday's coffee. It was a painful reminder that Ivy was gone; she'd never let the coffee sit like that. My arm hurt, and I held it as I ran the water to rinse out the pot. "Damn it, Jenks! Letting a vampire drain someone to death as a thank-you is twisted and sick! Especially when the person being murdered thinks it's acceptable. Piscary is an animal! You think I like that he's the only one I can go to for protection? You think I like giving the focus to him? If I thought he'd do anything other than stick it into hiding, I'd give it to someone else. But I won't let Kisten die."

Jenks's wings drooped as he landed beside Mr. Fish, the sun shining through them to make sparkles on my hands. Feeling like an ass for my outburst, I put cold water in the pot and wiped it dry with a hand towel. "Sorry," I said, knowing that this *animal* was my best long-term insurance to stay alive. *How did I get here?* Depressed, I pushed the coffeepot away, not feeling up to making coffee anymore. "Kisten must think I'm a boob for falling asleep," I muttered.

"He knew you were tired." His brow was creased, and he sounded almost bitter. "Don't worry about him. Kisten probably has plans you don't even know about." Jenks lifted into the air and gave himself a shake to sift the last of the soot into the sink. "Besides, I've got some news that's going to make you piss your pants."

I didn't want to hear whatever gossip he had dug up, and I held my upper arm and tried to remember where I had left my shoulder bag. I had to talk to Kisten. Damn it, this wasn't fair. He was running away like an old cat to die in the woods. That was the terrifying part—that he accepted his murder willingly. Like he deserved to be treated like a thing.

"Listen to me," Jenks said with a false eagerness as he got in front of me. "You're not going to believe who called this morning."

I felt funny, standing in my sun-drenched kitchen with Jenks hovering close—too close—while I tried to remember where I had left my bag. My hand had crept up to my neck, and I forced it down. I was getting the oddest feeling—like I should have a string around my finger or something. Confused, I focused on Jenks. "Kisten isn't answering his phone. Where is he?"

"Tink's titties, Rache!" he exclaimed, his wings clattering. "Get off it! Let the man be a man. Besides, if you call or go see him, they'll find him that much sooner."

I slumped against the sink, stymied. There was that. My car was well known, and I wasn't about to take the bus and risk getting stranded somewhere. Giving up on finding my bag, I headed into the bathroom as a mildly pressing need grew worse. "Are you sure he's okay?" I asked, rubbing my arm through Jenks's shirt. That was the last time I was going to sleep in Ivy's chair. It was harder than it looked.

"Trust me." Jenks followed me in with a soft, almost subliminal hum. "Going to see him won't help him at all. Make everything worse. Let it go, Rache."

It was excellent advice—though not any I wanted to take—and I sourly stared at Jenks, standing on the washer lid with his feet spread and his hands on his hips. I had to use the bathroom, but he looked immovable. "Do you mind?" I said, and he sat down, his wings stilling.

I couldn't make him leave, and I wasn't going to use the can with him sitting there, so I grabbed my toothbrush. My mouth tasted like dead weeds, and I put an extra glop of minty toothpaste on the brush. "You know where he is, don't you?" I accused while I leaned over the sink to check out my perfect teeth, and when Jenks flushed, I continued, "He left without his clothes? He went to a girlfriend's house, didn't he? Someone who doesn't have any ties to Piscary."

Jenks said nothing, avoiding my gaze—and looking really, really guilty. I knew that Kisten had someone he was tapping for blood, and the fact that whoever it was might willingly defy Piscary if worse came to worst was a guilty relief. Besides, a vampire chick was probably tougher than me in a pitched fight. As long as she didn't hand him over. *If she does, I'm going to freaking kill her,* I thought in a pang of angst, then prayed I'd never have to make that decision.

"How long until you can get yourself cleaned up?" Jenks said, and I made a telling face.

"Ah 'ot 'icker if 'ou weren't in 'ere," I said around the foam, ticked off that Jenks knew where Kisten was and I didn't. If I really pressed him, Jenks would tell me. Probably even come with me to keep my ass above the grass when the bad guys followed me to Kisten's hideout. *Crap on toast, I don't like feeling this helpless.*

Jenks's wings blurred. "Glenn called," he said, as if it were a great honor.

Whoop-deee-freaking-do. "Mmmm?" I prompted around the toothbrush. My hair was down about my shoulders, and I frowned as I brushed my teeth. Jenks's kids' work usually had to be picked apart, but this braid was completely gone. I winced when my toothbrush hit my inner lip. Bending over the sink, I spit, eyes widening at the thread of pink in with the paste.

"What does Glenn want?" I asked as I leaned to the mirror and curled my lower lip down to see a red line. *When did I do that?* "More Tabasco sauce?"

"He's got a warrant," Jenks said, hovering so close that I had to back up until there were twin images of a nervous pixy between me and my reflection. "Or he will soon."

Okay. Now I was interested. "For who?" I rinsed and spit, glad there was no more blood.

Jenks grinned, looking relieved. "For Trent."

My head jerked up. "What!" I shouted. "He did it? Glenn got a warrant? Why didn't you tell me!"

Silver dust slipped from Jenks, and he returned to the washer. "He has the verbal okay, and he's on his way to the FIB's headquarters in Detroit to get the original paperwork. That's why I let you sleep. He doesn't want you to do anything until he has the papers in his hand. Hours yet. You need any help in the kitchen?"

"Holy crap!" I exclaimed, pulse quickening. I looked at what I was wearing, then at the shower, fingers undoing a button. I had to get cleaned up. This was just too cool.

"It was you," Jenks said, his features glowing with pride. "Thanks to your tip that Trent confessed to the murders, Glenn got approval to take another crack at Brett's body. He lifted a print off Brett's toenail before they moved him back to a person and destroyed it. It matched one they got from Trent from when you got him hauled in last year."

"Hot damn!" I whispered, too excited to be disgusted that I had more than Trent's admission that he had abducted, tortured, and killed another person in the name of . . . whatever holy mission he thought he was on. "I've got to get dressed. I have to go to work." I put a hand to my snarled hair and hesitated. "Uh, Glenn's going to let me bring him in, right?"

"Yup." Jenks hovered an inch from the cool porcelain, wings faintly humming. "He said he's turning this over to you, seeing as you're . . . Just a minute, I want to get this right. He said you're not a detective person but a smack-them-up-and-bring-them-in person. All he wants is for you to wait until he has the paperwork in his hands. That's why he's going up there to get it himself. He's afraid it will get lost in the fax machine or something."

I didn't blame him. Not for one glorious moment. Ecstatic, I headed to the kitchen to see if I needed to make anything. "I've got a warrant for Trent for murder," I said, sliding the last yard or so in my socks to land in the threshold. "I'm going to tag him! I'm going to get him off my back for good! And I don't have to rescue a demon familiar to do it!"

Jenks was smiling at me. "You are so funny," he said. "It's like Christmas for you."

"Okay," I said, feeling the blood thrum in me as I found the sunbright kitchen. The window was open, but still, the faint scent of yew from the forget potion I'd been planning on making for Newt lingered. "Let me think. You going to be around this afternoon, Jenks? I'm going to need your help."

"Like I would miss this?" He was grinning, looking happy and relaxed.

Beaming, I threw my charm cupboard open and ran my hands through my amulets. I had enough of everything except disguise amulets, but I wouldn't need them to bring in Cincy's favorite bad boy. "I have to take a shower," I said, excited as I limped across the kitchen. "Are you sure Kisten's okay?"

Jenks landed on the spigot, his fitfully moving wings sending flashes of morning light everywhere. "I expect he's exactly the way he was when you left him."

I had to trust that. And he'd be okay now until the sun went down. As Jenks had said, the I.S. was probably watching me and would relay my movements to whoever was looking for Kisten. Actually, that might make tagging Trent more difficult, unless . . . "Get yourself cleaned up," I said to Jenks as I headed for the shower. "We have a wedding to go to."

"What?" Jenks yelped as he followed. "You're going to arrest Trent at his wedding?"

"Why not?" I halted in the threshold to the bathroom. My hand was on the doorframe, but I didn't want to shut the door on him. "It's the only place I'll be able to tag him without him siccing Quen on me. Not to mention the I.S. bothering me. I *am* invited." I felt my expression grow hard. "And Piscary, probably. I'd rather talk to him there than on his own turf." This was going to work in so many ways. It was perfect.

Jenks's sigh was loud. "Rachel, you're cruel."

"Right," I said, eyebrows rising. "Like Trent really wants to marry Ellasbeth?"

Shrugging, he darted out of the kitchen, shouting to Matalina if she knew where his good bow was. I got the shower going and stripped, my motions slowing as I found that my hip was sore from Ivy's chair—and my foot? I prodded the swollen, tender tissue as I waited for the water to warm, thinking I was way too young to get sore from sleeping in a chair. But the water was hot, and when I got into it, it soothed all the aches away. Kist was in hiding, and I could barter for his safety—our safety—once dusk fell. But before that, I would get to pick up Trent at last.

Damn, this was going to be a *good* day.

THIRTY-THREE

I put a hand out to brace myself against the seat ahead of me as the bus bounced forward through the heavy fog, gears slipping. Taking my car to Trent's wedding would have been easier, but this was safer when it came to getting pulled over by the I.S. and hauled in for driving with a suspended license. Then there was the little question of the ugly dent someone had put into my front fender, along with breaking the left turn light. It had happened somewhere between yesterday and today, and it ticked me off that it might have been the I.S. trying to up the citations.

I eyed my red nails peeping past the long lace sleeve, thinking the black weave looked nice against my pale skin. My shoulder bag sat beside me, and Jenks was swinging from a ceiling strap, the silver dust sifting from him making a bright spot on the otherwise dim bus. It was crowded, but everyone was giving me loads of room. Smirking, I glanced at my black butt-kicking boots showing past the hem of the delicate silk dress and wondered why.

Okay, even I knew the boots didn't go with the dress, but I wasn't going to tag Trent in heels. No one would see them anyway. I didn't know which dress Ellasbeth had picked out, but I wasn't going to wear that ugly green thing. God! I'd be the laughingstock of the I.S. Besides, my foot still hurt, and heels would have me in agony.

Nervous, I squinted in the glare of the oncoming traffic. We were almost to the basilica, and my pulse was quickening. I had my splat gun in a thigh holster Keasley had given me—like I could really believe he was just a harmless old man now?—and a spindle of line energy in my head. The present on my lap held the focus; I had gone out and picked it up as a general delivery at the post office this afternoon. Trent wasn't getting it, but it was better than trying to find a place for it in my bag, still full of the accumulated crap of the week. I thought it ironic that I had used the carefully preserved paper and bow from Ceri's gift to wrap it.

I looked up from the floor in anxiety. Ceri had come over after hearing what I was going to do, and though she'd pursed her lips in disapproval, she did help the pixies braid my hair and work in the flowers. I looked gorgeous. Except for my boots. She had asked if I needed backup; I told her that was Jenks's job. The reality was I didn't want to see her and Ellasbeth in the same room. Some things you just don't do.

I wasn't too worried about making this run with only Jenks as backup. I had the law on my side, and in a room full of witnesses, a publicity-conscious Trent was going to come quietly. After all, he was up for reelection soon, which was probably why he was getting married, the flop. If he was going to kill me, it would be a private affair. At least that's what I was telling myself.

Brakes huffing, we turned a sharp corner. The old woman across from me was eyeing my present, and when her gaze dropped to my boots, I shifted my knees so my dress would cover them. Jenks snickered, and I frowned.

We were almost there, and I shuffled through my bag for my cuffs, enduring the looks as I hiked up the dress and clipped them onto the thigh holster, carefully adjusting the slip and dress back over it. They'd jingle when I walked, but that was okay. I glanced at the cute guy three seats down, and he nodded as if telling me they were hidden.

I turned my phone to vibrate and went to tuck it in a pocket, frowning when I realized the dress didn't have one. Sighing, I tucked it in my meager cleavage, getting a thumbs-up from Mr. Three Seats Down. The plastic was cold, and I started when it slipped a little too far. I couldn't wait for Glenn to call me with the news he had the warrant in his hand. I'd talked to him a few hours ago, and he'd made me promise to do nothing until he did. Till then I'd be the perfect bridesmaid in black lace.

A smile curved up the edges of my lips. Yeah. This was going to be fun.

Jenks dropped to the back of the seat ahead of me. "Better stand up," he said. "We're almost there."

My focus sharpened. The blocky structure of the cathedral loomed ahead, the floodlights bathing it in a beautiful glow in the fog and almost-full moonlight. Tension spiked. Hiking my bag onto my shoulder, I held my present close and stood.

The driver's attention flicked to me, and he pulled off. The entire bus went silent, and my skin crawled as I edged to the front, all eyes on me.

"Thank you," I muttered as the driver opened the door, then jerked back when my dress caught on a screw poking out of the ceiling-to-floor bar.

"Ma'am," the driver said as I laboriously unhooked it, "pardon my asking, but why are you taking the bus to a wedding?"

"Because I'm going to arrest the groom, and I didn't want the I.S. stopping me en route," I said flippantly, then flounced down the steps, Jenks's dust putting gold sparkles in my hair.

The door sighed shut behind me, but the bus didn't move. I glanced through the door at the driver, and he motioned for me to cross in front of him. Either he was a gentleman or he wanted to see me walk into the church in my beautiful bridesmaid dress and kick-ass boots.

Jenks snickered. Pulling the damp air deeply into my lungs, I ignored the faces pressed against the window, hiked up my dress to keep it from getting dirty, and crossed the one-way street through the fog glowing from the bus's headlamps.

An usher waited in a pool of humid light, the big, burly guy taking a stance at the top of the stairs before the doors. "I'll get him," Jenks said. "You might mess up your hair."

"Naaaah," I said, conscious of the bus behind me, now tilting since everyone was on the one side watching. "I'll do it."

"That's my girl," he said. "Will you be okay for a second? I want to do a periphery."

"Yup," I said, taking the steps with my dress hitched up high.

Jenks zipped off, and when I reached the landing before the doors, I settled my dress and smiled at the guy. He was dark like Quen, and I wondered if he was one of the Withons' personal attendants. "I'm sorry, ma'am," he said with a soft surfer-boy accent. "The wedding has started. You'll have to wait and join the party at the reception."

"You're not nearly as sorry as you're going to be if you don't get out of my way." I thought it a fair enough warning, but he saw the pretty dress and the present in my hands and assumed flake. Okay, I was a flake, but I was a flake in ass-kicking boots.

I went to edge past him, and he touched my shoulder. Oooooooh, big mistake.

Jenks came back right about then, whooping as I spun, gripping the guard's wrist and swinging my elbow into his nose without ever dropping the present. "Oh! That had to hurt!" the pixy cried as the man stumbled back, hand over his broken nose, eyes tearing and hunched in pain.

"Sorry," I said. Shaking out my dress, I drew myself up and pulled on the door. From behind me came a harsh toot from the bus. Framed in the threshold, I turned and gave them all a bunny-eared "kiss-kiss."

Still, the man wasn't unconscious, and I ought to move before he remembered to do something. I strolled in, my dress getting me past the hangers-on between the front doors and the christening pool with no resistance save whispers.

Adrenaline shivered through me as a wave of flower scents hit me. The church was dim with candlelight, and the soft intonations of the holy guy up front created a sensation of comfort. By the looks of it, they were just getting started. Good. I had to go along with this until I got Glenn's call, and I didn't know when that would be.

Someone in the back row turned, starting a slow chain reaction. My pace bobbled, and I took a deep breath. Shit. The mayor was here, and Takata? Oh, God, I was going to arrest Trent in front of Takata? Talk about performance anxiety.

As expected, Piscary was in the front row with Ivy and Skimmer, and I stifled a surge of anger at him for *giving* Kisten to someone to murder for some twisted pleasure and the clout he had with the I.S. to get away with it. But I needed his help, so as much as I hated it, I'd have to be damningly politically correct.

I couldn't look at Ivy. Not yet. But I recognized her stiff carriage from under a gray, wide-brimmed hat beside Piscary. Ivy's dad was here, too, and what had to be her mother beside him, looking like an ice queen from Asia next to his elegant, rugged fatigue. Mr. Ray and Mrs. Sarong made an unusual showing together, banding up since they lacked their usual packs. Al was standing up with Trent, and, catching sight of me, he grinned, the pure-Al expression looking odd on Lee's strongly Asian features. Quen was beside him, his face blank. He mouthed something at Trent, and Ellasbeth's grip on his arm tightened.

The bride's side was entirely full of thin, tan people. They hadn't listened to me, and they all dressed alike to look as if they were extras from a Spielberg movie at a Hollywood commissary. I thought they ought to be more careful if they didn't want their little secret to get out. Jeez, they all looked the same to me.

The holy guy's spiel faltered when the usher stumbled in from outside. I glanced back in warning, seeing his hand still over his nose, a white handkerchief stained with blood.

Piscary slowly turned, drawn by the scent of blood. He smiled delightedly at me, making my own blood burn. He knew I hated him, and he liked it. The usher went pale at Piscary's attention, and when Quen motioned for him to leave, he beat a hasty retreat, trying to hide the blood.

"Sure about this, Rache?" Jenks said. "You could always retire and open a charm shop."

I thought of Kisten, a spike of fear coming from nowhere. "I'm sure." Hiking up my shoulder bag, I tucked the focus under an arm and headed for the altar. Jenks took to the rafters, and whispers started in my wake. The eyes of Cincy's finest were on me, and as my boots smeared the flower petals, I prayed that I wouldn't slip on them and fall on my ass.

The holy guy gave up trying to remember his place and fumbled in his Bible for his crib sheet, jowls shaking while he tried to act normal. That he was ignoring me spoke volumes. Quen inclined his head at me, and when the holy guy's voice faltered to a stop, Trent turned.

Okay. I'll admit it. He was absolutely stunning in his white tux, his almost translucent fair hair perfect, the tips shifting in the slight draft. Elegant and polished, he made anger look *damn* good. From his black-orchid boutonniere to his embroidered socks, he was the apex of elite power and grace. And he was really, really ticked, by the choleric look in his green eyes.

Ellasbeth spun with him, her elaborate dress with the arranged train rustling all over Creation. If Trent was stunning, she was stunning taken to the nth power, her icy beauty done up with perfect makeup and an exquisite gown. Her defined cheekbones were faintly blushing, and I marveled that the makeup artist had managed to hide her tan and give her a porcelain beauty. Her hair still looked like a cheap imitation of Trent's, though, especially in the candlelight.

The maid of honor was in that ugly green dress, and I gave her an apologetic wince. Figures Ellasbeth would have picked that one. "Sorry I'm late," I said cheerfully, my voice loud in the expectant silence. "I was held up on the bus. Traffic, you know." Setting the focus in its disguise of a wedding gift on the steps, I shuffled off my shoulder bag and settled in behind the maid of honor, clasping my hands demurely before me. *Yeah. Right.*

"Rachel," Trent started, his hand slipping from Ellasbeth's.

"No, no. Go on," I said, making shooing motions, though my insides were wound tighter than a pixy on Brimstone. "I'm all set."

Ellasbeth's painted lips were pressed tight. *A veil would have been nice,* I thought, then mused disparagingly upon my own makeup, slapped on almost at the last minute. Green eyes vehement, she took Trent's arm and turned her back on me, shoulders trembling. The holy guy cleared his throat and started in where he had left off, talking about devotion, understanding, and forgiveness. I tuned him out. I had to get my pulse down; I might be here a while.

The cathedral was beautiful, the scent of Queen Anne's lace faint in the closed air. Flowers decked every available flat surface and a few vertical ones, with little bouquets pinned to ribbons. There were exotic vines, and lilies, but it was the simpler blooms I liked the best. The world-renowned stained-glass windows were muted from the fog and moonlight, and the shadows of the nearby trees moved against them in the breeze like dragons circling. The candlelight flickered, and the smooth voice of the holy guy was like dust given resonance.

I blinked when I realized Al was making eyes at me from across the couple-to-be. Beside him Quen was scowling. They were in marvelous black tuxes that looked like dress uniforms from a classic eighties space opera. Nervous, I adjusted my dress. I'd gotten a spot on it somewhere, and I wished I had a bouquet to hide it with, but that's what you get when you're late.

I turned my attention to the audience to find Jenks's twinkle in the rafters. He was dusting heavily, and Takata sneezed in the artificial sunbeam he was making.

"Bless you," I mouthed to him, and his bushy eyebrows rose. The middle-aged rock star looked worried, but the scarred Were woman beside him—Ripley, his drummer—was clearly amused. Thank God Takata was in a suit instead of the orange monstrosity he'd been wearing the one time I'd seen him. He even had his blond tangle of curls in order, and I could see the charm about his neck that did it.

Glancing over the congregation, he mouthed back, "What are you doing?"

"Working," I said without a sound.

I glanced at Mr. Ray and Mrs. Sarong behind him. They look like little kids plotting. I wouldn't worry about it. It would be over soon.

Finally I grew brave and looked at Ivy. Fear slid through me. She was numb. Blank and empty. I'd seen that look on her before, but never this deep. She had shut herself down. Beautiful in her elegant gray dress and a wide-brimmed hat, she looked remarkably like her mother, a pew behind her. She sat stiffly between Skimmer and Piscary. The blond living vampire glared at me jealously, clearly part of Piscary's camarilla now despite the little detail that the city had let Piscary out because of Al, not her skills in the courtroom. I had to believe Ivy would be all right. I couldn't rescue her. She had to save herself.

Seeing my pain at Ivy's state, Piscary smiled at me, mocking and confident. My breath hissed in when my demon scar sent a surge of tingling sensation through me. Damn it, I hadn't counted on that. Ticked, I mouthed at him, "I want to talk to you."

Piscary inclined his head, looking fabulous in some authentic outfit from Egypt. Apparently thinking I wanted to discuss Ivy, he lifted her slack hand and kissed the top of it.

I stiffened, suddenly realizing that Trent was watching me out of the corner of his eye. Actually, the entire church was paying more attention to me and Piscary than the couple on the stage. If Ellasbeth's clenched jaw was any indication, she was pissed.

Grimacing, I tried to find a kick-ass posture while wearing a lace dress and flowers in my hair. "Not Ivy," I mouthed. "I want your protection. Both me and Kisten. I'll make it worth your while."

Piscary seemed confused at my request, but he nodded, deep in thought. Al's amused grin went sour, and behind Takata, Mr. Ray and Mrs. Sarong started talking in hushed voices that every Inderlander could probably catch. Skimmer's satisfaction turned to hatred, and Ellasbeth . . . Ellasbeth was gripping Trent's arm hard enough to make her knuckles white.

The tinkling sounds of someone's phone burst rudely out into the solemn cadence of the holy guy's speech, and my eyes widened. It was coming from . . . me?

Oh, my God! I thought, mortified as I jammed my fingers down my cleavage, scrambling. It was my phone. *Damn it, Jenks!* I thought, glaring at the ceiling as "Nice Day for a White Wedding" played out. I had put it on vibrate. Damn it, I had put it on vibrate!

Face flaming, I finally fished the thing out. Jenks was laughing from the upper windows, and Takata had his head in his hands, clearly trying not to laugh. A nervous titter went through the church, and I looked at the incoming number. Glenn. Adrenaline hit me.

"Excuse me," I said, really excited. "I am *so* sorry. I had it on vibrate. Really."

Takata laughed outright, and I reddened upon remembering where I'd fished it out from.

"Ah, I have to take this," I said. Ellasbeth was furious, and when the holy guy gestured sourly for me to go ahead, I flipped it open and turned my back on everyone. "Hi," I said softly, and my voice echoed. "I'm at the Kalamack wedding. Everyone's listening. Whatcha got?" *Crap, could this get any more awkward?*

There was a crackle of static telling me Glenn was still on the road, and he said, "You're at his wedding? Rachel, you're one crazy-ass witch."

I halfway turned and shrugged at the holy guy. "Sorry," I mouthed, but inside I was running full out. At least Glenn had gotten my unspoken reference to people being able to hear him and would word his responses carefully.

"I've got the paperwork," Glenn said, and my tension spiked. "You can go to work."

I shifted my weight to feel the comforting bump of my splat gun, hoping I wouldn't need it. "Hey, uh, Jenks never said how much you're going to give me for this."

"Oh, for Christ's sake, Rachel, I'm on the interstate. Can we discuss this later?"

"Later gets me nothing," I said, and the congregation started to stir.

Trent cleared his throat, the anger of a thousand desert sunrises in it, and I shot him a look. Behind him Quen was starting to look suspicious. I wasn't going to get my fee out of them after pulling this little stunt, and I wanted something to show apart from my satisfaction of tagging Trent.

"I want your department to get my church resanctified," I said, and a ripple of surprise shifted through the people. Nothing like waving your dirty laundry in front of Cincinnati's finest. Piscary especially looked interested. This had better work, or I was dead tomorrow.

"Rachel . . ." Glenn started.

"Oh, never mind," I said nastily. "I'll do this pro bono, like I always do for the FIB." Like everyone didn't know who I was talking to by now? My back was to the pews, but Jenks was watching, and I felt reasonably safe.

"I'm calling you some backup," Glenn said, and I put a hand to my forehead.

"Good," I said, around an exhale. "I don't want to haul my tag in on the bus." I heard Glenn take a breath to say something, and, catching Trent shifting from the corner of my eye, I blurted, "Thanks, Glenn. Hey, if this doesn't work out—"

"You want red roses on your grave, right?"

That wasn't it, but he had hung up. Closing the phone, I hesitated, then dropped it back down my front as I turned.

Trent was not happy. "That was a fascinating look into your life, Ms. Morgan. Do you do children's parties, too?"

Nervousness rose in me, quickly followed by a spike of adrenaline. It lit through me, almost as good as sex. My thoughts zinged back to Ivy telling me I lived my life making decisions that would put me in dangerous situations just to feel the rush. An adrenaline junkie, but at least I was making money at it. Usually.

Ivy. She was staring at me, a glimmer of fear marring her deep blankness. "Jenks?" I said loudly, and when he chirped his wings, Quen tensed.

The congregation gasped when I leaned to pull aside my dress to show my calf-high boots. Fumbling with the silk slip, I grabbed my cuffs. "Under temporary jurisdiction of the FIB, I'm authorized to arrest you, Trent Kalamack, for suspicion of the murder of Brett Markson."

A unified gasp rose like a wave from the audience.

"*That's it!*" Ellasbeth shouted, and the holy guy snapped his book shut and took a step back. "Trenton, I've put up with your little tart of a witch in my bathtub. I put up with your insisting she be in *my wedding.* But her arresting you just to stop our marriage is *intolerable!*"

She was royally pissed, and I yanked a pliant Trent from his grooms-men. Quen moved, then leapt backward, a flash of dragonfly wings be-tween us. Al was laughing in big, booming guffaws, but I didn't see anything funny. Except maybe the witch-in-his-bathtub comment.

"Rachel—" Trent's words cut off, and his beautiful face went indig-nant at the twin clicks of metal ratcheting about his wrist. Quen tried to outflank Jenks, his pockmarked face dark with anger when Jenks stopped him, an arrow pointed at his eye.

"Try me, Quen," the pixy said, and the congregation went silent.

Trent stood with his cuffed hands before him. "Uh, uh, uh," I mocked, picking up my shoulder bag and getting ready to bug on out of here. "Trent, remind Quen what happens if he interferes with me. I've got a warrant." *Oh, yeah.* Turning to Trent, I said, "You have the right to remain silent, but I doubt you will. You have the right to an attorney, which I imagine Quen will be calling soon. If you can't afford one, hell has frozen over and I'm the princess of Oz, but in that case, one will be appointed to you. You understand your rights that the entire congrega-tion of Cincy's finest has heard me recite?"

Green eyes angry, he nodded. Satisfied, I tugged his shoulder and started him toward the steps. Trent's mix of anger, shock, and disbelief gave away to anger. "Call the appropriate lawyer," he was saying to Quen as I dragged him. "Ellasbeth, this won't take long."

"Yeah, call your lawyer," I echoed, scooping up the focus.

Al's laugher echoed up into the rafters. I hesitated, waiting for the windows to break or something. There was an evil delight to it, and it seemed to free the seated people from their shock. They burst into a sudden noise of conversation, startling me. Ivy's face remained blank. Beside her, Piscary, too, was wide-eyed, trying to wrap his thoughts around this. Takata was worried, and Mr. Ray and Mrs. Sarong were arguing vehemently.

"Jenks!" I shouted, not wanting to walk down that aisle alone.

And suddenly he was with me. "Got your back, Rache," he said, his wings snapping with excitement, flying backward with his arrow still aimed at Quen. "Let's go."

Bag on one shoulder and focus under an arm, I guided Trent down the stairs, holding his elbow so he wouldn't trip and sue me for unnecessary roughness. *Da-a-a, da-a-a, da, dum. I got the bastard now,* echoed in my thoughts in a mockery of the wedding march. Someone's phone snapped a picture, and I grinned, imagining tonight's front page. I could hear sirens in the background, and I hoped they were the FIB, come to hustle me off the street, and not the I.S. to arrest me. I didn't actually have the warrant, but my contact did.

Forgotten by the altar, Ellasbeth made a frustrated sound of anger. "Trent!" she cried, and I almost felt sorry for the woman. "This is outrageous. How can you let her do this? I thought you *owned* this city!"

Trent halfway turned, and I steadied him on the steps with a hand on his shoulder. "I don't own Ms. Morgan, dear. I need a few hours to sort this out. I'll join you at the reception."

God, I hoped not.

As we passed Piscary, I slowed. "Could you meet me at the FIB?" I said, pulse pounding and breathless. "I have something for you."

The undead vampire kissed the underside of Ivy's wrist, making her shudder. "You are utterly inhuman, Rachel. Almost as cold as you are audaciously contemptible. It's a side to you that is . . . delightfully unexpected. I'm most interested in what you have to say."

Not knowing what to make of that, I nodded and pushed Trent back into motion. He was indignant, apparently figuring out that I was going to give the vampire the focus. Hell, Piscary "insured" four-fifths of the city, and David's company picked up the rest. It wasn't hard to figure out I wanted to be added to the list. Seeing Trent's understanding, I smiled. *Bastard.*

"Trent!" Ellasbeth shrieked. "You walk out of this church and I'm gone. I'm on the plane and I'm home! I agreed to marry you, not this . . . this *circus* you call a life."

"I don't have much choice—*dear,*" he said over his shoulder. "Will you curb your hysterics and tend to our guests? This is a minor glitch."

"Minor glitch!" I was walking sideways, nearly missing it when she threw her bouquet at the holy guy, screaming. "Quen! Do something! That's what you're paid for!"

My eyebrows rose. I was almost to the door, and no one had tried to stop me. Shock was a wonderful tool when used correctly.

Quen looked up from his phone. "I am, Ms. Withon. I've already established that Morgan is acting within the law, and I'm calling Trenton's trial lawyer."

Al was laughing, tears streaming down his face. His hand was against the altar for balance, and the flowers on it were turning black. Being in Lee's body let him touch it with impunity, but he was still a demon, and clearly his presence was being noted.

When we reached the entryway, it hit Trent that I was really tagging him. "This is ridiculous, Rachel," he said as I bitch-kicked the door open. Moonlight spilled in through the fog shining on the cement steps. "This is my wedding day. You are *way* out of line."

"Hauling your ass in is justice," I said, squinting from the flashing FIB lights. "Killing Brett was out of line. He didn't know anything. All he wanted was someone to look to."

I shoved Trent through the door before the heavy wood could arc closed, then pulled the damp, cool night air smelling of garbage and exhaust deep into me, relieved to see those FIB cruisers. Officers were all over the place, securing the area before anyone could follow me out.

"Hey! Hi!" I called while I waved, wanting to be sure they knew I was the good guy. "I got him. He's all yours! Just tell me where to put him."

I headed toward the nearest cruiser, pushing Trent before me. "Trust me, Trent," I said when we found the pavement. "You'll thank me for this someday."

"I didn't think you cared about my happiness, Ms. Morgan," he said as an excited officer touched his cap and opened the door for him.

"I don't," I said shortly. "Watch yourself." I put my hand on the back of his head, feeling a jolt of ever-after try to surge to him, checking it just in time. Shaken from my lack of control, I shoved him into the car and slammed the door shut. It was noisy, and I blinked when I realized the bus was still there. I waved, and everyone waved back, the driver tooting the horn. Satisfied, I stood a little taller and slicked my hair back out of my eyes.

Damn, when I was bad, I was good.

THIRTY-FOUR

The hem of my lacy bridesmaid dress whispered over the cracked gray tile in Edden's office. Sitting hunched in the chair before his desk, I nervously bobbed my foot. The FIB captain had taken possession of my elbow the moment I crossed the Federal Inderland Bureau seal inlaid in the floor of the lobby, dragging me into his office and telling his aide, Rose, to keep me here before stomping out in search of coffee, his son, Glenn, and a first impression that didn't come from me. That had been ten minutes ago. Unless he was grinding the beans himself, or waiting for Glenn to get back from Detroit, I figured he'd come in knowing more than I did.

The jitters had started. It was growing noisy in the lobby, voices raised in protest and demand. By the sound of it, the entire wedding party was out there. I glanced at Jenks, perched on Edden's pencil cup. He looked unusually nervous, having opted to stay with me instead of hanging with Edden as was his habit when we were at the FIB. Leaving the present on the floor, I stood to shake out my dress and went to peek past the blinds. I was getting the distinct idea that Edden hadn't known I was going after Trent Kalamack this evening.

"Maybe we should've gone to the I.S?" Jenks said, his wings making a distracting hum.

"The I.S!" I said, turning to gape at him. "Are you crazy?"

It sounded as if Mr. Ray was close to losing it, and wincing, I reached for the blinds, jerking my hand back when the door scraped open.

Edden stomped in, the muscular, almost squat man so close to my height that it didn't matter. He was in his usual khakis and white shirt with the sleeves rolled up, but the outfit had lost its just-pressed look sometime between dragging me in here and getting the two waxed-paper cups of capped coffee he had sandwiched between a hairy arm and chest.

Feeling guilty, I let the blinds slip from my fingers. The lacy dress made me feel stupid, and I tucked a wayward strand that had escaped my elaborate braid behind an ear and stood with my hands clasped before me like fig leaves. I felt about as vulnerable as if I had been naked, too. Edden had been instrumental in helping me save my butt when I'd quit the I.S., but he had his own bosses to please, and he didn't look happy. Of all the humans I'd met, only his son, Glenn, and my old boyfriend, Nick, were more comfortable with my being . . . not human.

His round face creased, he set both coffees on the desk and dropped into his chair on the exhale. Captain Edden was not tall, and the first hints of a soft widening of his waist added to his comfortable, late-fifties look. His military background showed in his quick mannerisms and slow decisions, only accentuated by the black hair cropped close to his skull. Lacing his stubby fingers across his middle, he stared at me in annoyance. His mustache was showing more gray than it had last time, and I couldn't help but cringe at the accusing look in his brown eyes.

Jenks clattered his wings as if in apology, and the captain glanced at him as if he ought to have known better before turning his disapproving attention back to me. "Would you be more comfortable running my department from my chair, Rachel?" he said, and I shifted forward to take a coffee just to have something between him and me. "What did you think you were doing, arresting Kalamack at his own wedding?" he added, and I sat down, the focus between my feet.

As if this were good news, Jenks brightened, flying up to land closer to the FIB captain to look satisfied and relieved. I thought it totally unfair that though Jenks and I were partners, I'd be the only one to suffer for any trouble we got into. Pixies were never held accountable for their actions. But then they usually didn't involve themselves this deep in "big people" affairs.

"If I arrested him anywhere else, he would have buried me," I said, singeing my finger and spilling some coffee when I removed the lid. Disgusted with myself, I sopped up the rivulet with my worn shoulder bag before it could drip to my dress. Jeez, I felt like one of those wackos haunting Fountain Square, with my ratty bag, my wrapped gift holding the focus, and wearing a gown that cost more than a semester of tuition.

"You being dead would make my life easier." Edden's face was tight when he leaned to get his coffee. "Listen to that!" he exclaimed, gesturing at the unseen lobby. "My people don't know how to handle this. That's why the I.S. exists! And you bring them all here? To me?"

"I thought you knew what I was doing," I said. "Glenn—"

My words cut off when Edden lifted a hand. His anger slid away, replaced with a rueful pride for his adopted son. "No," he muttered, his eyes dropping to the desk. "He slipped the paperwork in with the requisitions for the company picnic. You're invited, by the way."

"Thanks," I said, wondering if I'd live that long. Depressed, I took a sip of coffee, glad the FIB had their priorities in order and bought the good stuff.

Edden frowned, his pride at Glenn's bucking the system to further justice now fading back to anger. "Kalamack left the species box blank on his statement," he said. "You know what that means?" I took a breath to answer, but he had rushed ahead with, "It means he's not saying if he's Inderland or human and is accepting FIB jurisdiction. I have to deal with this. Me. And you want me to *pay you* for dumping this crap on me?"

My jaw clenched. "He broke the law," I said hotly.

The unusually enlightened human sighed, his entire body moving. "Yes, he did."

For a moment there was silence. Then Edden took the lid off his coffee. "Piscary is in my lobby," he said tightly. "He says you want to talk to him. How am I supposed to keep you alive through your testimony when Piscary comes to *my department* to kill you?"

I glanced at Jenks, who was starting to shed a faint trail of glittering dust in agitation. "Piscary didn't come here to kill me," I said, hiding my jitters behind a sip of coffee. "I asked him here. I want to arrange some protection from him for me and Kisten."

Edden went markedly still as I guiltily swallowed more coffee and set the cup down. The acidic drink hit my stomach, where it sat to make me feel ill. Piscary was a sick wacko—and the only one who could protect me and rescind Kisten's blood gift.

"You're buying protection from Piscary?" Edden shook his head, his few wrinkles deepening. "He wants you dead. You put him in jail. He's not going to forget that just because he's out. And the word is he made a blood gift out of your boyfriend." His gaze fell from mine in shame. "Rachel, I'm sorry. I can't do anything about that."

A hot feeling of betrayal rose through me, of innocence lost. I knew that nothing could stop Piscary from getting away with treating Kisten like a box of Godiva, but damn it, these were the people who were supposed to keep us safe from the big-bad-uglies. I hated this, but what I hated more was that I had to work in such a depraved system to stay alive. *Like I have much choice?*

"I'm sorry," Edden said again, and I glanced at him ruefully so he would know that I understood his position. Hell, I was standing right next to him.

Jenks's wings clattered, and I shifted the split in my dress to show the present sitting between my feet. My butt-kicking boots looked really odd down there, but I was glad I'd worn them. "I've got something he wants more than revenge," I said, praying I hadn't overestimated its worth. Though it grated on every fiber of my being, this had to work. *It had to.*

Edden bent forward to see the blue-foiled package, then leaned back. "I don't want to know what's in there. I *really* don't want to know."

I let my hem cover it. "I thought this was the safest place to hammer out an agreement with Piscary," I said meekly.

"My office?" he barked.

"Well . . ." I hedged. "Maybe a conference room?"

Edden's brown eyes went wide in disbelief, and I started to get a little upset. "Edden," I cajoled, "I don't have anywhere else to go. Kalamack *is* responsible for the deaths of those Weres. I'm trying to save my own butt here. All I have to do is swim through the crap to get to it. Now, are you going to throw me a preserver, or do I have to dog-paddle the whole way by myself?"

He tilted his head to see the clock on the wall above and behind him. I could almost read his thoughts. Why couldn't I have waited a few hours when he would have been off-shift?

"I wish you would include me in your thought processes," he said dryly.

"Just pretend you're still in the military," I said, hearing our conversation ending.

"Yeah," he said with a rueful chuckle as he stood. "I'd be safer on a front line than working with you." He took up his coffee and gestured to the door. "After you. The sooner we're done with this, the sooner I can go home."

Jenks's wings buzzed to life, and I stood, taking a moment to gather my present, my bag, and my composure. The butterflies had turned to fireflies, cramping my stomach. Edden opened the door, and when the noise hit me, I balked, thinking about how I needed the rush of danger to remind myself I was alive. Adrenaline junkie? I was embarrassed to admit that Jenks was probably right. It explained way too many things for me to simply dismiss because it was a stupid way to live. I couldn't help but wonder if I hadn't misjudged the risk this time and if it was going to turn around and bite me. But some of this *wasn't* my fault.

Landing upon my shoulder, Jenks said, "That little charm shop is looking mighty good right about now, eh, Rache?"

"Shut up, Jenks," I muttered, but I let him stay where he was—needing him.

Edden came to a halt beside Rose's desk and gazed over the maelstrom of officers trying to deal with upset Inderlanders. They looked as if they were doing okay. Maybe the essays Edden had asked me to write up for their handbook were helping.

Piscary was standing off a little by himself, his inquiring eyes on me and his grip possessively on Ivy as Skimmer spoke lawyer to a nervous woman with a clipboard. They were all sitting down, and my heart clenched at Ivy's blank stare. It was like she wasn't there. The news crews were visible through the black windows, lights glaring in the fog as they clustered outside the doors like wannabes trying to get into a club.

"I meant to tell you that's a pretty dress," the captain said, not looking at me as he rocked from heel to toe with his hands behind his back. "The boots are a nice touch."

I looked at them and sighed. "My foot hurts. They help." My foot, my arm, my back—they all ached like crazy. I felt like I'd been in a fight, not sleeping in Ivy's chair. *God, I hope she's okay.*

Edden chuckled at my dry sarcasm. "I thought you simply liked stomping around in them." Turning away, he gestured for a thin officer who looked less harried than the rest. "I hope you can work something out for your boyfriend."

Jenks's wings fanned faster. "Thanks," I said, carefully tucking away a strand of hair.

"Why don't you find a nice witch?" Edden said, shifting back a step to make room for the approaching officer. "Take the opportunity to get some space between you and Mr. Felps. I care what happens to you, and I hate to see you getting involved in vampire politics. People die when they do that."

I couldn't help my smile. "Gee, thanks, Dad. Can I have my driving privileges back?"

His eyes glinted. "You're grounded until you clean up your room, and you know it."

From my shoulder came a tiny snort, but Jenks was too close to see. *Clean my room?* I suppose that was a suitable metaphor. I had certainly put the city in a mess.

The officer that Edden had pulled from the melee stopped expectantly before us, and Edden drew him close. "Where's Kalamack? Ms. Morgan needs a room, and I don't want her anywhere near him."

I huffed in insult, and the man gave me an apologetic glance. "He's in five, but three is available," he said.

"No way," I said tightly. "I am *not* getting in a little interview room with Piscary. I want a conference room. Big enough so that I can have a few witnesses." *And kick some vampire ass if I need to.*

Edden crossed his arms over his chest to turn immovable. "Witnesses?"

"Witnesses." I gripped the focus tighter. This wouldn't work unless everyone knew I didn't have it anymore. "I want Mr. Ray and Mrs. Sarong." I turned to look over the open offices, each one occupied with a belligerent Inderlander and one or two nervous but doggedly determined FIB officers. "Quen," I said, finding him standing alone and on the phone as if none of this was touching him. "And Al," I finished, finding the demon flirting with the receptionist, now glowing from the attention of someone she thought was a wealthy eligible bachelor in a tux. Ellasbeth's dad was behind him, the upright man looking like he was ready to whip out his checkbook right here if it would help get his daughter married.

"Al?" Edden said, following my gaze to his receptionist, handing her phone number to the smiling man. "That's Mr. Saladan. Piscary said he exorcised the demon from him. My people have seen him in the sun."

I shook my head, feeling Al's gaze on me. "Piscary's lying. That's still Al."

The FIB officer with the clipboard paled. "That's a demon?" he squeaked.

Edden's brow furrowed. Putting a thick hand on each of our shoulders, he turned our backs to the room, all the while scanning the surrounding people to decide if they had heard him. "Rachel," he said, voice hushed but intent, "I'm not set up to deal with this situation."

His hand was warm through the lace on my shoulder, and I shivered. "Neither am I, but here I am. I can do this, Edden. I just need a quiet room. Your people don't have to do anything. No one's going to get hurt." But I couldn't promise it.

He was silent in thought. Deep concern in his gaze, he looked at the package in my hands, then turned to the officer with us. "How messy is Camelot?"

Camelot? I mused, and the man in question fidgeted. I could smell his fear on him, and Piscary was watching him. "It's full of mailings," the officer said. "June's newsletters still have to go out."

Edden's frown deepened. "It's the only room with a two-way that will hold all of them."

"Two-way!" I scoffed. "I want a room, not an FIB audience."

"I'm not going to let you go into a room alone with those people," Edden said. "You put me here, Morgan, and you're going to do it my way."

Jenks stifled a snicker, and I cocked my hip, copping an attitude in black lace and butt-kicking boots. "Whatever," I said, knowing I was at his mercy.

Satisfied, Edden drew the FIB officer even closer. "Grab a couple of guys and get the table cleared off. And have someone get Ms. Morgan's wish list in there."

My neck grew cold as Jenks took flight. "I'll get them," he offered, and the FIB officer looked relieved. Edden started to protest, but upon seeing Jenks already fronting the two Weres, he hesitated. Piscary was next, falling into step behind them. From his corner, Quen closed his phone and rocked forward before Jenks reached him, giving the pixy a nod. Al noticed the mass exodus and joined them, kissing the receptionist's hand in farewell.

"Damn," Edden swore softly, taking my elbow and angling us to the top of the hallway ahead of them. "I need to get me a pixy on the payroll."

I couldn't help my smile. "They're expensive," I warned him.

The comforting blank walls took us in, and the noise behind us dulled. "I thought they worked for sugar water and nectar," Edden said, and I slowed as I noticed we were passing interrogation rooms.

"I meant in terms of loyalty," I clarified, pulling him to a stop when I found Trent's room. A soft murmur came from behind the door, and when he saw my expression, Edden's face went hard. There was one more person I wanted to be present. Quen wasn't enough. I wanted Trent.

"No," Edden said, clearly knowing why I'd stopped, then pressed back against the walls as the Weres, Al, Quen, and Piscary all passed before us in silent expectation. Mrs. Sarong's heels clicked smartly, and Al gave me an amused grin over his smoked glasses. Quen was silent, his shoulders tense under the expensive fabric of his tux. Jenks was with them, and I gave him a nod as he went along to serve as my ears.

Skimmer and Ivy were with Piscary, and my heart clenched as Ivy did nothing when I tried to catch her eyes. She looked pale and empty, her perfect face still blank and beautiful, graceful in her sophisticated gray dress. It hurt to see her like that, and the memory of her voice rang in my head, the broken sound when she had begged me to keep the sun away from her after Piscary had raped her body and her blood and she thought she was dead. Pulling back, I forced myself to keep from reaching out to give her a shake. Piscary smiled in smug satisfaction at my pain, his hand upon the small of her back as he guided her forward.

I watched until they turned the corner. How could I do nothing? How could I stand here and watch her go by without doing something? She was my friend. Hell, she was more. And with that thought I felt my face go cold.

Kisten and Ivy offered me the same chance at finding blood ecstasy,

Kisten's offer packaged in a way my upbringing would have no problem dealing with, yet I'd said no to him. Continually. All the while, I was courting disaster trying to battle both my preconceived notions of myself and the risk of death to find the same thing with Ivy. Why?

And I closed my eyes, shutting out the world as I hammered the thought home. I wanted something lasting with Ivy. Yes, this spring I had come to grips with the idea that I'd probably moved into the church unconsciously hoping she'd bite me. True, I had beaten her off a few times before in fear, but I couldn't bring myself to do it anymore if the van incident this spring was any indication. I made no apology for wanting to try to find a blood balance with her. But only now did I realize what that meant. I was talking about a life commitment. Just because it might not involve sex didn't make it any less important or lasting.

"No way, Rachel," Edden said, and I stared in panic until I realized he was talking about my wanting Trent with us, not the possibility of Ivy and me together. Bound by blood and friendship. That it didn't necessarily preempt a secondary, more traditional relationship with a man—with Kist?—only added to the scary factor.

Edden's head tilted in confusion at my deer-in-the-headlights expression, and I dropped my gaze, feeling dizzy. Crap, why did I always pick the best times to figure things out?

"I need Trent there," I said, pressing the focus to my middle. "If he doesn't see me give this thing to Piscary, then it doesn't do me any good."

Edden grimaced, making his mustache stick out. "Quen can tell him."

The door to Trent's interrogation room opened, cutting our argument short. The FIB officer stopped, but it was too late, Trent had followed him out, accompanied by a second man in a suit. His lawyer, probably.

Trent looked totally unlike himself, yet nothing significant had changed. He was still dressed in his wedding finery, he still walked with grace, but there was an eerie wariness that had been absent before. His gaze fastened on mine with the usual intensity, but the edge of icy hatred was new. Disturbingly controlled, he drew himself upright, hiding the fatigue born of his efforts to lie his way out of his heinous crimes.

"Trent needs to be there," I blurted, trying to muddle things more. "He's a council member until proven guilty, and he needs to be present. This involves the city's security. You want to wait around for someone else to show up? You're pretty good if you think you can put a master vampire in a room with two alpha Weres, a demon, and a . . . a whatever Quen is," I said, remembering to keep his elven heritage a secret.

"Rachel . . ." Edden warned, but I had given Trent all he needed.

"If there is a city security issue, I have a right to be present," he said, regaining a modicum of his usual crisp presence. Trent didn't know what I was doing, but clearly I was trying to include him in it, and despite his probably wanting to put out a contract on me for tagging him, he'd go along with it. All things in their own time, apparently.

The officer and the suit flanking him had a hushed conversation, and when the FIB guy shrugged, Edden sighed. "Damn it, Rachel," he muttered, squeezing my elbow. "This is not how I do things."

Tired, I said nothing as I waited for his decision. My thoughts went to Ivy, then Kist.

The squat ex–military man rubbed a hand over his chin and took a firmer stance. "I'm in there with two other men."

"Just you, and you can cuff him to a chair," I came back.

Trent's frown deepened until it showed on his forehead. We all had to press back against the walls as three harried-looking officers carrying boxes of blue paper and envelopes passed. Apparently the room was cleaned up, and I started getting nervous again.

"All right," Edden said sourly. "Mr. Kalamack, would you please accompany me? Ms. Morgan seems to want to have a town meeting. We'll get you back to your processing as soon as possible so you can make bail."

Bail! I thought, not having imagined they would even offer it.

Trent saw my startled expression, and he allowed a hint of smugness to show. "Thank you, Captain. I would appreciate that."

Jenks flitted into the hallway to hover by the door. "Okay, Rache. They're all yours."

Mine, I thought as I steadied myself and followed Edden and Trent. But what by Tink's little red shoes was I supposed to do with them, now that I had them?

THIRTY-FIVE

Edden escorted Trent into the room ahead of me. Hesitating in the hall, I tugged the lacy collar of my dress straight, tucked a stray curl behind an ear, hiked my shoulder bag up, took a tighter grip on the wrapped present, and wished I could run to the bathroom.

"Charm shop," Jenks taunted from my shoulder, and I made a rude noise. There was a mild stir as everyone reacted to Trent's appearance. It wasn't going to get any easier. Knowing that Ivy was already in there, I squared my shoulders and walked in.

I scanned the room and saw where the Camelot remark had come from. A round table with its attendant half circle of chairs took up the right side of the large, rectangular room. Between it and the two-way mirror to my left was a wide space that gave me the impression of a stage. At the far right was a coffee-stained counter with a sink, covered in anything anyone could possibly use to put together a presentation: tatty binder clips, scratched report covers, three-hole paper punches, and a massive paper cutter that looked like it could chop wood for a campfire.

Piscary and Ivy sat at the back near the counter, Skimmer's thin grace standing submissively behind them in her strict black business suit. A flash of nervousness went through me, shortly followed by self-disgust. I was going to buy protection from the same man who had abused Ivy and given Kisten's death to someone as a thank-you gift. But what choice did I have? Someone powerful had to hold the focus. It didn't matter whether I liked him or not if he could keep me and Kisten alive and prevent a worldwide Inderland power struggle.

The two Weres sat near the middle of the table across from the door. Upon seeing me enter, Mrs. Sarong yanked Mr. Ray back into his seat before he could make an ass of himself. Trent was sitting beside the door, with Edden looming behind him. The elf wasn't in cuffs. Across from them Quen stood with his arms over his chest, looking good in his tux/uniform.

My attention went to Al. He was a vision of upright elegance in his black tux, standing with his back to me before the two-way mirror. The demon was breathing heavily on the glass to mist it up, using a gloved finger to scribe ley line symbols I couldn't understand. I didn't want to imagine the fear of the men and women watching behind the glass.

Al turned, beaming over his round smoked glasses. "Rachel Mariana Morgan," he drawled, his accent proving that despite looking like Lee, he was all Algaliarept. "Watching you cuff Trenton was extre-e-e-emely entertaining. What *will* you do for your next trick?"

Glowering beside Mrs. Sarong, Mr. Ray grumbled, "Pull a flaming bunny out of her ass, maybe?"

Quen stifled a smirk, and I came forward, boots clunking and dress furling. Jenks left me for the overhead lights in a soft hum. Only Quen and Al watched him go, the rest clueless as to how much of a threat he was up there. The gown made me feel stupid, but everyone was overdressed. I tried to get Ivy's attention as I stood at the table a few chairs down, with Trent between me and Al. She never looked up, her gaze fixed on the nothing and her face peacefully blank. Skimmer let her hatred show, and I ignored the sophisticated, pretty, blond vamp.

I set the package and my shoulder bag on the table, pushing them together as I gathered my thoughts. "Thanks for meeting me here, Piscary," I said, forcing my hand off my aching upper arm. "You are the foulest thing I've ever seen, but I hope we can come to some agreement." *God, I'm such a hypocrite.*

Piscary smiled while petting Ivy's hand, and when Al took a breath to say something, I turned. "Shut up," I demanded, and he huffed, though I could tell he thought it all a big joke. "You're here as witnesses. All of you. That's it."

There was a nervous shifting of position from everyone but Quen, and, satisfied, I touched my stuff on the table and tried not to think about my full bladder. "Okay," I said, and Trent smiled mockingly at my nervousness. "As you all probably figured out, I still have the focus."

Mr. Ray stiffened, and Mrs. Sarong's grip on his wrist tightened.

"I've got the focus," I continued when he settled back. "And all of you want it." I sent my gaze to my right. "Trent, I imagine you want it for a power play, seeing as you offered me an insane amount of money for it." *And killed three Weres, but why bring that up?*

"We double his offer," Mrs. Sarong said crisply, and Trent laughed outright, bitter and mocking. It was a new side to him, and it wasn't attractive. The woman turned scarlet, and Mr. Ray hunched over, looking uncomfortable.

"It's not for sale," I said, before anyone else could interrupt, then turned to Piscary. "Piscary, you want me dead for obvious reasons," I added. "And so does Trent, probably, by now."

"Don't forget me, love," Al said, turning his back on the mirror. "I just want you for an hour. One hour and this would all go away."

Jenks clattered his wings in warning, and I steadied myself. "No," I said, though my stomach was starting to hurt. An hour with him would become an eternity.

Mr. Ray himself tugged out from under Mrs. Sarong's grip. "Give it to me or I'll hunt you down like an animal and take it." Then the man jumped, and Mrs. Sarong's smile made me speculate about what she had done to him under the table. Gold pixy dust sifted down to put the Were in a temporary sunbeam, and Mr. Ray looked up in surprise, clearly having forgotten about Jenks.

Wondering if he had just been pixed, I stifled a smirk. "Yes," I said dryly. "I know. Which is why I'm talking to Piscary, not you."

There was a heartbeat of silence, and Mr. Ray surged to his feet. "No!" he bellowed, his round face flashing red. "You sorry little whippet. You can't give it to that undead bast—"

His words cut off when Quen put a hand on his shoulder and shoved him down. "Close your mouth," Quen said. "Listen before you draw your battle lines, lest you alienate your allies."

Oh, that sounds just peachy damn keen. But at least it was quiet. Shifting my weight to my other foot, I glanced at Al—who was starting to match Mrs. Sarong in terms of pissed-off-ness, to Trent, who was clearly thinking furiously, and finally to Piscary. The undead vamp was smiling like the benevolent god he believed he was. A honey-hued hand sat atop the pale purity of Ivy's, and I imagined he thought I was going to barter the focus for her and Kisten. I wanted to, but Keasley was right. She had to escape him on her own, or she would never be free of him.

"I'll give it to Piscary," I said as sweat trickled down my spine. "But I want something."

All eyes were on me. Piscary's smile widened. He slipped an arm behind Ivy and pulled her gently close. There was barely a flicker behind her brown eyes. "Ivy is mine," he said.

My breath shook as I exhaled. "Ivy belongs to herself. I want you to rescind the blood gift you made of Kisten, take him back into your camarilla, and give me protection from yourself and those yahoos," I said as I tossed my head to indicate everyone else in the room. "I also want my church back, and the freedom to pursue my business interests without interference."

Trent stiffened. Quen uncrossed his arms and took a more balanced stance. Al turned completely around from where he'd been scribing more ley line symbols on the two-way mirror. Piscary blinked in surprise. "Kisten?" he murmured in question. "You want . . . Kisten?"

"Yes, I want Kisten back under your protection," I said belligerently. "Will you rescind his blood gift or not?"

Piscary made a small sound of surprised consideration. Then, as if shifting his thoughts, he said, "You would have to restrain from persecuting me, of course."

"That's not fair," Al protested indignantly. "I'm trying to get Cincinnati's gambling and protection, and that gives you an unfair advantage. I want a witch on my payroll, too."

I gritted my teeth. *I will not put myself on Piscary's payroll. I will not.* "I can work on that," I said to Piscary. "It depends upon how much you tick me off."

The small man in his traditional Egyptian robes steepled his fingers in consideration. "You want me to rescind my gift of Kisten, take him back into my graces, grant you protection from all of them," he said with an elegant gesture, "and have me still be subject to your unique sense of moral outrage?"

Al's shoes clicked smartly, and everyone tensed as he came to the table. Clearly enjoying everyone's unease at his approach, Al sat with a provocative motion at the head of the table. "I'll say it again, Rachel Mariana Morgan. You're not shy about asking for things."

I wished he'd stop using all my names. "Look," I said, seeing Edden relax now that the demon was sitting. "I know what the focus is, what it does, and that it works. I've got it, and I won't give it away for nothing." My gaze slid to Trent's. "And money doesn't keep me alive."

"I can keep you alive," he said, his gray voice confident, though Edden stood behind him to cart him off to a cell if he couldn't make bail. "You underestimate me if you think I can't."

I grimaced as I remembered him offering me an island to get me out of the city and under his thumb. I still didn't know why. Maybe because he'd known that my blood could kindle demon magic? But he was afraid of black magic. It didn't add up.

"Thanks, but no," I said tightly. "I'd rather deal with the undead." Mrs. Sarong was looking at my shoulder bag as if she might snatch it, and I pulled it closer. "The focus will cause more turmoil than the Turn. I can't destroy it without twisting demon magic, and despite what you all think, I avoid it when I can." I took a deep breath, turning to Piscary. "I'm assuming you will keep it hidden and on this side of the lines so the Weres don't overthrow vampire superiority?" I asked, and he nodded, the light glistening on his shaven scalp.

"They are not superior to us!" Mr. Ray bellowed, and Mrs. Sarong edged her chair away in a show of distancing herself from him, clearly tired of his lack of grace.

"And that's why you want it so bad?" I said sharply. "Without the focus you're second, maybe third, on the food chain. Deal with it. Everyone else does."

Tension had pulled all my muscles tight. I was losing control. Edden had a weapon, but there were two predators and one elven warrior in here, all deadly on their own.

Piscary alone looked confident. "You're afraid," he breathed, the rim of brown about his eyes starting to disappear. "You smell . . . so good."

Adrenaline dove through me, followed by the memory of him pinning me to the floor of his apartment, licking the blood from my elbow on his way to my neck. "And you stink like three-day-old carrion under your pheromones and witch charms. Do we have a deal or not?"

"Perhaps," he said shortly. "But you ask for too much. I'm going to have my hands full trying to keep that fluffy ball of damnation under control," he said, glancing at Al, as his smile grew to show his fangs. "That's why they let me out. I must do my civic duty."

Behind him Skimmer shifted uneasily, and glanced nervously at her. "You mean Al?" I questioned when the demon leaned back and put his shiny dress shoes on the table in satisfaction. "No problem. I'll have him back in the ever-after as soon as I make an interdimensional phone call."

I wasn't a demon practitioner. *I wasn't.*

"You little *canicula*!" Al swore, his feet hitting the tile as he stood. His glasses slipped, and he fumbled for them. "You can't! You don't know anyone's summoning name but mine!"

Edden moved, drawing his weapon. The safety clicked off, and Al stumbled to a halt, remembering he had a body now that couldn't go misty. Quen was tense, and Trent was stiff in his chair. I was the nearest to him, but he knew I wouldn't protect his lame elf ass. Besides, he was looking at me as if I had sprouted black wings with matching tail and horns.

Piscary, though, was as cool and calm as ever, Skimmer behind him looking scared at last, and Ivy blinking, the faintest worry lines showing upon her forehead. Compared to Piscary, Al was weak now, trapped in a witch's body and capable of doing only what Lee could. "You can't banish him," the undead vampire said coolly. "Not with him possessing another."

I lifted one shoulder in a nervous shrug. "Someone in the ever-after owes me a favor. Al's over here hiding from trouble. If I blow the whistle, someone will pick him up."

"You bitch!" Al howled, jerking when Edden aimed his weapon. "You don't know anyone but Newt, and Newt doesn't have a summoning name. Who gave you their name?"

"He's back into the ever-after?" Piscary said, smiling again to show his fangs.

"And out of your territory." My fingers trembled, and I glanced at Trent, bothered by his look of horror. "Territories," I added to make it plural, not liking that Trent thought I dealt in demons. "I'll do that for you for free, Trent."

Trent shook his head, his fair hair floating in the breeze of the building's air. "You consort with demons," he whispered, then turned to Quen, looking betrayed. Everyone he thought was untainted was not. Seemed like Trent had his own problems.

"I don't," I said, unclenching my teeth before I gave myself a headache. "Someone in the ever-after owes me. You have a problem with my calling in a favor to get rid of Al?"

His confidence shaken, Trent asked, "What did you give a demon for a favor owed?"

Stomach cramping, I turned to Piscary. "Do we have a deal or not?"

The vampire smiled to make me shudder. "Very much so."

Al growled, and as Edden held him at gunpoint, I shoved the package down the entire length of the table. "Mazel tov," I said, depressed, anxious, and jittery.

"It was the gift?" Trent stammered. "You brought it to the wedding?"

"Yup," I said with a false brightness. I felt sick. Buying Kisten's and my safety from Piscary was so wrong. But it was either that or deal with a demon, and I'd rather keep my soul clean and let my morals get dingy. I guess. But I felt filthy. This wasn't who I wanted to be.

"Son of a bitch . . ." Al said as Piscary's long fingers stretched forward to take it.

"Rachel!" Jenks shouted from the ceiling. "Get down!"

My breath hissed. Not looking, I dropped. The flat of my arms hit the tile, and I saw Al's feet move toward me. I rolled under the table to Quen. But Quen was gone.

"Get down!" Edden's voice bellowed, strong and demanding. I was on my hands and knees under the table, and I tensed for a gunshot. It never came.

A guttural snarl erupted from the back of the room, and I gasped when Al fell into my sight on the floor. Piscary was atop him. The undead vampire had launched himself across the room. He was protecting me. I had paid him to keep me alive, and that's what he was doing.

Shocked, I scrambled up.

Quen and I had exchanged places. The warrior elf had Trent backed into a corner by the door. Edden was standing before them, gun trained on Al. The Weres were by the back counter, wide-eyed. Ivy was blinking where she sat, looking at her reflection in the distant two-way mirror, oblivious to Skimmer's attempts to tug her upright and to the back of the room. The pretty vampire's eyes were black in fear, and her mouth was open in horror. I could smell burnt amber, and I patted at my clothes, looking for damage. But then I saw it. The doorknob had been melted. We weren't getting out of here anytime soon.

Oh, God. I wanted to live.

The lights were on in the room behind the mirror, and someone was trying to break the glass with a chair. Heart pounding, I backed up to the wall, my gaze on Piscary and Al.

"Jenks! Get back!" I shouted when I saw the sparkle of pixy dust. Snarling, fangs bared, Piscary grappled with Al. The demon was at a severe disadvantage in his witch body, and I went cold when I realized that Piscary had him. Hand covering my neck, I stood in shock as the vampire sank his teeth.

Al howled, managing to get an arm between them, then a knee. With a pained grunt, he tried to shove Piscary away, failing. Tears of remembered fear filled my eyes as the demon went limp with a moan, the vampire saliva starting to work.

My hand clutched my sore upper arm, and I looked away. My gaze found Trent behind Quen. He, too, appeared shocked. I don't think he knew until this moment the horror Quen and I had endured when we were attacked by an undead. They didn't care. They existed to feed. The walking and talking simply make it easier for them.

Edden was ashen-faced, but his pointed weapon stayed steady, waiting. The pounding on the mirror had shifted to a pounding on the door.

With a sodden thump, Piscary let Al drop. Wiping his mouth on the back of his hand, then delicately cleaning even that from himself with a black handkerchief, Piscary rose. His eyes were black. He had just fed, but we were trapped in here with him. Al's hand lifted, then fell.

The room tensed, and Jenks landed on my shoulder. He was pale, as shocked as the rest of us. "It's not over, Rache," he said, his voice frightened. "Get yourself in a circle."

I drew myself up to tap a line and set an informal circle, but a hint of burnt amber brought my attention to the front of the room. *Shit.*

A mist was forming over Al. Al wasn't dead. He was leaving Lee's body now that it wasn't useful anymore. Piscary didn't know it, standing satisfied and full of himself, smiling benevolently. Any circle I was going to make had to have a real beginning to stand against a demon. My bag and its stick of magnetic chalk was on the other side of the table. Hiking up my dress, I crawled up onto the table to jerk my bag to me. Backing into a corner as Piscary advanced, I scrabbled in my bag, fingers fumbling.

"Rache! Hurry up!" Jenks shrilled.

Heart pounding, I found it, yanking it out. It slipped, and I cried out in frustration as it rolled under the table. I dove for it, but Quen got there first, and both our hands landed on it.

"The demon isn't dead," the elf said, and I nodded. "I need this," he said, jerking the chalk from my fingers.

"Damn it, Quen!" I shouted, then screamed when a set of fingers fastened about my ankle and dragged me out from under the table. I twisted and, flat on my back, stared up at Piscary. He bared his fangs, and my heart gave a thud. From my neck came a pulse of feeling, but I was too scared for it to feel good. Piscary's eyes closed in twisted bliss, soaking it in like sunshine. Behind him a sheet of ever-after swirled and condensed into a vision of the Egyptian god of the underworld, his smooth chest bare and bells jingling from his scarlet-and-gold loincloth.

I never thought I'd be so glad to see Algaliarept. Too bad he was likely going to kill me after he finished staking Piscary.

"Piscary," I said breathlessly as the demon's goat-slitted eyes glinted red and a long canine tongue slipped out to catch a drop of hanging saliva, "You might want to turn around."

"Pathetic," the undead vampire mocked, and I stifled a gasp as he yanked me up.

"You only killed Lee, you stupid ass," Jenks said from above me. "Not Al."

The vampire took a deep breath, scenting the air. I shrieked when he shoved me away. I flew backward, hitting the cupboards. Struggling to breathe, I put a hand to my back.

"Rachel!" Jenks shrilled. "Are you okay? Can you move?"

"Yeah," I rasped, almost cross-eyed as I looked at him inches away from me. I scanned the room for Ivy, not seeing her. Someone screamed. It wasn't me this time, and I staggered up.

"Oh, my God," I whispered as Jenks hovered beside me. Al had Piscary. It was a vision from the depths of history as a jackal-headed god grappled with an Egyptian prince in royal robes who had set himself even with the underworld. The demon had his hands around Piscary's neck, his fingers pressing into the vampire's flesh as if it were dough, and he was trying to pinch his head right off. Piscary was fighting him, but now that Al was in demon form and pissed to the ends of the Turn, the undead vampire hadn't a chance.

Piscary couldn't die. It would ruin everything.

"Quen! Give me the chalk!" I wheezed, hand over my bruised throat. I had to save Piscary. Damn it, I had to save his worthless, stinking, perverted life.

From his corner, Quen hesitated.

"Who do you think Al will go after when he's done with Piscary!" I exclaimed, frustrated, and the elf threw it at me.

My heart leapt. Crap, why did people always throw stuff at me? I was a lousy catch. But I put my hand up, and the chalk hit it with a satisfying thump. Keeping one eye on the jackal-headed god and the dying vampire, I hunched over, tripping on my dress as I drew a circle around them, making it as big as I could to stay out of their way. Jenks went before me, and I followed the path he was dusting to get it circular.

"Ivy," I gasped when I found her, standing blank-faced before the mirror, watching her faint reflection, oblivious to everything. "Go to Quen. Get over by Quen. I can't help you."

She didn't move, and when Jenks shrilled at me to hurry, I lurched past her, praying she would be okay and cursing my helplessness.

I had to crawl under the table to finish the circle, and as I came out, the end of my silver line met the beginning. "Rhombus," I breathed, tapping a line. The gold of my aura flowed upward, the black of demon smut following to coat it a breath behind.

"No!" Al howled, his eyes red with fury as he dropped Piscary an instant too late.

The vampire hit the floor. Still conscious, Piscary grabbed the demon about the calves and pulled him down. Piscary was on him in an instant, fangs tearing ribbons of flesh like a wolf's. I scrambled up, shocked as he gulped them down to make room for more, trying to savage the demon into nonexistence. The sound was absolutely . . . horrifying.

"Let them kill themselves," Trent said from beside the door, pale and shaking.

"Demon!" I shouted, unable to risk calling Al by his summoning name. "I have bound you. You are mine. Leave here and go directly to the ever-after!"

The Egyptian god howled, saliva dripping red from his muzzle and his neck reduced to ribbons of exposed flesh. He had returned to his demon form, and he was vulnerable.

"Leave *now!*" I demanded, and with his anger ringing within the room, Al vanished.

Piscary fell through the space where Al had been, his arm hitting the floor to catch himself. Hand against his crushed neck, he found his feet. The room was silent but for Skimmer's gasping breaths, sounding almost like sobs. The Weres were in one corner and the elves in another. Edden was passed out on the floor beside the door. Just as well. He would have tried to shoot someone, and that would only have given him more paperwork.

I turned to Quen, the chalk still in my grip. "Thanks," I whispered, and he nodded.

Slowly Piscary collected himself, turning from a savage monster to a ruthless businessman, albeit one covered in blood. His eyes were utterly black, and a shudder rippled over me. Taking a step forward, he stopped at the edge of my bubble. He tugged down the sleeves of his elegant traditional dress robes and wiped the last of the demon flesh from his mouth, clearly waiting. My pulse slowed, and, praying I was safe, I slid a foot forward and broke the circle.

Hell, I had saved his undead life. Surely that meant something to him.

"You could have let him kill me," Piscary said, scanning the room until he found Ivy, her back to him as she touched her reflection.

"Uh-huh," I panted, scooping up my bag and tucking the chalk away. "But you're my ticket to normalcy, right? And the only way to get Kisten's blood gift reversed."

Piscary raised one eyebrow. "I can't rescind my gift of Kisten's last blood. I wouldn't even if I could. Kisten needed to be reminded of his reason for existence. And besides, that would have been rude."

Would have been? I thought, going cold. *As in past tense?*

"Kisten . . ." I stammered, suddenly feeling trapped. My hand clutched at my sore arm, and I felt sick. Jenks's wings rose to a pitch that made my eyes ache. *Kisten*. "What did you do?" I took a frantic breath. "What did you do to him!"

The vampire dabbed at the black blood leaking from him. It smelled like incense, potent and heady. "Kisten is dead," he said flat out, and I reached for the table, dizzy. "Not only dead but truly dead. Twice. He didn't have it in him to stay the course." Piscary pressed his lips and cocked his head in a mockery of interest. "I'm not surprised."

"You're lying," I said, hearing my voice tremble. My chest clenched, and I couldn't get enough air. Kisten couldn't be dead. I would know. I would have felt it. Something would have been different, everything, and nothing was. Jenks had said he'd called. *He couldn't be dead!*

"He went underground!" I exclaimed, frantically looking at everyone—wanting someone, anyone, to tell me I was right. But no one met my eyes.

Piscary smiled to show a glint of fang. He was getting too much joy from my despair for it not to be true. "You don't think I know when one of my own passes into undead existence?" he said. "I felt him die, and then I felt him die again." Face showing a twisted pleasure, he leaned toward me and whispered loudly. "It was a shock to him. He didn't expect it. And I licked up his despair and failure, reveling in it. His entire life was worth just that one . . . *exquisite* moment of failed perfection. Pity his living bloodline ended with him, but he was always so careful. It was as if he didn't want anyone to follow him. . . ."

Vertigo hit me, and I clutched at the edge of the table. *This cannot be happening.* "Who?" I rasped, and Piscary smiled like a benevolent, savage god. "Who killed him?"

"How pathetic," he said, then cocked his head. "Or do you really not remember?" he said in speculation, dropping his bloodstained handkerchief and focusing intently on me.

I tried to speak, but nothing came out. Horror that he might be speaking the truth numbed me. I couldn't think. My arm throbbed under my fingers, and when he leaned closer, I did nothing, too shaken to respond.

"You were there," he said distantly, reaching out to take my jaw in his hand and tilt my head so the light hit my eyes. "You saw. I can smell Kisten's final death all over you. You breathe it out. It lifts from your skin like perfume."

I was sleeping in the church, I thought in denial, then felt my world shift with a nauseating spin as things added up. I had woken sore and hurt. I had a cut on my lip. The kitchen had smelled of candles and lilac—the materials for a forget potion. My damned foot was so swollen that I couldn't wear anything but my boots.

What had I seen? What had I done?

I stumbled back when Piscary took a step forward. I didn't believe this! I had given him the focus for what? Kisten was dead. Tears prickled. *Oh, my God, Kisten is dead. And I was there.*

Piscary reached for me, and I flung my hand up to block, only to have him capture my wrist. Fear spiked to my middle, and I froze. The room seemed to waver as the people in it drew their breath, and Piscary breathed deep, scenting me. Relishing my fear.

"You're stronger than Ivy let on," he said softly, almost introspective. "I understand why she's fixated on you. Perhaps there's a use for you, if you can walk unscathed from a room where one undead vampire met his end and another barely escaped to see another night."

I jerked away, my frantic gaze going to Edden. Tension crept along my spine as I backed up. There had been another? I didn't remember it, but I had to believe him. *What have I done to myself? Why?*

"Or maybe . . . you're too dangerous to be allowed free range, anymore. Time to break you to the bit, perhaps."

Disoriented, I did nothing when Piscary put a golden-skinned hand around my throat. "No!" I shouted, but it was too late. My word escaped with a gurgle. Adrenaline flamed through me, and I struggled as Piscary backhanded Jenks with a slow nonchalance. The pixy shot across the room, hitting the wall and falling to the floor.

God help me. Jenks . . . "I gave you the focus!" I rasped, toes brushing the tile when he lifted me. "You said you'd leave me alone!"

Piscary pulled me closer. "You put me in jail," he said, his breath smelling of blood and burnt amber. "I said I'd keep you alive, but I owe you some serious pain. You'll only wish you were dead." He put up a warning hand when Quen moved, and the elf stopped.

Horror trickled through me. *This isn't possible!* "I saved your life!" I rasped when his fingers let up so he could hear me beg. "I could have let Al kill you."

"Your mistake." He smiled at me with sin-black eyes. "Say good-bye, Rachel. Time to start your new life."

"No!" I screamed, then tapped a line. I pushed at him, willing the energy to flow, but it was too late. Crushing me to his chest, Piscary savagely sank his teeth into me.

My shriek of terror filled my ears. My heart hammered as if trying to find a way out of my chest, but my muscles had gone slack. Pain flowed, and I couldn't move. It was agony. I heard my breath come in gasps, pushing my blood into Piscary all the faster.

A dark shadow approached like fast water, and Piscary backhanded Quen without breaking from me. I heard a thump and a pained grunt.

Just kill us, I thought, wanting Quen to blast us both to hell with a ball of ever-after. How could it end like this? It wasn't supposed to end like this. It couldn't end like this!

"Piscary!" Ivy pleaded, and my heart leapt at the emotion in her voice. "Let her go!" she cried, and I saw her slim hand take his shoulder, gripping with fierce intensity. "You promised. You promised if I came to you that you'd leave her alone!"

I groaned as he pulled from me, his teeth ripping tears in my neck. I couldn't . . . I couldn't move!

"It's too late," Piscary said, and I hung in his grip, unresisting. "This has to be done."

"You said you wouldn't hurt her." Ivy's voice was heavy, as gray as morning fog.

Piscary held me upright, one arm crushing me to him. "You've been careless," he said flatly. "This is the last time I'm going to pick up after you. You should have bound her to you when I told you to. By rights I have to kill her. An unpredictable animal needs to be culled."

"Rachel would never hurt me," Ivy whispered, and I tried to speak, feeling my heart break. I took a breath, seeing my sight graying at the edges. I was slipping. I couldn't stop.

"No, Ivy girl." Piscary's face was gentled in concern as he leaned over me and touched her face with false love, leaving my blood on her jawline. I could hear Skimmer crying in the corner, adding to the travesty. "That's both their lure and their downfall. I'm going to kill her for you. If I don't, I'll only use her to torture you, and I've tortured you enough. It's my gift to you, Ivy. She won't feel a thing. I promise."

Ivy stared at him, her face lost in terror as Piscary bent to me again, making a small sound of pleasure when he licked the blood leaking from my neck, wallowing in it. She stood beside him, struggling to overcome a lifetime of conditioning. Her eyes filled, spilling over. My vision blurred, and she touched Piscary's shoulder lightly.

"Stop," she said before his teeth could find me again, but it was a whisper. "Stop!" she said louder, and hope struck through me. Piscary hesitated, his grip tightening.

"I said no!" Ivy shouted. "I won't let you kill her!"

Backing up a step, she swung her foot in a roundhouse to hit Piscary's head.

It never landed. Piscary hissed, dropping me to collapse between their feet. I took a raspy breath, and my fingers searched my neck. I was dizzy, weak. He'd bitten me. How bad? How bad was it?

"Ivy girl?" the undead vampire questioned from somewhere above me.

"No," Ivy said. Her shaking voice was determined, but even I could hear her fear.

"No?" Piscary said lightly, and I tried to push away, to get out from between them. "You aren't strong enough to best me."

My heart pounded, and I managed to find the wall, fingers scrabbling weakly as I turned to sit with my back to it. Lee's body was gone from under the mirror, and I found that Trent had dragged it to the door, his tux's coat covering him like a blanket. *Lee is alive?*

In the space between the table and mirror, Ivy dropped into a fighting stance. "Then I'll die trying, and kill you myself. She's my friend. I won't let you hurt her."

A smile of satisfaction blossomed over the older vampire's face. "Ivy," he crooned, "my sweet Ivy. You defy me at last. Come here, little fish. It's time you leave the weeds and swim as the predator you are."

No, I thought in horror, seeing that everything—the terror, the pain, the agony—had all been meant to manipulate Ivy into standing up to him, completing his vision of finding an equal in her.

"It will hurt like the sun," Piscary warned, arms open to embrace her as she backed away, face white. "Your last blood will be sweet in me."

Edden, again conscious, scrabbled to me, and I slapped weakly at him as he tried to look at my neck. "Shoot him," I breathed, almost vomiting when I reached up and found my neck ripped open. "He's going to kill her," I whispered, but Edden didn't seem to care. Ivy had defied Piscary. He was going to kill her so they could live an undead existence together. "Ivy, no." I said, louder since Edden wasn't listening. "You don't want . . . this."

Piscary raised one eyebrow. "Patience, witch," he said, then reached for Ivy.

Terror overcame training, and Ivy backpedaled. She screamed, high and shrill, and the sound struck through me. He had her against the mirror, his mouth on her neck as he dug deep to end it fast.

She didn't resist him. She wanted to die. It was the only way she could fight him and hope to save me. She was letting him kill her to save me.

"No," I sobbed, trying to rise, but Edden had my arm. He wasn't letting go. "No!"

A blond shadow darted to them. Grunting, Skimmer swung the arm of the paper cutter like an ax against the back of Piscary's neck. It hit his flesh with a meaty thump.

Piscary jerked. He drew away from Ivy, showing her neck bloodied and torn. Blood flowed from her. He had bitten deep, a death bite.

Crying in fear and her fury, Skimmer swung again. My stomach churned at the thunk as it met the front of Piscary's neck this time. His hands slipped from Ivy, and Skimmer swung yet again, screaming in a blind frustration as she angled to hit him in exactly the same spot.

The blade went through the third time, and Skimmer stumbled and fell sobbing to her knees as Piscary collapsed. The bloodied blade still in her hand rang as it hit the floor.

"Sweet mother of God," Edden swore, his grip falling away.

Slumped against the mirror, Ivy stared at Piscary in disbelief. His severed head looked up at her, his eyes blinking once before the pupils turned silver black and empty. He was dead. Skimmer had killed him. Thin streams of red blood pooled from the ruin of his neck, slowing to nothing.

"Piscary?" Ivy whispered like a forgotten child, then collapsed.

"No!" Skimmer shrieked. Crying, she crawled to Ivy. Her hands went red as she tried to stop the blood from flowing from Ivy's neck. "God, please, no!"

The door crashed open, the sound of the drill they used to open the door, fading away as people rushed in. Two fell on Skimmer. She fought them, but her movements were blind and easy to overcome. Three more descended upon Ivy, and I heard the rhythmic chants as they started CPR. Oh, God. She was dead. Ivy was dead.

I crawled under the table, forgotten as feet rushed about to pull Trent from his corner and escort Mr. Ray and Mrs. Sarong out. A sheet was draped over Piscary. Both parts of him.

Ivy was dead. Kisten was dead. Jenks . . .

"No," I whispered, eyes filling as I slumped. *Jenks,* I thought in despair, throat heavy with an immovable lump. *Where's Jenks?* Piscary had hit him.

The pain was easing, the heartache wasn't. Jenks. Where was Jenks? My neck was cold, and I wouldn't touch it. My breath escaped me in a sob. Oh, God, I hurt. From under the table, I saw shiny dress shoes and three people kneeling before Ivy. Her hand lay outstretched as if looking for her salvation. As if looking for me. She was dying, and nothing could stop that.

But Jenks was somewhere, and someone might step on him.

I crawled to the back of the room, looking for him. The focus lay forgotten on the floor in an open box amid the nest of black tissue paper. I shoved it out of the way to find the shimmer of fallen gold beside my bag.

My heart seemed to cease. I felt nothing but pain. It was all I was. "Jenks," I croaked. *Please, no,* I thought, tears blinding me as I hunched over him. My hands, sticky with blood, trembled as I picked him up. He wasn't moving, his face pale and one of his wings bent.

"Jenks," I sobbed, the release shaking me as I felt him light in my hand. Jenks was dead. Kisten was dead. Ivy was dying. My would-be protector had tried to kill me, only to be killed in turn. I had nothing. I had absolutely nothing. There were no more choices, no more options, no more clever ways out of a tough situation. *And the rush,* I realized in a brutal wash of despair, *is a false god I've chased my entire life. One that cost me everything in the blind search for sensation.* My entire existence amounted to nothing. Running from one thrill to the next with no regard to what really was important.

What in hell is left for me?

Everyone I had cared for was gone. It had taken me too long to find them, and I knew deep into my soul that their like would never come again. I had come too far from my beginnings, and no one else would understand who I really was—or, more important, who I wanted to be— under all the crap my life had become. I was now something no one could trust, not even me. I openly consorted with demons. My blood kindled their curses. My soul was coated with the stink of their magic. Every time I tried to do good, I hurt myself and those who loved me.

And those I loved, I thought, the tears blurring my vision.

Well, the hell with that, I thought as I fumbled for the open box with the focus in it. There was one final way to find an end to this, and now . . . now I had no reason not to.

A profound feeling of apathy took me, hollow and bitter, and my fingers shook as I wiped my face and pulled the hair from my eyes. Past the edge of the table, feet moved and voices were raised in urgency, but I was forgotten. Alone and apart, I pulled the focus out of its open box, knowing what I was going to do and not caring. It was going to hurt. Probably kill me. But there was nothing left in me except pain, and anything was better than that. Even oblivion.

Watching my hands as if they belonged to someone else, I scribed a circle encompassing most of the tile under the table with my metallic chalk. My heart felt like ash, unstirred by the power of the ley line as I touched it to make a shimmering black sheet bisect the table above me.

"Where's Morgan?" Trent said suddenly, his voice cutting through the excited babble. I could hear the CPR chant, but I'd seen Ivy's neck. She would die, if she wasn't dead already. She had wanted me to save her soul, and I had failed. It was gone, as if she had never been, never smiled, never taken joy in the day.

Edden's work shoes moved restlessly. "Someone check the bathroom."

Cold despite the warmth of the line running through me, I clenched the focus to me and scribed three more circles, intersecting them to form four spaces. I was crying, but it didn't matter. I was inside the circles. I was *inside* the circles.

"Morgan," Trent accused in a tired voice, and he bent at the waist, finding me. "It's over. You can come out of your bubble now."

I ignored him. My fingers hummed with force, and from my bag I pulled the candles I had bought for my birthday. *Why, God? What in hell did I ever do to you?* Trent's face went pale, and he sat down when the Latin spilled from me as I lit and placed them. First the white one, then the black, and lastly the yellow one, the yellow one that would represent my aura. There was no gray, so I put a second black one in the middle, confident that because my soul was the color of sin, the magic would work. This one I left unlit. It would burn when the curse was twisted and my fate was immutable.

Quen tried to pull Trent up, and, failing, he bent to look himself. "Bacchus save us," he whispered, knowing what I was doing. The focus no longer had a protector. Everyone knew I had it. I couldn't give it to Piscary—the bastard was dead. I had to get rid of it another way. Just because I had screwed up, that was no reason to send what was left of the world into war. The blackness on my soul would have no meaning if there was no love, no understanding, no one to share my life with. I just wanted it to all go away, to stop. And because I didn't think I was going to survive this, it was all to the better.

Edden bent at the waist, swearing when he reached out to find that the shimmering black shadow between us was real. From the hallway came Mrs. Sarong's complaining voice, going faint as she was led away. "What is she doing?" Edden said. "Rachel, what are you doing?"

Killing myself. Numb, I set the focus in its spot and myself in the other. The third space where my ring of hair would go was empty. I was in the circle; I didn't need a symbol of connection. My chest clenched, and I drew my will together. Jenks's body lay outside my circle. Ivy's was beneath the mirror. Kisten was dead. I had no reason not to do this. I had no reason at all. Piscary had ripped everything from me in less than twenty-four hours since his release. Not bad. Maybe he was a little more pissed than I'd thought.

"Rachel!" Edden said, louder over the chants of the EMTs who had arrived to push the FIB officers away. "What are you doing?"

"She's getting rid of the focus," Quen said tightly.

"Why didn't she just do that in the first place?" Edden said, his expression annoyed. "Rachel, come out of there."

Quen's voice was empty. "Because it will take a demon curse to do it."

Edden was silent for a moment, and I jumped when I felt his fist hit my bubble. "Rachel!" he exclaimed, then swore as his knuckles met my bubble again. "Get out! Now!"

But I couldn't stop and I didn't want to. Almost having forgotten, I touched my finger to my oozing neck, and, using the blood, I scribed a figure on the unlit black candle. I still didn't know what the figure stood for, and now I never would. Silence ached through me when the EMTs knelt before Ivy, their heads bowed as they slowly put their things away.

Tears spilled, and I started to get angry. I touched the interlaced circles, willing energy to fill them. I didn't even need to use my trigger word—it happened just as I willed it.

Edden swore again as the tainted bubbles rose about me, and I wondered if he knew that the arcs of gold where the circles intersected were what my aura was supposed to look like.

"Will it kill her?" Trent whispered.

Let's find out, I thought bitterly, not believing I could hold the power of a demon curse. And when they killed me—which they would for working demon magic inside a public building in front of credible witnesses—the power of the curse would die with me. Problem solved.

Except a small part of me really wanted to live. *Damn it, hope is a cruel god.*

Fingers still shaking, I knelt in my tiny space and clasped my hands, willing the trigger words back into my memory. They came. Exhaling, I said harshly, *"Animum recipere."*

Quen's breath hissed, and he pulled Trent back.

The power of the curse flowed into me, warm like sunshine. I stiffened as the scent of burnt amber coated me, tasting bittersweet, like dark chocolate. It felt good. It tasted sweet. My thoughts wailed in despair. *What in hell have I become?*

Jaw clenched, I knelt under the table, my unseeing gaze lifting upward and my breath held against the sensations. It felt good, and that was wrong. The power of creation coursed out of the focus and into me, familiar and welcoming. It sang, it lured, it whispered behind my eyes of the lust of the chase, the joy of the capture, the satisfaction of the kill. Within me stirred the need to dominate. I remembered the feel of the earth beneath my paws and the scent of time in my nose, filling my memories, making me want more.

And this time instead of denying it, I accepted it. *"Non sum qualis eram,"* I said bitterly, angry tears spilling from under my closed lids. I would take the curse into me, and I would keep it. It would end everything. There was no reason not to.

I felt the white candle go out, and I opened my eyes to see a thin trail of smoke showing me the lost path to eternity. I had set the taper with the word for protection, but I was beyond its reach. Nothing could protect me. The focus was empty, and the curse was inside me, beating like a second heart, crawling through my aura and clouding my sight. I could feel it, alive like a twin awareness beside my own. But I wasn't done yet. I still had to seal the magic.

A wild impulse to flee filled me, born of the curse. Gritting my teeth, I forced myself to stay still, chaining the second awareness with my will. But it fought me, slipping deeper when I struggled to keep it separate. Eyes fixed on the black candle, I willed it to go out. With a soft puff, the light was gone. The curse's need to run grew stronger. My hands started to shake uncontrollably.

My bowed head swung to the gold candle. It would seal the curse into me so it couldn't unravel. It flickered in a wind only I felt, and then, as soft and surprising as a butterfly wing upon one's cheek, it went out. The last black candle burst into light. The curse was twisted anew.

A groan slipped from me, and I felt light-headed. It was done. I was a demonic curse. I could feel it within me, poison seeping from my soul to my mind. Now all that remained was to see if it would kill me.

Lips parted in the shock at what I had done, I lifted my head to find Trent sitting under the table in his white tux shirt without a coat. He was watching me, Quen behind him ready to drag him away. I blinked, my chest burning. There was just enough time for me to take a breath, and then the reality imbalance from twisting the curse hit me.

I jerked, my head hitting the bottom of the table and my elbows breaking the circles. Gasping, I convulsed as a wave of black coated me. I couldn't breathe. My cheek hit the cool tile, and I clenched in pain. The curse saw my will weaken, and its need to run redoubled, twining into mine until they were the same. I had to run. I had to flee! But I couldn't move . . . my damned . . . arms.

"Will she be okay?" Trent asked, worry and bewilderment in his voice.

"She's taking on the payment for the curse," Quen said quietly. "I don't know."

Someone touched me. I screamed, hearing only a guttural groan. The curse dove deep into my psyche, melding with me. There was no way out for it anymore, and it flowed into every facet of my memory and thought, becoming me. I was dying from the inside out. And through it all the smut of the imbalance burned, threatening to stop my heart.

"I take it," I panted, and the hurt ebbed. "I take it," I sobbed, clenching into a ball. It was mine. The curse was all I had left. A frightening need to run was filling me. It was the demon curse, but we were the same. Its need was mine.

Why am I fighting this? I thought suddenly, the agony of the demon smut burning my blood. And with that last, bitter feeling, I let my will die.

My fear vanished in a ping of singular thought, the heartache left in a blink of bewilderment that I cared, and the turmoil of mental anguish evaporated in the sudden realization that everything had changed.

My eyes opened. Peace filled me. It was as if I was reborn. There was no anger, no heartache, no sorrow. My breath filled my lungs in a smooth, unhurried motion. I stared at the world in a pause of time, my cheek resting on the cool tile, and I wondered what had happened. My body hurt as if I had fought and won, but there was no torn-apart corpse lying before me.

And then I saw my prison beside me, knocked askew from where I had placed it behind the trappings of demon magic. *Oh. That.*

Eyes narrowing, I reached for it. It would never hold me again.

"*Celero inanio,*" I snarled, not caring it was a demon curse, not caring I didn't know how I knew it. The bone shattered where I touched it, superheated to flake into fragments. I jerked my hands back and sat up, the pain surprising but nothing against my satisfaction. That prison would never hold me again, and I welcomed the imbalance for breaking the laws of physics as it flowed into me, coating me in a comforting layer of warmth, protecting me. *On to other things . . .*

Above me I felt the flat smoothness of wood and above that a crisscross of metal, plaster, carpet, and space. I was in a building—but I didn't have to stay here.

Someone was watching me. Actually, a lot of people were, but one was looking at me like a predator at its prey. My eyes searched the silent, questioning faces until they found the vivid green eyes of an elf, framed by dark hair. *Quen*, I thought, giving him a name, and then I saw the open door beyond him.

"Watch out!" someone yelled.

I leapt for it, tripping on my dress. Someone fell on me to pin me to the floor. I fought silently, lashing out with my fists. A man was yelling at me to be still. The memory of the clatter of pixy wings was like a knife through my soul, and I felt the last of myself, of Rachel Morgan, vanish, hiding from the heartache.

There was a grunt as my fist found a tender spot, and in the slight release, I clawed for the door. Someone grabbed my wrists, and I cried out when they were wrenched behind my back.

Snarling, I fought to be free, then went still as I lay on the floor, a crafty smile curving over my face. I didn't have to fight with my body; I could fight with my mind.

"Someone strap her!" shrilled a pixy from above. "She's tapping a line!"

"Rachel! Stop!" a woman cried, and I whipped my head at the familiar voice.

"Ivy?" I warbled. My breath hesitated at seeing her sitting slumped against the wall, a hand pressed to her neck and pale from blood loss. Reason tried to force its way through my brain, but a heady feeling of power shoved it out. Men stood between me and the door. The woman on the floor wasn't enough to best the curse's demands.

Shivering, I twisted to sit upright. Latin spilled from me, the words coming from somewhere in my past, my future, from everywhere.

"I'm sorry, Rachel," a gravelly voice said behind me. "We don't have ley line bands."

I turned, savage in my need to hurt someone. A fist swung at me. Stars exploded, lighting my conscious thought, dying away to leave only the blackness of sweet oblivion.

But as my breath left me in a gentle sigh and I fell, I could swear that the drops of warmth upon my face were those of tears, that the shivering arms holding me from the cruel coldness of the tile had the luscious scent of vampire. And someone . . . was singing about blood and daisies.

THIRTY-SIX

I was moving. It was warm, and I was wrapped in a blanket that reeked of cigarettes. Something was on my sore wrist, and since there wasn't an erg of ever-after in me, it seemed someone had found a zip-strip. Probably the one I had in my bag. The thrum of a big engine was soothing, but the sudden shifts of motion made me sick.

"She's awake," Jenks said, his voice holding an incredible amount of worry.

"How can you tell?" came Ivy's voice from the front, and I cracked my eyes. I was in the back of a FIB cruiser, wrapped in a blue FIB blanket and slumped across the backseat.

"Her aura brightened," Jenks snarled. "She's awake."

My breathing quickened. The fog was lifting, making me even more confused. I was thinking everything twice, almost as if trying to filter the world through an interpreter. A wave of fear took me when I realized it was the curse. I wasn't just holding it, it was a part of me. The damned thing was alive?

"Rachel . . ." Ivy said, and I winced. Pain iced through me as a wave of panic I didn't understand rose. I could move, but I couldn't, wrapped up tight.

"Where . . . where are we going?" I managed, then opened my eyes wide when we turned a corner and I almost rolled off the seat. Ivy was up front, and Edden was driving, his neck red and his motions quick.

"The church," Ivy said.

A barrier of plastic separated us. "Why?" I had to get out of here. Everything would be better if I could just run. I knew it.

Her eyes were black in fear. "Because when vampires are afraid, they go home."

The curse inside me was gaining strength, and I wiggled. "I have to get out," I breathed, knowing it was the curse but unable to stop myself.

Jenks squeezed between the ceiling and the divider, and I blinked when he stopped inches from my nose. "Rachel," he coaxed, "look at me. Look at me!"

My darting eyes, following the passing building, returned to him.

"You're okay," he soothed, but his voice was making me nervous. "The EMTs gave you something to relax you. That's why you can't move. It will wear off in about an hour."

It was wearing off *now*. "I have to get out," I said, and Jenks darted back when I threw off the blanket and sat up.

"Whoa!" Edden said from behind the wheel. "Rachel, take it easy. We'll be there in five minutes, and then you can get out."

I wiggled the door latch to no avail. It was a cop car, for God's sake. "Stop the car," I demanded, looking for a way out and not finding it. Panic was settling in. I knew I was safe. I knew I should ease back in the seat and sit. But I couldn't. The curse inside me was stronger than my will. It hurt, and when I moved, the confusion was less.

"Let me out!" I shouted, smacking a fist into the plastic.

Edden swore when Ivy turned in her seat, and with one motion, broke the plastic with a sharp back fist. "Tamwood! What the hell are you doing!" he shouted, the car swerving as he tried to watch the road and Ivy both.

"She's going to hurt herself," she said, clearing the shards and wiggling over the seat.

I pressed into the corner of the car, scared of her. "Stay away from me!" I exclaimed, trying to get control of myself, but I couldn't.

"Rachel, relax," she said, but her hand was reaching for me.

My breath hissing in, I moved to block it.

Ivy moved blindingly fast. She twisted her hand, catching my wrist. Yanking me forward, she wrapped her body around me, hauling me onto her lap.

"Let go!" I shrieked, but she had me firmly.

"Edden," Ivy panted, her lips next to my ear. "Pull over. You have to give her another shot or she's going to hurt herself."

"Keep driving," Jenks said. "I'll do it."

Pulse beating wildly, I struggled. Ivy grunted when my head smacked into her face, but she wouldn't let go.

"Can't you hold her still for a bleeding minute?" Jenks said from in front of me, and I twisted wildly. He wanted to drug me. The little bug wanted to drug me so I couldn't move. I wanted to move. I had to run. It was why I existed, and I couldn't let them take it from me!

"Let. Me. Go!" I grunted.

Edden flipped on the lights and pulled over. Traffic passed as we stopped right on the bridge. The thickset man wedged himself half over the front seat. Grabbing my arm at the wrist and elbow, he held it steady.

"No-o-o-o-o!" I howled, struggling, but he had that one part of me unmoving, and I shrieked at the tiny prick of a needle.

"Hold still, Rache," Jenks said as I gasped for air. "You'll feel better in a minute."

"You son of a fairy whore," I seethed. "I'm going to step on you. I'm going to pluck your wings off and eat them like chips."

"Looking forward to it," the pixy said, hovering at my eye level and peering at me. "How you feel now?"

"I'm going to stuff your stump with poison ivy," I said, blinking as Edden let my arm go. "And buy a terrier to dig you out. And then I'm going to . . . to . . ." *God, this stuff works fast.* But I couldn't remember anymore, and I felt my muscles go limp. The curse went somnolent, and I had a brief instant of clarity before the drug took complete control. Golden sparkles blotted my vision, turning black as I shut my eyes. "I thought you were dead, Jenks. . . ." I said, starting to cry. "Are you okay, Ivy?" My voice shook, and I couldn't open my eyes anymore. "Are you dead? I'm sorry. I messed everything up."

"It's okay, Rache," Jenks said. "You're going to be okay."

I wanted to cry, but I was falling asleep. "Kisten," I slurred. "Edden, go see Kisten. He's at Nick's," and then my lips quit working. Ivy's arms were around me, keeping me from rolling to the floor as Edden twisted back into the front seat. The siren wailed a short bleep, and he pulled back onto the road. I heard Ivy whispering softly in my ear, "Please be okay, Rachel. Please."

The gentle sound of her words became the shushing of my blood in my head, and I listened, hovering on the edge of consciousness, bathed in the oblivion of whatever drug they had given me. It was a relief not to have to fight the curse. I'd made a mistake. I'd made a horrible, immense, irrevocable mistake. And I didn't think there was a way out of it.

It was a shock when I realized my cheek was cold. I wasn't moving anymore either, and the echo of voices came from everywhere, confusing me as I tried to give them meaning where there was none. The warm arms around me slipped away, and I felt dead. I think I was in the church. Yeah, I was lying on the floor like a sacrificial lamb. That was about right.

"I don't know if I can," a soft voice said. It was Ceri, and I tried to move. I really did, but the drug wouldn't let me. The confusion was starting up again. It seemed as if the more awake I was, the more the curse could exert itself. I was beginning to feel anxious and jittery. I had to get up. I had to move.

"I can help," came Keasley's gravelly voice, and an unexpected fear joined my bewilderment. Keasley was my friend, but I couldn't let him touch me. He was a witch. A witch could put me back in prison. A witch had done it before. I wouldn't let it happen. I had finally gotten free, and I wouldn't go back!

I could feel the drug slipping away, but I couldn't move yet, so I pretended to be dead. I could be still as well as run. I'd been still for millennia. And then, when the time was right, I *would run*.

"It's not that I can't do the curse," Ceri said, and I felt someone brush the hair from my eyes. "But her psyche is mixed with it. I don't know if I can lift the curse away without taking a chunk of her. I'm calling Minias. He owes her a favor."

Panic slid through me. Not a demon. He would see. He'd put me back! I couldn't go back. Not now. Not when I had tasted freedom! I had to get *up*!

I winced at the brush of air and the clatter of wings. "She's waking up again," that damned tiny voice shrilled.

A presence smelling of aftershave and shoe polish came close, making the floorboards creak. "She's had enough to put down a horse," said a man, and I tried to pull back when my arm was lifted. "I don't want to give her any more."

"Just do it," Ivy said, and I tried to slow my breathing. "We have to get that thing out of her, and we can't do it if she's fighting us!"

Again the prick of the needle, and I fought it. Blackness swirled, and I was running, running, my pulse strong and my feet moving like water. But it was a dream like all the other times, and I cursed the pain it left behind when a new voice—soft and demanding—lifted through me and stirred me to life.

It was a Were's voice. Low. Strong. Independent. I wanted it so badly I almost choked on my desire to be free. I tried to get his attention. He would take me. He had to take me. He knew how to run. This witch didn't. Not even in her dreams.

"I can legally make life-and-death decisions for her," the Were said, and I heard the rattle of paper. "See? It's right here. And I make the decision that she will exchange the favor you owe her for your helping Ceri. You will make sure Rachel is herself before it's called done, and you will not harm anyone in this room until it is finished and you're gone."

I cracked an eyelid, rejoicing in it. With sight came a confusion of double thought. The witch in my thoughts tried to stop me, but I piled pain and confusion on her, and she ceased thinking. This was my body, and I wanted it to move as I said.

A pair of purple slippers shifted on the hardwood floor, about a yard from me. A shimmering band of black was between us, but I knew the terrible stink of demons, a hundredfold worse than the green reek of elves.

"The mark is between Rachel and me," the demon said, and my hope died. It would put me back in a little box of bone. But I wanted to run. I would be free!

The Were came closer, and I sang to him, but he didn't hear me. "I'm her alpha!" he exclaimed. "Look at this paper. Look at it, you damned demon! I can make this decision for her. It's the law!"

I stiffened at the clatter of wings, hating them. It was that pixy again. Damn it, why wouldn't it leave me alone!

"Guys . . ." the pest said, hovering at my nose and peering into my eyes. "She needs a little more of that happy juice."

The slippered feet padded closer, and someone turned me. I stared up at the demon, feeling my hatred grow. His kind had created me. Created me, bound me, and then trapped me in a little box made of bone that couldn't move.

A sliver of satisfaction lifted through me when the demon's eyes widened and he backed away. "Bless me back to the Turn, she really does have it in her," he whispered, still retracting. "I'll do it," he said, and I struggled to move. He was going to put me back into my cell. I would kill him first! I would kill them all.

"Sleep," the demon commanded, and I shuddered as a blanket of black imbalance shifted over me, and I slept. I had no choice. The demon had willed it, and they had made me.

THIRTY-SEVEN

The room was dim, and I was hot. I could smell my conglomeration of perfumes over an unfamiliar, throat-catching incense, but the heavy weight atop me had the familiar feel of my afghan. The sound of birds coming in my open, dusky window was soothing, and the warm spot beside me said Rex had been here. My curtains were closed, but pre-dawn light filtered in as they moved in the breeze to tell me along with my clock that it was just before sunrise.

I took a slow breath, feeling the air slip in with barely a twinge of pain. Just muscle aches. A chanting heavy with ceremony came from the sanctuary, and the ting of a bell. The scent of incense wasn't vampiric but herbs and minerals. To be quite honest, it stank.

I managed to sit up. My heart quickened, and I put my back to the headboard. Wincing, I touched my neck and the bandage there. It felt okay, and my hand moved to my middle when it rumbled.

My face lost all expression as I realized that the confusion was gone.

I sat on my bed, worriedly remembering Ceri and David. A pulse of fear shot through me. Minias had been here, and I had literally been out of my mind. Where was the curse? Ceri was going to take it out. *Oh, God, Ivy.* She had been savaged by Piscary. But I remembered her in the car. She had been alive. Hadn't she?

I flung the covers off, ready to find out who was here and demand some answers—but when the cooler air hit me, I realized I had a more pressing problem.

"Uh . . . I have to go to the bathroom," I murmured, swinging my feet to the floor, not nearly as fast as I wanted to. A myriad of aches and pains hit me. I was shaky, too. Carefully, I stood with my hand atop the bedpost for balance. Last time I checked, I had been in that gorgeous bridesmaid dress. Now I was in a pair of panties and a long T-shirt. Atop my dresser among my perfumes and sitting on Nick's file were my hairbrush, a tube of antibiotic ointment, and some bandages.

I shuddered when something passed through my aura with the tinkling of silver bells to leave me with the sensation of wintergreen. I'd never felt the like, but it hadn't hurt. More like the pristine pricks of snow on your upturned face. Uneasy, I pulled up my shirt to see the bruises and scrapes in my bedroom mirror. I wasn't dead. Hell wouldn't have me in a Takata STAFF shirt, and heaven would smell better.

I heard the front door shut, then silence. Moving slowly, I headed to the door, feeling every muscle protest. I had to use the bathroom in the worst way. But as my hand reached for the knob, I froze. My nose was tickling. I was going to sneeze.

A thread of alarm unrolled as I took a deep breath, trying to stop it. My hand went to my bandaged neck to hold me in place as a sneeze shook me. Hunched, I sneezed again, then again.

Crap. It's Minias.

"Where's my scrying mirror?" I whispered, panicking as I looked over my dark room. Lurching to my closet, I flung the door open. I had put it in here. Hadn't I?

Pain jolted me as I dropped to my knees, flinging aside boots and magazines as I searched. I sneezed again, grimacing at the throb in my neck. I couldn't see in the darkness of my closet, but a cry of relief passed my lips as my fingers found the cool glass. Staggering to my feet, I backed out and into my room.

My hair swung into my eyes, and I plopped onto my bed. I put my hand on the glass and froze, trying to remember the word. But it was too late.

I spun where I sat at the soft pop of displaced air, springing to my feet with the mirror in hand. Minias stood in the shadowed darkness between me and the closed door, his funny hat atop his brown curls, that exotic purple robe draped over his wide shoulders, and the glint of bare toes catching the faint light.

"No!" I exclaimed, terrified, and Minias raised his hand. I didn't wait to see what he was going to say. Hefting my scrying mirror, I swung it at his head.

It connected, pain reverberating up my arm. Minias yelped, and the mirror shattered into three heavy pieces. Wide-eyed, I fell back, shaking my stinging hand and tapping a line.

Ugly words I didn't understand fell from the demon, and, continuing to backpedal, I made a circle. But it wasn't set from a drawn line. I knew it wouldn't stand.

Striding forward, Minias jabbed one finger into my circle, and it fell.

I retreated to kick him, but he caught my foot before it reached him.

Fear iced through me when he didn't let go, hopping me backward and pushing me onto the bed. "You stupid witch," he said in disdain, then slapped me.

Stars exploded, and I think I passed out, because the next thing I knew, Minias was bending over me. Gasping, I thrust my palm, jamming his nose. The demon fell back, swearing at me. "Get out!" I exclaimed.

"I'd love to, you asinine witchanderthal," the demon said, voice muffled by the hand holding his nose. "Will you relax? I'm not going to hurt you unless you keep hitting me."

My gaze darted to the closed door, and he brought his hand from his nose, glancing at it to see if he was bleeding. He murmured a word of Latin, and a glow from my dresser mirror lightened the predawn gloom. My mouth was dry, and I scooted to the headboard. "Why should I believe you?" My throat hurt as if I'd been yelling, and I held a hand to it.

"You shouldn't." Minias looked at his fingers in the new light, then let the hand drop. "You're the most backward person I know. I'm trying to finish up this arrangement so I can return to my quiet life, and you want to play demon summoner and demon."

Pulse easing, I flicked my gaze to the door and back to him again. Someone had gone outside, and I hadn't heard a car start. It had to be Ivy. If she'd been in the church, she would have heard us and come. "I'm safe?" I said softly so my throat wouldn't hurt, wondering if I could trust him. "We're in the middle of a deal?"

Minias took a firmer stance, his head canted in exasperation and his hands clasped before him. "I'm *trying* to finish it *up*. The way your Were worded it, I'm not done until I'm sure the curse is out of you and you're back to your usual backward self. And until it is, everyone that was in the room is under a measure of protection. So yes, we are in the middle of a deal." His gaze went to mine, and I shivered. "But you're not safe."

I curled my feet up under me, not liking this at all. "I'm not paying for you to come over here," I babbled. "I was trying to answer. You didn't give me enough time to answer."

"Good Lord!" Minias exclaimed, crossing his arms over his chest and leaning back against my dresser. Bottles spilled, and he jerked forward. "It's only a little imbalance," he said, fingers fumbling to stand a bottle upright before he turned to ignore the rest, making me think that for a demon he didn't have much experience in dealing with people. "You make your dates pay for everything, too, don't you?" he added. "No wonder you can't keep a boyfriend."

"Shut up!" I yelled, hurting my throat. *Oh, God. Kisten.* Piscary had been lying. He had to have been. Otherwise I was going to have to decide if I was above revenge or not. And I wasn't good at telling myself I couldn't have something when I wanted it.

Minias's eyes ran over the lines of my room as I sat on my bed in my underwear and a shirt and tried not to shake. "You have such interesting thoughts," he said lightly. "No wonder witches are ephemeral. You drive yourself crazy. You should simply do what you want without the soul-searching." His goat-slitted eyes fixed on me, and I felt my stomach drop. "It will be easier in the long run, Rachel Mariana Morgan."

My pulse had slowed, and I was starting to believe I was going to survive this. "Rachel is fine," I said, not liking him saying my middle name.

A single eyebrow rose. "You seem to be all right. Any urges to run under the moon?"

Refusing to shrink away, I let him get close enough that the scent of burnt amber settled deep in me. "No. Where's the focus?"

"Feel the need to tear out people's throats?" he asked.

"Just yours. Who has the focus? You took it out, where is it?"

He straightened, and I realized again how tall he was. "Ceri took it out, not me. And if there had been a way to help her do it wrong, I would have."

"Just tell me who has the damned focus!" I exclaimed, and he snickered.

"Your alpha," he said, and my stomach knotted. *David? We're back to square one.*

"It settled in him as if it wanted to go," the demon added, and my heart seemed to stop. David didn't possess the focus; it possessed him? Like it had been inside of me?

"Where is he?" I said, springing off my bed. But there was nowhere to go.

"How should I know?" Minias lifted a bottle and sniffed the top, recoiling. "He's handling it better than you are. It was made for a Were, not a witch. Taking it in you was stupid. Like dropping a chunk of sodium metal into a bucket of water." The bottle hit the dresser with a clink.

I shifted uneasily, not knowing if I should believe him. "He's okay?"

"Better than," Minias drawled, his fingers still toying with my perfumes. "Giving the focus to the Weres is going to turn around and bite you, but it did accomplish what you wanted." His goat-slitted eyes focused on mine, and my tension rose. "The Weres are happy, and the vampires think it's destroyed. Right?"

Right. "I'm fine," I said tartly, my fear coming out as cheek. "You can go now."

"The elf did it," he said, shaking his head. "Al has more drive and talent to teach than I gave him credit for. He taught her extremely well to be able to untwist a curse like that and leave you . . . relatively unscathed. No wonder he kept her for a thousand years."

Face scrunched up, he smelled another bottle and set it down. "Al is furious," he said casually, and even my false bravado vanished. "They caught him seconds after you threw him back to our side of the lines. He's in his own personal hell. And you still owe him a favor." Sniffing a third perfume, he looked at me from under a lowered brow. "I wonder what it will be?"

"I'm fine. Get out," I repeated.

"May I have this?" he asked, holding the bottle upright.

"If you leave, you can have them all."

The bottle vanished from the cradle of his fingertips. "One last thing," he said, an odd glint in his eyes. "The focus?"

I stiffened, a trickle of fear growing in the pit of my being. "Yeah?"

"It wasn't what Newt was looking for when she tore your church apart."

He began to vanish, and I stepped forward, frightened. "What was she looking for?"

I haven't the slightest idea, echoed in my thoughts.

"Wait!" I shouted. "Does she remember me? Minias! Does she remember me?"

I searched the night for sound and my mind for thoughts, but he was gone. Another instant and the light he had set glowing in my mirror faded to nothing.

Crap. What had she been looking for if it hadn't been the focus?

The thump of the front door closing echoed through the brightening air, and I looked to the front of the church. A car started, and tension brought me straight when I recognized Ivy's soft footsteps in the hall. "Ivy . . ." I said, then put a hand to my throat when it hurt.

I jumped when my bedroom door was flung open and a gray shaft of light spilled in. "Rachel," Ivy said, her features lost in shadow.

"Last time I checked," I said, deciding that mentioning Minias wouldn't help anyone.

"You're okay," she whispered, coming in and gripping my arm. "It's you. Right? Just you?" Her eyes were wide from the shadow, and there was a bandage on her neck. Seeing my blank stare, she took me in a surprising hug. "Thank you, God."

My tension, born of surprise, vanished and I relaxed, my face next to hers as I took in her scent as if it were water. I didn't care if it was chock-full of pheromones meant to relax me, to make it easier for her to bite me. That's not why she was holding me. She had been worried. And she was alive. A dead vampire wouldn't have cared if I was myself or not. Ivy was alive. *Maybe Kisten is, too.* Please let Piscary have lied to me.

"It's me," I said, remembering Ivy and Edden grappling with me in the back of a car when I'd been lost to the curse. "Uh, I have to go to the bathroom."

Ivy stepped back. "You scared me," she said.

"I scared myself," I said, catching myself against the bedpost as I scuffed forward.

"Jenks!" Ivy yelled when my bare feet edged into the hallway. "She's okay! She's up!"

"What is that stench?" I said, sniffing the distastefully harsh scent of bad incense.

"We got the church unblasphemed," she said, following me out. "The guy just left. I think you embarrassed him, so he did some research. All he had to do was find and replace the original scrap of holy cloth that the sanctity was focused on. Jenks's kids found it, and the rest was easy."

I nodded, thinking that odd sensation I'd felt when waking up must have been the blasphemy falling away. Then I wondered what the guy was going to do with the fouled cloth. Put it in the ever-after, maybe? That's what I'd do. I wobbled three more steps to the bathroom, then turned. "You're alive, right?" I asked, remembering the EMTs stopping their efforts.

From my doorway Ivy laughed. I must have really scared her. I'd never seen her show so much emotion. Clearly *happy*, she smiled. "I'm alive," she said, looking beautiful with her eyes wet. "Piscary didn't . . ." She took a breath. "I passed out when Piscary gave me enough vamp saliva to stop my heart, but the FIB guys kept me alive and the EMTs gave me an antitoxin. I never died," she said happily. "I still have my soul."

Good, I thought. Something had gone right for a change. I was afraid to ask her about Kisten. "I have to go to the bathroom," I murmured, the situation turning critical.

"Oh!" she said, suddenly embarrassed. "Sure. I'll, um . . ."

Her thought was cut short when Jenks blew in from the back rooms. "Rache!" he shrilled, shedding gold sparkles. "You okay? Tink's bordello, you're one wild woman. I've never *seen* anyone do the things you did. Who taught you to swear in Latin?"

He was flitting madly between Ivy and me, and I put a hand to the wall so I didn't lose my balance trying to watch him. "It was the curse, not me," I said.

"How's your knees?" he said, dropping down to look at them, and my head snapped up when he darted to the ceiling. "You hit them pretty hard when Ceri took you down."

"I don't remember that either," I said, crossing my legs and praying. "Could you get out of my way? I have to go to the bathroom."

"Holy crap," Jenks said, rising up to follow Ivy and me. "I thought you were going to kill Edden. He's the one who gave you the black eye."

So that's why my face feels puffy, I thought, shuffling down the hallway. "What day is it?" I asked, wondering how long it had been since I ate.

"Monday." Ivy was hovering tight to my heels. "Wait. It's Tuesday now."

"Oooooh, the spirits did it all in one night," I said, squinting as I flicked on my bathroom light. My eyes hurt. I turned to find them staring at me as if I'd said something scary. "What?" I protested, and Jenks landed on Ivy's shoulder.

"You sure you're okay?"

"Yes, but if I don't get into this bathroom, I'm going to make a puddle."

Jenks took flight, and Ivy took three steps back. "You want something to eat?" she said, and I hesitated in my motion to shut the door.

"Anything but Brimstone," I said, and her face flushed guiltily. The door closed between us, and I put both hands on the washer, leaning over it and shaking. It wasn't blood loss. And I wasn't beaten up that badly. I was fatigued. Something—maybe someone—had fought a battle in me, and I didn't remember any of it. The focus was gone, so it had lost. *I* was the one picking myself up off the battlefield and hobbling to the next fight.

I hoped it would be easier than this last one.

Pushing myself upright, I went to the mirror. My hand moved to peek behind the bandage on my neck, then dropped. I didn't want to know just yet. Turning my head, I looked myself over, deciding that it wasn't bad. A complexion amulet would take care of the black circle under my eye, and the fat lip made me look pouty. There was a bruise on my shin and another on my hip just below where the T-shirt ended. My back hurt when I bent over to check out my knees, but nothing would need more than a day or two to return to normal. It was almost a disappointment. Having been a demon curse, however brief, should leave some kind of mark. A streak of silver hair, or bewitching eyes. Maybe crows on one's roof or a hound from hell at your heel. But what do I get? Blowing out my breath, I stood and squinted at my reflection.

A black eye. Swell.

Ivy's voice murmured as she talked on the phone, and after taking care of my most urgent need, I decided a shower could wait until after I got a few questions answered and my stomach filled. The dryer contained a pair of jeans instead of Kisten's clothes, so with a new depression, I tucked my STAFF shirt in, invoked a complexion charm, ran a toothbrush over my teeth, and called it good. The smell of coffee sifting in under the door made me feel ill, I was so hungry.

Movements slow from the expectation of bad news, I headed out. The bright light of a new day spilled into the hallway from the kitchen. This was the third morning I'd gotten up at dawn instead of going to bed, and I was tired of it.

"Rachel just woke up," came Ivy's voice before I had gone two steps, and I slowed. She wasn't on the phone; we had someone in our kitchen. "She's not talking to anyone until she gets a chance to eat and catch her breath, and she's not talking to your shrink, so you can just get back into your cruiser and the hell back to the FIB where you belong."

My eyebrows rose, and I hastened forward. *What's Glenn doing here?*

Shit. *Kisten,* I thought miserably, answering my own question. *He's dead.*

"Felps wasn't at Sparagmos's apartment," I heard Edden say, and my reality shifted. Not only was Kisten's death still uncertain, but this wasn't Glenn, it was his dad. I didn't know if that was better or worse. "We need to find him, and Rachel might be able to help," he finished.

"Give the woman some peace!" Jenks said. "Piscary said he was dead. Find him on your own. The I.S. isn't going to stop you. They don't care."

I pushed into motion, ready to try anything if it would lead to Kisten's still being alive. "But if he's alive, he might be hurt," I said as I entered, and Edden turned from his position at the back of the kitchen. There was someone else with him, looking spare next to Edden's squat bulk, and my bare feet squeaked to a stop. *Edden had brought the FIB's shrink out with him?*

Edden glanced at the young man beside him. Ignoring the threat of Ivy standing before the sink with her arms crossed, Edden came forward, his brow pinched in worry. He was in his usual khaki slacks and white shirt, and the gun in his shoulder holster said he was working. "Rachel," he said, glad to see me. "You look a lot better."

"Thanks." I blinked in surprise when he gave me a hug. The scent of

Old Spice puffed up, and I couldn't help my smile when he awkwardly dropped back. "I didn't hurt you, did I?"

He smiled and rubbed his elbow. "Don't worry about it. It wasn't you."

I exhaled in relief, though still feeling guilty, and I looked over the kitchen for anything to eat. Nothing was cooking, but the coffeemaker was gurgling its last. The cake had been frosted, and it sat on the counter as a sad testament of how things were supposed to be. Depressed, I sank down at my spot at the table. "Kisten wasn't at the apartment?" I asked, desperate hope almost painful as it settled in around my heart, and I glanced at the other guy, now shifting awkwardly. "Jenks said he called to say he was going underground. And Piscary has lied before. If Kisten might be alive, I'll do anything."

Edden's friend went to speak, changing his mind when Ivy pushed away from the sink and slunk to her chair before her computer—her safe spot. Jenks stayed at the window, standing on the sill where he could keep an eye on his kids. I hadn't realized how noisy they were at sunrise.

"Edden thinks human psychology can bring back your memory," Ivy said, scowling. "Human science can't best a witch charm. It's only going to tear you up, Rachel."

Ignoring her, Edden turned to the man, and he came forward with a hesitant confidence. "Dr. Miller, this is Rachel Morgan. Rachel, I want you to meet Dr. Miller, our psychiatrist."

I leaned forward in my chair and shook his hand. The hope that Kisten might be alive was desperate and painful, and the color of the amulet Dr. Miller was wearing shifted from a deep purple to white. "Nice to meet you," I said, indicating he should sit down, and he and Edden took two chairs to my right.

The young man had a nice grip, which wasn't surprising if he was the FIB's shrink. What did surprise me was the slight lifting of everafter that had tried to pull through me when we touched. He was human—I didn't sense any redwood coming off him at all, and he worked for the FIB—but he could do ley line magic. And his amulet was metallic—clearly a ley line charm.

He was taller than me, and his brown shoes made an odd statement against his gray slacks and gray-pinstriped white shirt. His black hair was cut to an easy style. His frame was spare, and he was wearing wire-rimmed glasses before his brown eyes.

Glasses? I mused, No one wears glasses unless . . .

My suspicion was borne out when Dr. Miller tucked them away with a grimace. Crap, they were for seeing auras without tapping into one's second sight, which humans generally couldn't do unaided without a lot of practice. Great. Nothing like a good first impression.

The amulet he wore shifted to a reddish gray, and the FIB's psychiatrist gave me an apologetic smile as he scooted his chair in. "It's a pleasure to meet you, Ms. Morgan," he said from between Edden and me. "Call me Ford."

Jenks's wings clattered, and he flew to land on the table, standing with his hands on his hips so the hilt of his garden sword showed. "That thing reads emotions, doesn't it?" he said belligerently. "Is that how you do your job? You use that to know if people are telling the truth or not? Rachel isn't lying. If she says she doesn't remember, she doesn't remember. She'd want to find Kisten if she could."

Ford glanced down at it again, taking it off from around his neck and setting it on the table. "The amulet isn't reacting to her, it's reacting to me. Sort of. And I'm not here to find out if Ms. Morgan is lying. I'm here to help reconstruct what I can of her artificially muted memory with the intent to find Mr. Felps."

I felt a stab of guilt, and his ley line amulet flashed a brief gray-blue once more.

"If she allows it," he added, fingering the metallic disk. "The longer we wait, the less she will remember. We are under a time constraint, especially if Mr. Felps is in trouble."

Ivy's eyes were closed as she struggled to hide her emotions. "Rachel, he's dead," she whispered. "For the FIB to play on your hope to make their job of finding him easier is wrong."

"You don't know he's dead," Edden protested, and a chill took me when she opened her eyes. They were black with pain.

"I'm not going to listen to this," she said.

I stiffened when she rose and walked out. Jenks hovered uncertainly, then buzzed out after her. The smell of the coffee pulled at me, and I went to pour myself a mug, filling two more for Ford and Edden. The first gulp hit me like a balm, doing as much as the soft breeze coming in the window to soothe me. Maybe there was something to this up-at-dawn stuff.

"What do I do?" I said as I put the coffee before the two men and sat.

Ford's smile was brief but sincere. "If you would put this on?"

The amulet settled into my hand, and I felt the hum of ever-after running through it, tugging on me as if trying to pull it from my fingertips. "What does it do?"

He hadn't let go of the charm yet, and feeling his fingers slide against mine, I looked up in almost shocked surprise. His lips quirked in a smile when the amulet in my hand turned to a delicate lavender. I was starting to see a pattern here.

"Your friend was correct. It's a visual show of your emotions," he said, and I cringed. I could guess what lavender meant, and I forced my thoughts to remain puritan pure as I looped it over my head. Unlike an earth-charm amulet, this one only had to be within my aura to work, not touching skin.

"But you said it was responding to you, not me."

A brief look of pain passed over his features. "It is."

My eyes widened. "You mean you can feel other people's emotions? Naturally? I've never heard of that before. What are you? You don't smell like a witch."

Chuckling, Edden took his coffee and retreated to the corner of the kitchen, pretending to watch Jenks's kids in order to give us some privacy.

Ford shrugged. "Human, I guess. My mother was the same way. She died from it. I've never heard of anyone else like me. I'm trying to find a way to make it work for me instead of against me. The amulet is for you, not me, so you know exactly what I'm feeling from you. The intensity of emotion is shown by brightness and the type of emotion by color."

I started to get a sick feeling. "But you can feel my emotions whether I'm wearing the amulet or not?" I asked, and when he nodded, I added, "Then why am I wearing it?"

Edden shifted nervously at the window. I knew he wanted us to get on with it.

"So that when we're done and you take it off, you have the illusion that I'm not listening anymore."

Jenks came in right about then, changing his mind about landing on my shoulder at the last moment to park it on Edden's shoulder when he saw my look. It made sense, even if it was a lie. "That's got to be hell," I said. "Someone ought to make a muffler for you."

Ford's expression blanked. "Do you think you can?"

I shrugged. "I don't know."

His brown eyes were distant, and the amulet around my neck went pearl gray. Taking a deep breath, he brought his attention back.

I couldn't help but wonder at the misery of sensing everyone's emotions all the time. *Poor guy,* I thought, and the amulet burst into blue. His lips parting, Ford blinked at me, clearly feeling my pity for him. The amulet shifted to red, and my face flamed to match it. Embarrassed, I reached to take the amulet off. "This isn't going to work," I said.

Ford's hands enveloped mine, stopping me. "Please, Ms. Morgan," he said earnestly, and I swear I could feel the amulet warming in our hands. "This is a tool. The reality is that people are far more adept at reading facial expressions than this amulet can indicate. It's simply a way to make a data point of something as nebulous as emotions."

I sighed, my entire body easing, and the amulet peeping between our fingers went a neutral gray. "Call me Rachel."

He smiled. "Rachel." His hands left mine to show that the disk was a silvery purple. Not the purple of anger, as when I thought of the I.S., but lavender. Ford liked me, and when I smiled, he went red in embarrassment.

Jenks snickered, and Edden harrumphed. "Can we get on with this?" the FIB captain complained.

Letting the amulet drop to where I couldn't see it, I straightened, suddenly nervous. "Do you really think Kisten is still alive?"

His brow knitting, Edden crossed his arms over his chest and leaned back. "I don't know. But the faster we find him, the better."

Nodding, I settled into the chair and glanced at Ford for direction. I'd been to family counseling with my mom when my dad died, but this was different.

Ford angled the chair so that his legs ran perpendicular to the table, rather than under it. "Tell me what you remember," he said simply, hands folded.

Jenks's wings increased in pitch, then went silent. I took a sip of coffee, closing my eyes as the liquid slipped down. It was easier if I didn't look at the amulet. Or Ford's eyes. I didn't like the idea that I couldn't hide my emotions from him.

"I left him at Nick's apartment to wash his clothes," I said, feeling a pang of heartache. "It was a few hours until sunset, and I had to move the car before it was recognized. I was going to go back."

My eyes opened. If Piscary was right, I did go back.

"And you don't remember anything after?"

I shook my head. "Not until I woke up in Ivy's chair. I was sore. My foot hurt." *My inner lip was cut.*

Ford's eyes went to my hand clutching my upper right arm, and I forced my hand down. Even I was starting to realize it was my subconscious trying to tell me something.

"Don't try to remember, then," he said, and I felt some tension leave me. "Think about your foot. You hurt yourself, and that's hard to wash away completely. Who did you kick?"

My breath exhaled slowly. I closed my eyes, and my foot seemed to throb. *Not who, but what,* I thought suddenly. My hair had been in my mouth, and it blocked my vision, making me smack into the archway to the door instead of the handle. The damn door was so freaking narrow, and it hadn't been my fault. The floor had moved, throwing me off balance.

I felt my face go blank, and I opened my eyes. Ford had leaned forward, knowing that I had remembered something, and his eyes seemed to demand an answer. The amulet between us glowed a slurry of purple, black, and gray—anger and fear. I didn't remember the night, but there was only one place Kisten would go with narrow doors where the floor would move.

"Kisten's boat," I said, standing up. "Edden, you're driving."

THIRTY-EIGHT

We sped down the paved road, hitting the potholes caused by last year's frost and snowplows. The back roads outside of the Hollows didn't get much attention as the cities grew larger and the country grew wilder. Edden had called in support, and we quickly found out that Kisten's boat wasn't at Piscary's, but a FIB officer on patrol remembered seeing a boat matching its description downriver at an old warehouse dock.

That's where we were headed, lights on and sirens off, speeding through the outskirts of the Hollows and beyond until we were at the edges of where even I wouldn't go after dark. It wasn't that the neighborhood was bad. It was that there was no neighborhood at all. Not after forty years of abandonment. Entire neighborhoods had been bulldozed under and left to go fallow when the survivors of the Turn fled to the cities. Cincy had been no exception.

Trees arched overhead, and I could tell that the river was close by the winding road and the occasional glimpses of silver water. I was up front with Edden, and Ivy was in the backseat with Ford. That she wanted to come had surprised me, until I realized her earlier words had been meant to quash her hope that Kisten might still be alive. Or undead. Or something.

Jenks was with her, working hard to keep her distracted and calm. It wasn't working, if her black eyes and Ford's growing nervousness were any indication. Putting them together might not have been a good idea, but I didn't want to sit next to him either.

"There!" I exclaimed, pointing to the outline of an abandoned brick building peeking from behind huge, ancient trees. It had to be the place. We hadn't seen anything but empty lots framed by large trees for half a mile. I tried to quell my nervousness even as I searched my feelings for having been here before. Nothing looked familiar. The hot morning sun glinted on the leaves and the river as we slowed and pulled into the weed-choked gravel drive. My heart gave a painful thud when I saw Kisten's boat.

"That's it," I said, fumbling for the door even before the car stopped. "That's the *Solaris*." Jenks left Ivy, hovering as I undid my belt.

"Rachel, wait." It was Edden, and I scowled when he hit the button and the lock engaged. The Crown Victoria rocked to a halt, and he put it in park. Ivy tried her door, but it was a cop car and wouldn't open from the inside even if Edden hadn't locked it. "I mean it," he said as a stuffy silence filled the car, broken by the agitated hum of Jenks's wings. "You're going to stay in the car until backup gets here. There could be anyone in that building."

Jenks snickered and darted under the dash to flip Edden off from the other side of the windshield. I glanced at the two-way radio and the chatter coming from it. It sounded as if the nearest person was five minutes away. "If it's undead vampires you're worried about, they won't be coming out for a suntan," I said as I manually unlocked the door and lurched out. "And if it's anyone else, I'm going to kick their ass."

Ivy scooted into Ford's space, and while the man sat wide-eyed and scrunched in the corner, she kicked the door. The lock snapped, and she slid out, unruffled and moving with the eerie grace of those that belong to the night. Jenks was gone, and we followed him to the boat with a grim determination. We were halfway there when Edden caught up.

"Rachel, stop."

Ivy's expression was awful, and after a single glance that showed the depth of her fear, she continued without me.

"Get your hand off me," I exclaimed, voice loud with misplaced anger as I yanked away from his grip. "I'm a professional, not some distraught girlfriend." Well, I was that too, but I knew how to act at a crime scene. "You never would have found him if not for me. He might need my help, or are you admitting you manipulated me, knowing he was dead already?"

Edden's face creased up in the bright light, and it made him look old. Behind him Ford sat leaning against the front of the car. I wondered what his range for reading emotions was. I hoped it was less than the twenty feet that separated us now.

"If he's dead . . ." Edden said.

"I can handle myself!" I shouted, the fear that he was right making me reckless. "I'm going in there! It's not a crime scene until we know there's a crime, so get a grip!"

Ivy had reached the boat and swung up the four-foot height to the deck in an enviable motion. I jogged to catch up, my swollen eye hurting from under the complexion charm and my foot throbbing. "Kisten?" I shouted, hoping for his voice. "Kisten, you here?"

From the corner of my sight, Ford remained leaning against the car, his head bowed.

Feeling awkward, I levered myself up onto the deck. Different muscles protested, and I got from my knees to my feet, tossing my hair out of my eyes. Ivy was already below the deck. Jenks still hadn't shown, and I didn't know if that was good or bad. I shivered at the dampness of the dew-wet deck, trying to remember being here. Nothing. Nothing at all.

The boat hardly moved with my weight, and I half slid to the cockpit door, grasping for handholds. "Ivy?" I called as I went belowdecks, fear winding between my soul and reason when she didn't answer. The silence ate away at my hope like bitter acid, drop by drop, breath by breath. If Kisten was conscious, he would have answered. If he was undead, he would be dead from the sun unless he had made it to the warehouse. Either option was bad.

It was quiet as I passed through the kitchen, only the sounds of my heartbeat and a plane high overhead. Ivy would have said something if she'd found him. The smear of blood on the high window looking out over the far shore shook me. A handprint.

"Kisten?" I whispered, but I knew it wasn't his. And it wasn't mine. It was his killer's.

The tears pricked. I couldn't remember anything. Why in hell had I done this to myself?

The sight of the splintered door between the kitchen and the living room brought me to a breathless halt. My foot started to throb, and my heart raced. I couldn't look away. I knew. . . .

My breath came back in a gasp when Edden's bulk landed outside the window, jarring me. The boat scarcely moved under his weight either. As if in a dream, I stepped to the door, reaching to touch it to make sure it was real. Sharp, smooth slivers brushed my fingertips, and I felt dizzy.

The light was eclipsed, and I didn't turn when I felt Edden and Ford fill the doorway.

"I did this," I whispered, my hand falling. I didn't remember it, but my body did, my foot throbbing and my pulse fast. I stared at the shattered frame. My foot had broken the doorframe.

Gaze unfocused, I leaned against the cupboard for balance as remembered panic took me. I remembered crying. I remembered my hair in my mouth, and trying to escape. My arm had hurt so badly I couldn't manage the door, so I'd kicked it open. My eyes closed, and I felt it all over again. Scattered images were all that was left. I had kicked the door in, and then the back of my head had met a wall.

I touched the back of my head as it began to hurt. There had been someone else here. And at the faint hint of unfamiliar, vampiric incense that still lingered, I knew it had to have been Kisten's killer. It had happened here, and I had been a part of it.

"I did this," I said, turning to the two men. "I remember doing this."

Edden's face was tight, and he held a drawn pistol pointed at the ceiling. Ford was behind him looking like the professional psychiatrist he was, out of place and gathering information I wouldn't want his opinion on.

The soft sound of dragonfly wings brought my tear-streaked face around to see Jenks, his wings sparkling in the light coming in the low windows.

"Rache, you better come in here."

Oh, God.

"Ivy?" I called out, and Edden shoved his way into the cramped space.

"Get behind me," he said, face grim, and I pushed through the broken frame before him, desperate to find her. Either Kisten was dead and no threat, or he was undead and destroyed from the sun, or his killer was still here, or Ivy had found Kisten and she needed me.

The living room was clean and empty, smelling of water and sunshine through the open windows. Pulse fast, I followed Jenks into the hall, past the bathroom, and to the back bedroom. The rasp of Ivy's ragged breath sent a chill through me, and I jerked from Edden's grasp only to stop dead just inside the door.

Ivy stood alone with her back to the dresser, arms over her middle, and her head bowed. Before her, on the floor slumped upright against the bed, was Kisten.

My eyes closed, and a lump filled my throat. Grief slammed into me, and I staggered to stand against the doorframe. *He was dead.* And it hadn't been easy.

Edden's soft curse behind me cut through my awareness, and I took a gasping breath. "You son of a bitch," I whispered to no one. "You son of a bitch bastard." I was far too late.

Kisten's barefoot body was dressed in a clean pair of jeans and a shirt I'd never seen. His neck and body had been savaged, and his arms and torso were torn as if he had tried to defend himself. Silvered blue eyes told me he had died undead, but the blood pooled in his legs and heels said that he hadn't been drained, simply killed twice. Dark blood matted his once-bright hair, and his smile was gone.

I took another breath, trying to keep upright, though the room was starting to waver.

"I'm sorry, Rachel," Edden said softly, his hand landing on my shoulder in a show of comfort. "I know he meant a lot to you. This wasn't your fault."

At that the tears started to dribble out, one by one. "Kisten?" I warbled, not wanting to believe he was gone. I had been here. I had tried to keep him alive. I must have. But I hadn't been able to, and the guilt must have been why I'd tried to forget.

I took a helpless step closer, wanting to fall on my knees and pull him to me. "I'm sorry, Kisten." I started to cry in earnest. "I must have tried. I must have."

From behind me in the hall, Ford said, "You did."

Both Ivy and I turned. He looked ragged as both of our personal hells resonated in him. "It's in your thoughts," he said, and I just about lost it. Giving up, I sank to my knees before Kisten, the tears flowing unchecked as I tried to arrange his shirt collar to hide his ravaged skin.

"I don't remember," I gushed. "I don't remember any of it. Tell me what happened."

Ford's voice was strained. "I don't know. But you're feeling guilt and remorse. There's hatred, but not at him. Someone made you forget."

I looked up, wanting to believe. Everything was blurry, unreal.

"You didn't forget because you couldn't handle it," he said, guilt in his voice for having labeled me weak. "Someone made you forget against your will. It's all there in your emotions."

Blinking fast, I tried to clear my sight. The pain in my chest wouldn't go away and let me think. Someone had been here besides me. Someone else knew what had happened. Someone had forced me to forget? Why?

A new fear pulled my attention to Ivy, still standing apart and miserable as Kisten lay cold and dead between us. She hadn't wanted Ford to help me to remember. Had she . . . had she killed him because he'd bitten me?

"I don't remember," Ivy whispered as if knowing my thoughts, her head bowed and arms wrapped around herself to keep from falling apart. "I could have. I don't remember."

Edden put his weapon back in the holster, snapping it shut. Arms crossed aggressively, he took a firm stance. I stood, torn between anger at him and fear for Ivy.

"She wouldn't do it," I said, frightened, and I went to give her a shake. "You wouldn't do that, Ivy. Look at me! You loved him!"

She shook her head, her black hair hiding her face.

"She was Piscary's scion," Edden said. "She would if he told her to."

"She loved Kisten!" I exclaimed, appalled and scared. "She wouldn't do it!"

Edden took a harder line. "Word on the street is she'd kill him if he touched your blood. Did he?"

Guilt seemed to stop my heart, and I looked frantically for a way out. Jenks stood on the dresser, miserable. We were in the same room where I'd bitten Kisten in a blood passion I scarcely knew how to comprehend. He hadn't bitten me, but it didn't seem to matter now.

Ivy brought her head up at my silence. Her beautiful face was twisted in pain. "I might have done it," she whispered. "I don't remember. Everything up to Piscary attacking you is a . . . a jumbled nightmare. I think someone told me you tasted Kisten. I can't remember if someone told me or if I made it up." Tear-wet eyes rose to mine, framed by black hair iced in gold. A terrible fear lay in her gaze. "I might have. I might have done it, Rachel!"

My stomach was in knots, but the terror was gone, and in a sudden surge I understood. She hadn't wanted to come out here, afraid she might find she'd killed him. She hadn't wanted Ford to help me remember for the same reason. Someone had killed Kisten, but I knew to the bottom of my soul that it hadn't been Ivy, though centuries of evolution and conditioning made her want to.

"You didn't kill him," I said, putting my arms around her to help her believe. Her muscles tensed, and she started to silently tremble. "You didn't. I know it, Ivy. You wouldn't."

"I don't remember," she sobbed, admitting her fear. "I don't remember anything but being angry and confused and out of control." She moved, and I let go so she could pull her head up. "Did you bite him?" she whispered, her eyes begging me to say no.

I was glad I wasn't wearing that amulet so at least I could pretend Ford wasn't watching the drama play out. If I said yes, she would assume she had killed Kisten. But to lie was not possible. "I bit him," I said, the guilty words coming quick so I could get it out before she decided she'd killed him to end the pain inside her. "He gave me a pair of caps for my birthday. He knew you'd made a pass at me. Looking back on it, I'm sure I did it to convince him that I wasn't going to leave him. That he was important to me."

Ivy moaned and pulled away.

"Damn it, Ivy!" I exclaimed, wiping at the slowly leaking tears. "You wouldn't kill him for that! You loved him! Piscary never touched that part of you. He couldn't! You were never his. He only thought you were! Kisten said Piscary never asked you to kill me, but Piscary did, didn't he?" I said, watching her. I could hardly breathe, and her misery hesitated as she tried to remember. "He told you to kill me, and you said no. You wouldn't kill me for Piscary, and you wouldn't kill Kisten for him either. I know it, Ivy. That's why you shut yourself off. You didn't kill him. *You didn't.*"

For six heartbeats she simply stared, thoughts sifting through her. Behind her I saw Ford drop his head into his hand, trying not to eavesdrop—but hell, that was his job. She took a deep breath, and all her muscles went limp. "Kisten," she finally breathed, falling to her knees to touch him, and I knew she believed. Her hands went to his hair, and she started to cry.

The first heavy cry was her undoing, and proud, stoic Ivy finally let go. Huge, racking sobs shook her shoulders. Tears for his death, yes, but for herself as well, and I felt my own eyes fill and spill over as I dropped down to hold her beside his cold stillness. Kisten was the only person who had known the depth of depravity to which Piscary had sunk them, the heights of ecstasy. The breath-stealing power he had granted them, and the terrible price he extracted for it. The only one who had forgiven her for what she was, who understood who she wanted to be. He was gone, and there'd be no one else who could possibly understand. Not even me.

"I'm sorry," I whispered, rocking her while her ragged sobs broke the silence as we sat on the floor of the tiny bedroom in a backwater tributary of the Ohio River. "I know what he was to you. We'll find out who did this. We will find out, and then we'll track them down."

And still she wept, as if her grief would never end.

And then grief came for me as well, cold and hard, grief defined by bright blue eyes and the smile I loved so much and would never see again. As my hand found his, bitter salt tears spilled from my eyes, in sorrow and pain and regret that I had so utterly failed him.

THIRTY-NINE

Two weeks later

I jiggled the handle of the canvas bag to the crook of my arm so I could open the door to the church, squinting up at the VAMPIRIC CHARMS sign glowing wetly. Ivy wanted ice cream, and since she didn't want it enough to go out in the rain for it, I had been suckered into it. I'd do just about anything to see her smile again. It had been a rough two weeks. 'Course, we needed cat food, too, and dish soap. And we were out of coffee. It was scary how fast my quick run to the store had turned into a three-bag trip.

The door to the church creaked open, and I slid inside. Leaning against the closed door for balance, I wedged my shoes off. It was dark, seeing as the moon wasn't up and the clouds were thick. I paused just inside the sanctuary, flicking the light switch with my elbow. Nothing.

"Crap on toast," I muttered, smacking it a few more times just for fun. "Jenks!" I shouted. "The fuse in the sanctuary blew again!"

I didn't really expect an answer, but where was Ivy? She had to have noticed.

Shifting the bags awkwardly, I headed for the kitchen. Three steps in, I froze. I could smell unfamiliar vampires. Lots of them. And old smoke. And beer.

"Shit," I whispered, adrenaline whipping through me.

"Now!" someone yelled, and the lights flashed on.

Panicked, I dropped the bags and fell into a fighting stance, blinded by the sudden glare.

"Surprise!" came a chorus of voices from the front of the church, and I spun, heart pounding. "Happy birthday!"

I stared, my mouth hanging open and my hands in fists as the pint of Choco-Chunk rolled to Ivy's feet. She was actually smiling, and I slowly stood straight. My heart was still hammering away, and Jenks was making darting loops from me to her, shedding a brilliant gold.

"We got her!" he was shouting, and what looked like all his kids took up the refrain, filling the air with color and sound. "We got her good, Ivy. Look at her. Not a clue!"

Shocked, I fumbled for the bags. David, Keasley, and Ceri were at the couch, and Ivy was standing by the far light switch. Everyone was smiling, but then, as Jenks had said, they'd gotten me good.

There were no vampires here other than Ivy, and the only drink I could see were the three two-liters of soda on the coffee table. The smell of vampire, cigarettes, and old beer was coming from the battered pool table now set up to one side of the sanctuary. It hadn't been there when I had left. Seeing it, I felt my throat close up. It had been Kisten's. "But my birthday was last month," I said, still confused.

Ceri came forward. There was a cone hat on her head, but she somehow made it look more dignified than one had any right to expect. "We didn't forget," she said, giving me a quick hug. "We were distracted. Happy birthday, Rachel."

I honestly didn't know what to say. Keasley had on a hat, too, and when he saw me look at him, he took it off. The pixies, though, kept theirs on, darting about like mad.

My gaze went to the pool table, and tears pricked at my eyes. From there I looked to the surrounding faces. Under their smiles they were pleading, almost desperate for me to pretend everything was normal. That life was getting back to what it should be. That I wasn't missing a huge piece of myself. That there was one person that should be here who wasn't, and never would be again.

So I smiled.

"Wow," I said, coming to take the ice cream Ivy had picked up off the floor. "This is great! And yeah, I'm surprised." I let the bags of groceries slip to the couch and took off my coat. "I really don't believe this. Thanks, guys."

Ceri gave my upper arm a squeeze in support, and then her expression blanked. "I forgot the cake!" she exclaimed, green eyes going wide. "I left it on my table!"

"There's cake?" I said, wincing when Jenks flicked on the stereo and Marilyn Manson's "Personal Jesus" blared out before he turned it down. Ceri must have made it, because we'd thrown the old one out. I hadn't been able to eat it while Kisten lay in the morgue, and now that he was cremated and in Ivy's room, I felt no different. But tonight other people's feelings were involved, and I realized I was going to have to eat Ceri's cake or risk hurting her feelings.

Jenks flitted back to me, shooing his kids away from the soda. "Hell, yes, there's cake!" he said, loud to cover Ceri's distress. "Can't have a birthday without cake. I'll help you, Ceri."

The pretty elf shook her head. "You stay," she said, halfway to the door. "No need for you to leave. I'll go get it. I'll be right back." She jerked to a stop and retraced her steps, smiling and bright. "Here," she said, taking her hat off and putting it on me. "Wear this."

Ivy snickered, and I reached up to touch it. "Thanks," I said, cursing my outright fear of hurting her feelings. Great. I was going to be eating cake in a silly hat. Damn it, no one had better have a camera.

Keasley's brown, arthritic hands gathered up the handles of the canvas grocery sacks. "I'll take those. You entertain," he said, pulling them from the couch. Hesitating, he turned, bending his once-tall height to give me a fatherly kiss on the cheek. "Happy birthday, Rachel. You're quite the young woman. Your father would be proud of you."

If they were trying to cheer me up, they were doing a lousy job of it. "Thanks," I said, feeling my throat start to take on a lump.

I turned, looking for something to do. Ivy was supervising Jenks handing out soda to his kids in little cups made from the plastic plugs they put in pressboard furniture to hide the holes. David caught my eye and started over. His worn brown boots showed from under his blue jeans, and he scuffed to an uncertain halt. I hadn't seen him since the night I'd been lying on the floor, drugged as he told Minias that he had a legal right to make decisions for me. David had saved my life as much as Ceri.

"Happy birthday," he said, clearly wanting to say something more.

Hell, a handshake wasn't going to do it, and as a wash of gratitude warmed me, I reached out and brought him close, taking him in a hug. His arms were solid and real. Comforting. The complicated scent of Were filled my senses, and I closed my eyes, feeling my chest grow heavy when I noticed the differences between being held by him and Kisten. *I'd never hold Kisten again.*

I clenched my jaw and refused to cry. I didn't want to talk about Kisten. I wanted to pretend we were all normal. But I had to say something. I couldn't let David think I wasn't grateful for what he'd done. "Thank you," I said into his shirt. "Thank you for saving my life."

"It was an honor." His voice rumbled from him to me through his chest, and his hold on me grew more certain now that he knew that the depth of my emotion was coming from gratitude.

"I'm sorry about Brett," I said miserably, and his grip tightened.

"Me too," he said, and I heard the pain in his voice, the loss of more than a fellow Were, but a possible friend. "I want to make him a member of our pack posthumously."

"I'd like that," I said, throat closing. Giving my arms a squeeze, he let go and backed up.

I met his eyes, surprised at the flash of fear. It was the curse. It was afraid of me, and it was only David's alpha confidence that held it in check. Anyone else might have misunderstood the fleeting, deep-seated terror, but I'd had that thing in my thoughts. I knew what it was. And it was dangerous. "David . . ."

"Don't," he said, his dark eyes fixing on me to stop my words. "I did the right thing. I turned five women, and it killed three of them. If I have the curse in me, I can help Serena and Kally." His anger left him as he got lost in a memory. "And it's not that bad," he finished, gesturing helplessly. "I feel good. Whole. Like this is the way I was supposed to be."

"Yeah, but, David . . ."

He confidently shook his head. "I have this under control. The curse is like the devil itself. I feel it in me, and I have to weigh my thoughts to decide if it's me or the curse, but it's happy to be able to run again, and I have that as a threat. It knows if it makes me angry, I'll come to you and you'll take it out and put it in a prison of bone."

"It's right," I said, remembering the fear in his eyes from just my touch. "David, this is so dangerous. Let me take it out. Everyone thinks the focus is destroyed. We can hide it—"

He held up a hand, and I stopped. "With the curse in me, Serena and Kally can shift without pain. Do you really want to take that from them? And it's okay. I didn't want a pack, but . . . sometimes our choices are made for us. The curse belongs to the Weres. Leave it where it is," he said firmly, as if the conversation were done.

Slumping against the back of the couch, I gave up. David ducked his head and relaxed. He had won, and he knew it. Ivy glanced at me from where she was handing out soda when Jenks whispered something in her ear, and her questioning gaze turned into a smile. Taking two plastic cups, she moved to sit against the pool table where she could watch everyone.

"Do you want something to drink, Rachel?" David asked, and Ivy raised one to say she'd already poured me something.

"Ivy's got it," I said, and he touched my arm before going to see what Keasley wanted.

I wasn't thirsty, but I went over to Ivy, leaning against the table beside her. Her thin eyebrows were high, and she silently handed me my drink. My gaze strayed to her neck. Piscary had bitten her so cleanly that the bites had healed with almost no scar. My neck still was a nasty mess, and it would likely stay that way. I didn't care. My soul was black, and the outward scarring seemed to fit.

Piscary had been dead for two weeks, and the minor camarillas were chomping at one another's heels to find out who would be Cincinnati's next master vampire. The mourning period was nearly over, and all of Cincy was gearing up for the squabbles and power plays. Ivy's mom had a good shot at it, which didn't fill me with any confidence. Though Ivy would be exempt from being a blood source, she'd probably have more backroom responsibility. All of Piscary's vampires had banded together under her; if a different camarilla came out on top, their lives wouldn't be worth the grape leaves Piscary had used to wrap around his lamb sandwiches. Ivy said she wasn't worried, but it had to be preying on her.

Now she cleared her throat in warning, and I forced my hand down from my own neck before I accidentally set the scar resonating to her pheromones. The scent of the pool table rose around me, the combined scent of vampires, cigarette smoke, and beer bringing back memories of me knocking around the balls as I waited in a peaceful, empty dance club for Kisten to finish locking up and our evening to begin.

Again my throat closed, and I set my drink down. "Nice pool table," I said miserably.

"I'm glad you like it." At my shoulder Ivy blinked fast but didn't look at me. "It's your birthday present from Jenks and me."

Jenks darted up with a clatter of wings. "Happy birthday, Rachel," he said with a forced brightness. "I was going to give you some color-changing nail polish, but Ivy thought you'd like this better."

Unshed tears made my vision swim, but I wasn't going to cry, damn it. I stretched out my hand and ran my fingers over the rough felt. It had stitches, just like me. "Thanks," I said.

"Damn it, Ivy!" Jenks said as he darted erratically from me to her. "I told you it was a bad idea. Look, she's crying."

I sniffed loudly, glancing up to see that only Keasley had noticed. "No," I said, my voice a shade too tight. "I love it. Thank you."

Ivy took a drink, maintaining a silent, companionable misery. I didn't need to say a word. I couldn't. Every time I had tried to comfort her the last two weeks, she'd fled. I'd learned it was better just to meet her eyes and look away with my mouth shut.

The pixy landed on her shoulder in silent support, and I saw her tension ease.

The pool table might be mine in name, but I think it meant more to Ivy. It was the only thing besides Kisten's ashes that she had taken. And the fact that she had given it to me was an affirmation that she understood that he'd been important to both of us, that my pain was as important as hers. *God, I miss him.*

The ice in my drink shifted to smack my nose when I took a sip. I wasn't going to cry. Not again. Edden wanted me to come in and talk to Ford about my memory, "for your own piece of mind, not the case," he had said. But I wasn't going to. I might have had my memory loss forced upon me, but now that it was gone, it could stay gone. It would only cause more pain. The FIB were bucking the system and trying to find out who had killed Kisten by way of who had made the deal between Piscary and Al to get him out, but that was a dead end.

The ringing of the doorbell cut through my mournful musings, and

I started. "I'll get it," I said, pushing from the pool table and heading for the door. I had to do something, or I was going to make myself cry.

"It's probably Ceri," Jenks said from my shoulder. "You'd better hurry. Cake and rain don't go together very well."

I couldn't help my smile, but it froze and broke to nothing when I yanked open the door and found Quen standing there, his Beemer running at the curb. Anger rose at the reminder of the murdered Weres. I knew too many people in the morgue. I didn't want to live my life like that. Trent was a slimy, murdering bastard. Quen should be ashamed to work for him.

"Hi, Quen," I said, putting an arm up to block his entrance. "Who invited you?"

Quen took a step back, clearly shocked at seeing me. His gaze went behind me to the party, then returned. He cleared his throat, tapping the legal-size envelope he had against his hand. The rain seemed to glisten on his shoulders, but he was completely unaffected by it. "I didn't know you were having a get-together. If I can talk to Jenks a moment, I'll go," he said. His gaze lingered on my head, and when he smiled, I snatched Ceri's hat off.

"What, not going to hang around for cake?" I snapped, snatching at the envelope. I'd take his money. Then buy a lawyer to put him in jail with Trent, currently out on bail.

Quen jerked the envelope out of my reach, his face creasing in bother. "This isn't yours."

Pixy kids were starting to gather around the doorframe, and Jenks made an ear-piercing chirp. "Hi, Quen, is that mine?" he said as his kids scattered, laughing.

The elf nodded, and I cocked my hip, not believing this. "You're going to stiff me again?" I exclaimed.

"Mr. Kalamack isn't paying you for arresting him," Quen said stiffly.

"I kept him breathing, didn't I?"

At that, Quen lost his ire, chuckling as he touched his chin and rocked back on his heels. "You have a lot of nerve, Morgan."

"It's what keeps me alive," I said sourly, starting when I found Rex at the foot of the belfry stairway, staring at me. *God! Creepy little cat.*

"Do tell." He hesitated, looking past me before he brought his attention back. "Jenks, I've got your paperwork." He went to hand the envelope to him, then hesitated again. I could see why. The envelope was three times Jenks's weight if it was an ounce.

"Just give it to Rache," Jenks said, landing on my shoulder, and I smugly held out my hand for it. "Ivy's got a safe we can put it into."

Quen sourly handed it over, and, curious, I opened it up. It wasn't money. It was a deed. It had our address on it. And Jenks's name.

"You bought the church?" I stammered, and the pixy darted off my shoulder, literally glowing. "Jenks, you *bought the church?*"

Jenks grinned, the dust slipping from him a clear silver. "Yup," he said proudly. "After Piscary tried to evict us, I couldn't risk you two lunkers losing it in a poker game or something."

I stared at the paper. *Jenks owned the church?* "Where did you get the money?"

In a flash of vampire incense, Ivy was beside me. She pulled the paper from my slack fingers, eyes wide.

Quen shifted his weight, his shoes gently scuffing. "Good evening, Jenks," he said, his voice carrying a new respect. "Working with you was enlightening."

"Whoa, wait up," I demanded. "Where did you get the money for this?"

Jenks grinned. "Rent is due on the first, Rache. Not the second, or the third, or the first Friday of the month. And I expect you to pay to get it resanctified."

Quen slipped down the steps with hardly a sound. Ceri was coming up the walk, and the two passed with wary, cautious words. She had a covered plate in her hands: the cake, presumably. She glanced back once as she rose up the stairs, and I moved so she could come in. Ivy, though, was too struck to move.

"You outbid me?" Ivy shouted, and Ceri slipped between us and into the sanctuary, Rex twining around her feet. "That was you I was bidding against? I thought it was my mother!"

The click of Quen's car door opening was lost in the hush of rain, and Jenks still hadn't answered me. Quen glanced at me across the top of his car before he got in and drove away. "Damn it, pixy!" I shouted. "You'd better start talking! Where did you get the money?"

"I . . . uh, pulled a job with Quen," he said hesitantly.

The masculine murmur of Keasley and David rose, and I shut the door against the damp night. Jenks had said "job," not "run." There was a difference. "What kind of job?" I asked warily.

If a pixy could hover guiltily, Jenks was. "Nothing much," he said, darting past Ivy and me into the sanctuary. "Nothing that wouldn't have happened anyway."

My eyes narrowing, I followed him back to the party, setting Ceri's hat on the piano in passing. Ivy was right behind me. "What did you do, Jenks?"

"Nothing that wouldn't have happened on its own," he whined, shedding green sparkles onto the pool table. "I like where I live," he said, landing behind the side pocket in his best Peter Pan pose. "You two women are too flaky to put my family in your hands. Just ask anyone here. They'd agree with me!"

Ivy huffed and turned her back on him, muttering under her breath, but I could tell she was relieved her new landlord wasn't her mom.

"What did you do, Jenks?" I demanded.

Ivy's eyes narrowed in a sudden thought. Faster than I would have believed possible, she snatched up a pool cue and slammed it down inches from Jenks. The pixy shot up into the air, almost hitting the ceiling. "You little bug!" she exclaimed, and Ceri grabbed Keasley and the cake and headed toward the kitchen. "The paper says Trent's been released."

"What!" Appalled, I gazed at Jenks up near the ceiling. Keasley jerked to a brief halt in the hallway, then continued on. David had dropped his head into his hands, but I think he was trying not to laugh.

"The fingerprint they lifted from Brett and the paperwork was lost," Ivy said, smacking a beam with the cue to make Jenks dart to the next one over. "They dropped the charges. You stupid pixy! He murdered Brett. She had him, and you helped Quen get him off?"

"Wha-a-a-at," he griped, moving to my shoulder for protection. "I had to do something to save your pretty little ass, Rache. Trent was thi-i-i-is close to taking you out." His voice went high in exaggeration. "Arresting him at his own wedding was stupid, and you know it!"

My anger evaporated as I remembered Trent's expression when the cuffs ratcheted shut. God, that had felt good. "Okay, I'll give you that," I said, trying to see him on my shoulder. "But it was fun. Did you see the look on Ellasbeth's face?"

Jenks laughed, doubling up. "You should have seen her dad's," he said. "Oooooh, doggies, that man was more upset than a pixy papa with eight sets of girls."

Ivy set the pool cue on the table and relaxed. "I don't remember it," she said softly.

Her lack of memory was disturbing, and trying to ignore that I was missing chunks of my week, too, I looked up as Ceri and Keasley came back in, the cake almost on fire from all the candles they'd stuck into it.

I couldn't very well stay mad when they started singing "Happy Birthday," and I felt the tears prick again that I had people in my life who cared enough to go through the misery of trying to pretend everything was normal when it wasn't. Ceri settled the cake on the coffee table, and I hesitated only briefly at my wish. It had been the same every year since my father had died. My eyes closed against the smoke as I blew the candles out. They smarted, and I wiped them with no one saying anything as they clapped, teasing to find out what the wish was.

Taking up the big knife, I started slicing the cake, layering perfectly triangular pieces on paper plates decorated with spring flowers. The chatter became overly loud and forced, and with Jenks's kids everywhere it was a madhouse. Ivy wouldn't look at me as she took her plate, and seeing as she was the last, I settled myself across from her.

David followed Ceri and the cat to the piano, where she started playing some complicated tune that was probably older than the Constitution. Keasley was trying to keep the pixies occupied and out of the frosting, entertaining them with the way his wrinkles disappeared when he puffed his cheeks out. And I was sitting with a plate of cake on my lap, absolutely miserable and having no cause for it. Or not really.

The awful feeling of loss I had felt in the FIB conference room rose from nowhere, pulled into existence by the reminder of Kisten's death. I'd thought Ivy and Jenks were dead. I'd thought everyone I cared about had been severed from me. And that I had given up and accepted the damage of a demon curse when I thought I'd nothing left to lose had opened my eyes really fast. Either I was an emotional wimp and had to learn to handle the potential loss of everyone I loved without caving or—and this was the one that scared me the most—I had to come to grips